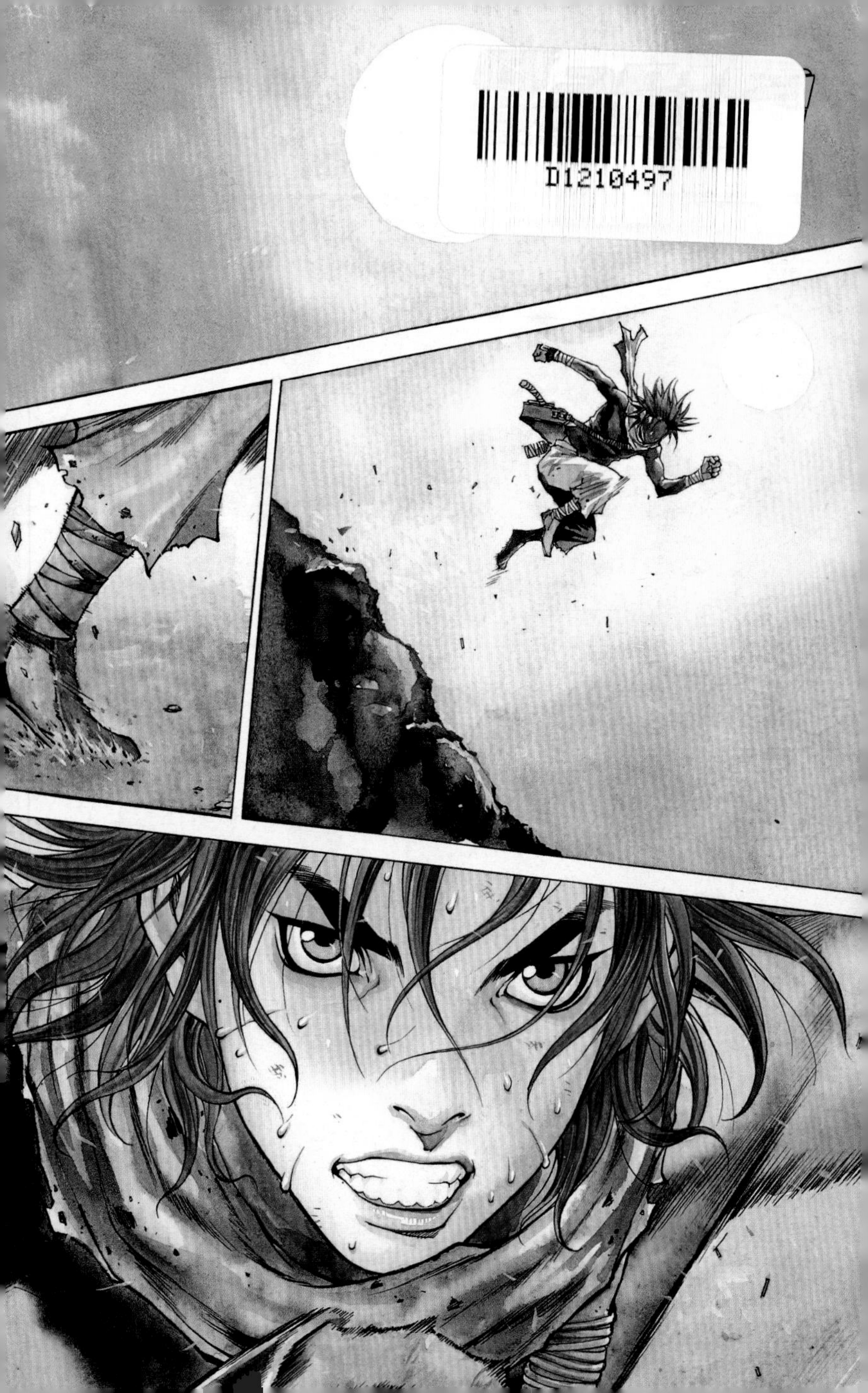

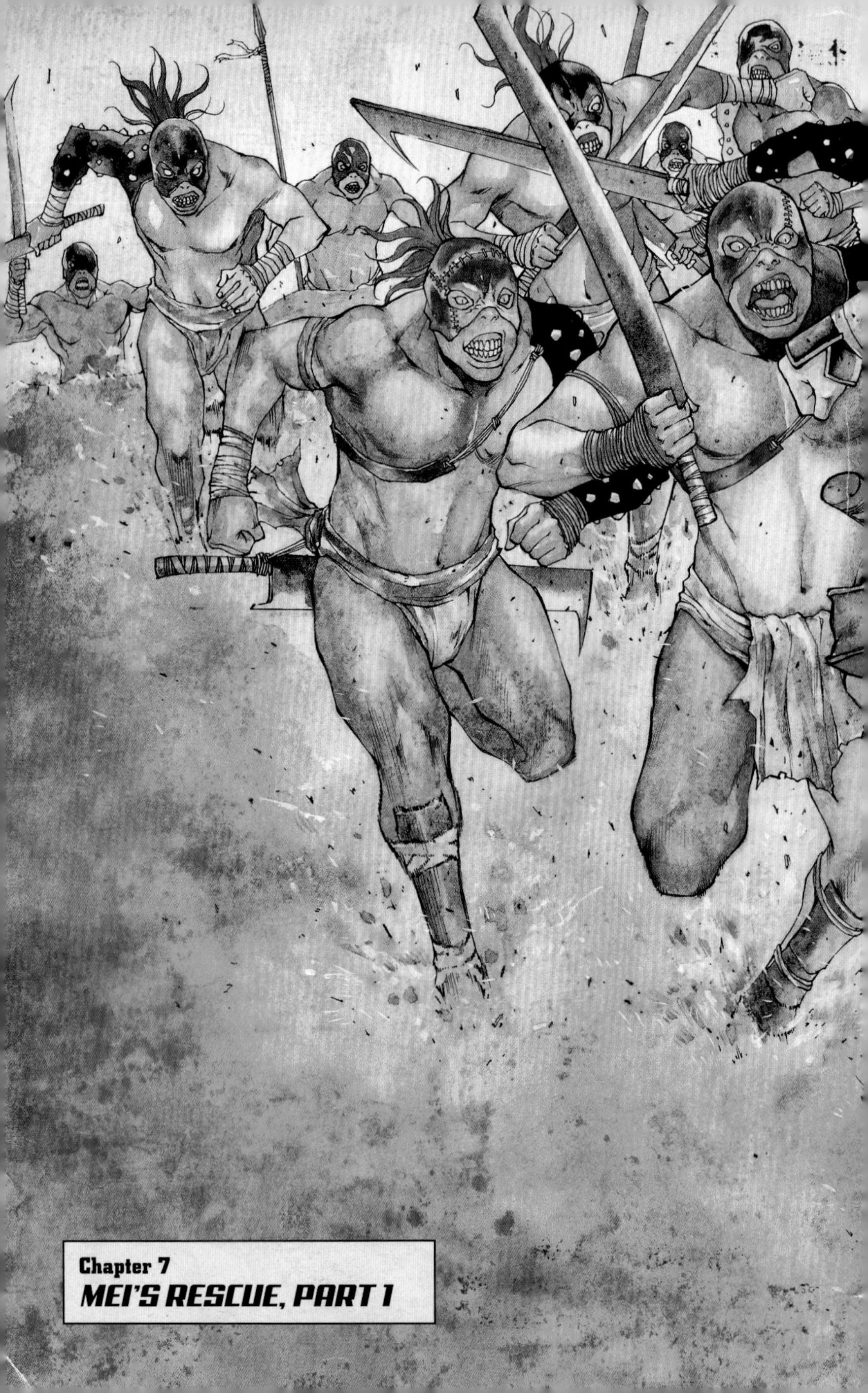

Chapter 7
MEI'S RESCUE, PART 1

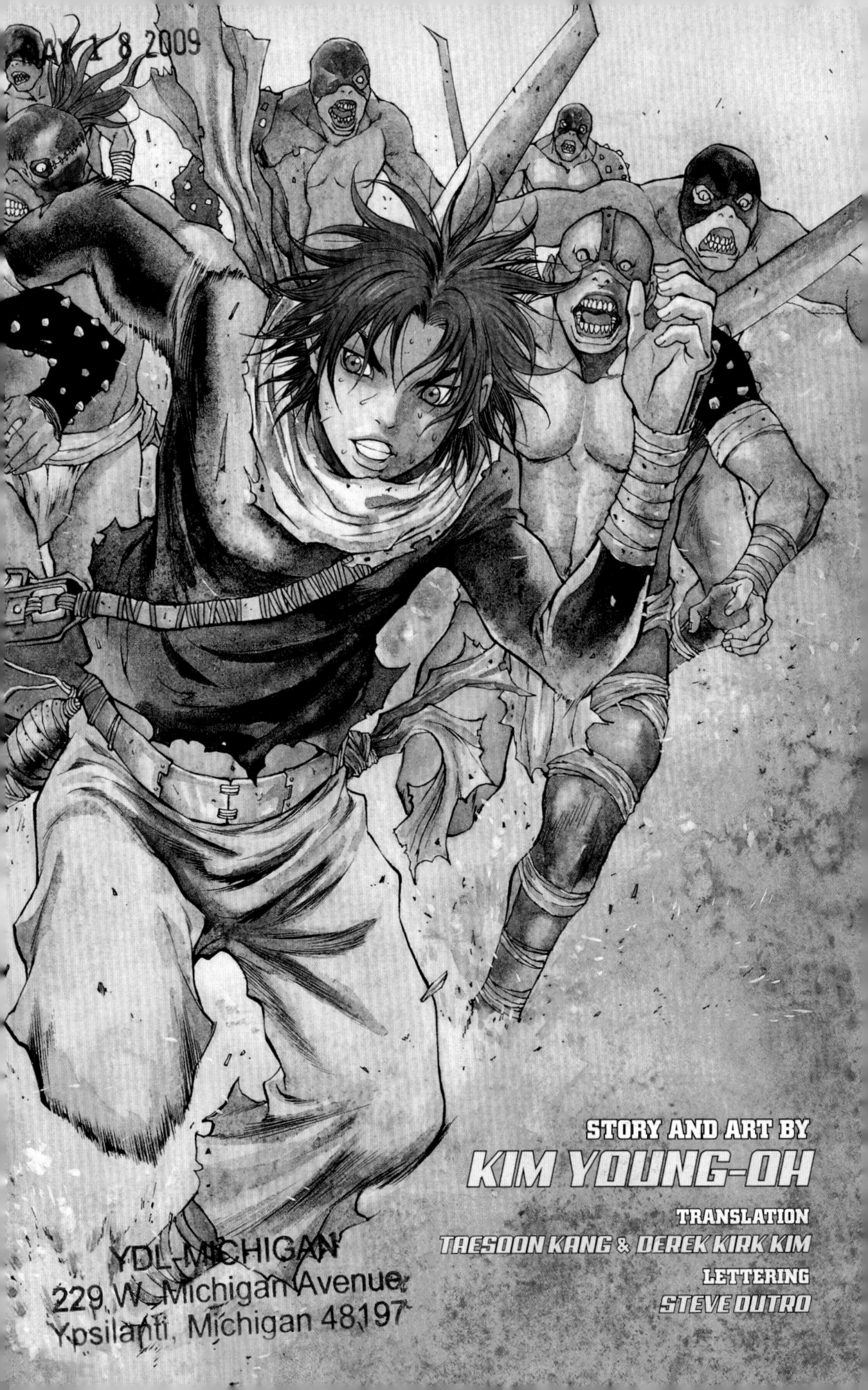

STORY AND ART BY

KIM YOUNG-OH

TRANSLATION

TAESOON KANG & DEREK KIRK KIM

LETTERING

STEVE DUTRO

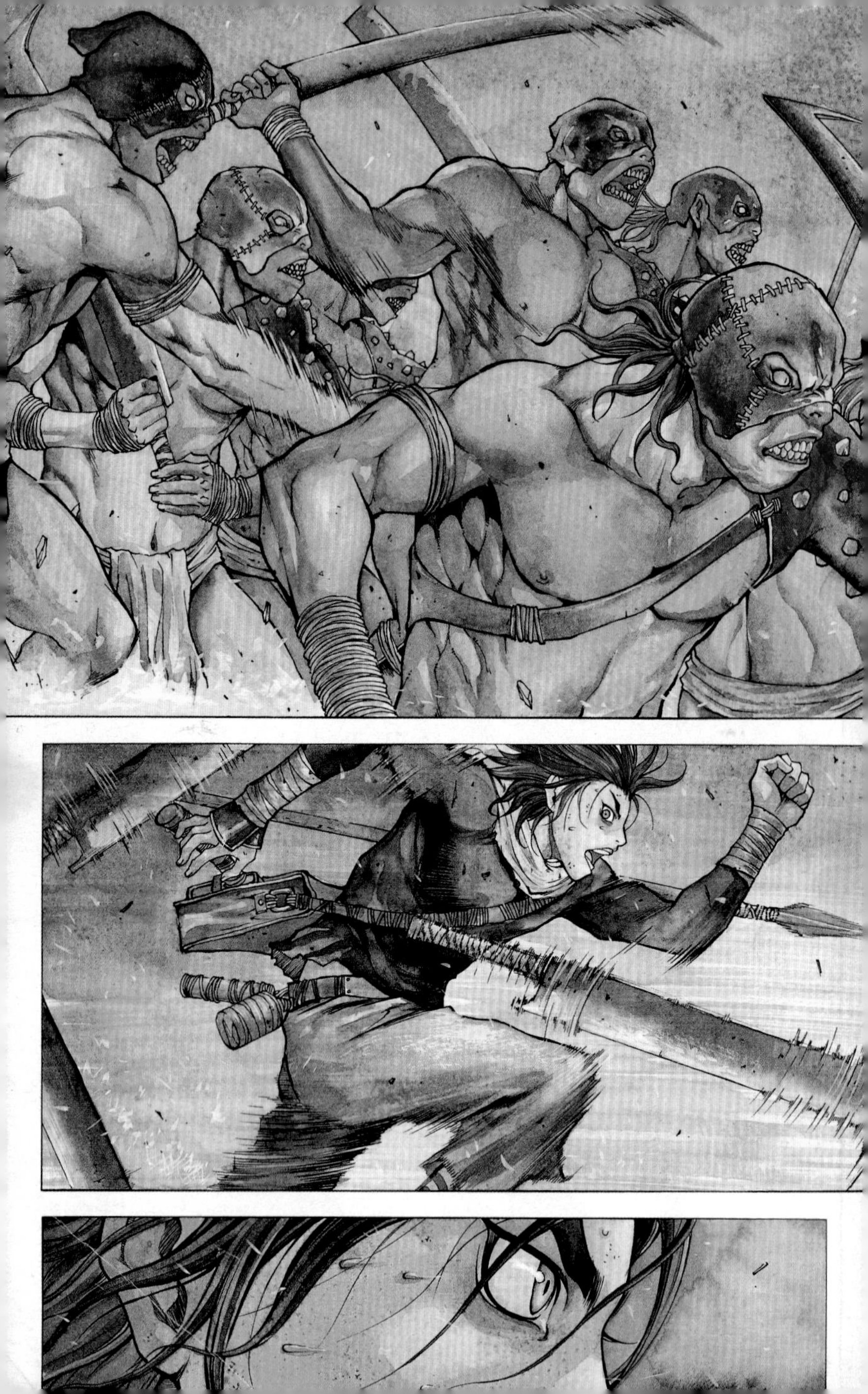

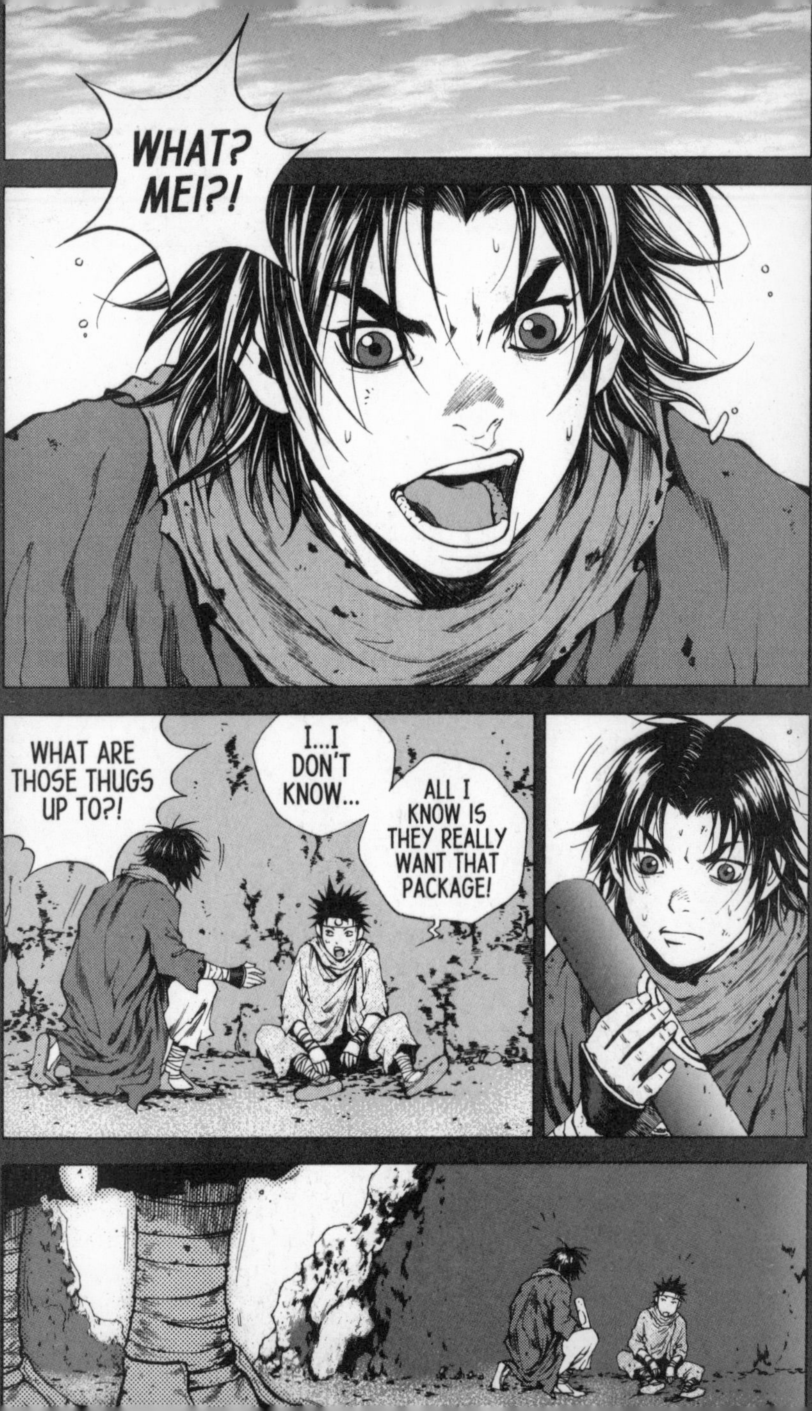
WHAT? MEI?!
WHAT ARE THOSE THUGS UP TO?!
I...I DON'T KNOW...
ALL I KNOW IS THEY REALLY WANT THAT PACKAGE!

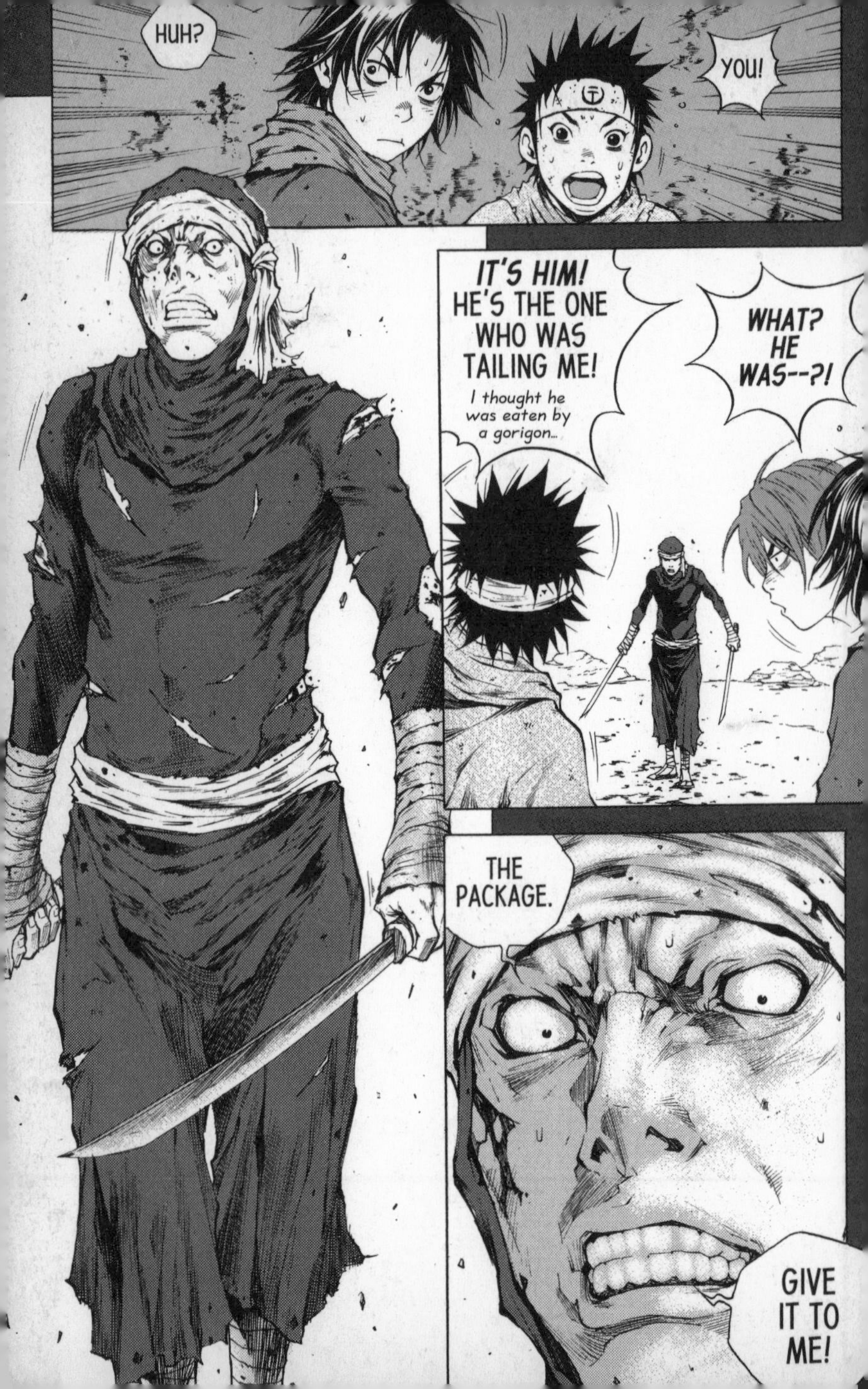

HUH?
YOU!
IT'S HIM! HE'S THE ONE WHO WAS TAILING ME!
I thought he was eaten by a gorigon...
WHAT? HE WAS--?!
THE PACKAGE.
GIVE IT TO ME!

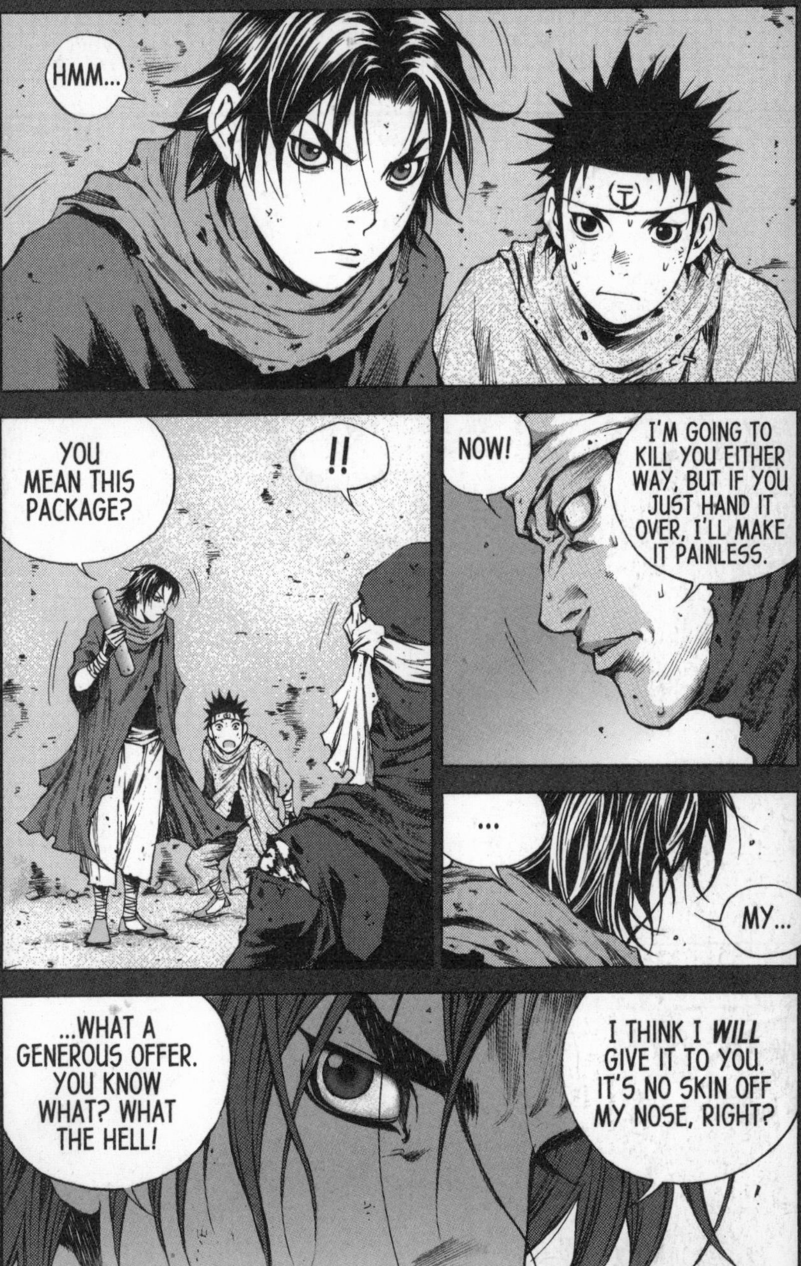
HMM...
YOU MEAN THIS PACKAGE?
!!
NOW!
I'M GOING TO KILL YOU EITHER WAY, BUT IF YOU JUST HAND IT OVER, I'LL MAKE IT PAINLESS.
...
MY...
...WHAT A GENEROUS OFFER. YOU KNOW WHAT? WHAT THE HELL!
I THINK I *WILL* GIVE IT TO YOU. IT'S NO SKIN OFF MY NOSE, RIGHT?

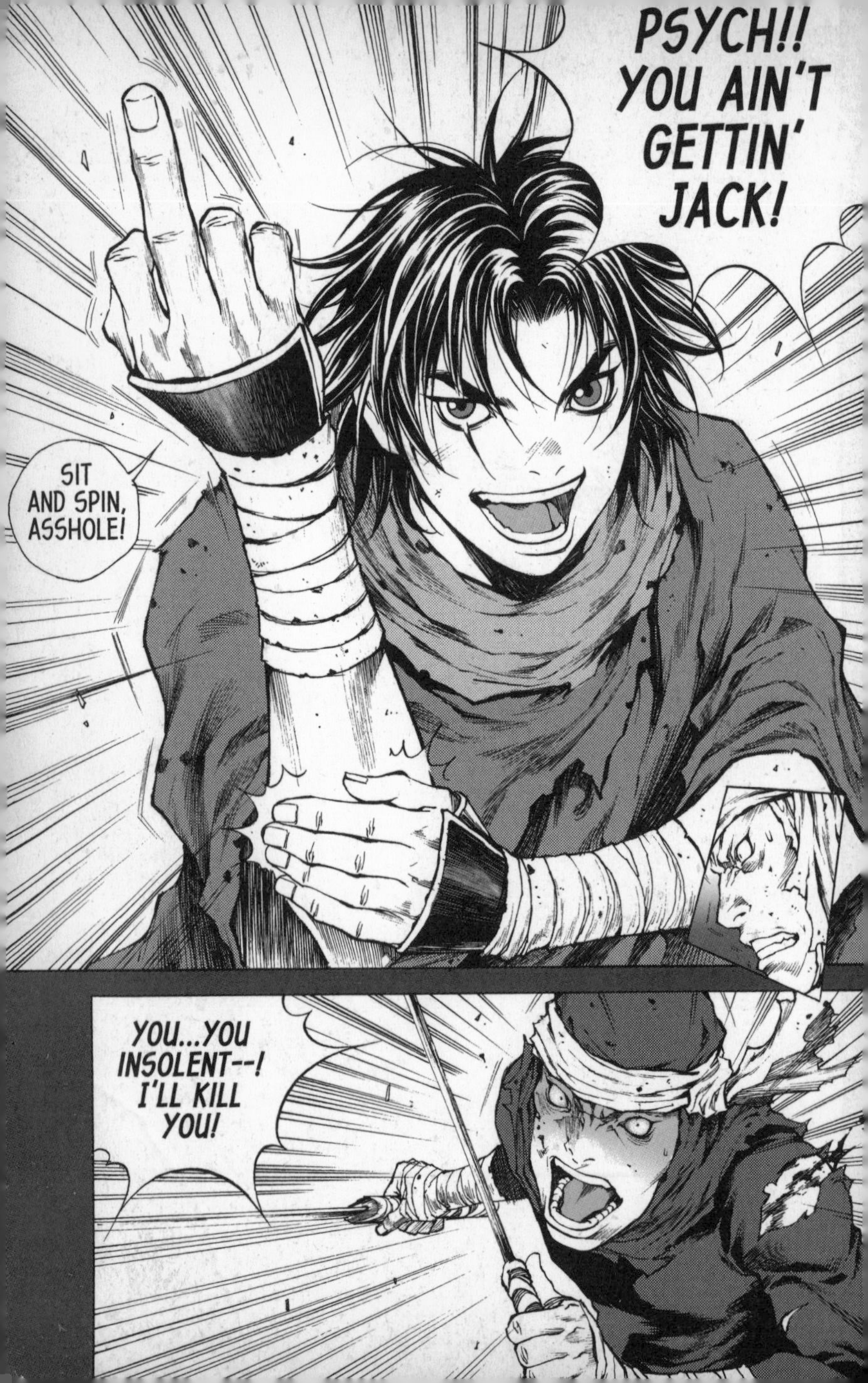
PSYCH!! YOU AIN'T GETTIN' JACK!
SIT AND SPIN, ASSHOLE!
YOU...YOU INSOLENT--! I'LL KILL YOU!

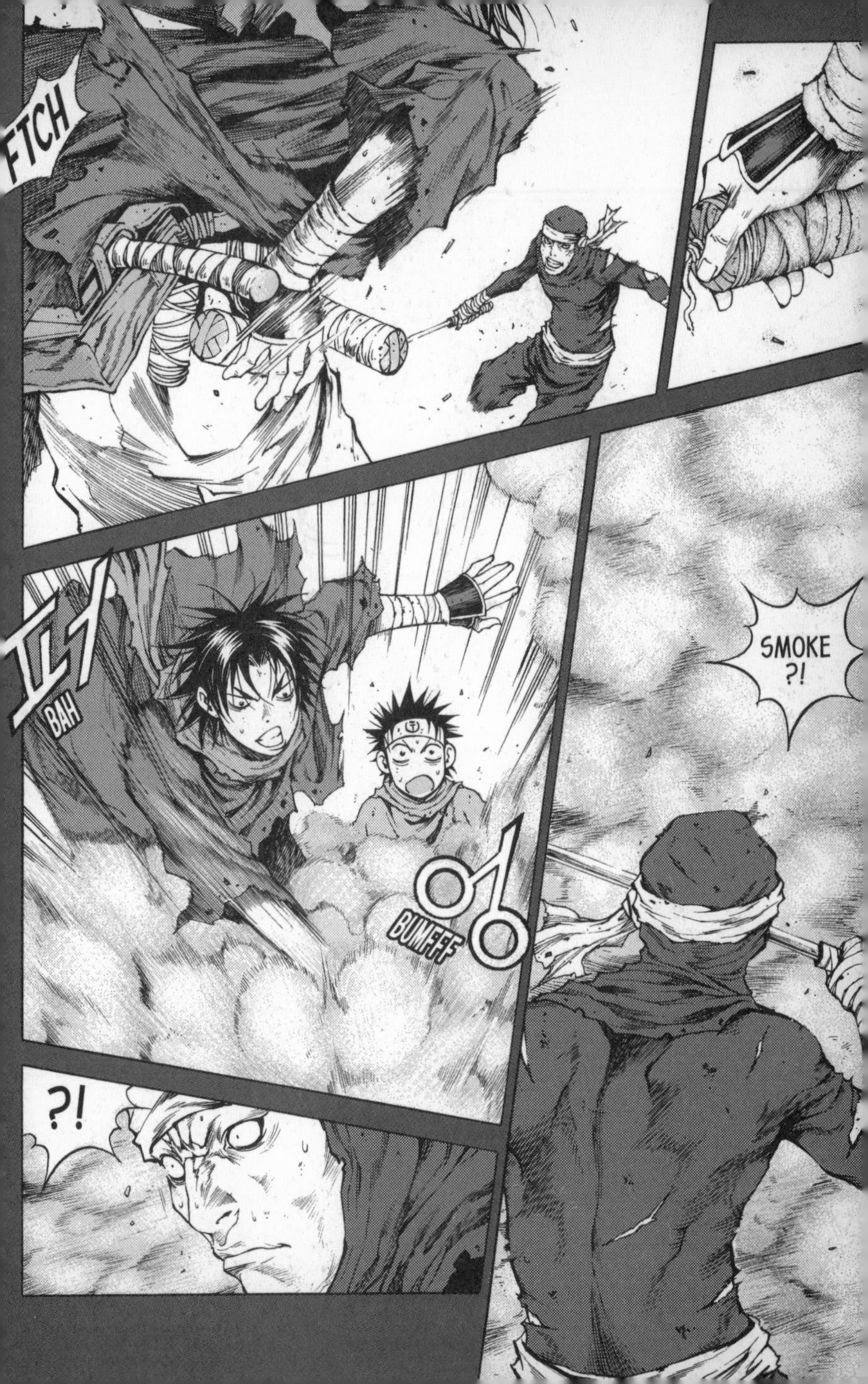

FTCH
SMOKE ?!
BAH
BUMFFF
?!

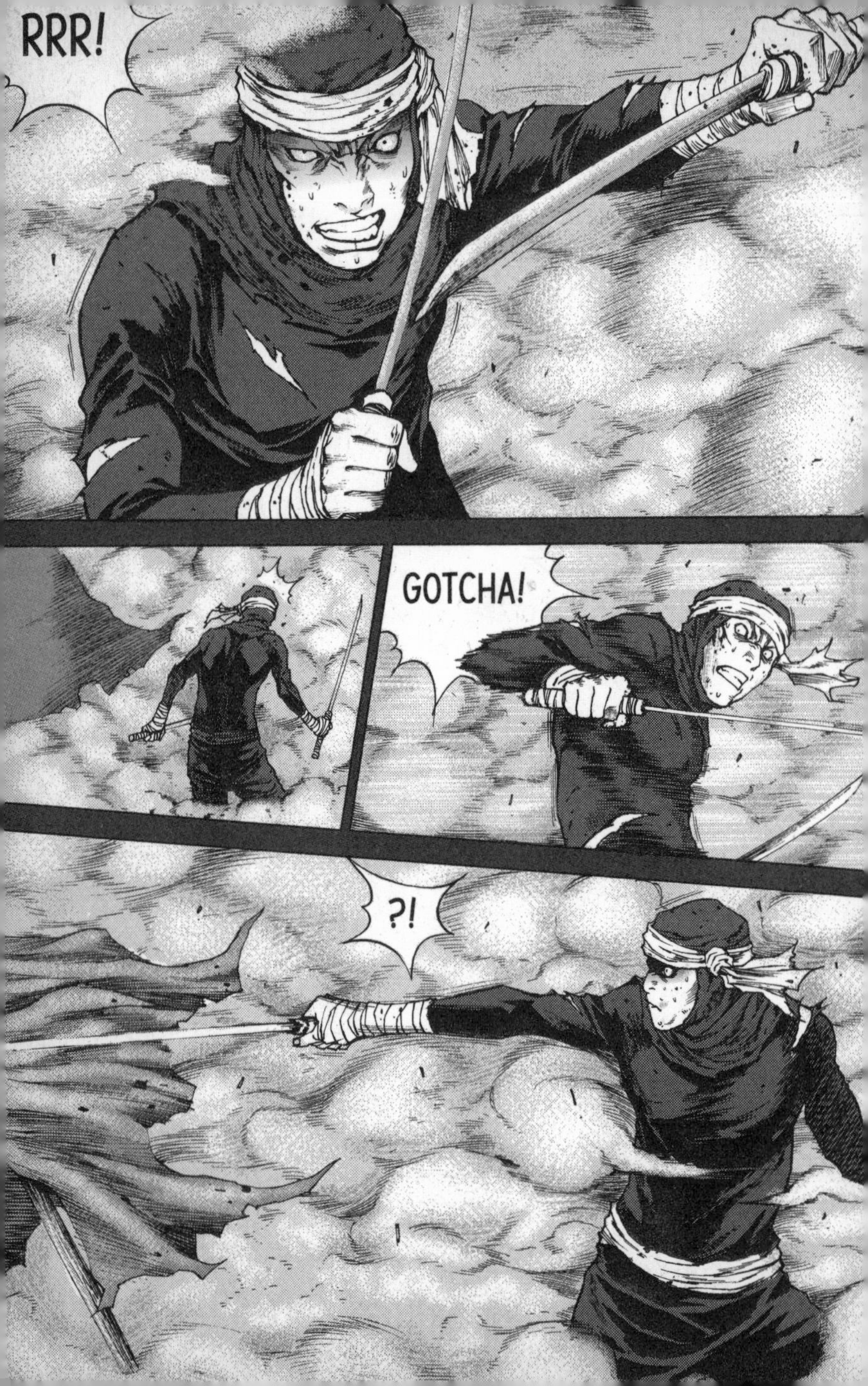
RRR!
GOTCHA!
?!

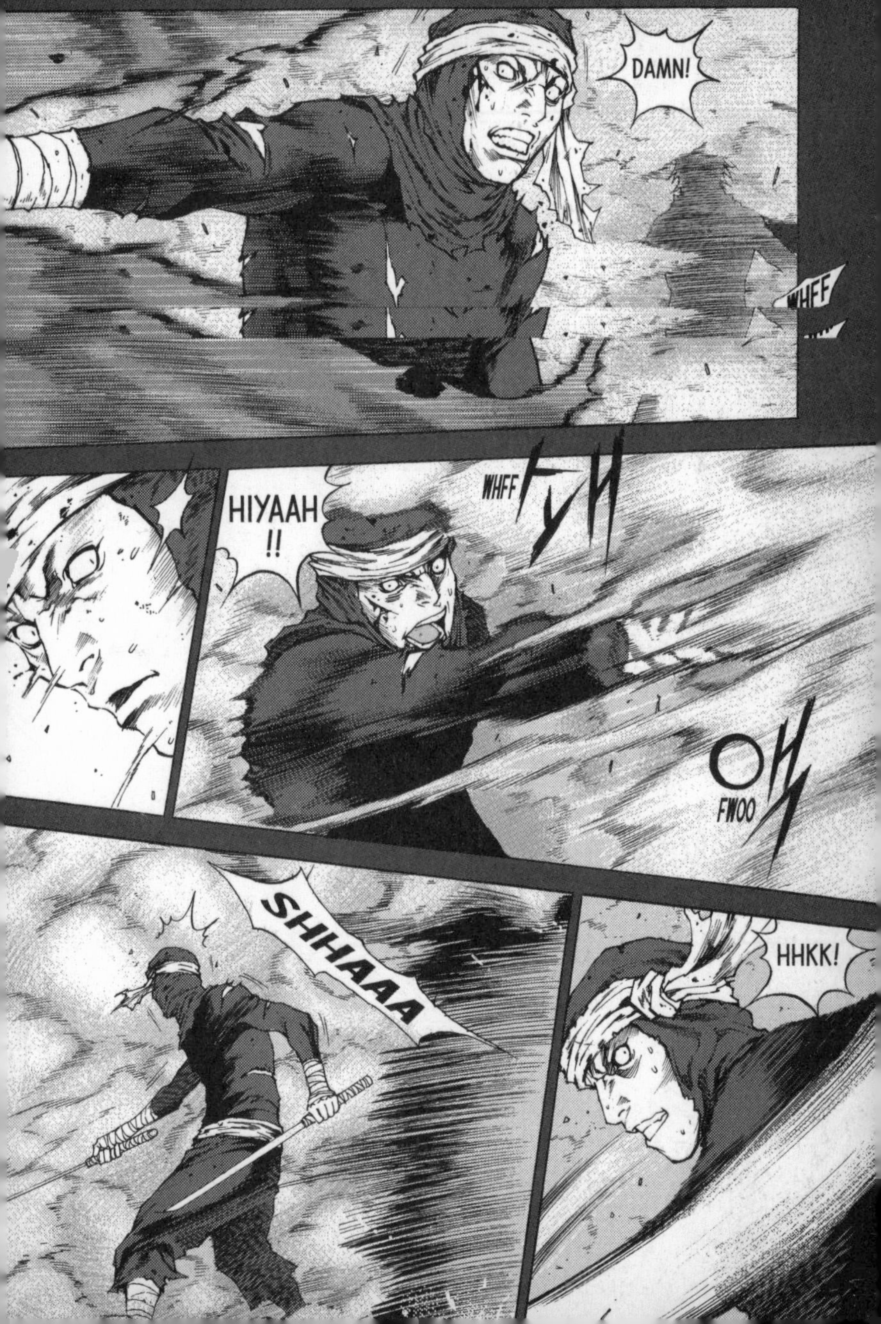
DAMN!
WHFF
HIYAAH !!
WHFF
FWOO
SHHAAA
HHKK!

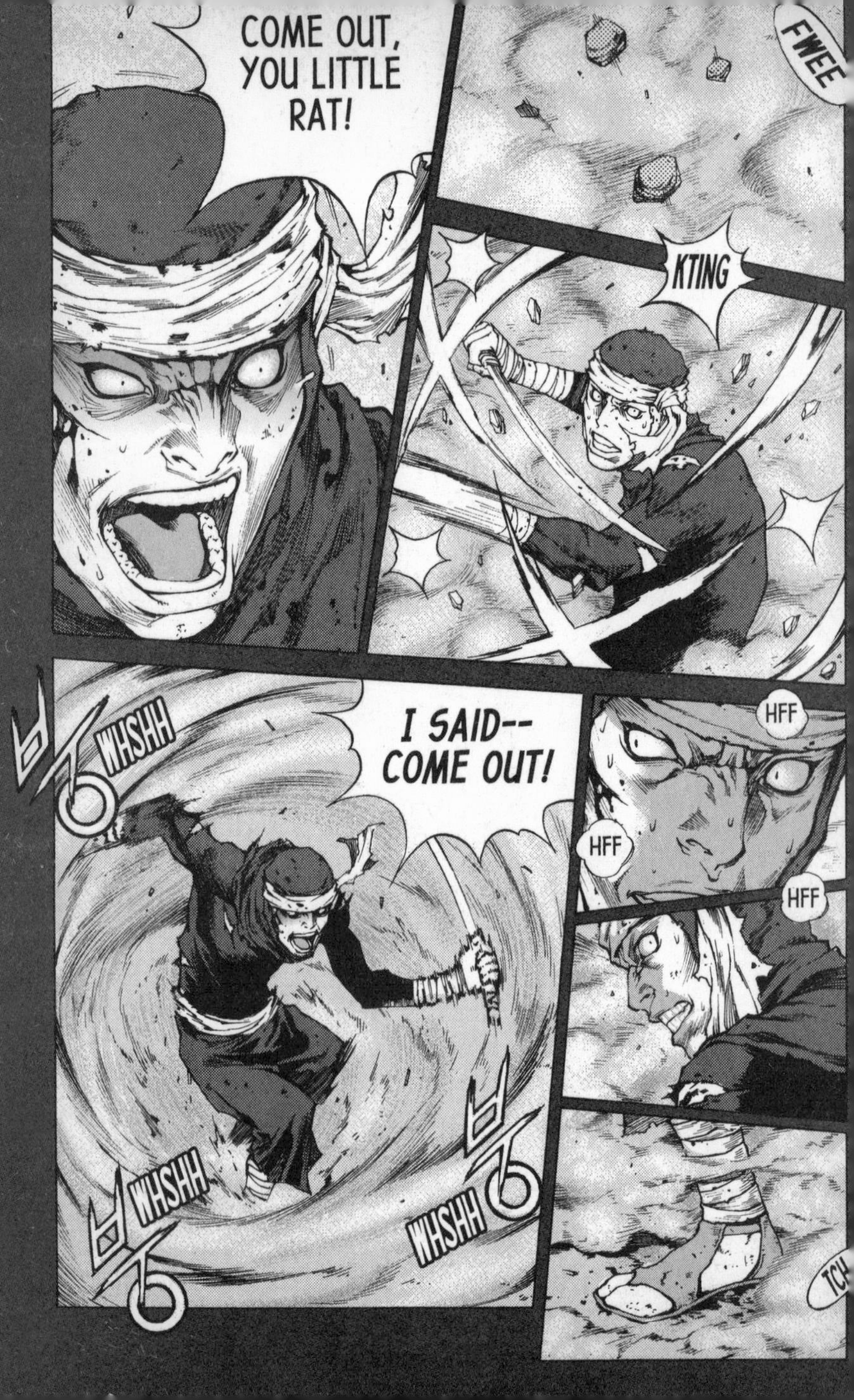
COME OUT, YOU LITTLE RAT!
FWEE
KTING
WHSHH
I SAID-- COME OUT!
WHSHH
WHSHH
HFF
HFF
HFF
TCH

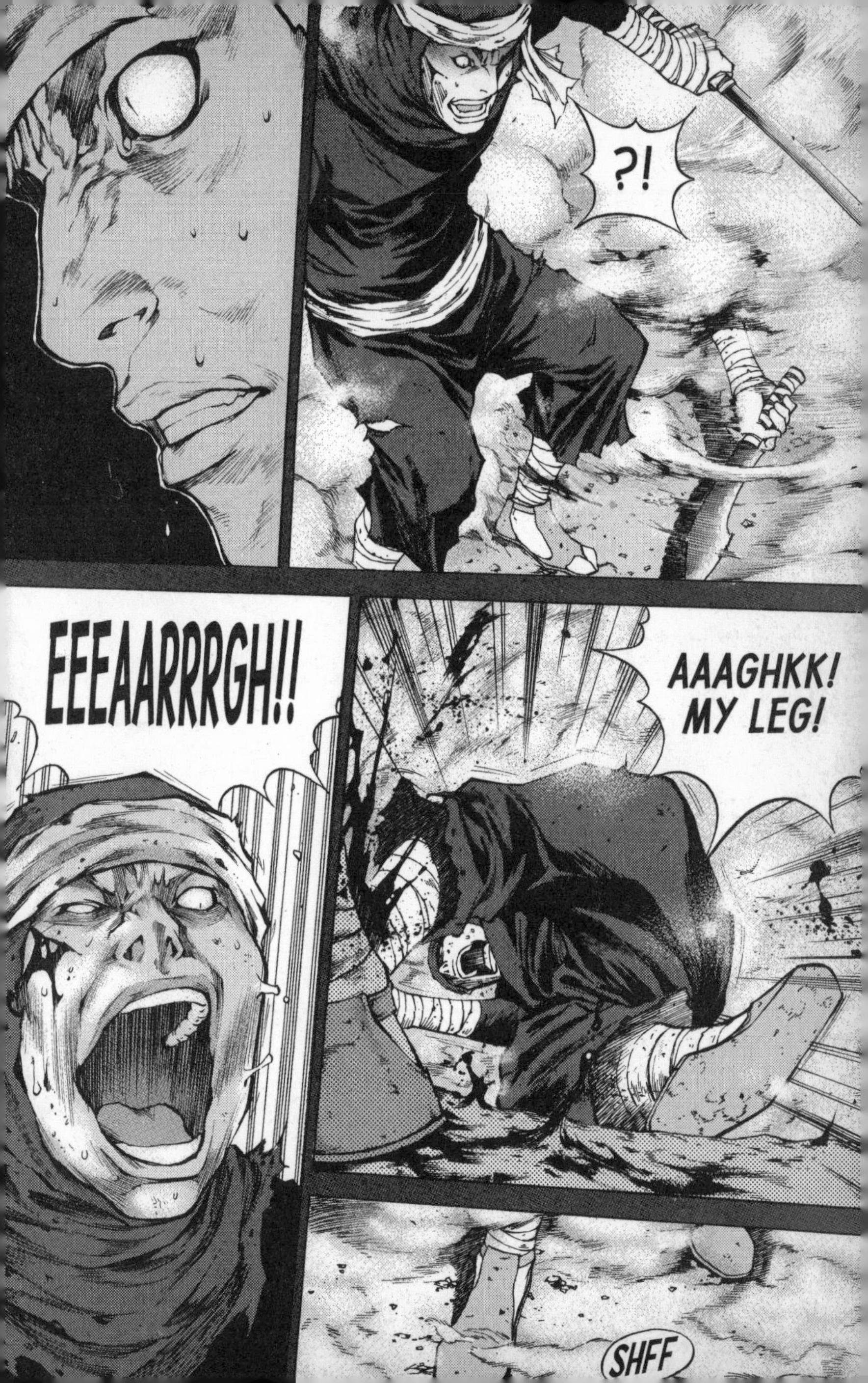
?!
EEEAARRRGH!!
AAAGHKK! MY LEG!
SHFF

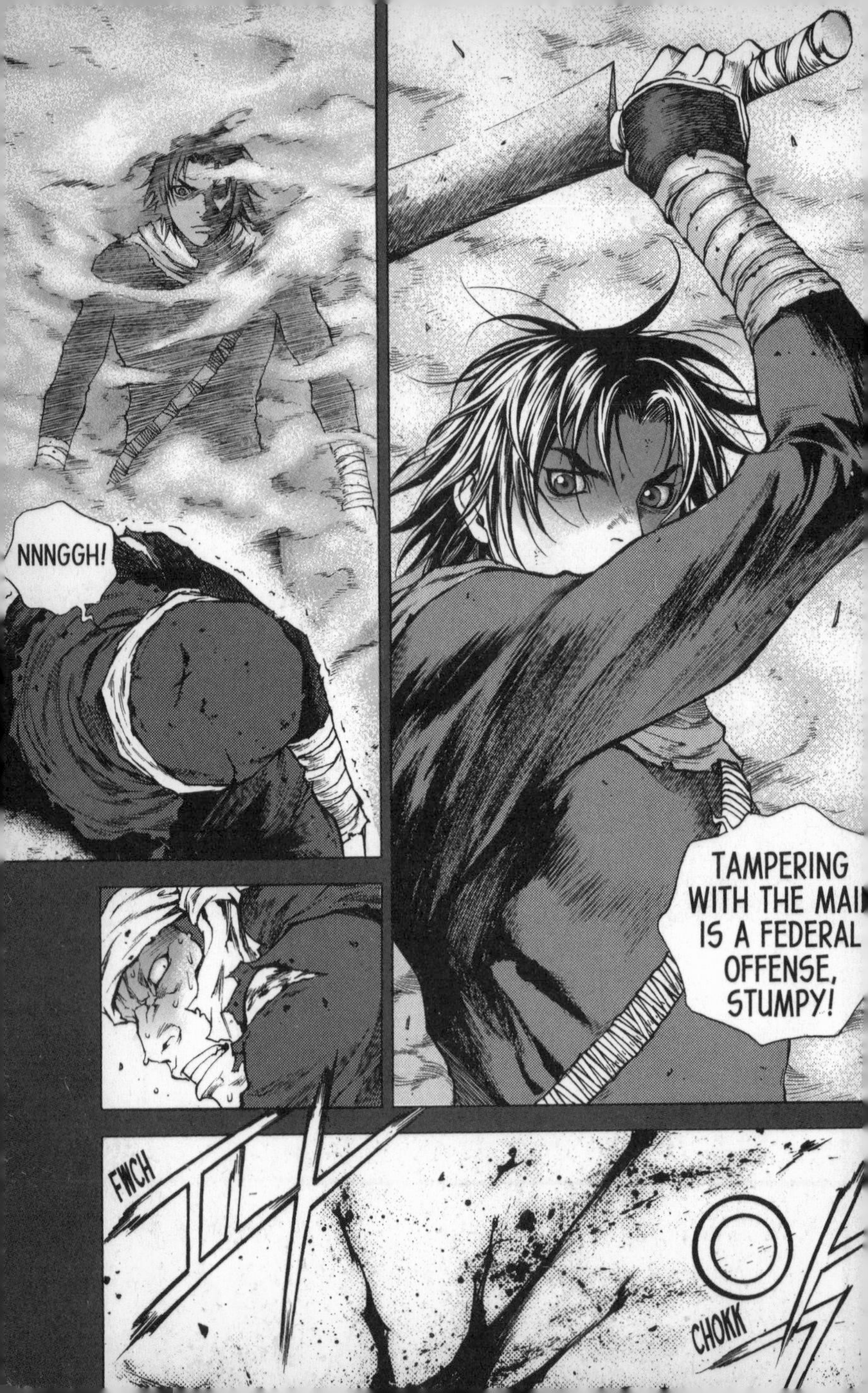
TAMPERING WITH THE MAI IS A FEDERAL OFFENSE, STUMPY!
NNNGGH!
FWCH
CHOKK

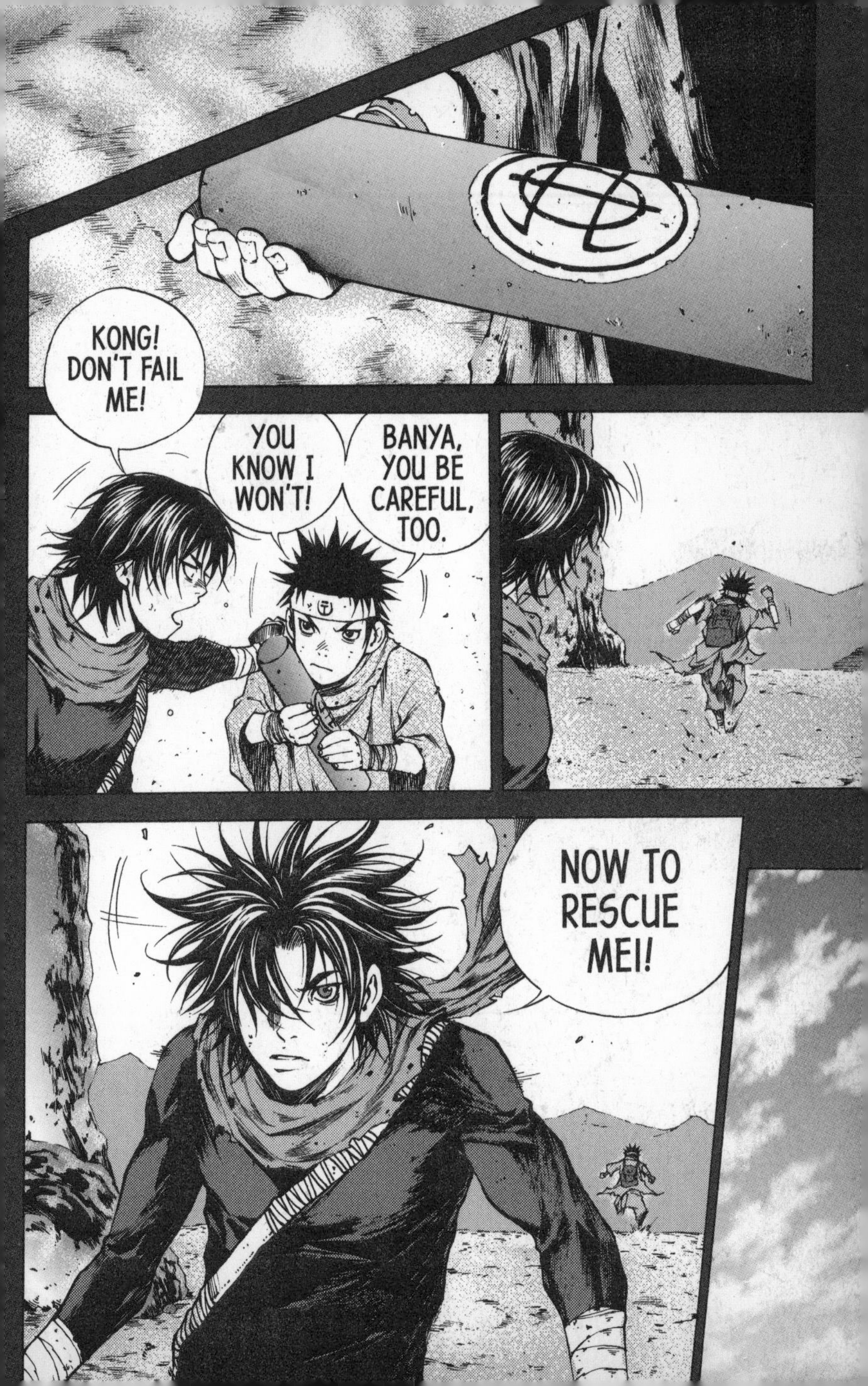
KONG! DON'T FAIL ME!
YOU KNOW I WON'T!
BANYA, YOU BE CAREFUL, TOO.
NOW TO RESCUE MEI!

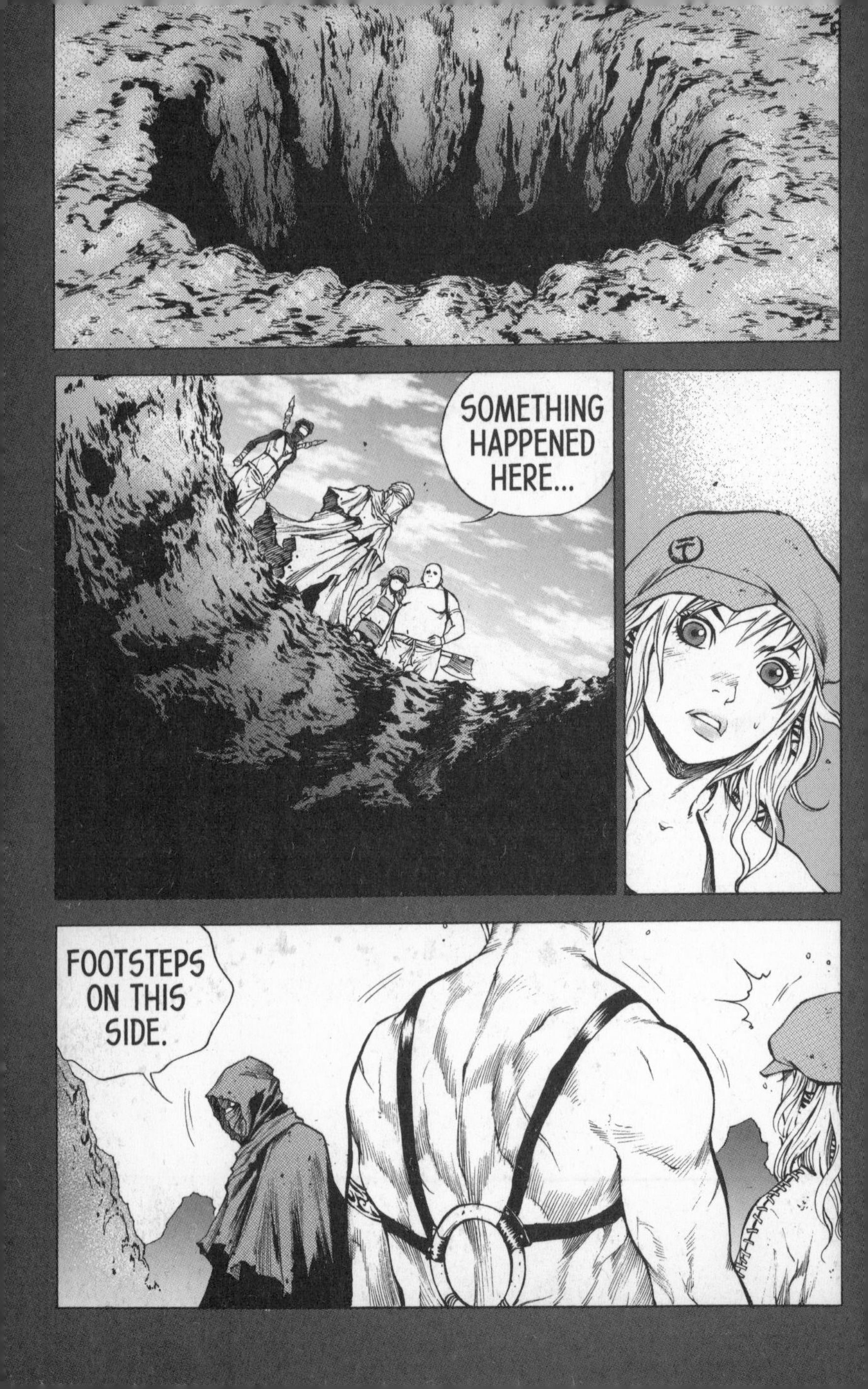
SOMETHING HAPPENED HERE...
FOOTSTEPS ON THIS SIDE.

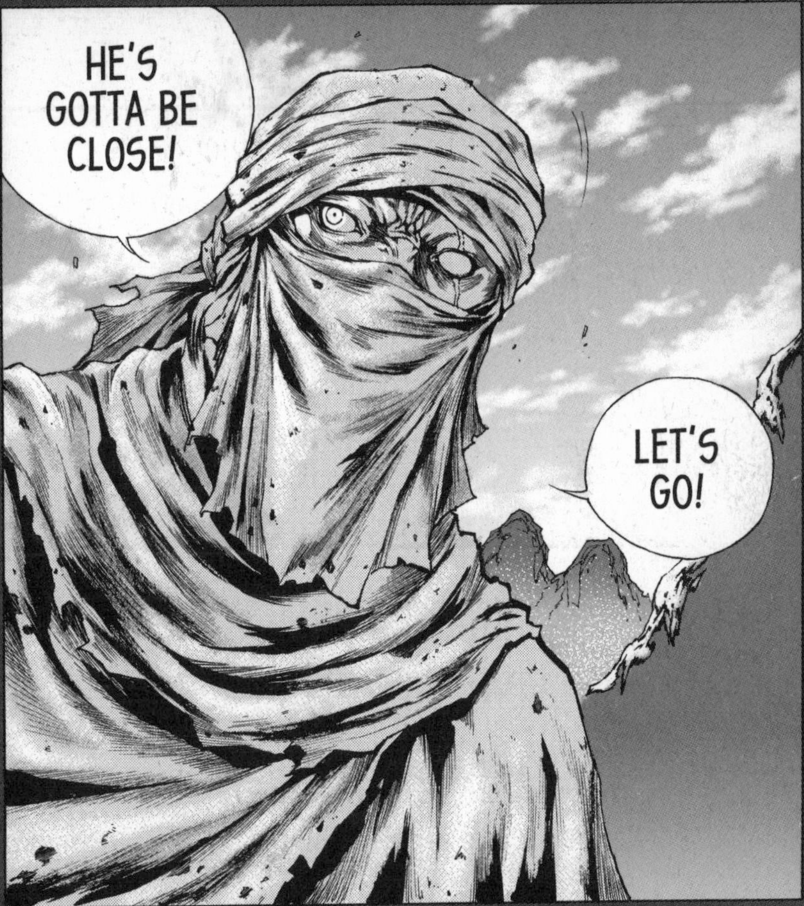
HE'S GOTTA BE CLOSE!
LET'S GO!

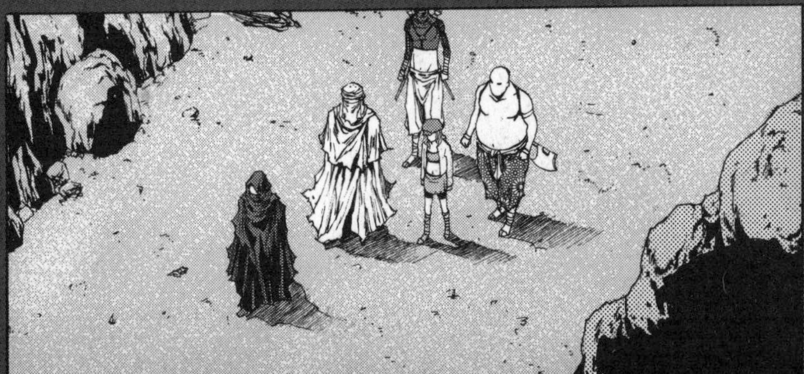

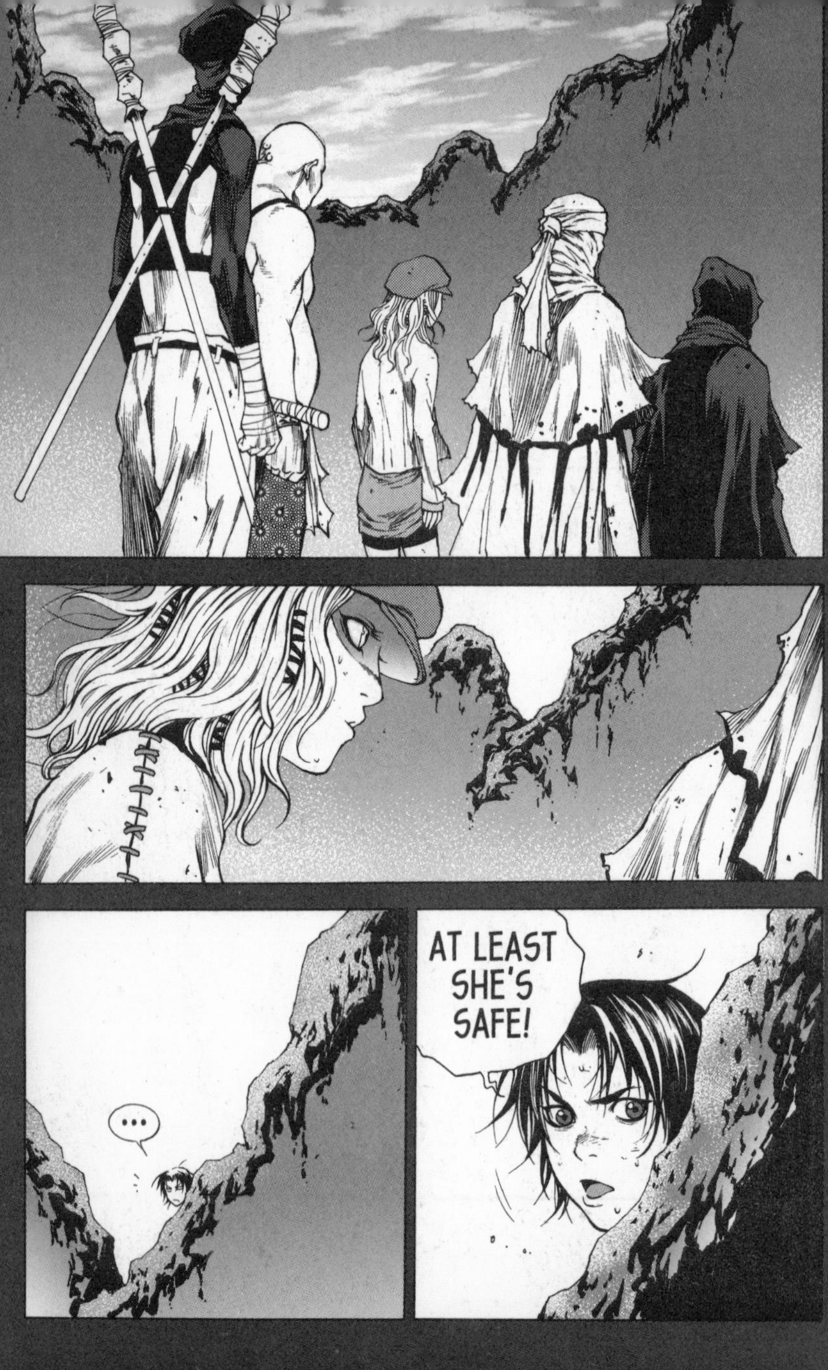
...
AT LEAST SHE'S SAFE!

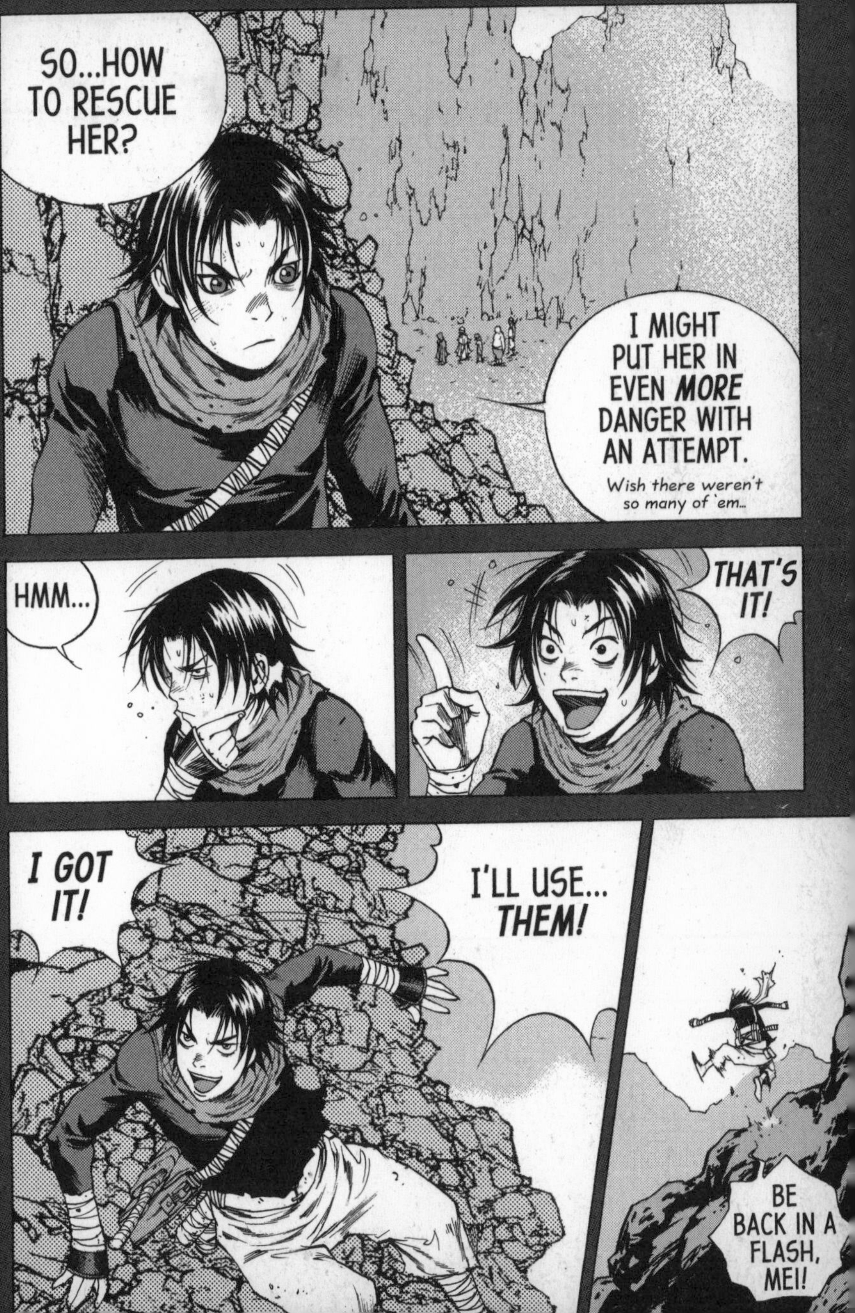
SO...HOW TO RESCUE HER?
I MIGHT PUT HER IN EVEN *MORE* DANGER WITH AN ATTEMPT.
Wish there weren't so many of 'em...
HMM...
THAT'S IT!
I GOT IT!
I'LL USE... *THEM!*
BE BACK IN A FLASH, MEI!

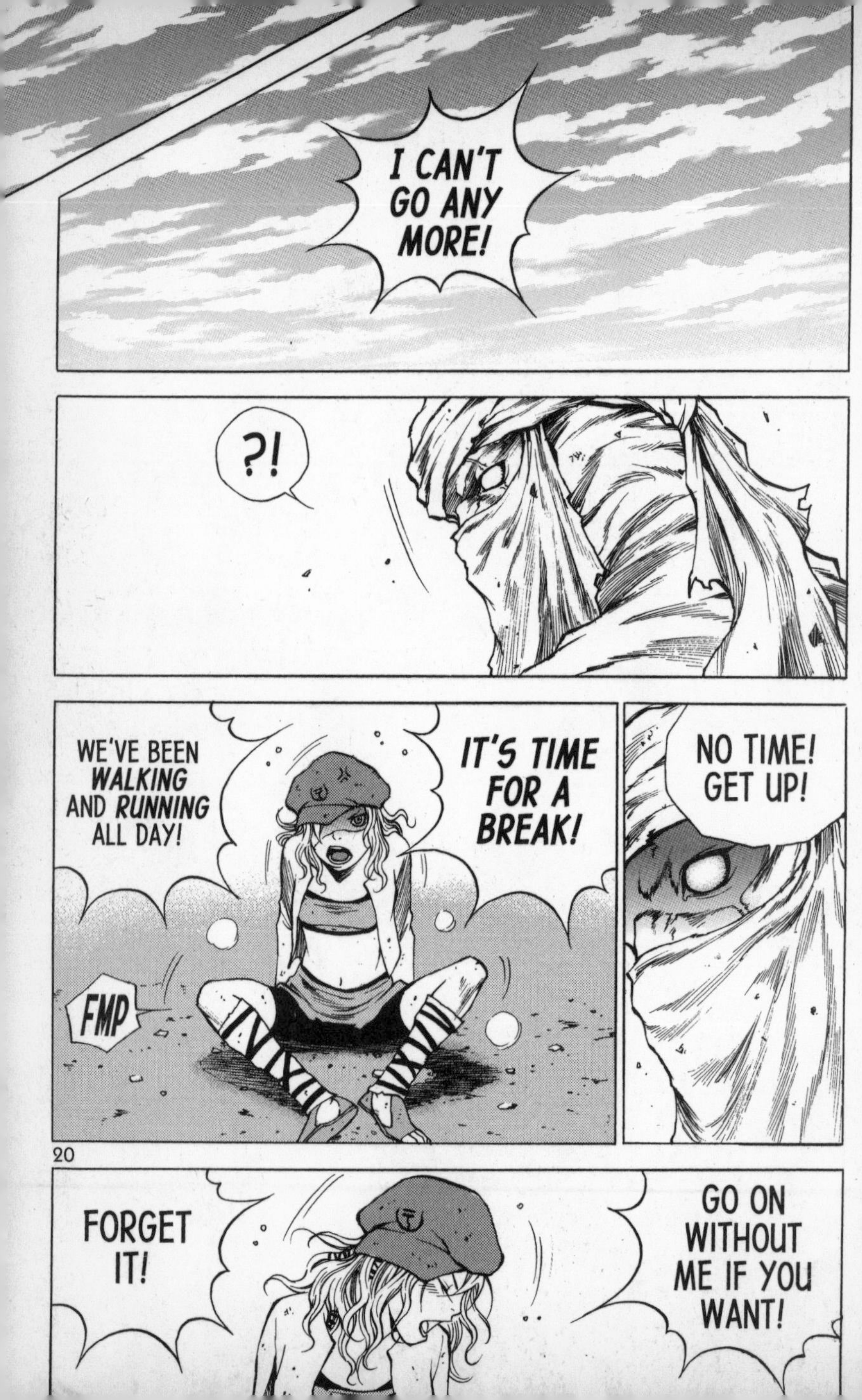
I CAN'T GO ANY MORE!
?!
WE'VE BEEN WALKING AND RUNNING ALL DAY!
IT'S TIME FOR A BREAK!
FMP
NO TIME! GET UP!
FORGET IT!
GO ON WITHOUT ME IF YOU WANT!

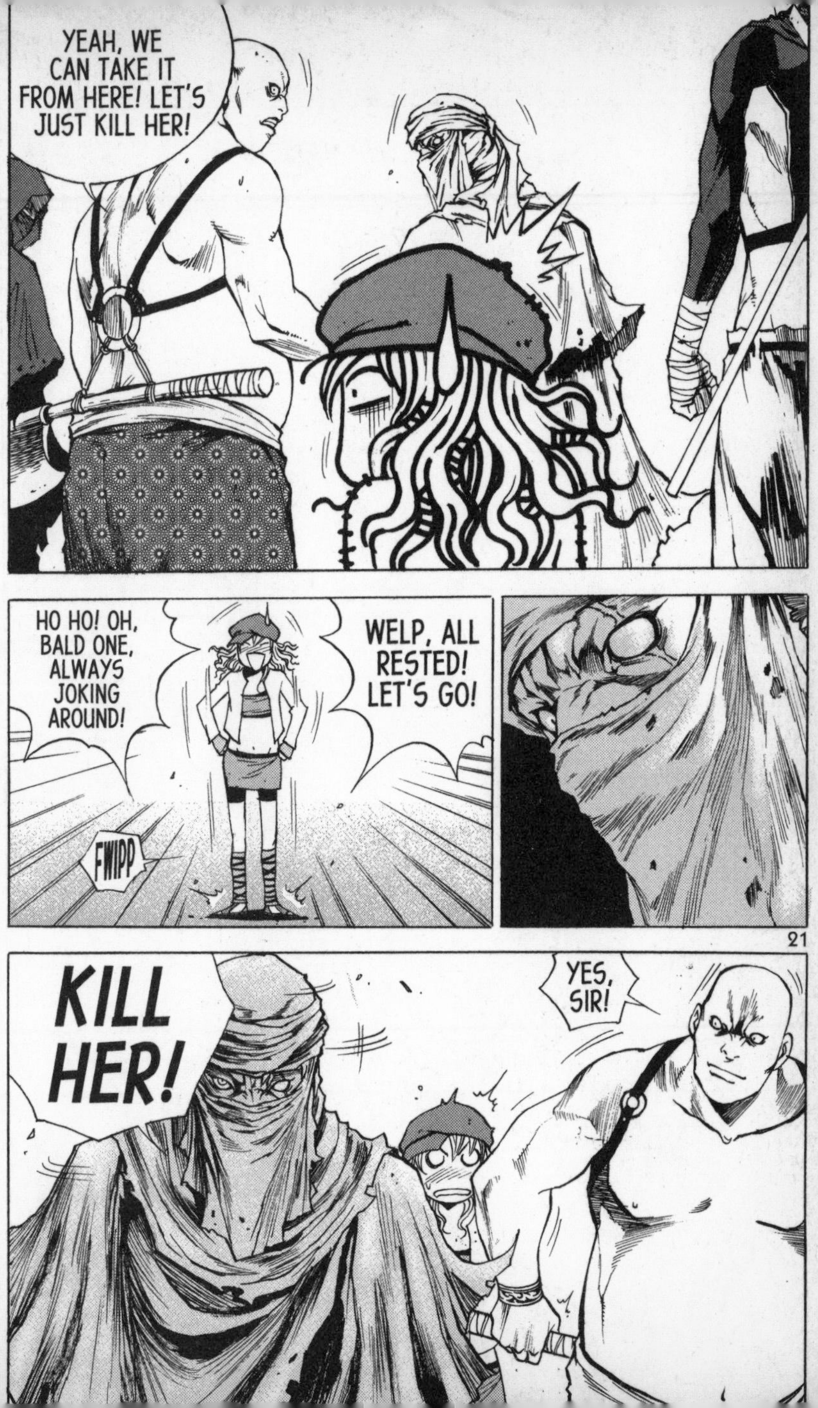
YEAH, WE CAN TAKE IT FROM HERE! LET'S JUST KILL HER!
HO HO! OH, BALD ONE, ALWAYS JOKING AROUND!
WELP, ALL RESTED! LET'S GO!
FWIPP
KILL HER!
YES, SIR!

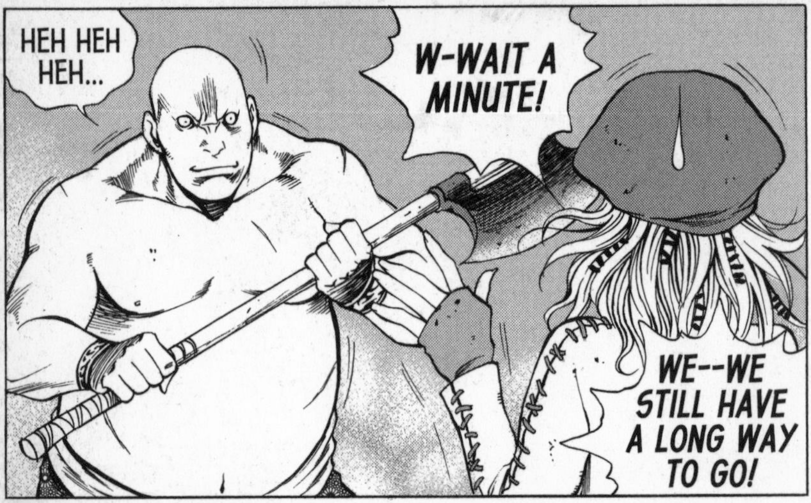
HEH HEH HEH...
W-WAIT A MINUTE!
WE--WE STILL HAVE A LONG WAY TO GO!

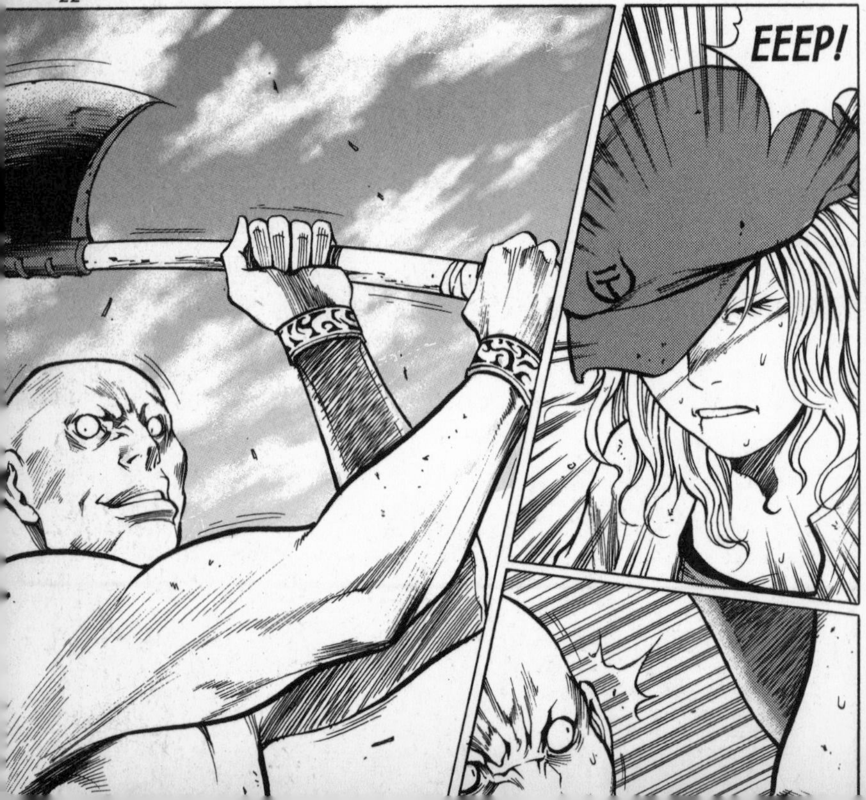
EEEP!

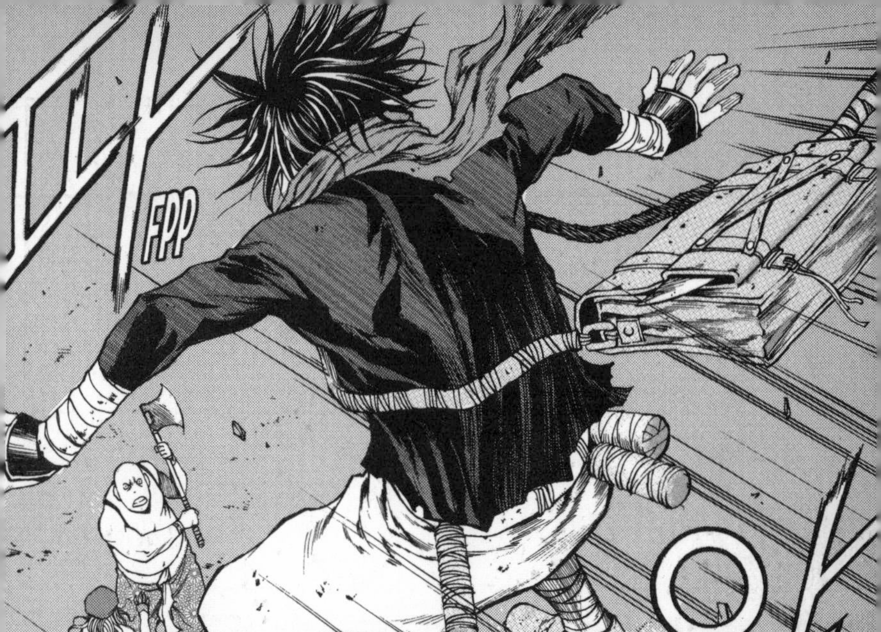
FPP
PAHH

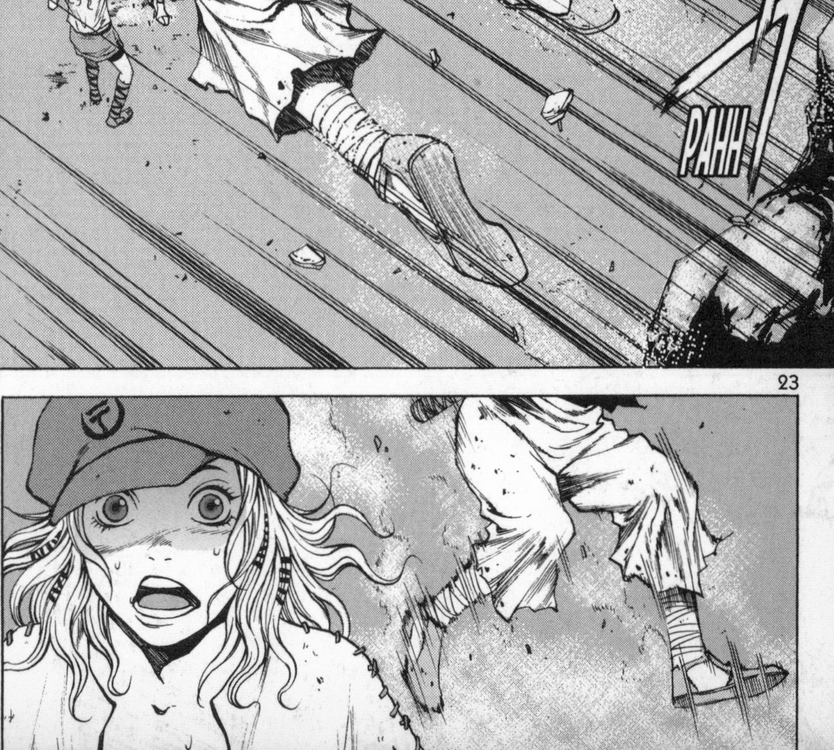

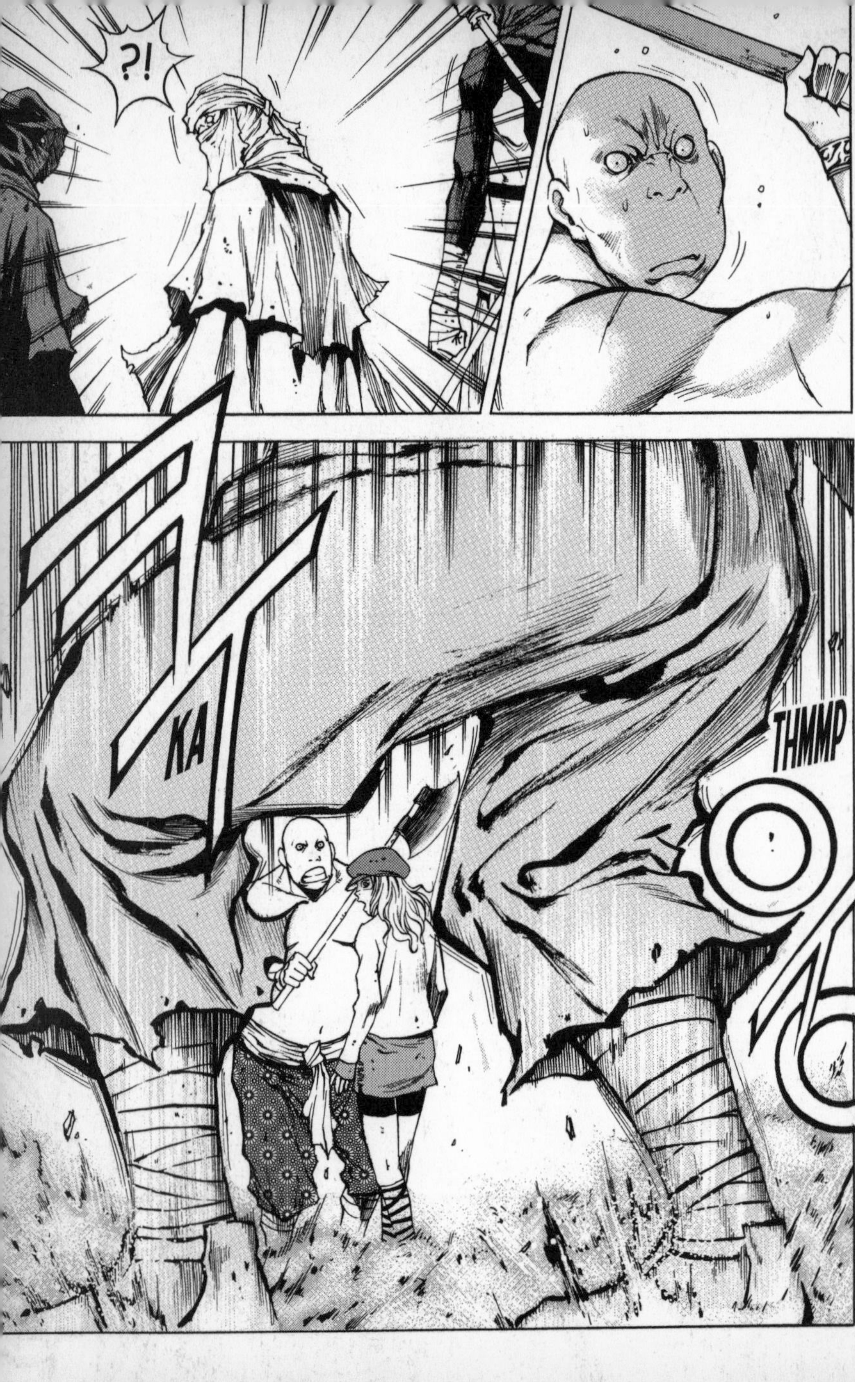
?!
KA
THMMP

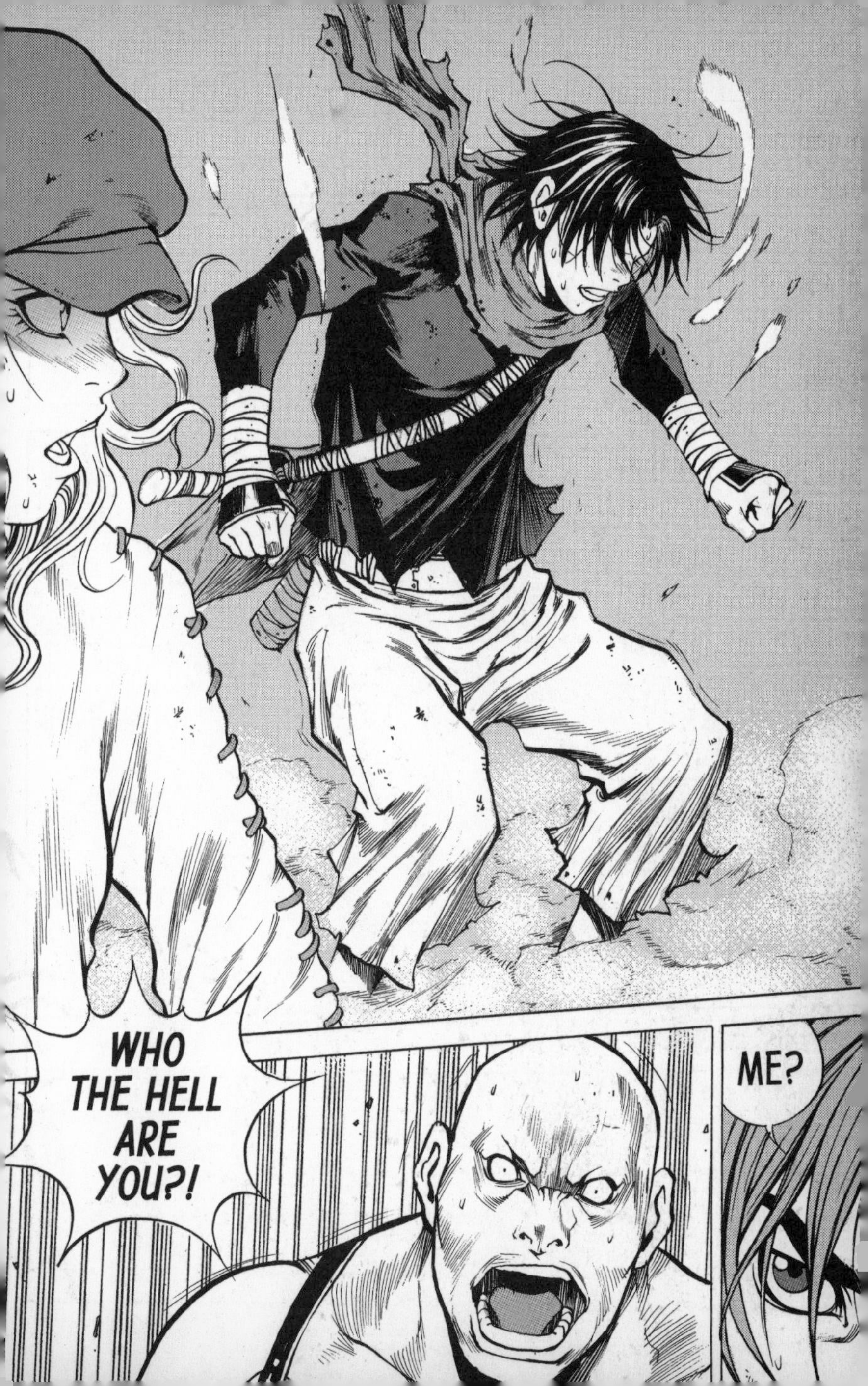
ME?
WHO THE HELL ARE YOU?!

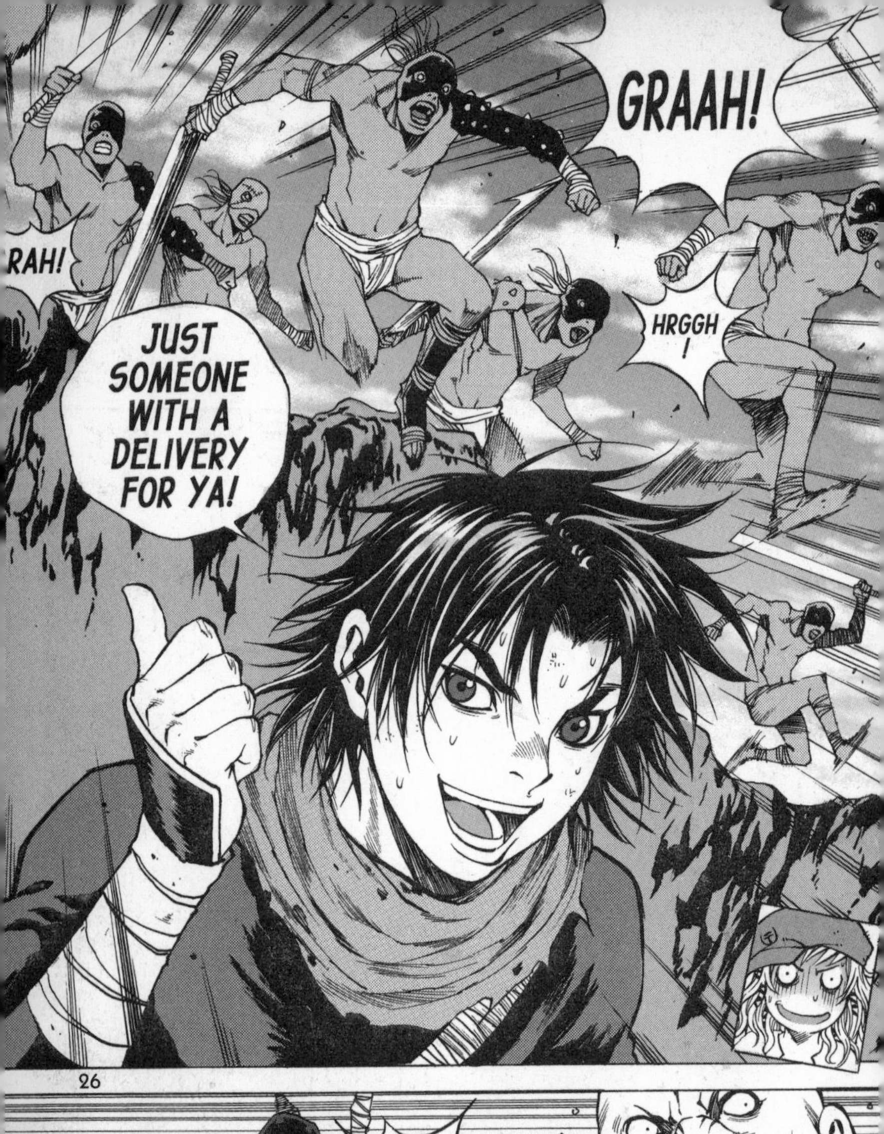
GRAAH!
HRGGH!
RAH!
JUST SOMEONE WITH A DELIVERY FOR YA!

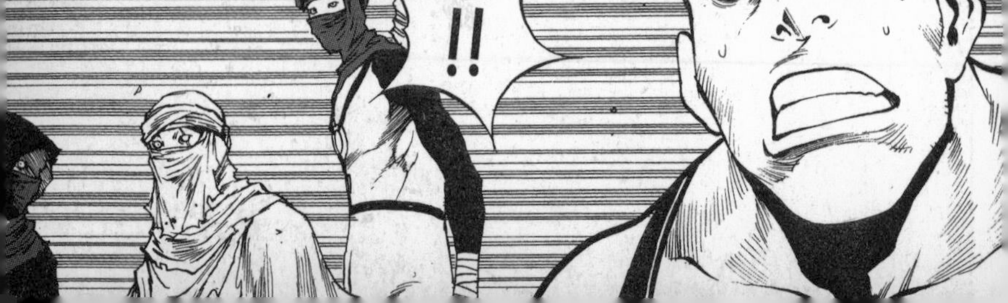
!!

IT'S
HIM!

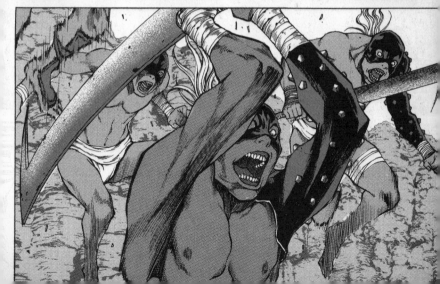

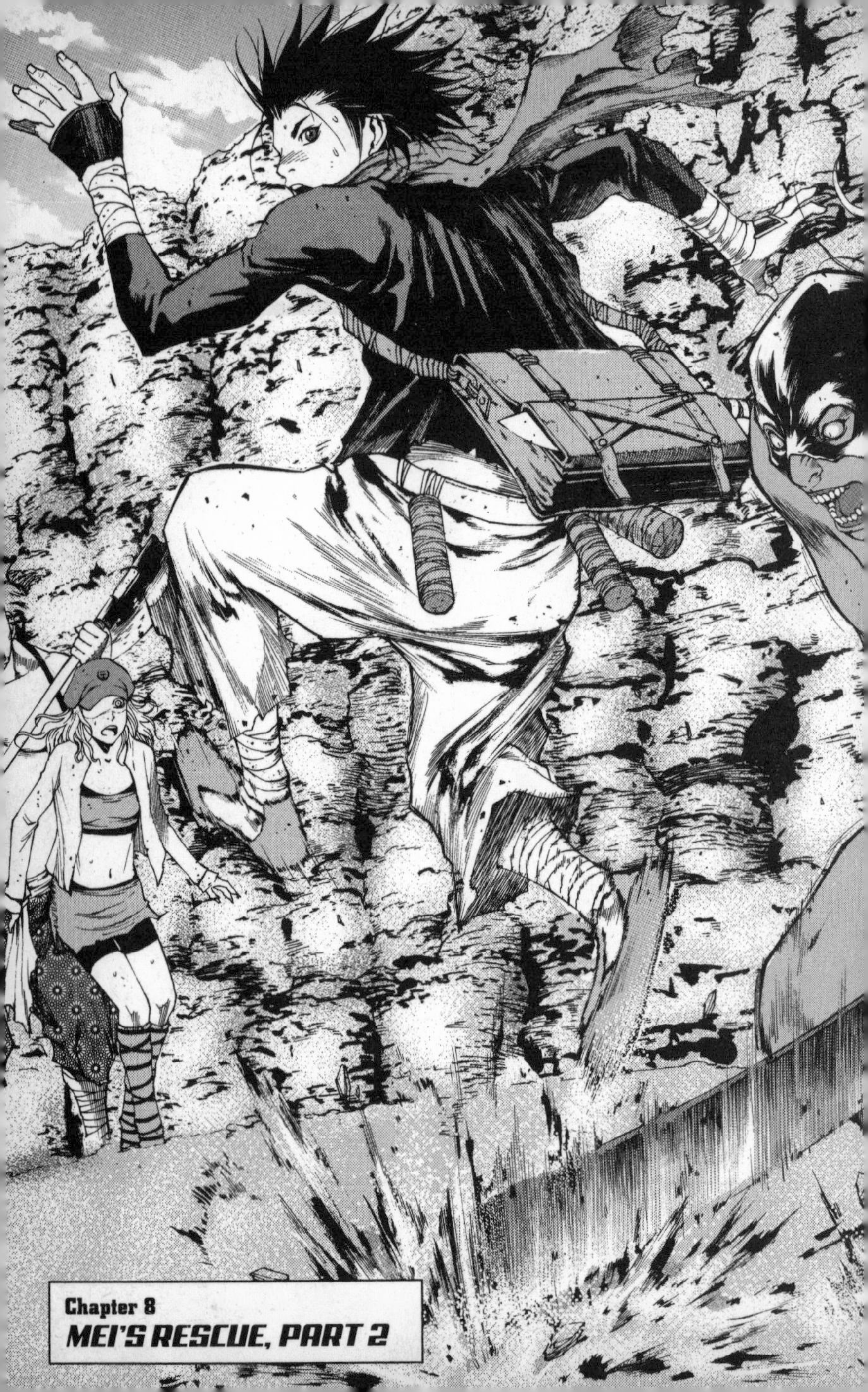

Chapter 8
MEI'S RESCUE, PART 2

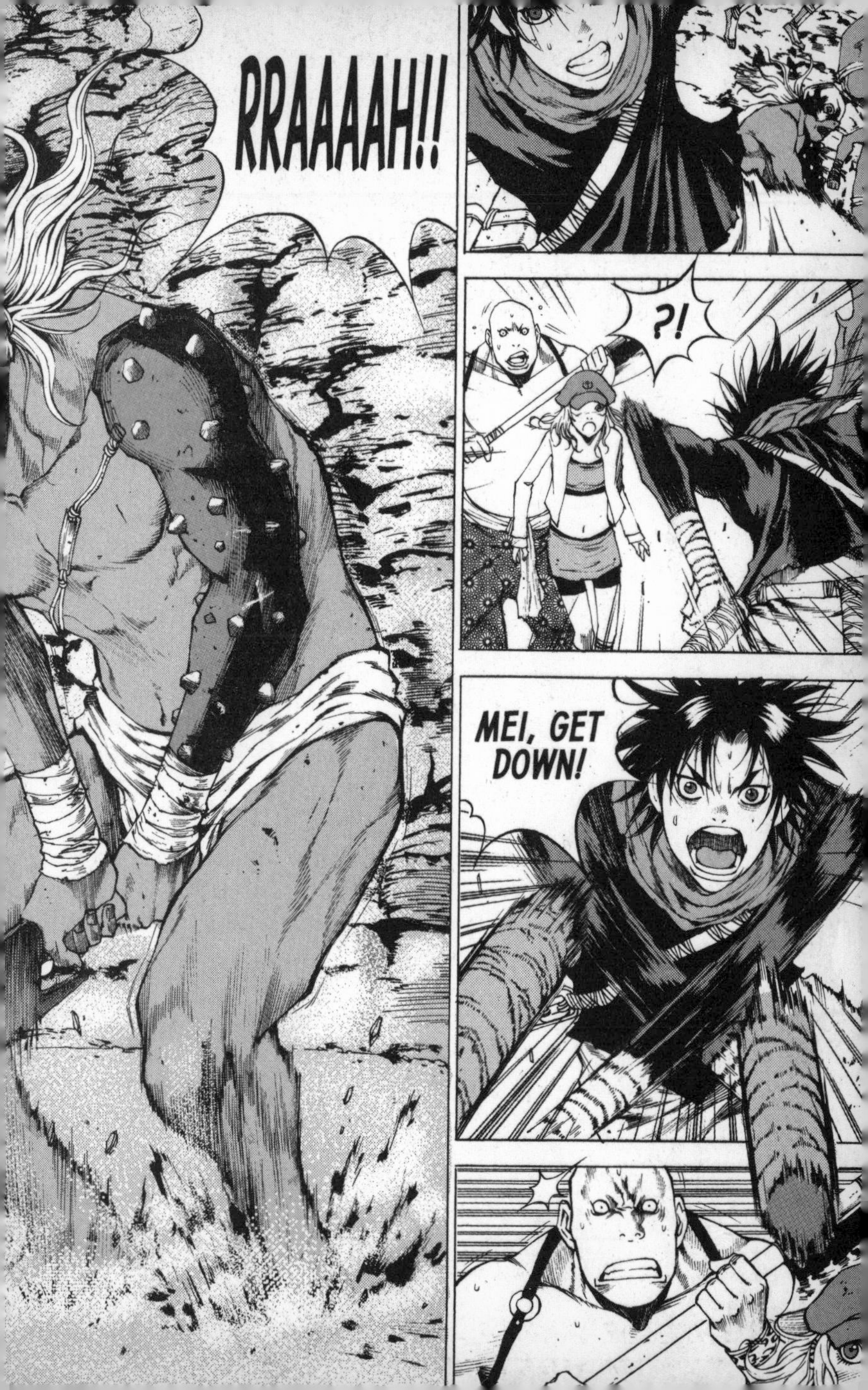
RRAAAAH!!
?!
MEI, GET DOWN!

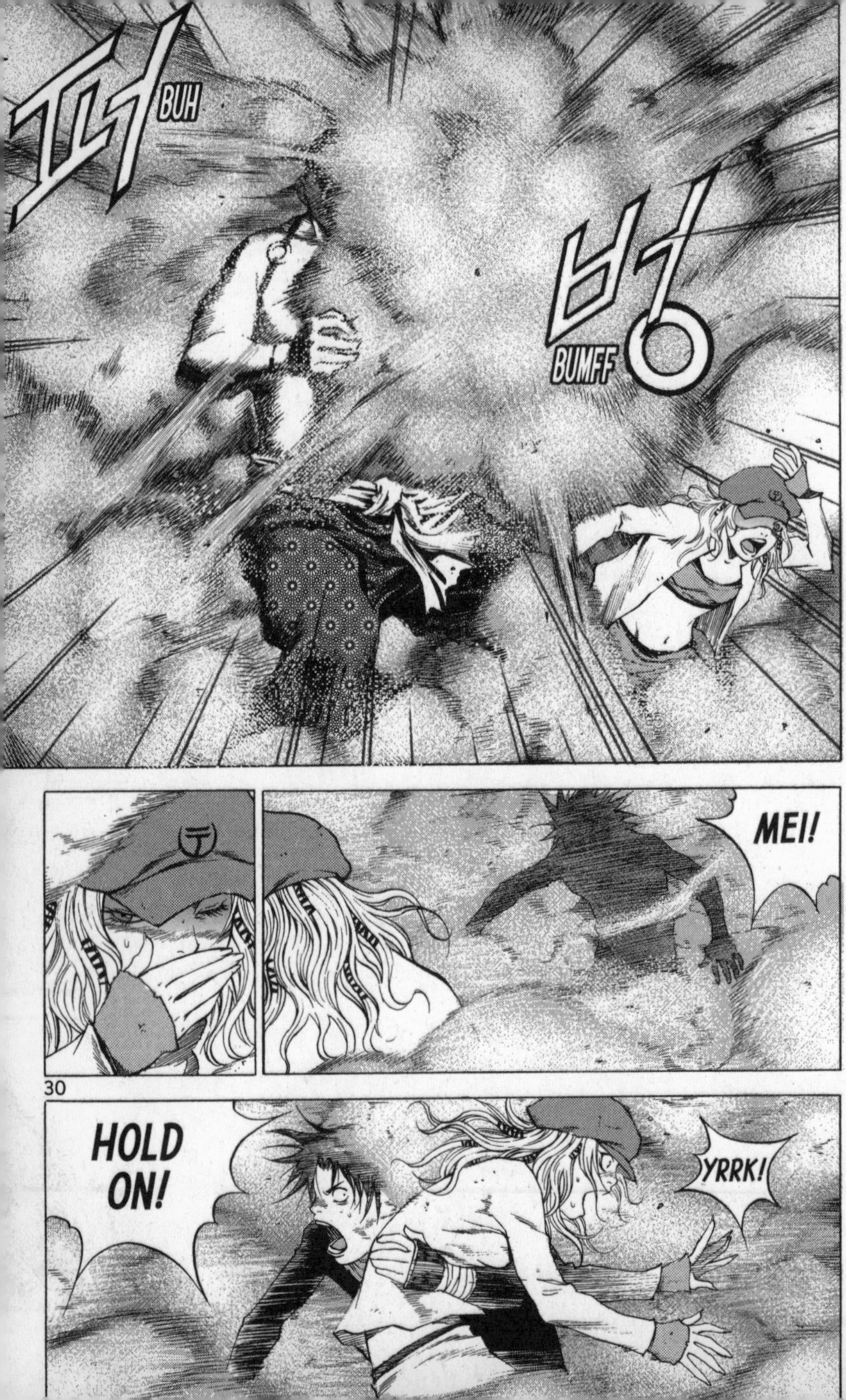
BUH
BUMFF
MEI!
YRRK!
HOLD
ON!

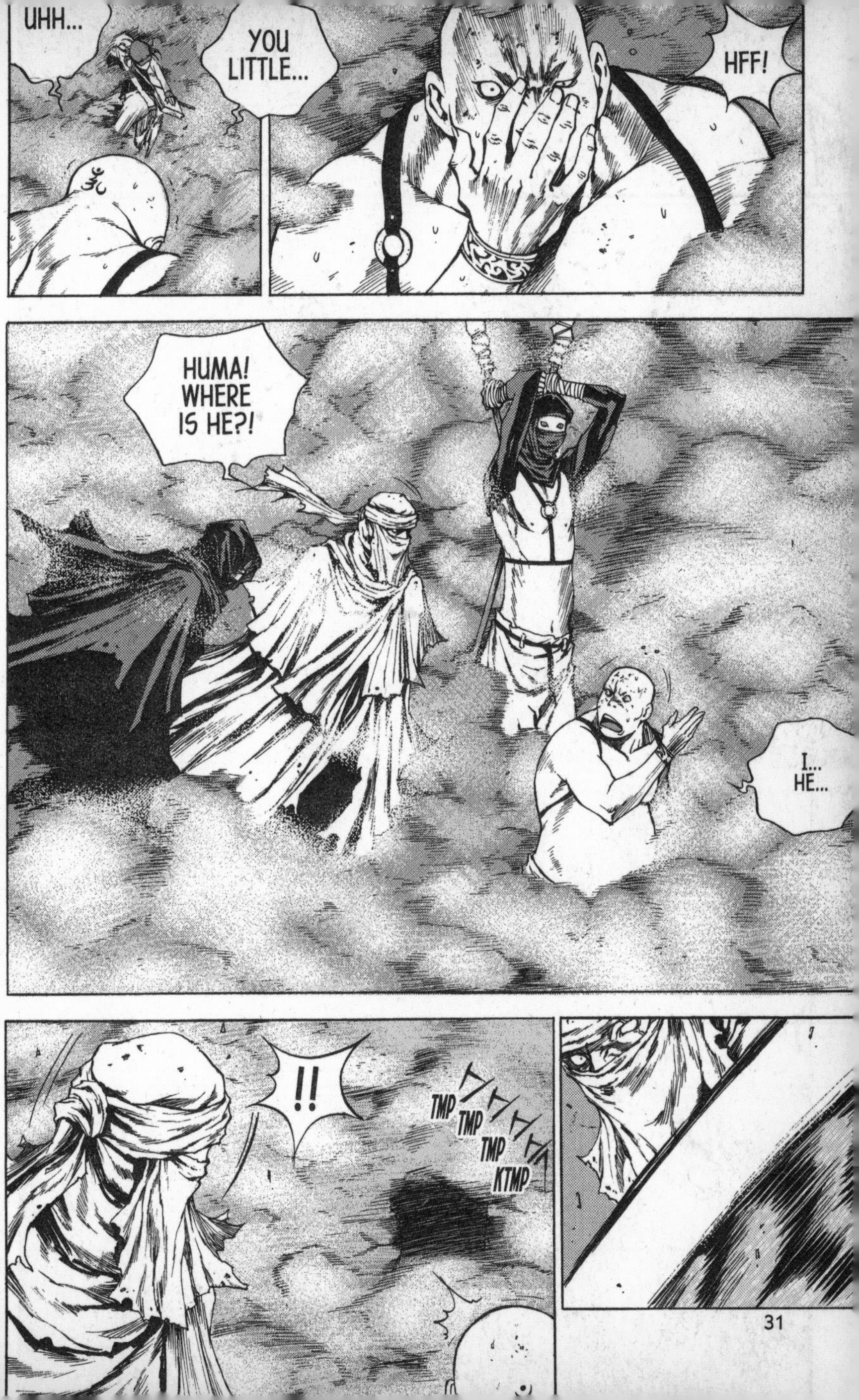
UHH...
YOU LITTLE...
HFF!
HUMA! WHERE IS HE?!
I... HE...
!!
TMP TMP TMP KTMP

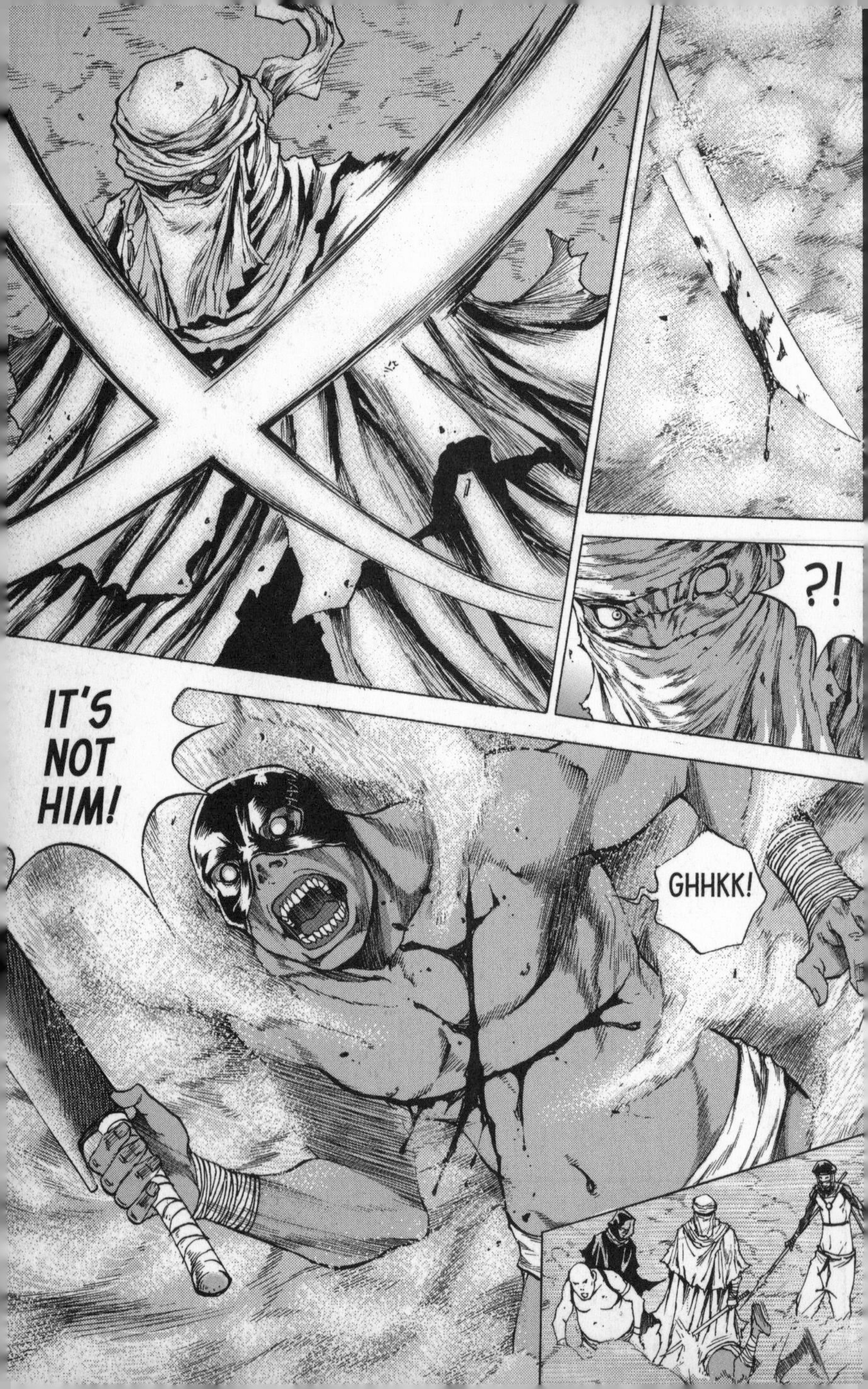
?!
IT'S NOT HIM!
GHHKK!

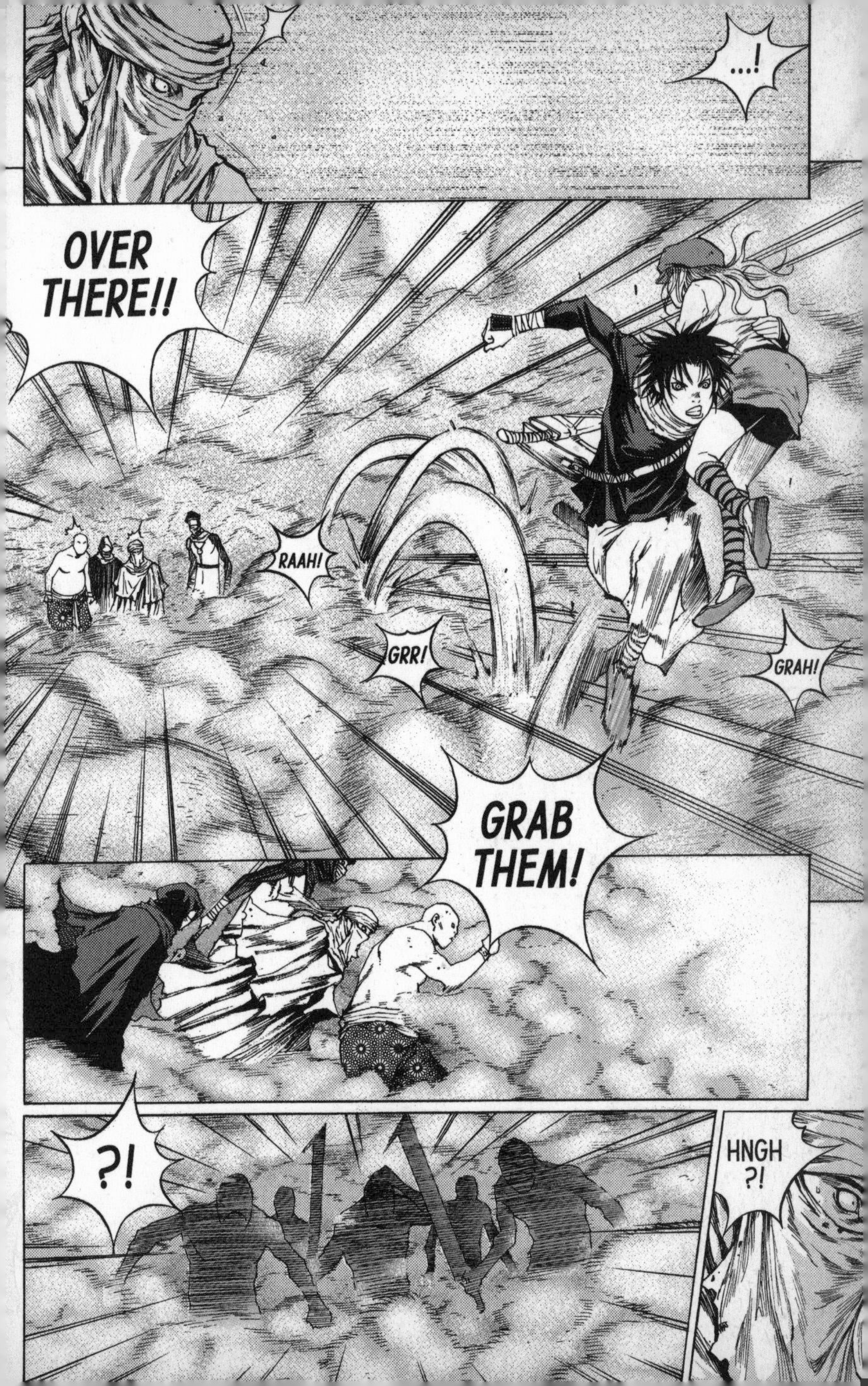
...!
OVER THERE!!
RAAH!
GRR!
GRAH!
GRAB THEM!
?!
HNGH ?!

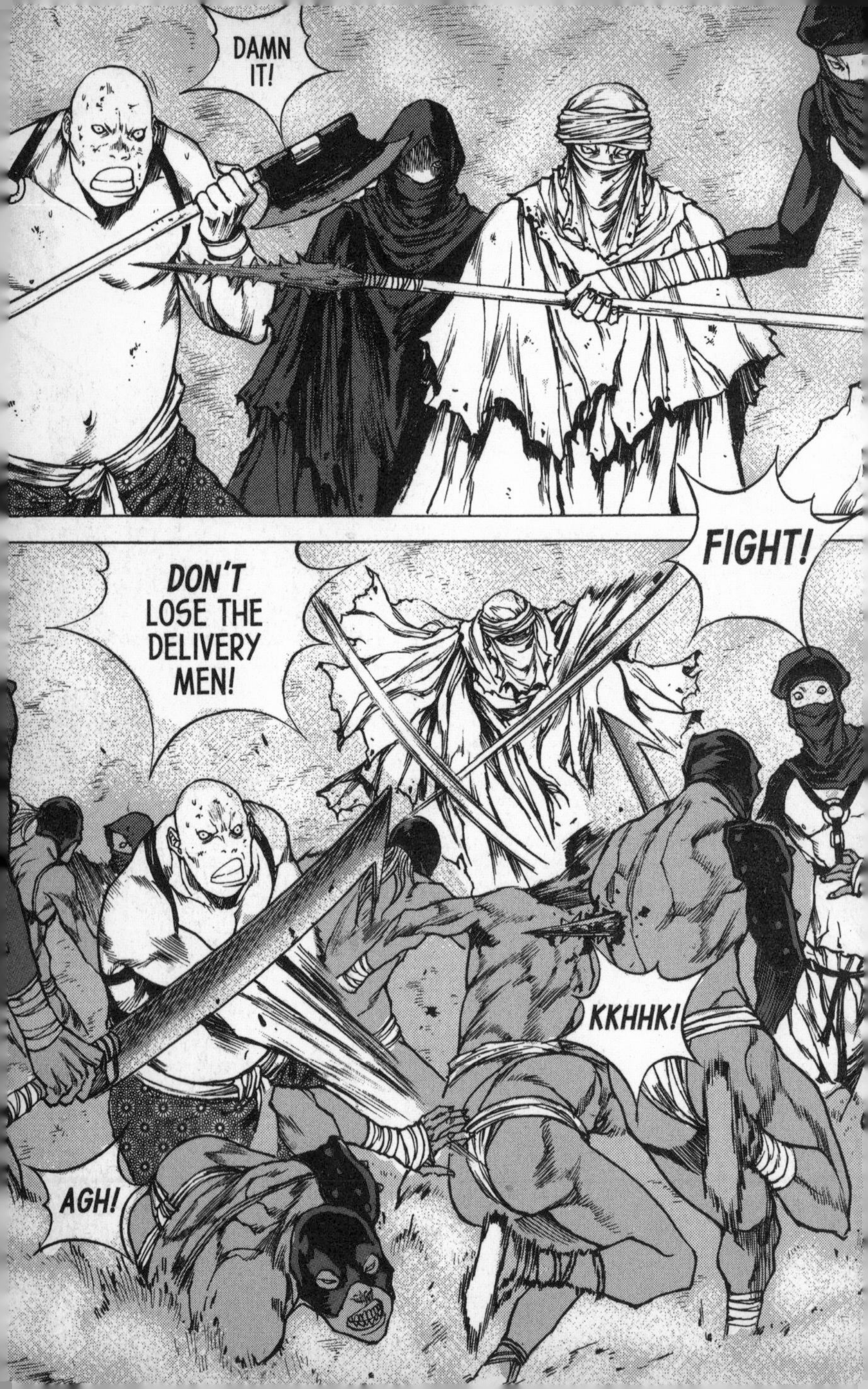
DAMN IT!
FIGHT!
DON'T LOSE THE DELIVERY MEN!
KKHHK!
AGH!

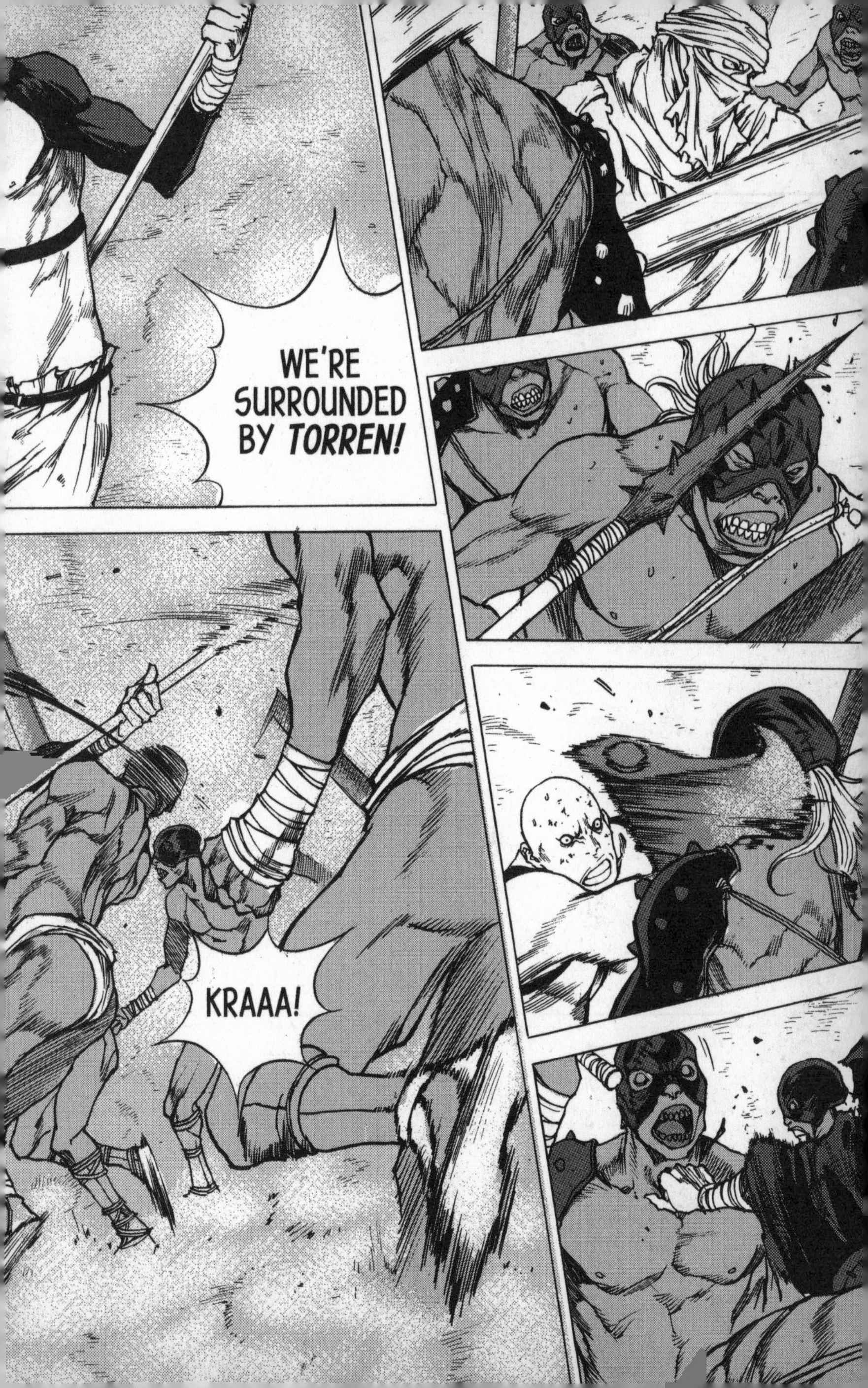
WE'RE SURROUNDED BY *TORREN!*
KRAAA!

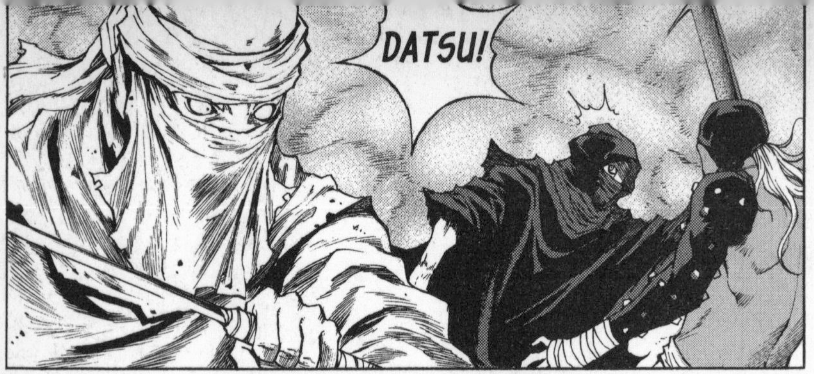
DATSU!

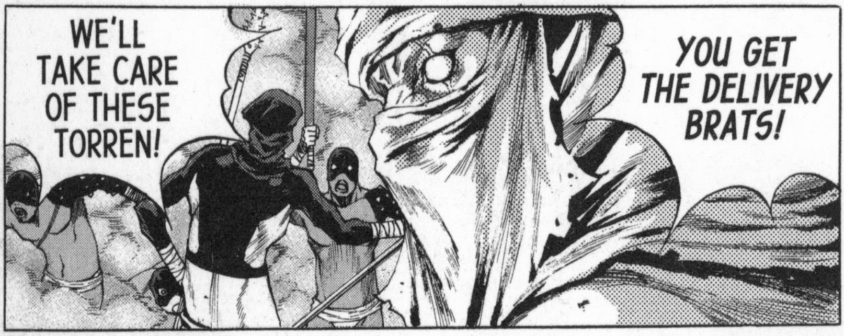
WE'LL TAKE CARE OF THESE TORREN!
YOU GET THE DELIVERY BRATS!

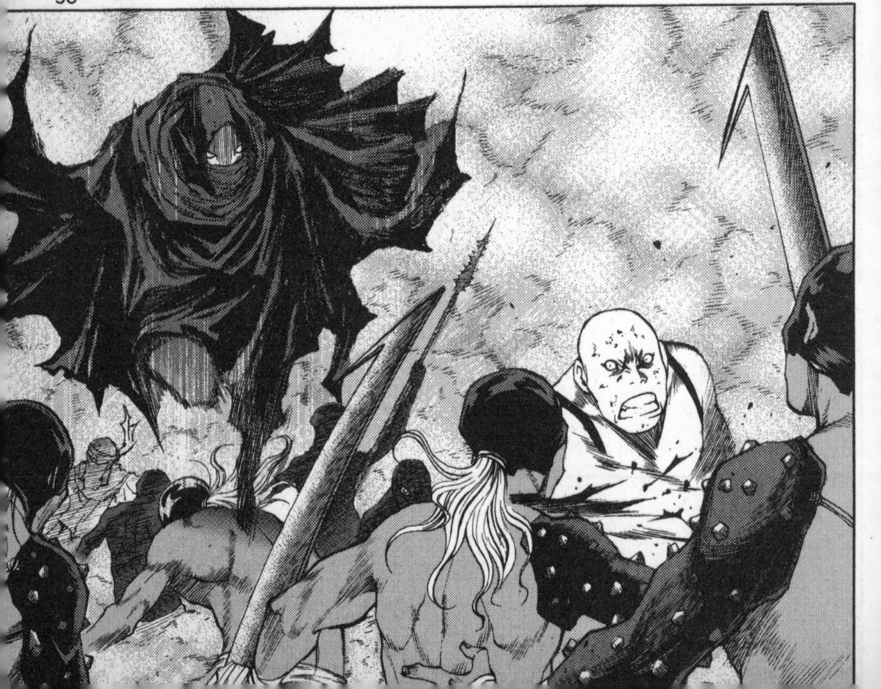

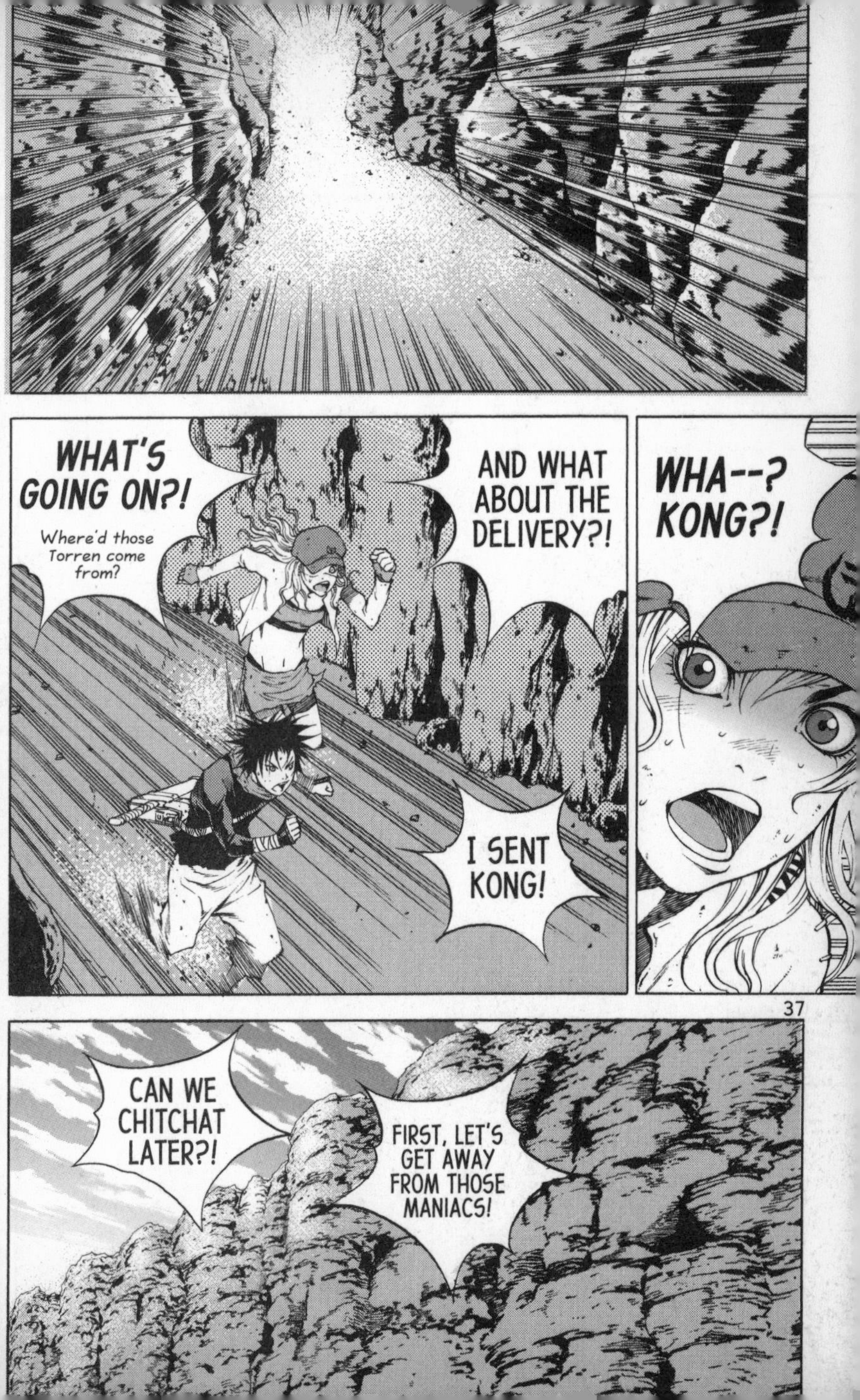
WHAT'S GOING ON?!
Where'd those Torren come from?
AND WHAT ABOUT THE DELIVERY?!
I SENT KONG!
WHA--? KONG?!
CAN WE CHITCHAT LATER?!
FIRST, LET'S GET AWAY FROM THOSE MANIACS!

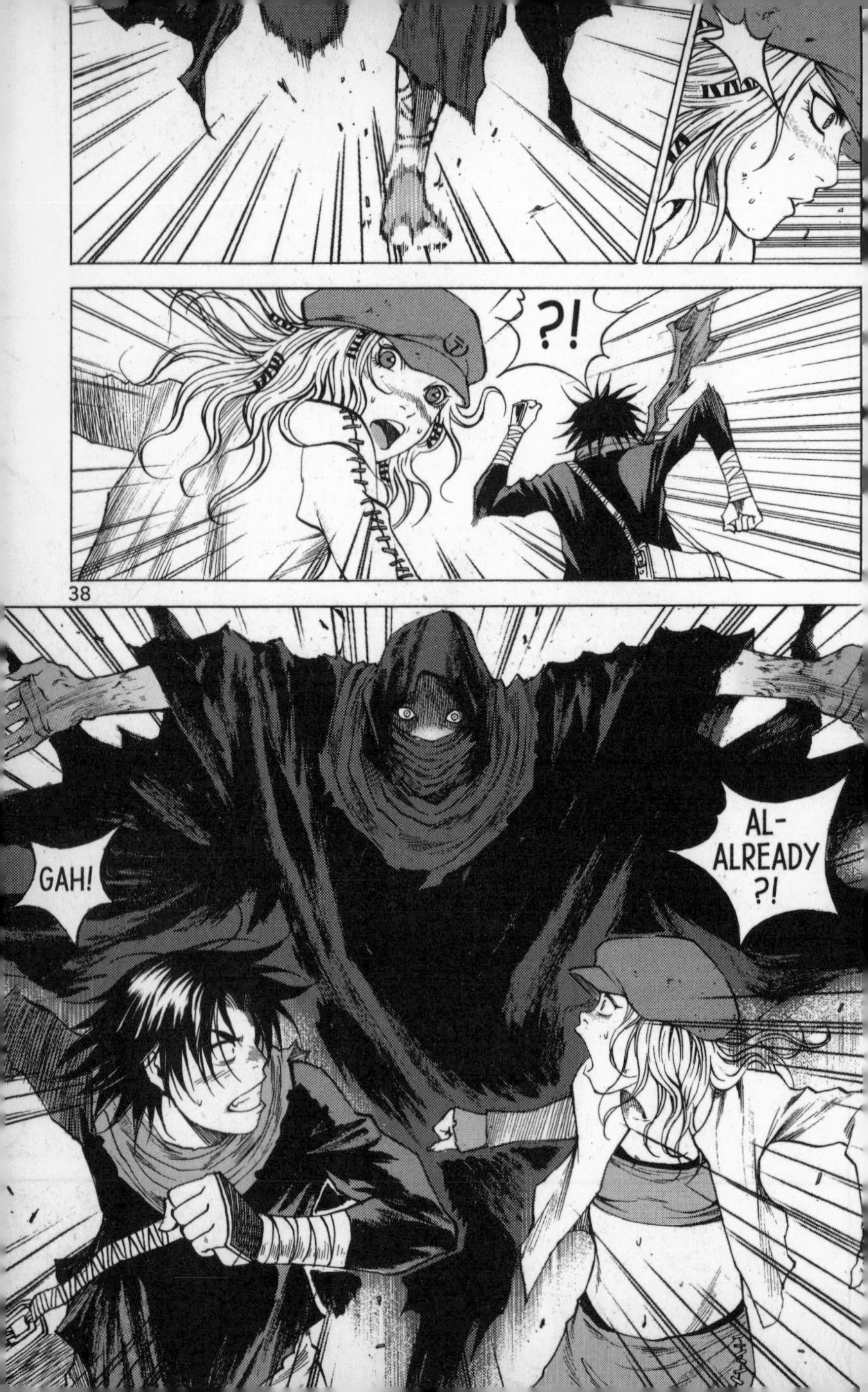
?!
AL-
ALREADY
?!
GAH!

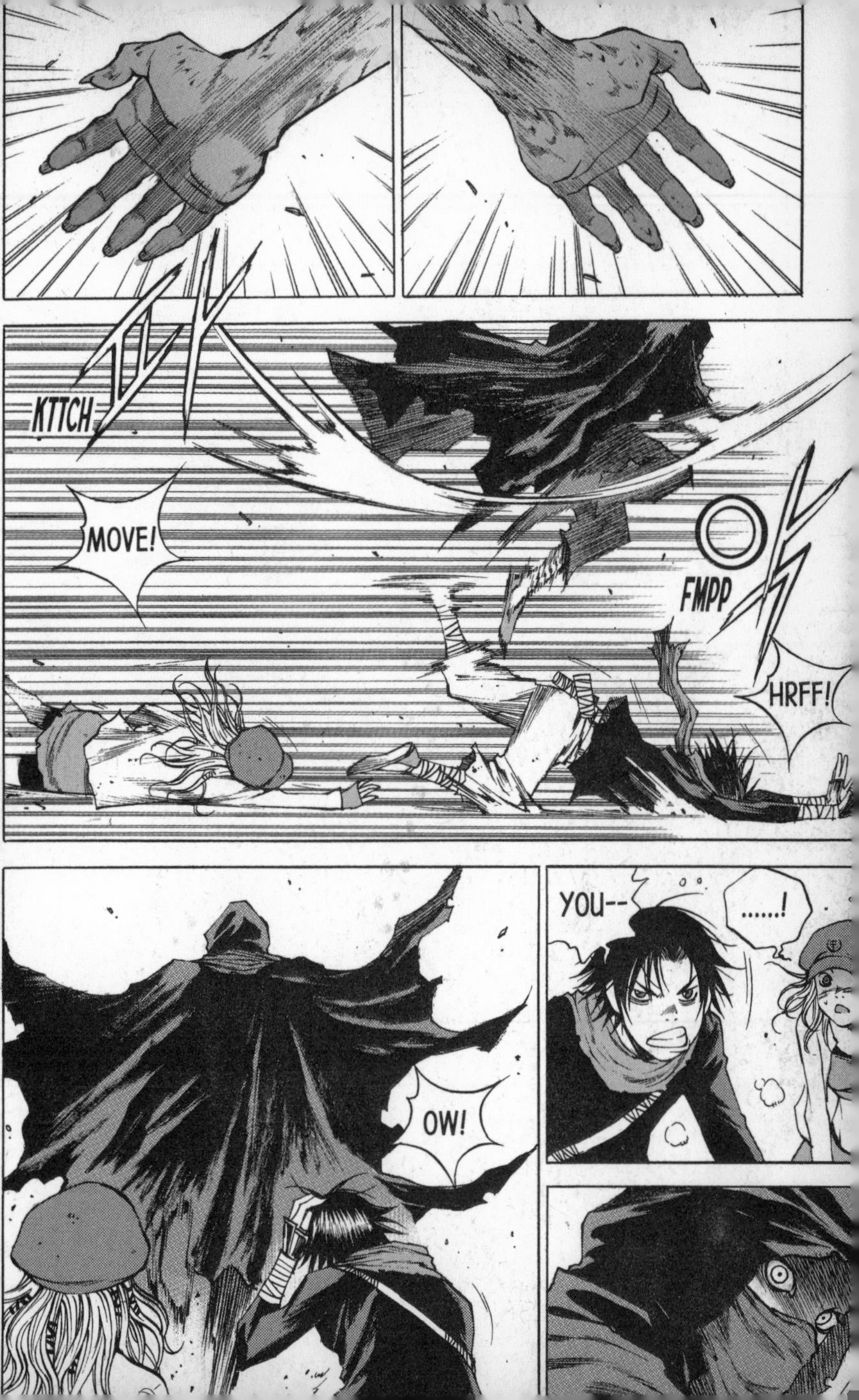
KTTCH
MOVE!
FMPP
HRFF!
......!
YOU--
OW!

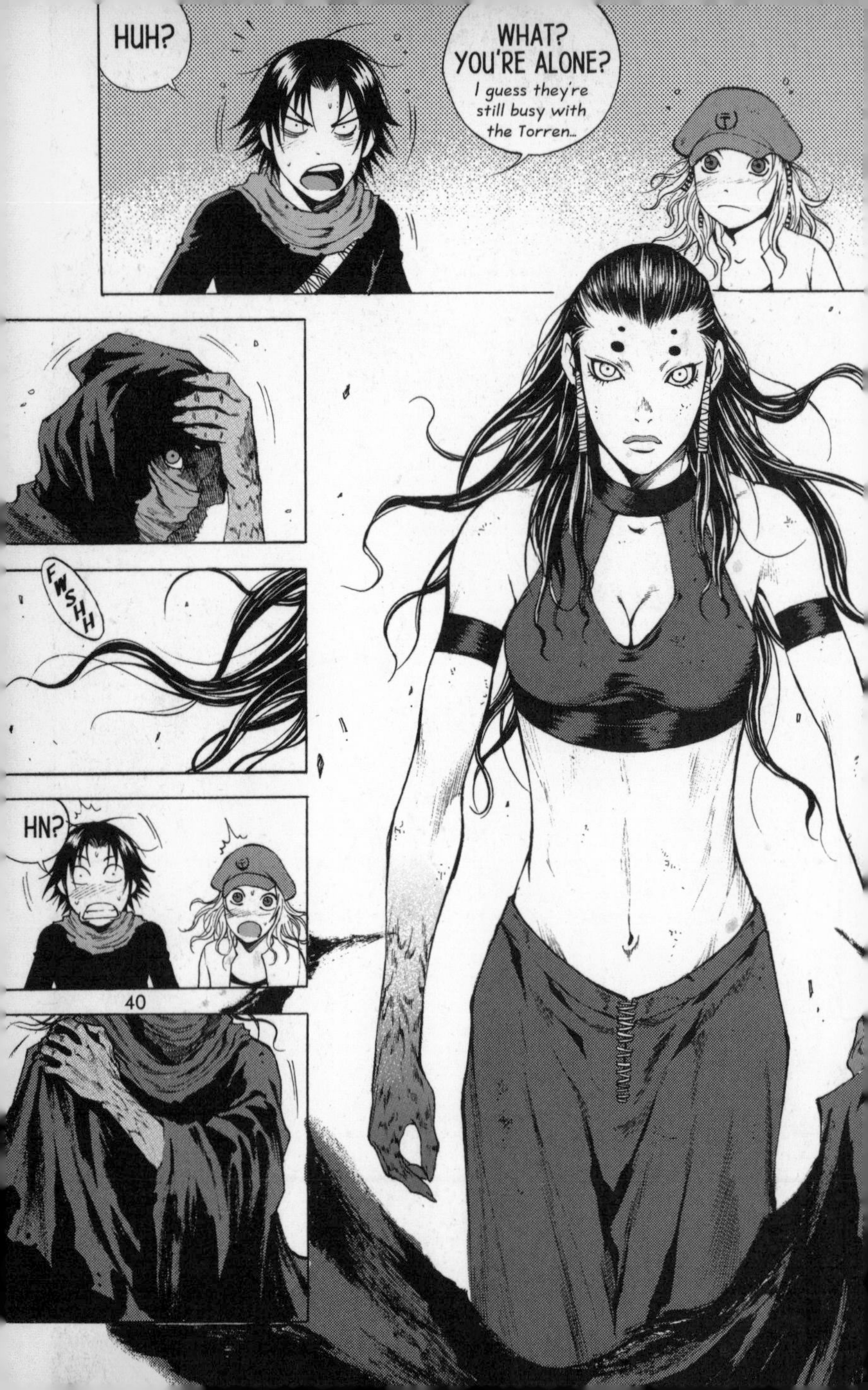
WHAT? YOU'RE ALONE?
I guess they're still busy with the Torren...
HUH?
FWSHH
HN?

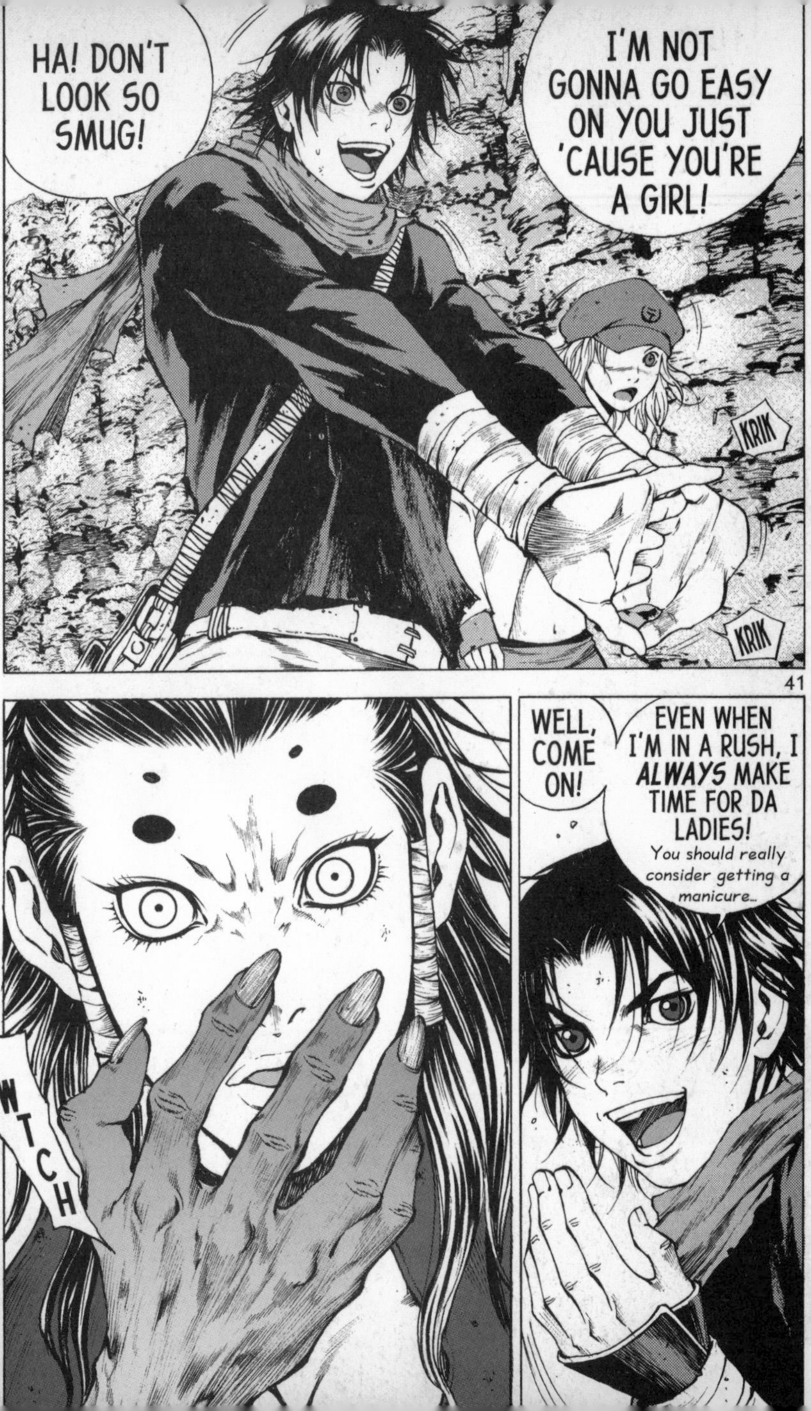
HA! DON'T LOOK SO SMUG!
I'M NOT GONNA GO EASY ON YOU JUST 'CAUSE YOU'RE A GIRL!
KRIK
KRIK
FWTCH
WELL, COME ON!
EVEN WHEN I'M IN A RUSH, I *ALWAYS* MAKE TIME FOR DA LADIES!
You should really consider getting a manicure...

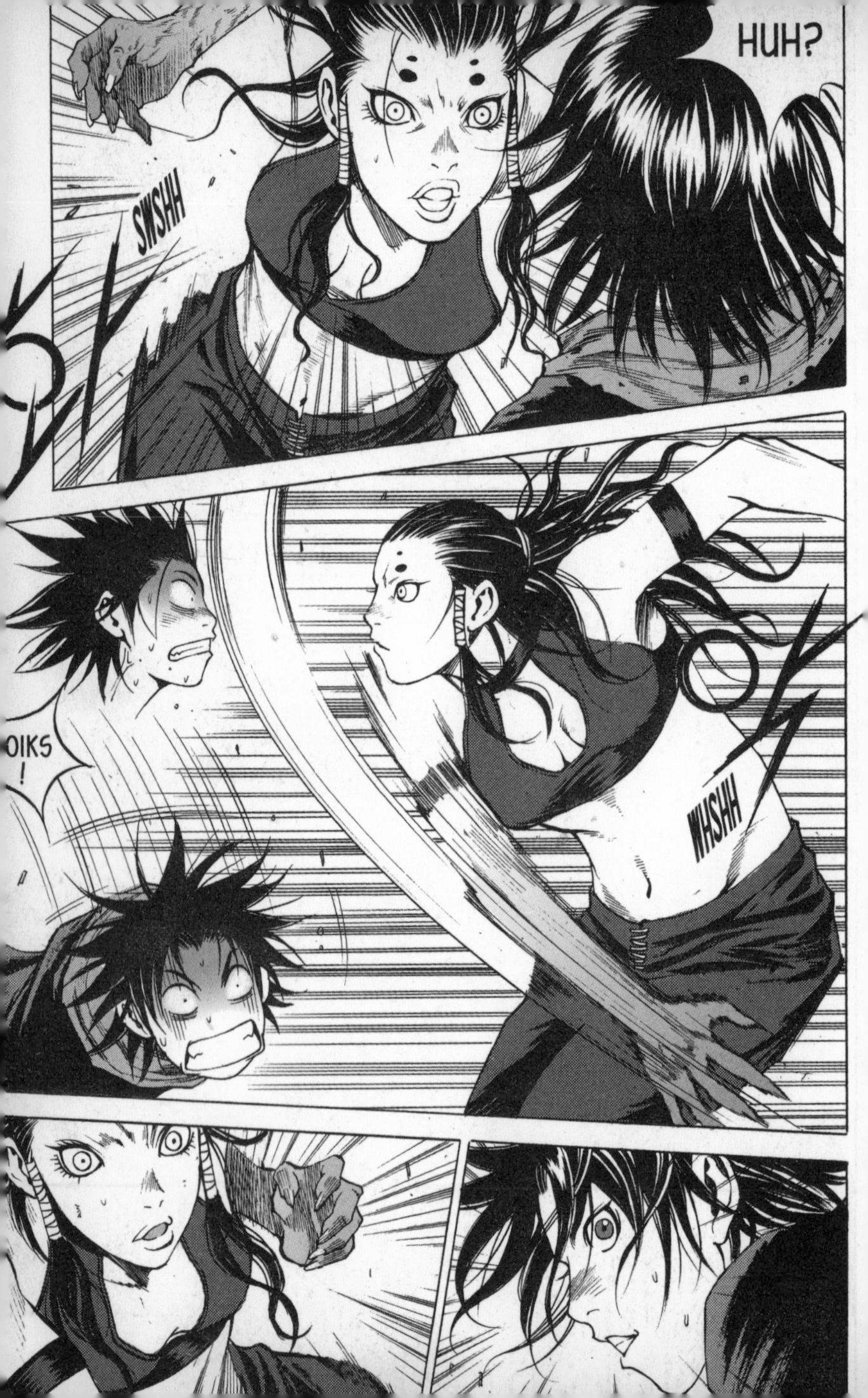
HUH?
SWSHH
WHSHH
OIKS
!

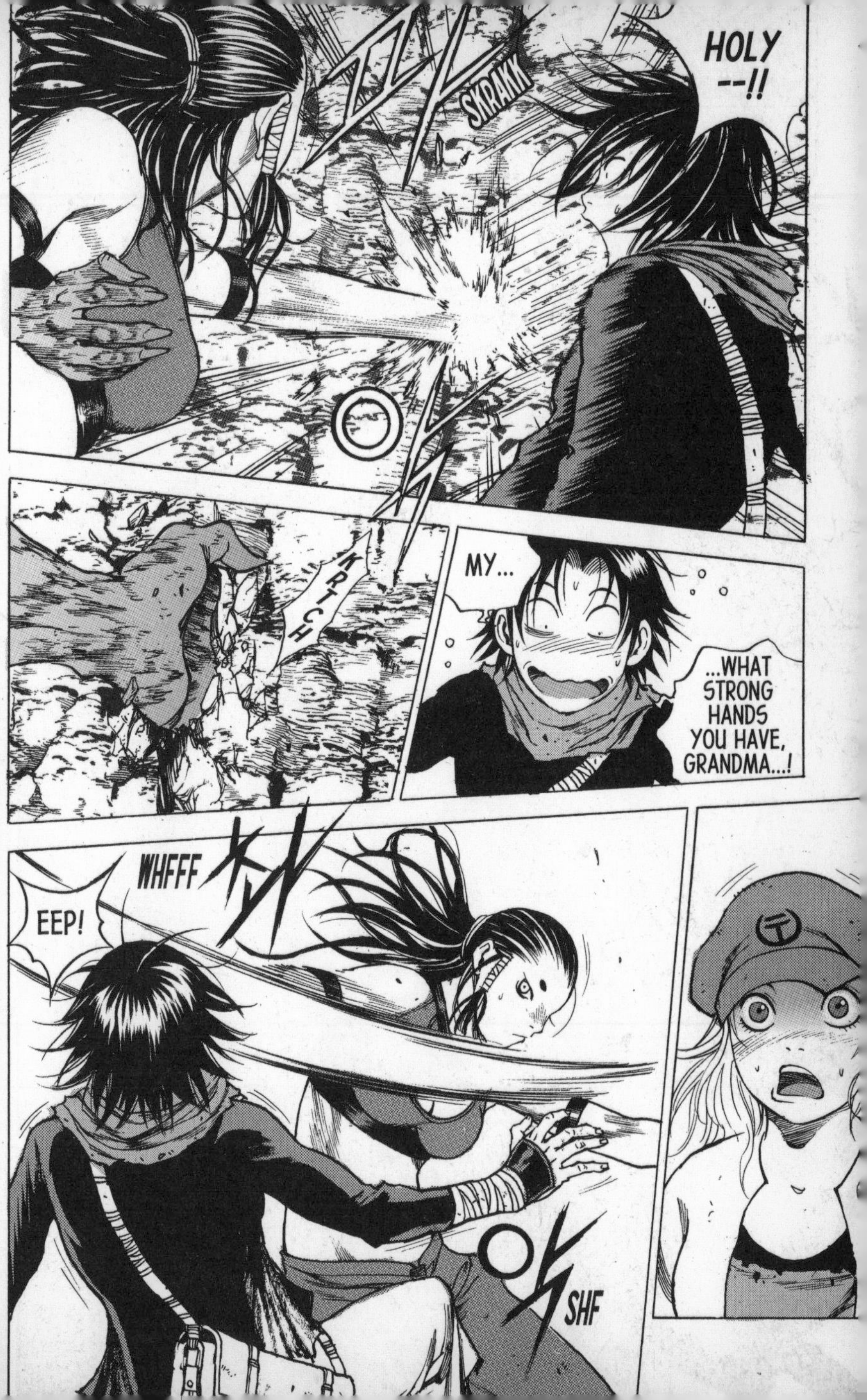
HOLY --!!
SKRAKK
KRTCH
MY...
...WHAT STRONG HANDS YOU HAVE, GRANDMA...!
WHFFF
EEP!
SHF

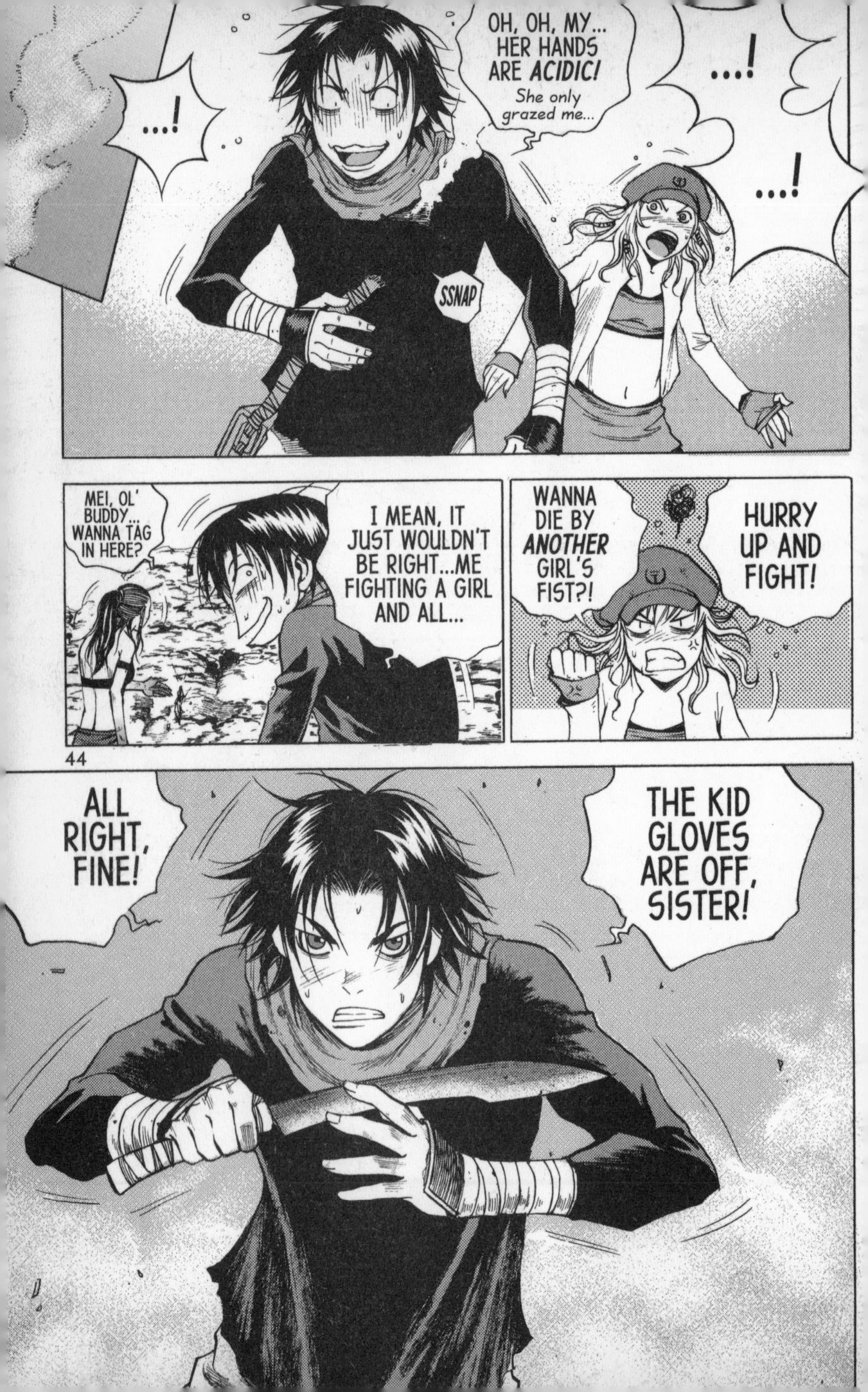
...!
OH, OH, MY... HER HANDS ARE *ACIDIC!*
She only grazed me...
...!
...!
SSNAP
MEI, OL' BUDDY... WANNA TAG IN HERE?
I MEAN, IT JUST WOULDN'T BE RIGHT...ME FIGHTING A GIRL AND ALL...
WANNA DIE BY *ANOTHER* GIRL'S FIST?!
HURRY UP AND FIGHT!
ALL RIGHT, FINE!
THE KID GLOVES ARE OFF, SISTER!

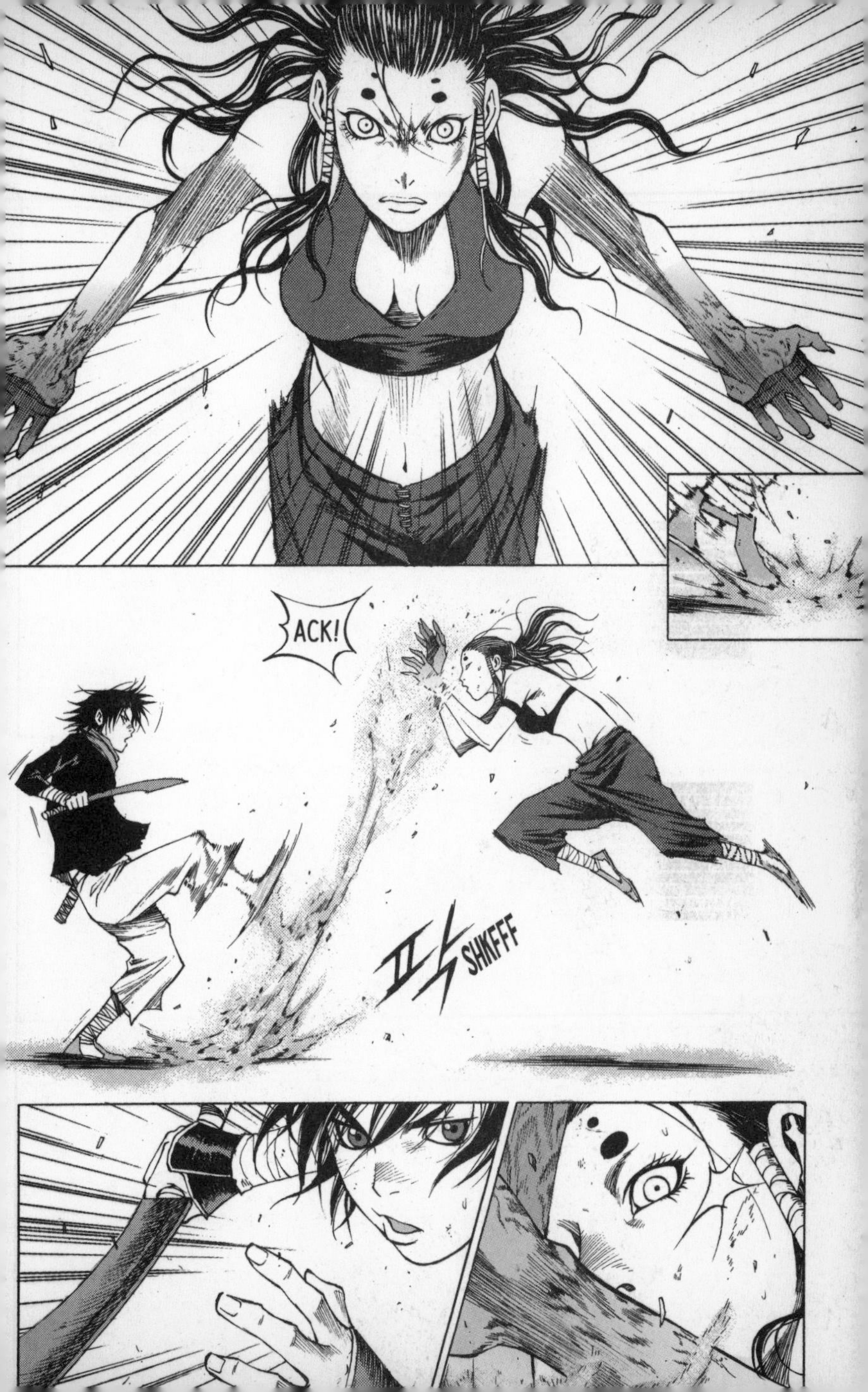
ACK!
SHKFFF

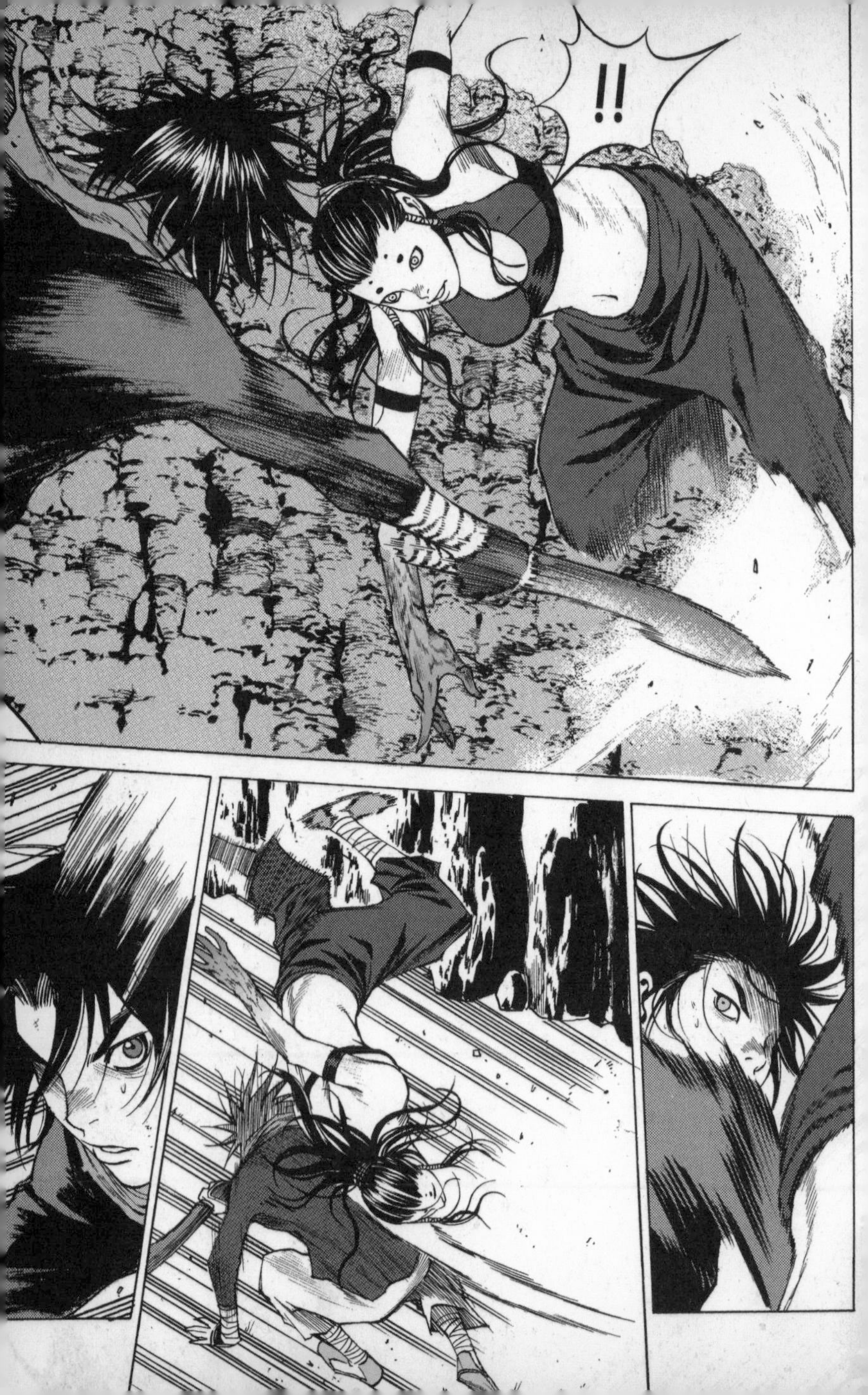
!!

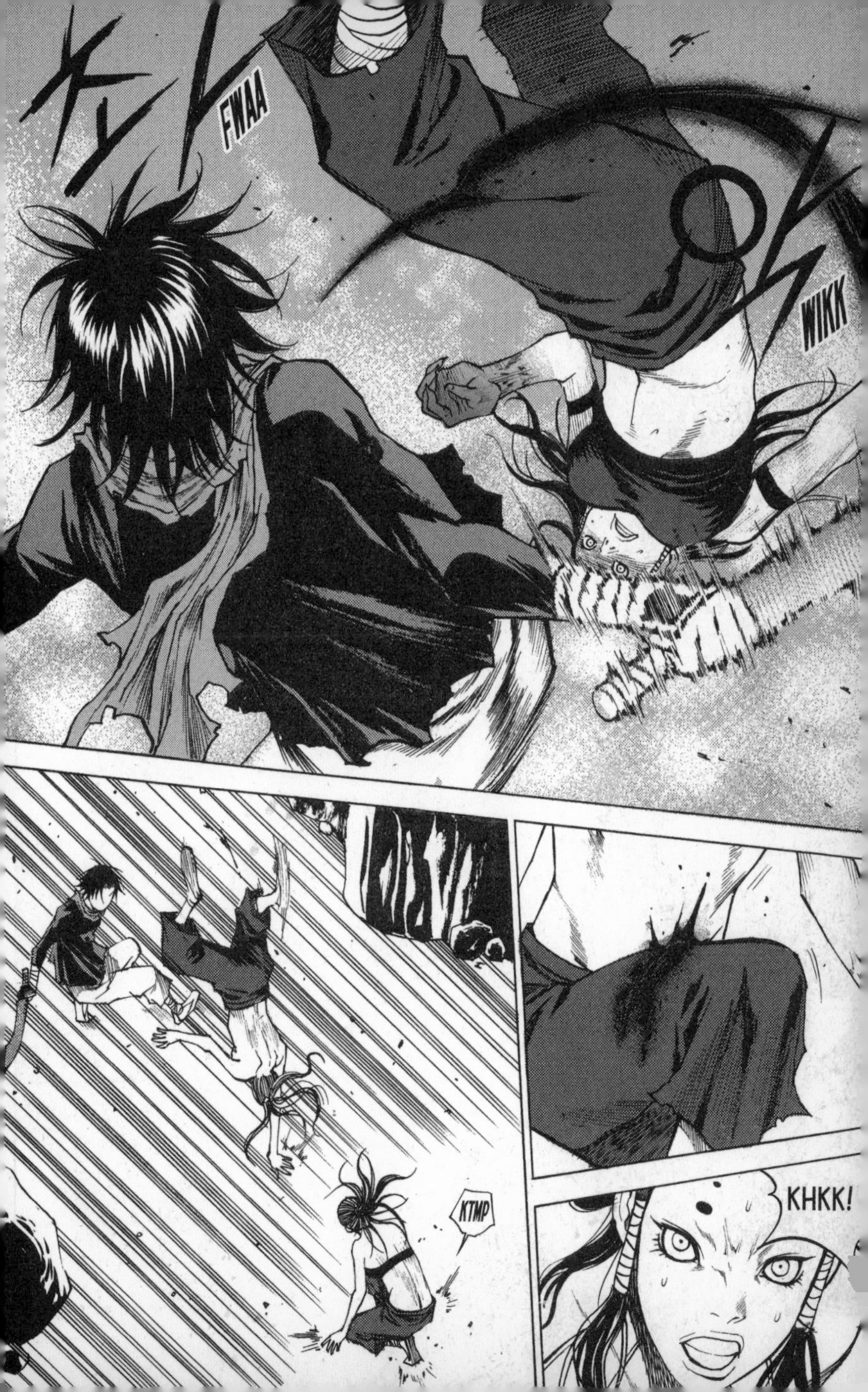
FWAA
WIKK
KHKK!
KTMP

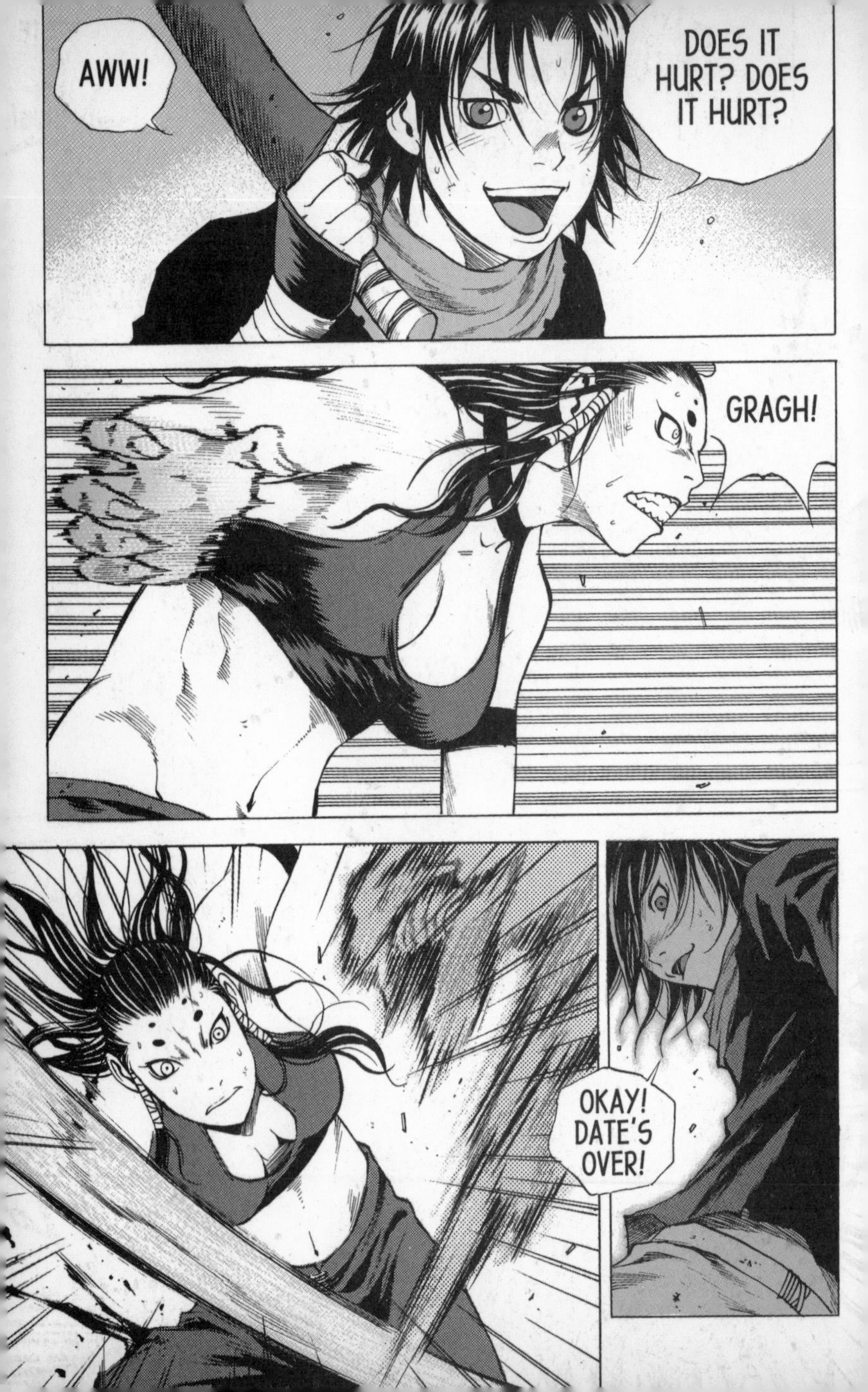
DOES IT HURT? DOES IT HURT?
AWW!
GRAGH!
OKAY! DATE'S OVER!

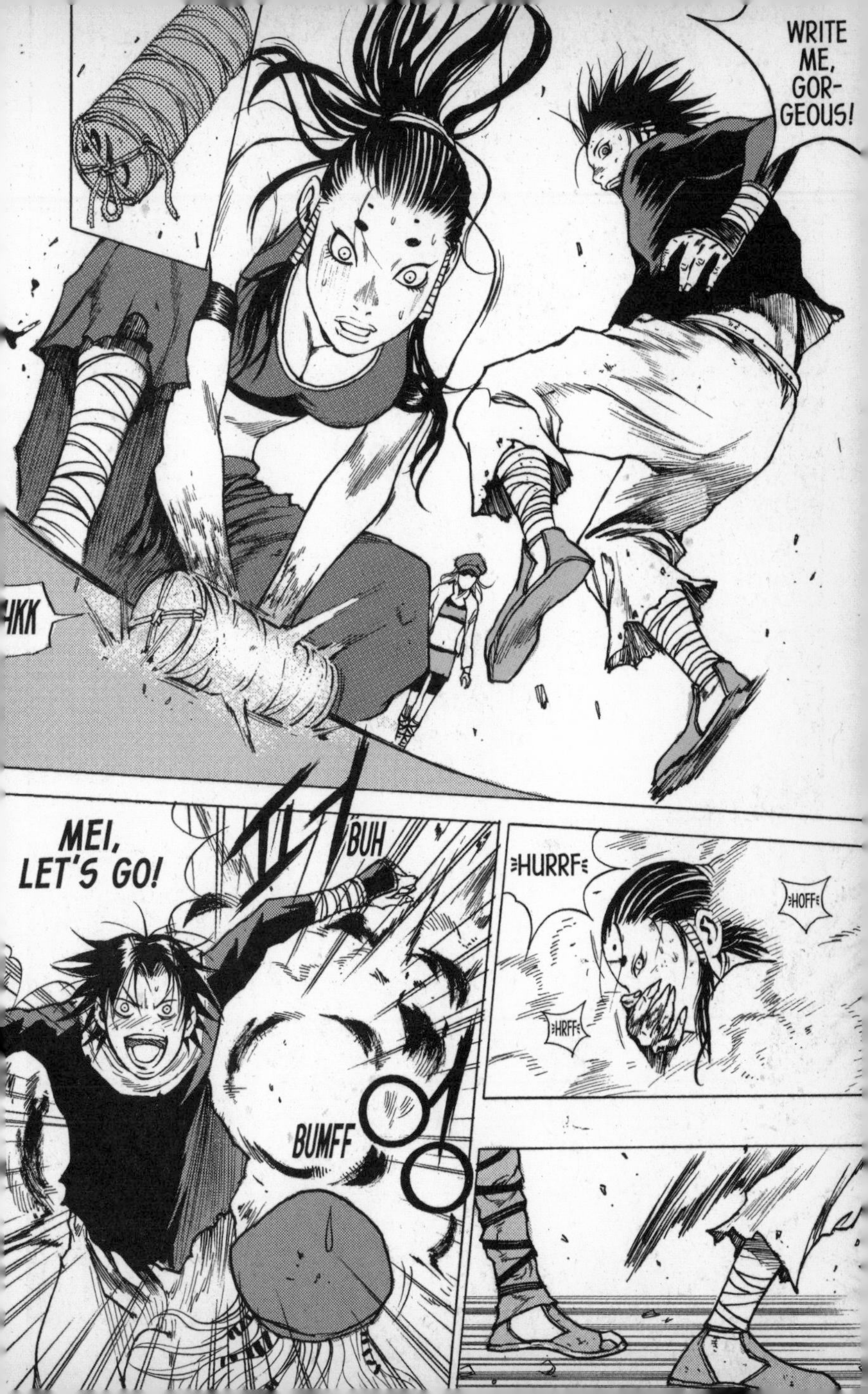
WRITE ME, GOR-GEOUS!
HKK
MEI, LET'S GO!
BUH
HURRF
HOFF
HRFF
BUMFF

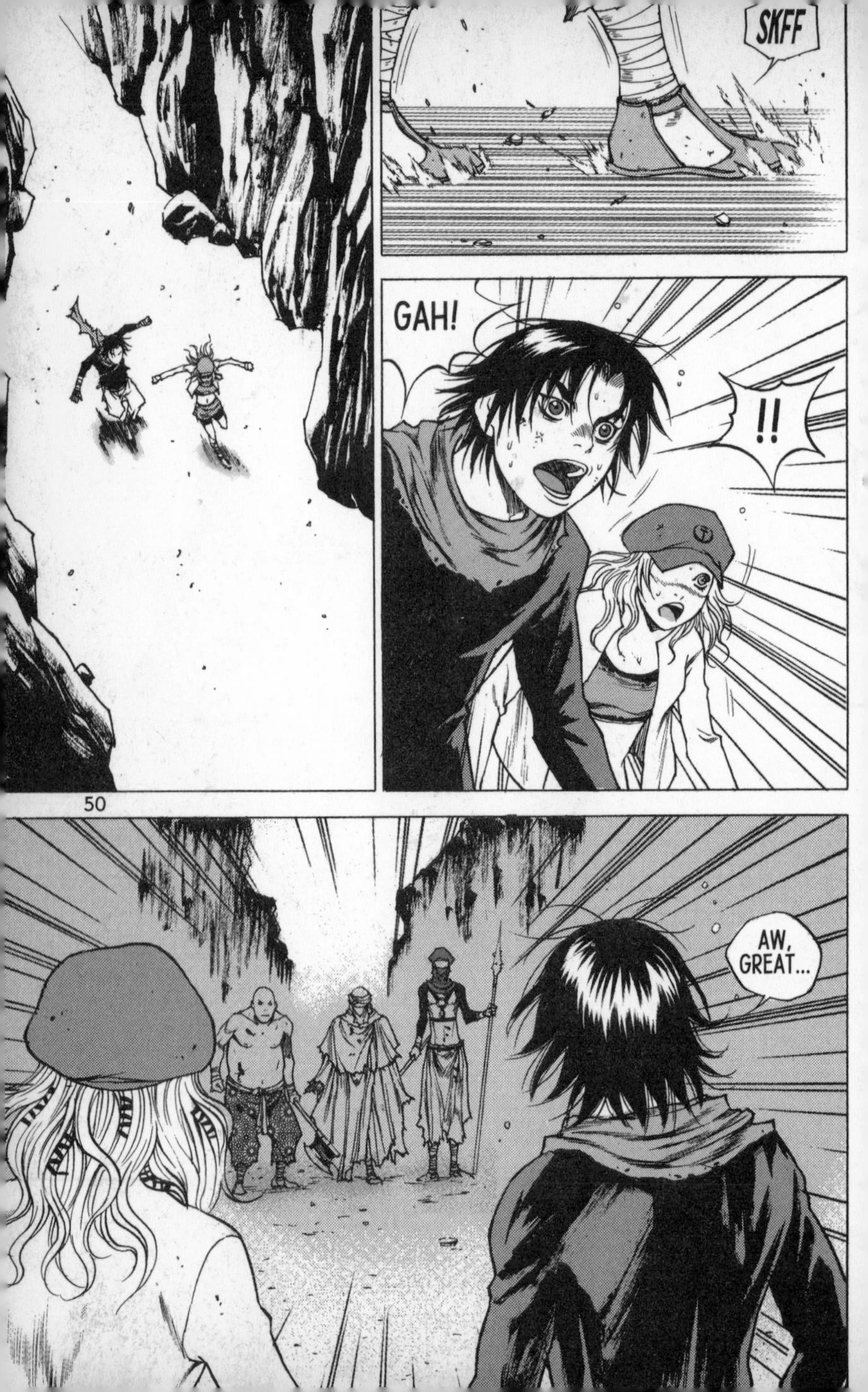
SKFF
GAH!
!!
AW, GREAT...

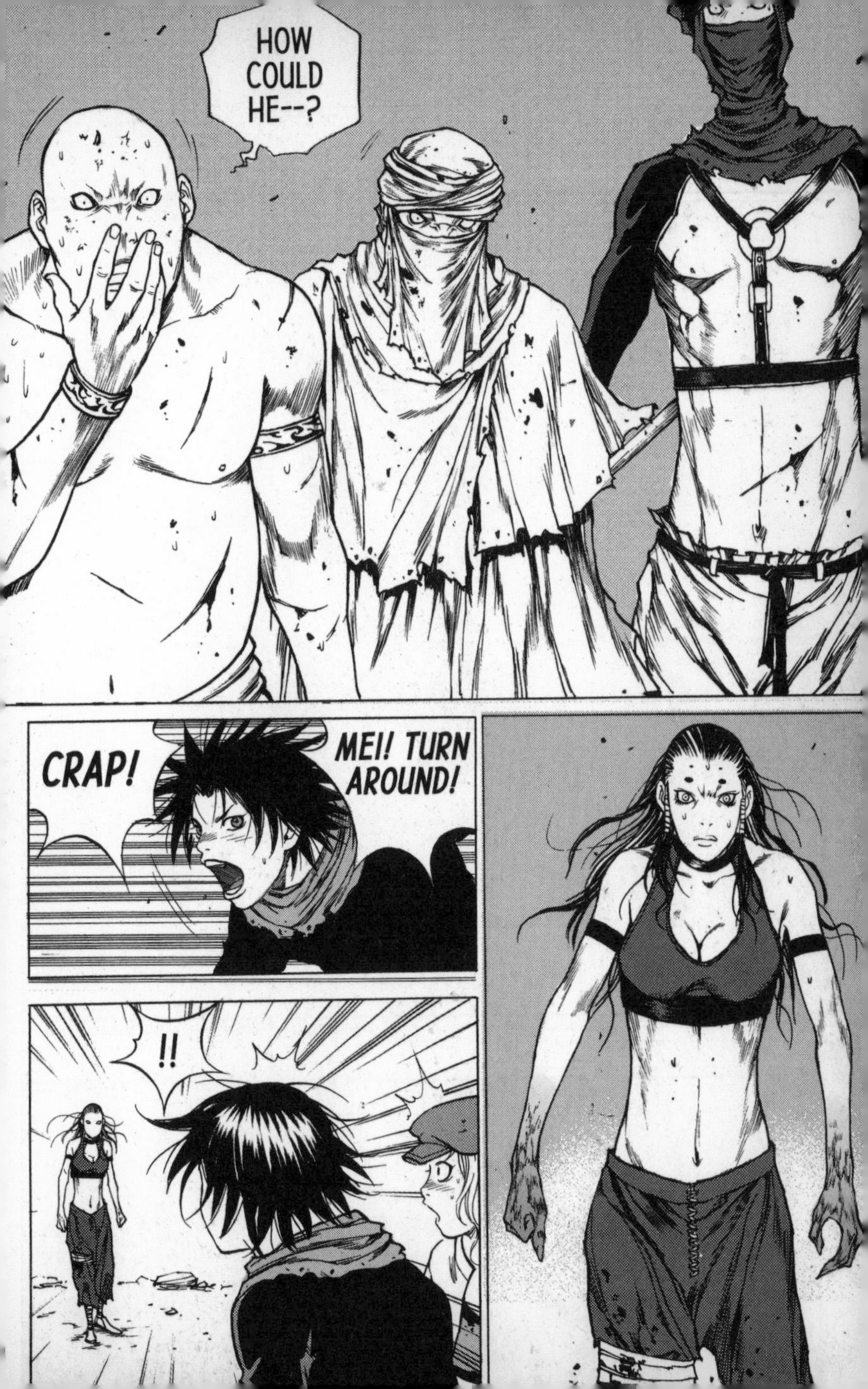
HOW COULD HE--?
MEI! TURN AROUND!
CRAP!
!!

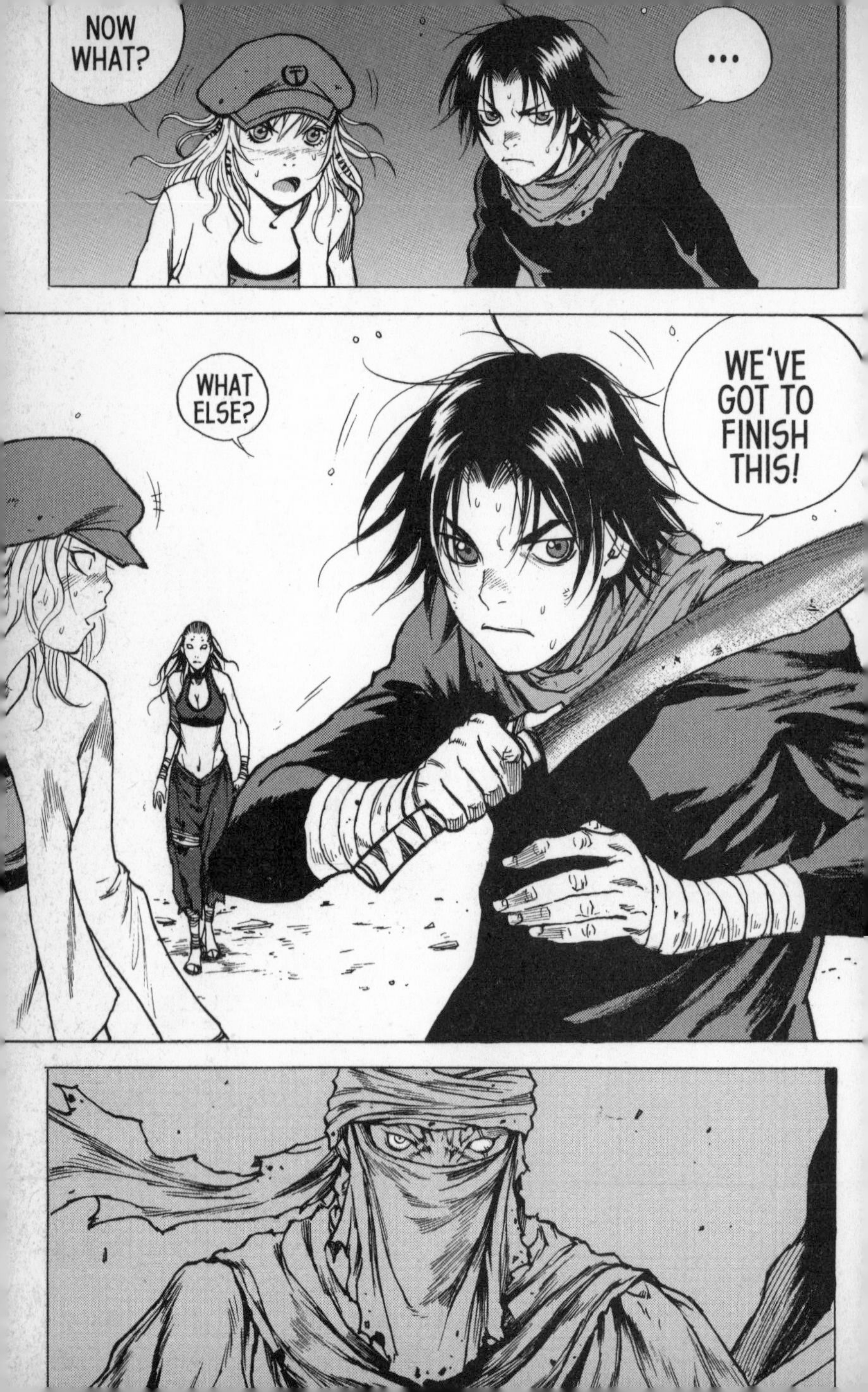
NOW WHAT?
...
WHAT ELSE?
WE'VE GOT TO FINISH THIS!

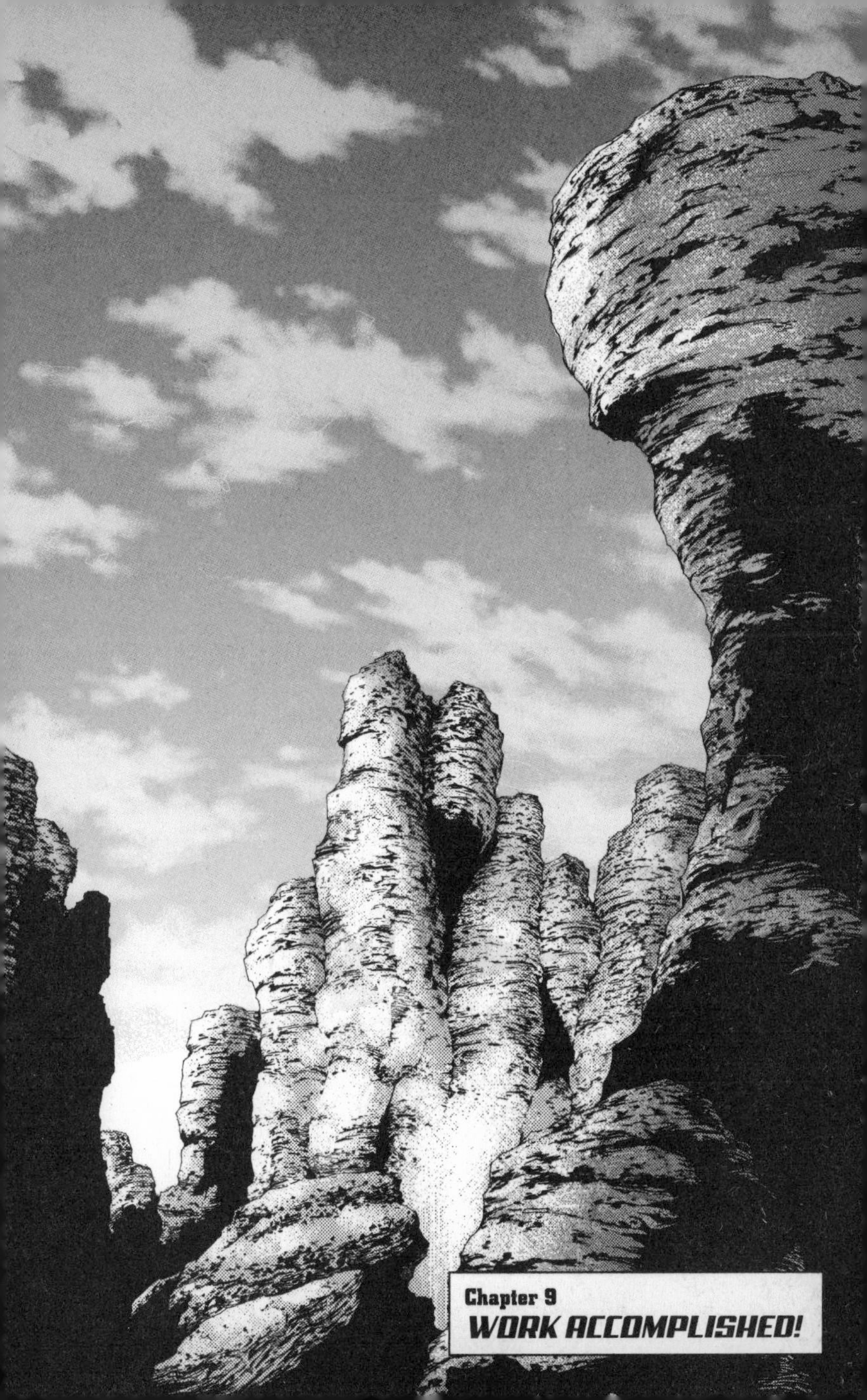
Chapter 9
WORK ACCOMPLISHED!

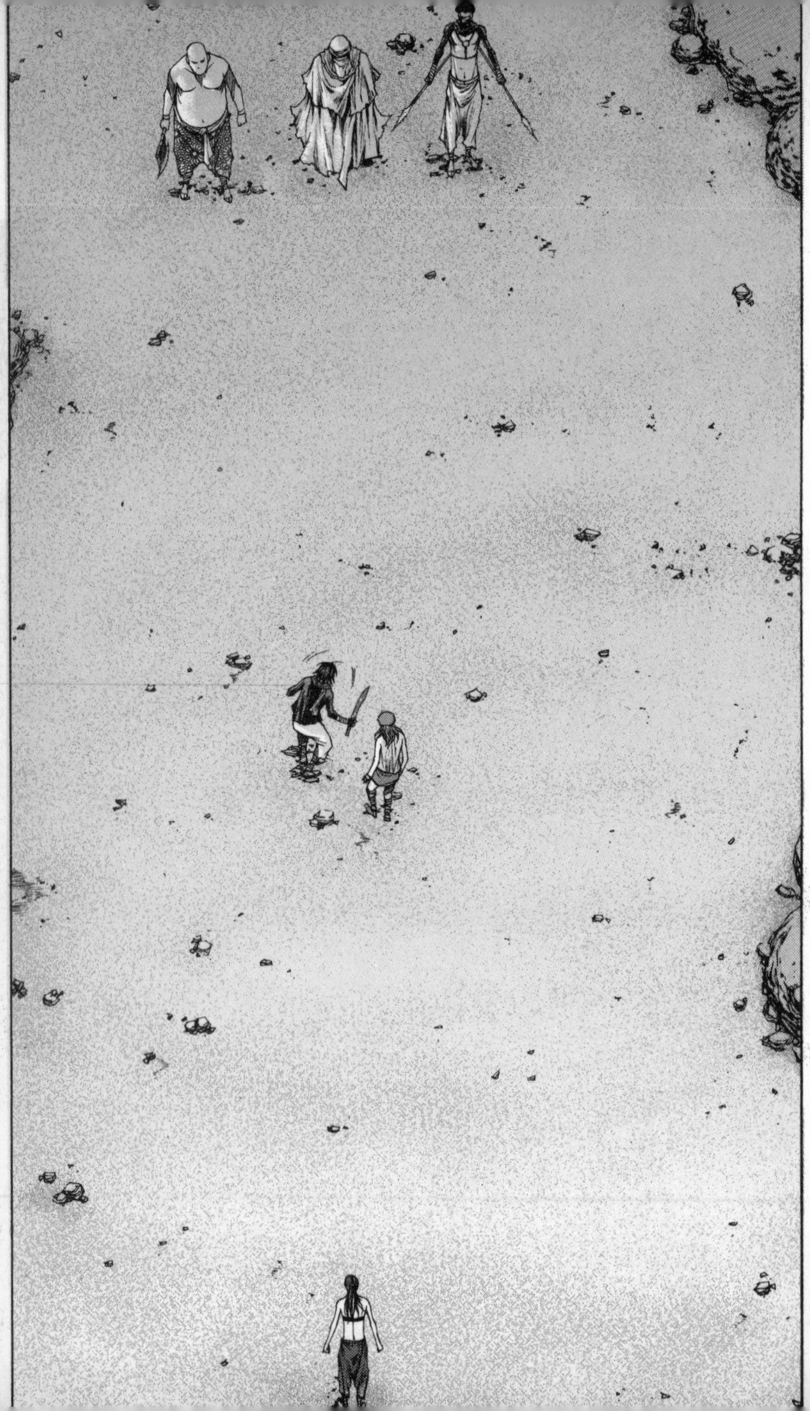

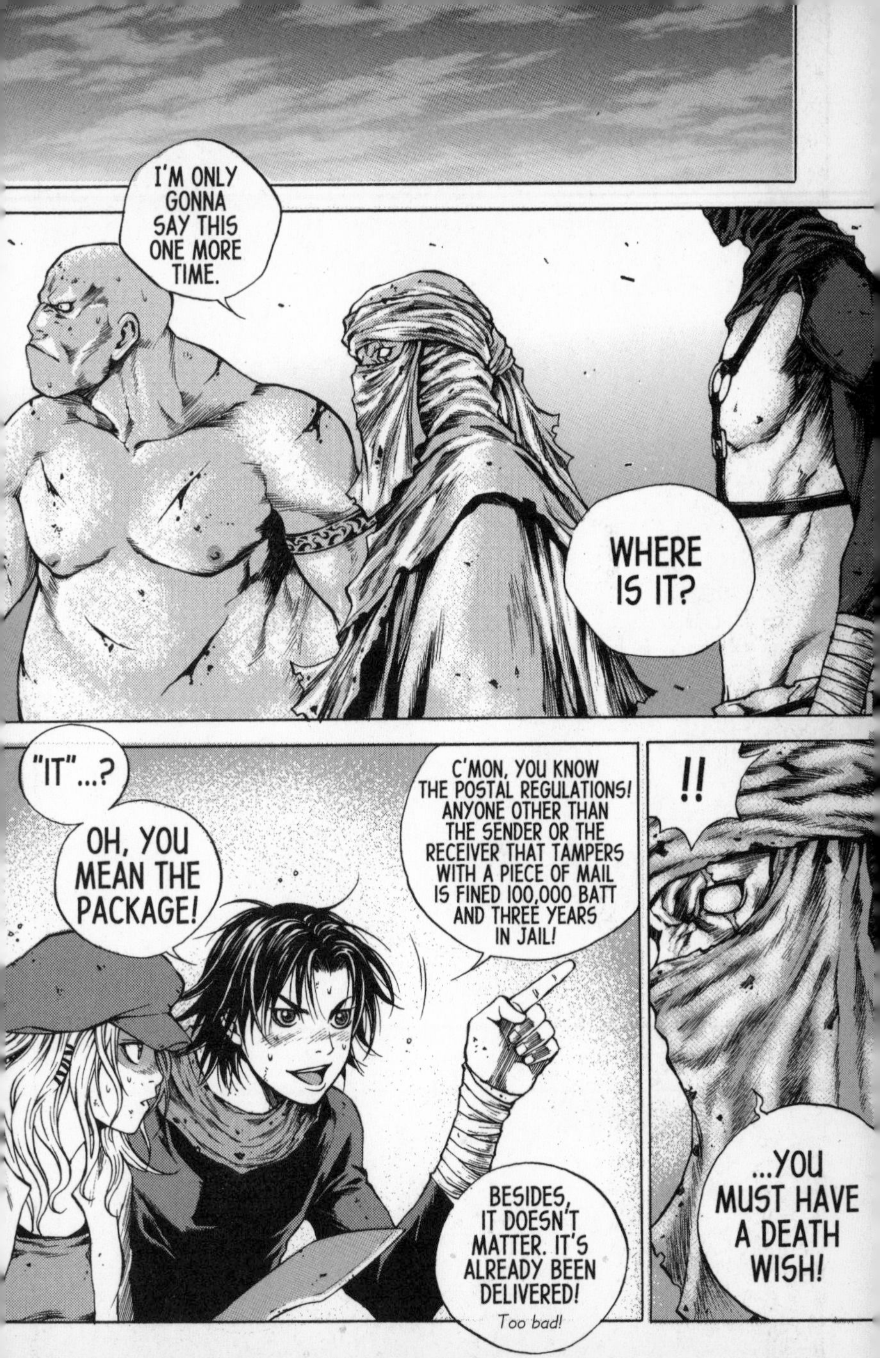
I'M ONLY GONNA SAY THIS ONE MORE TIME.
WHERE IS IT?
"IT"...?
OH, YOU MEAN THE PACKAGE!
C'MON, YOU KNOW THE POSTAL REGULATIONS! ANYONE OTHER THAN THE SENDER OR THE RECEIVER THAT TAMPERS WITH A PIECE OF MAIL IS FINED 100,000 BATT AND THREE YEARS IN JAIL!
BESIDES, IT DOESN'T MATTER. IT'S ALREADY BEEN DELIVERED!
Too bad!
!!
...YOU MUST HAVE A DEATH WISH!

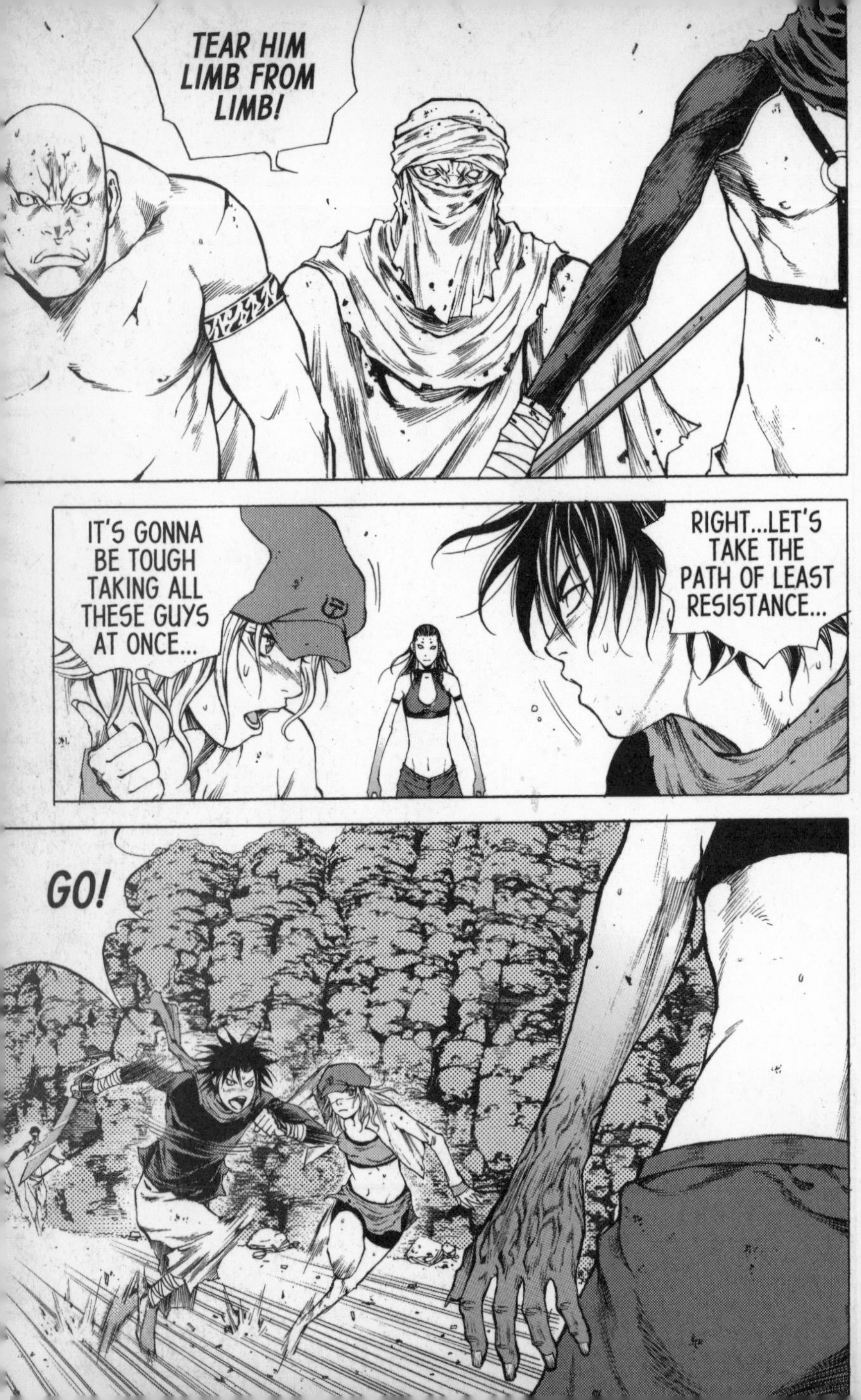
TEAR HIM LIMB FROM LIMB!
IT'S GONNA BE TOUGH TAKING ALL THESE GUYS AT ONCE...
RIGHT...LET'S TAKE THE PATH OF LEAST RESISTANCE...
GO!

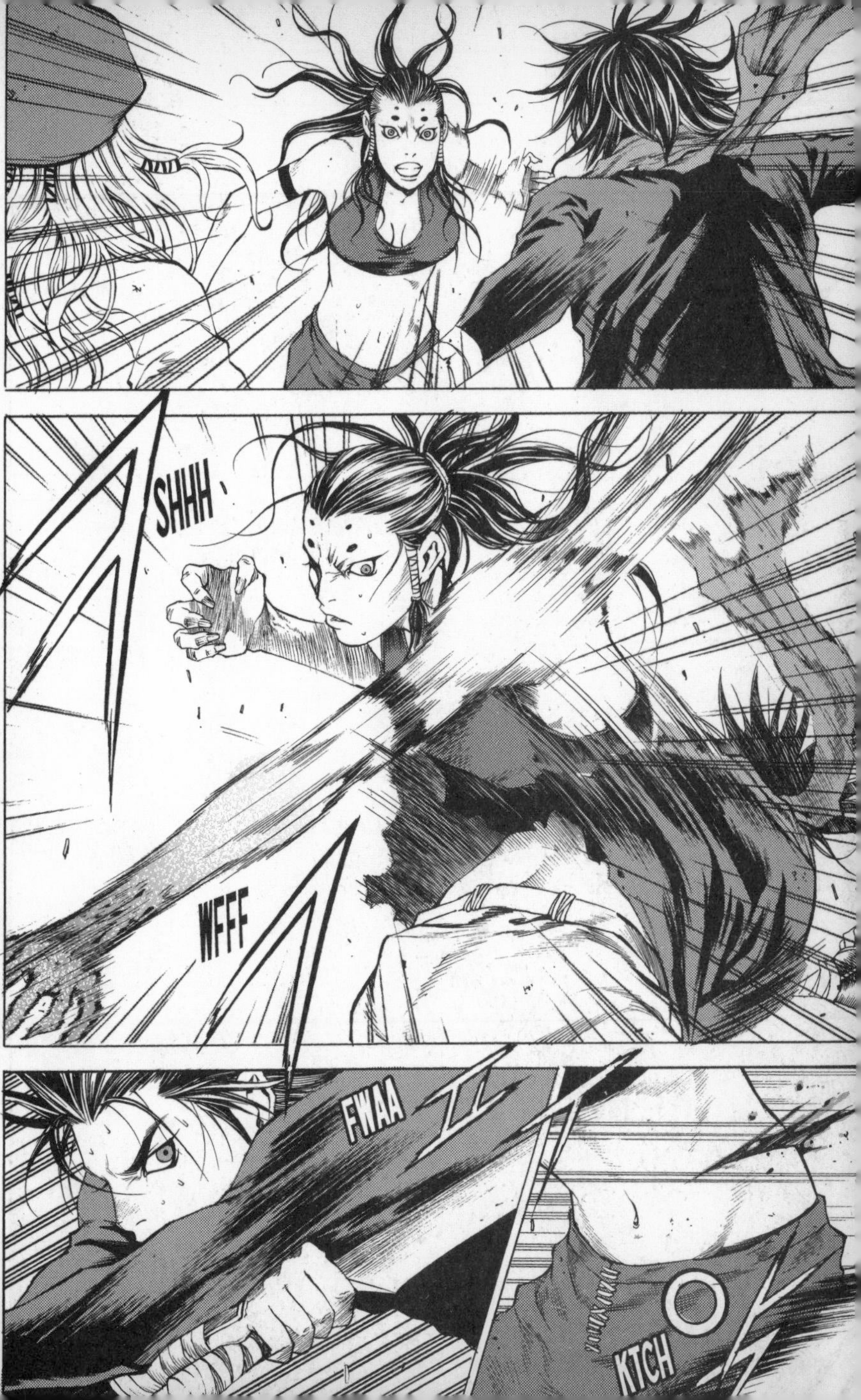
SHHH
WFFF
FWAA
KTCH

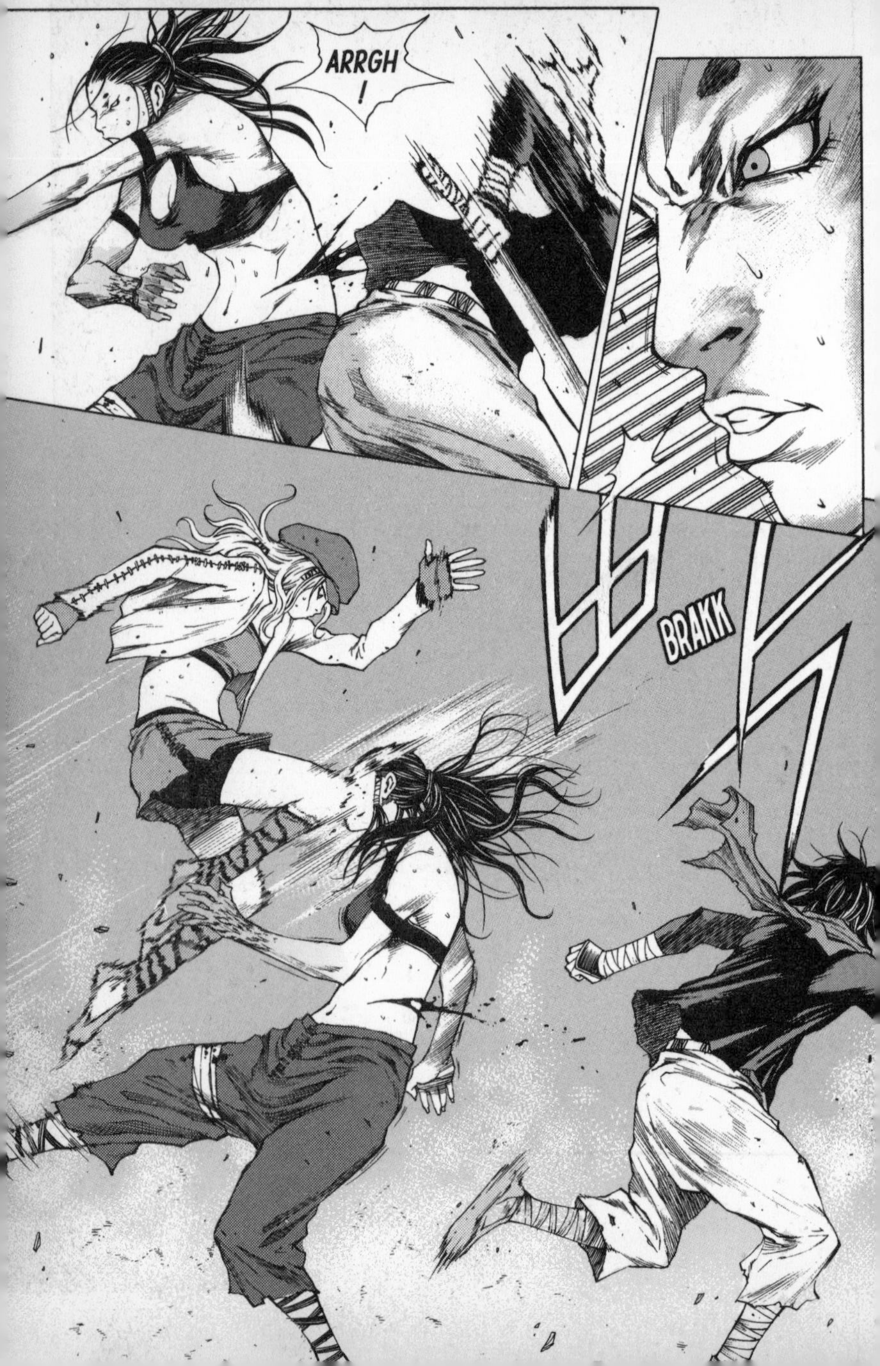
ARRGH
!
BRAKK

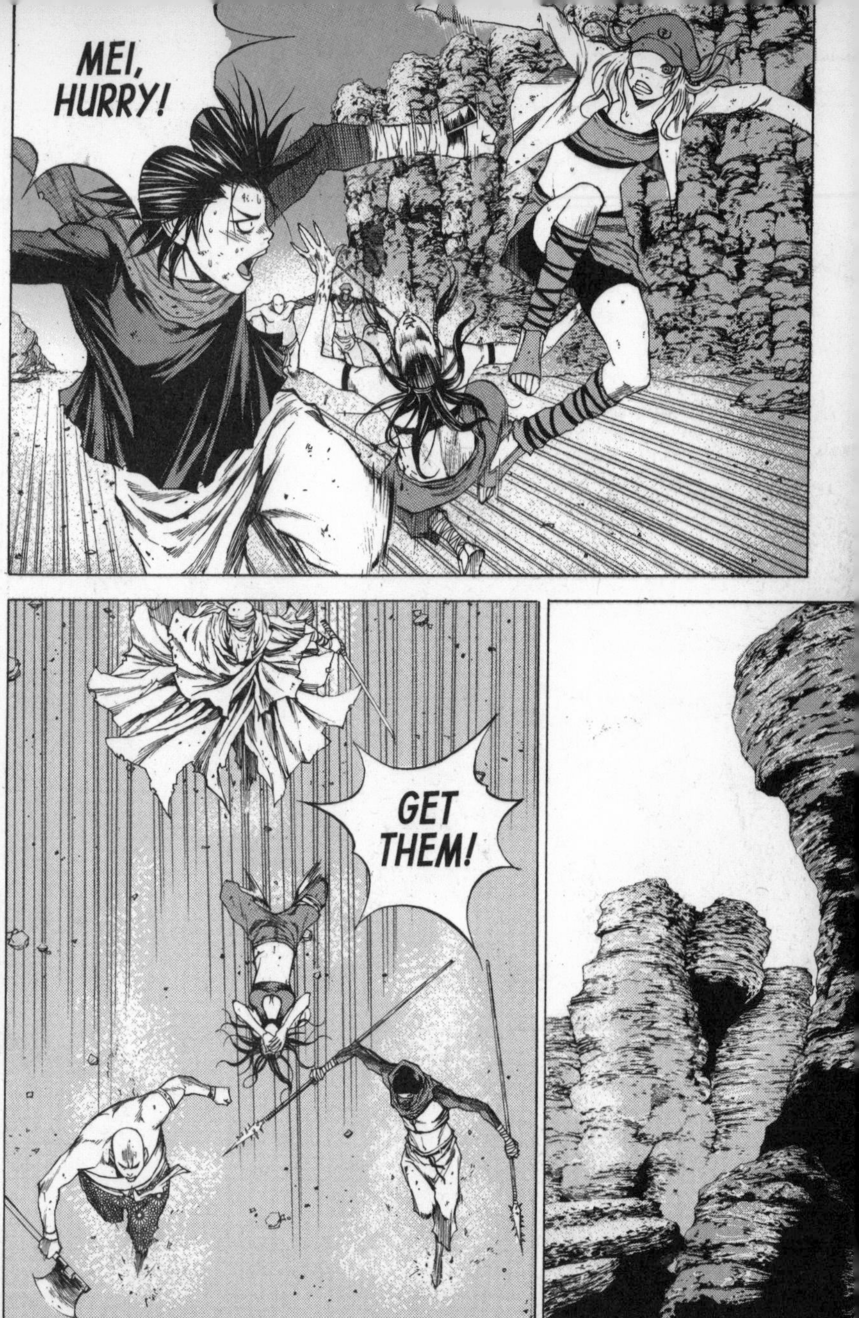
MEI, HURRY!
GET THEM!

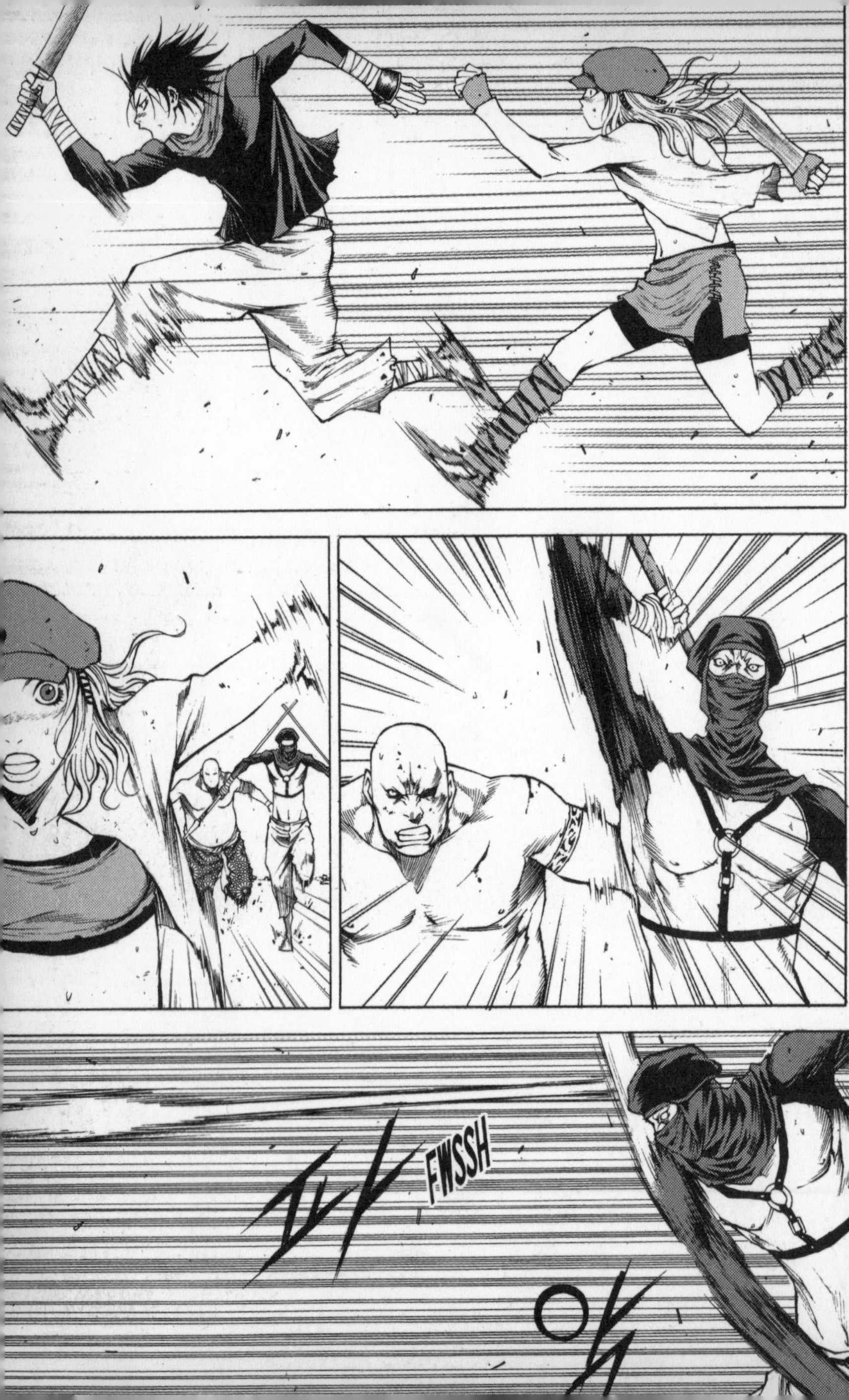
FWSSH

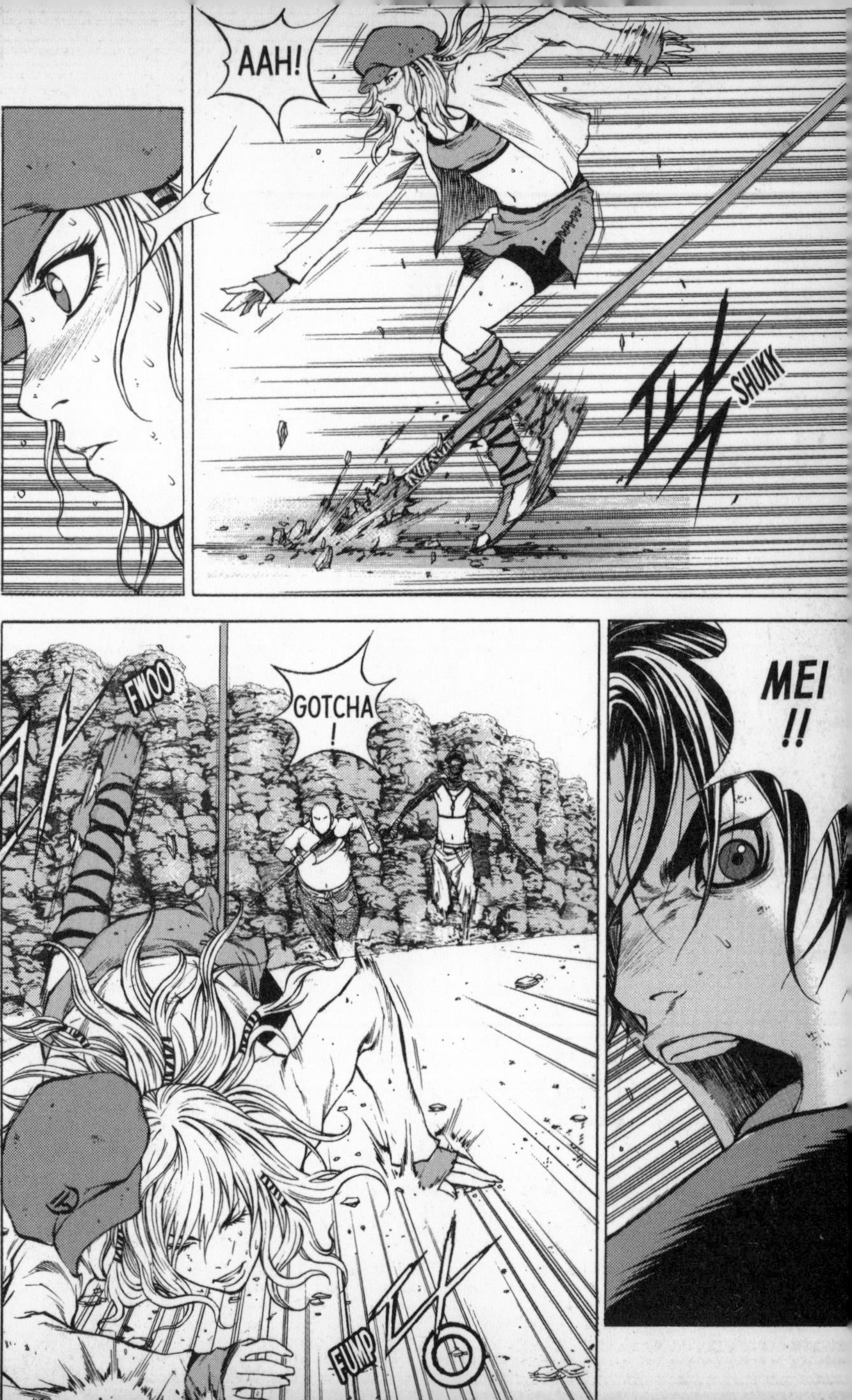
AAH!
SHUKK
MEI !!
GOTCHA !
FWOO
FUMP

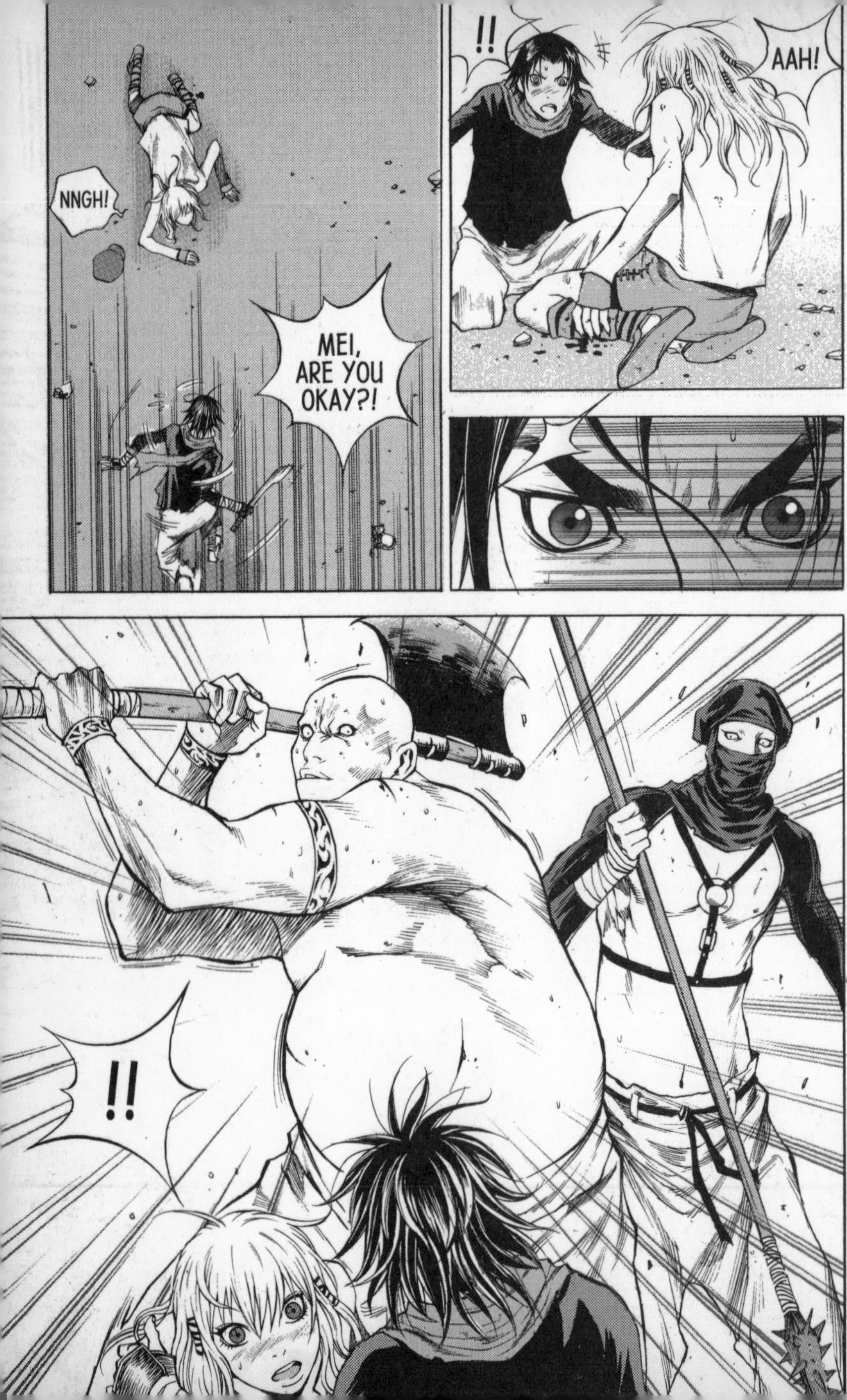
NNGH!
MEI, ARE YOU OKAY?!
!!
AAH!
!!

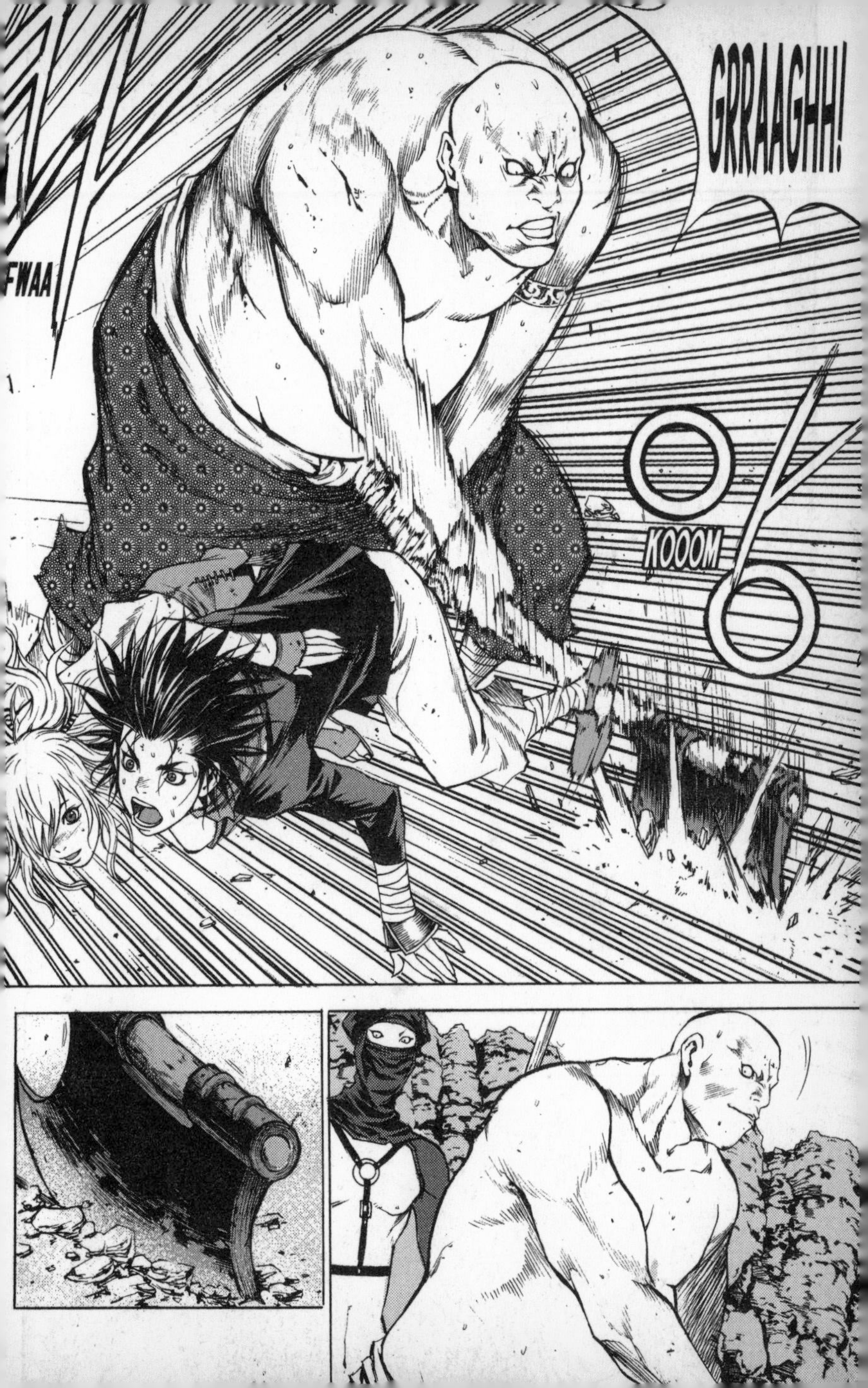
GRRAAGHH!
FWAA
KOOOM

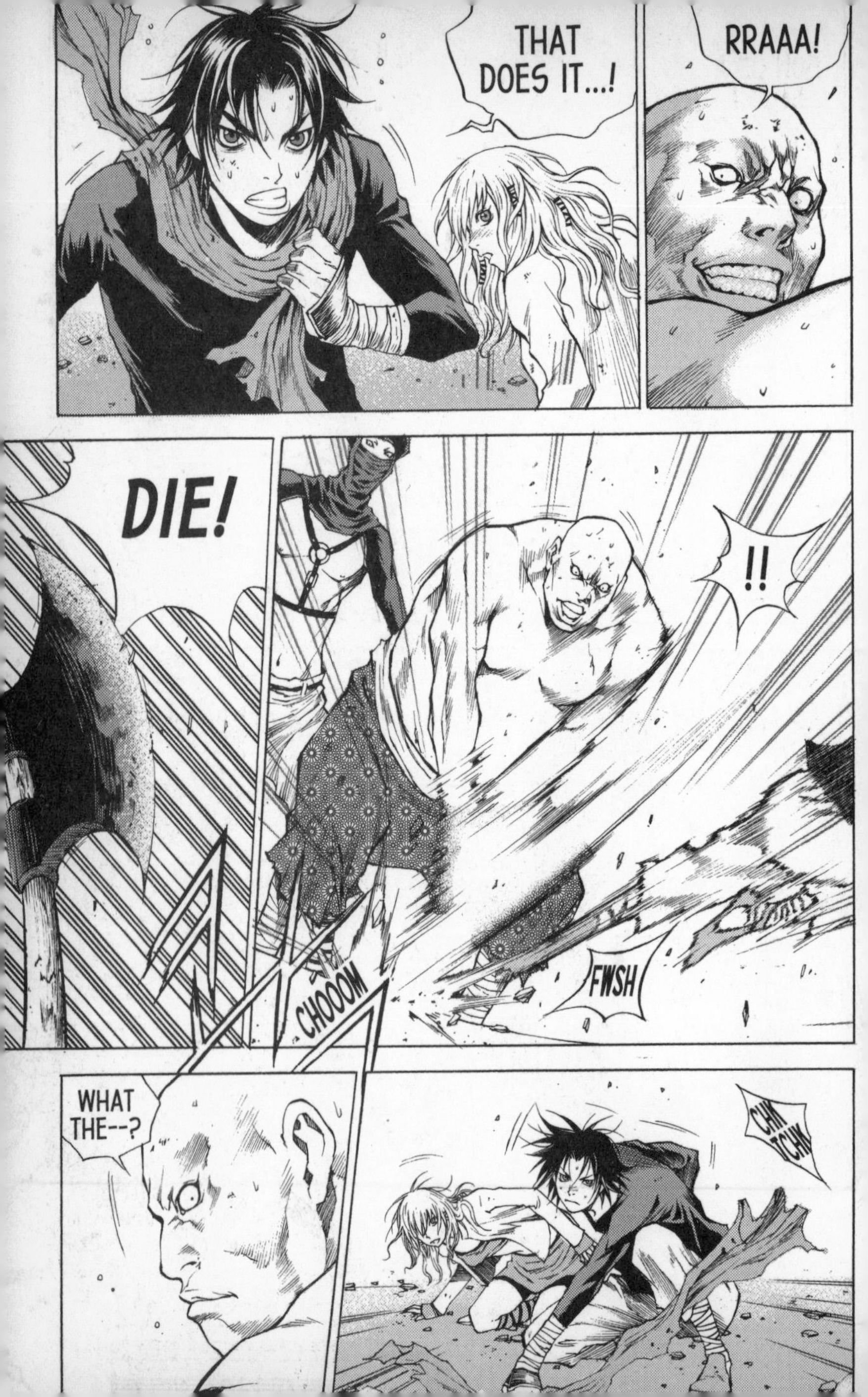
RRAAA!
THAT DOES IT...!
!!
DIE!
FWSH
CHOOOM
CHK TCHK
WHAT THE--?

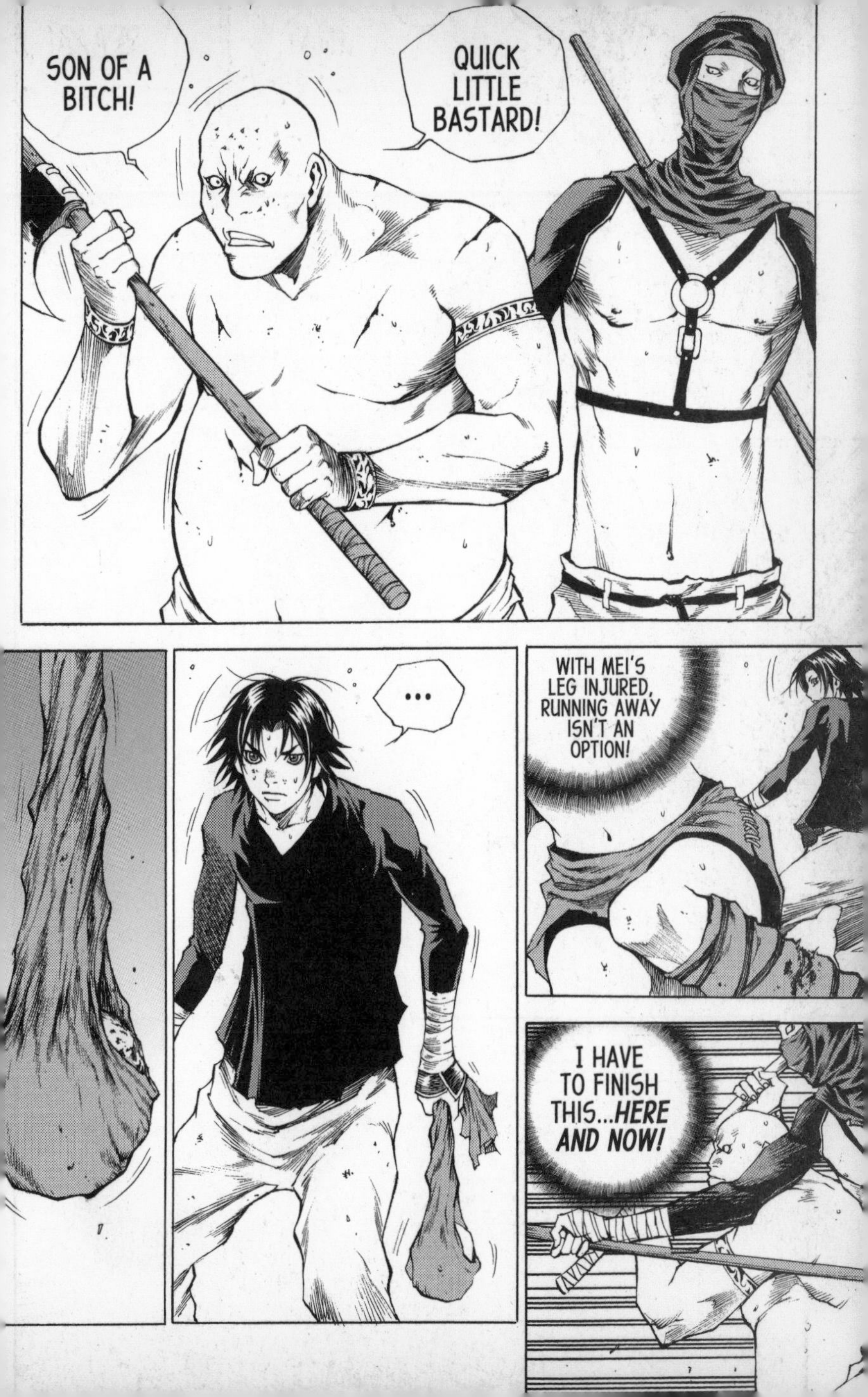
QUICK LITTLE BASTARD!
SON OF A BITCH!
...
WITH MEI'S LEG INJURED, RUNNING AWAY ISN'T AN OPTION!
I HAVE TO FINISH THIS...*HERE AND NOW!*

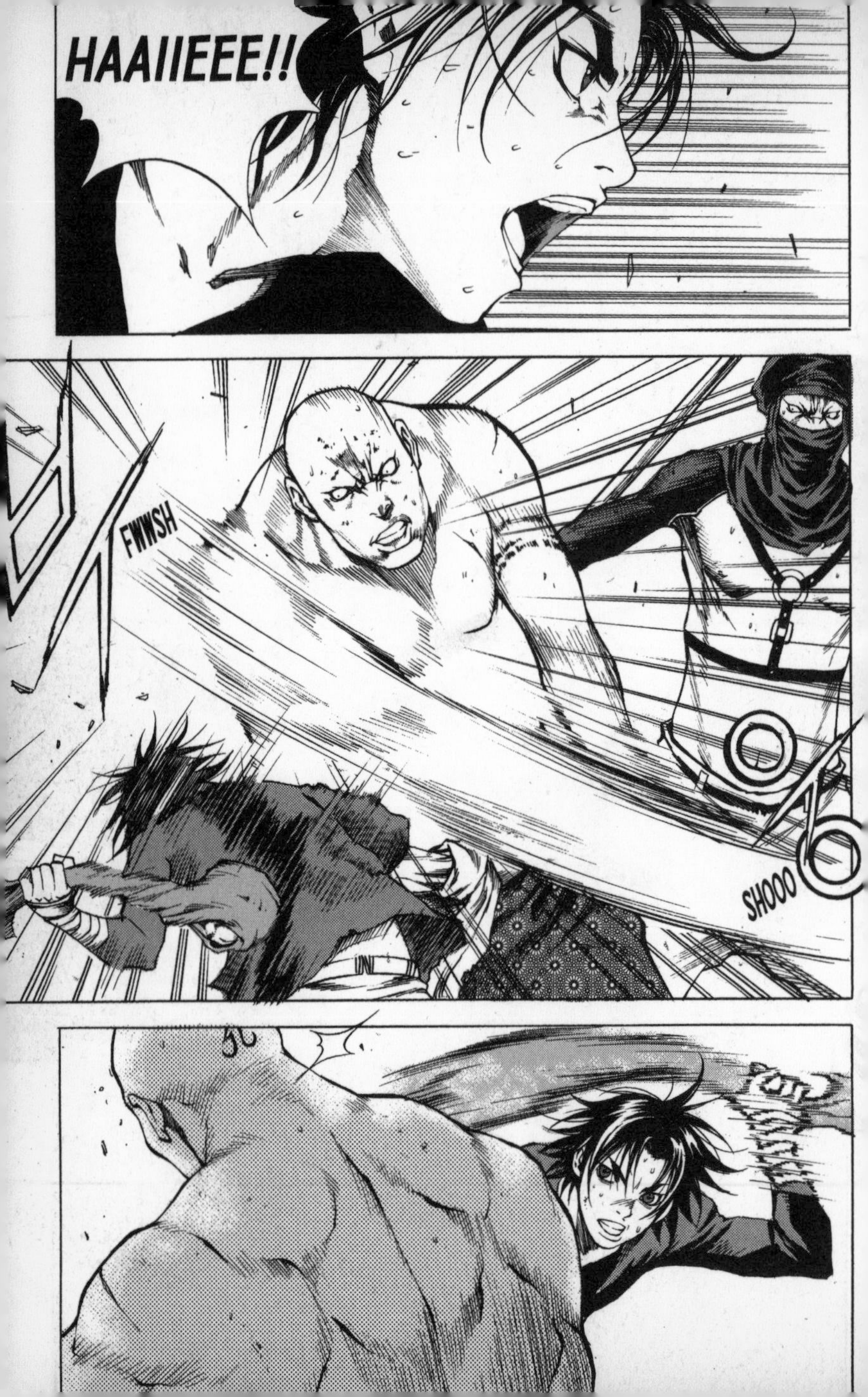
HAAIIEEE!!
FWWSH
SHOOO

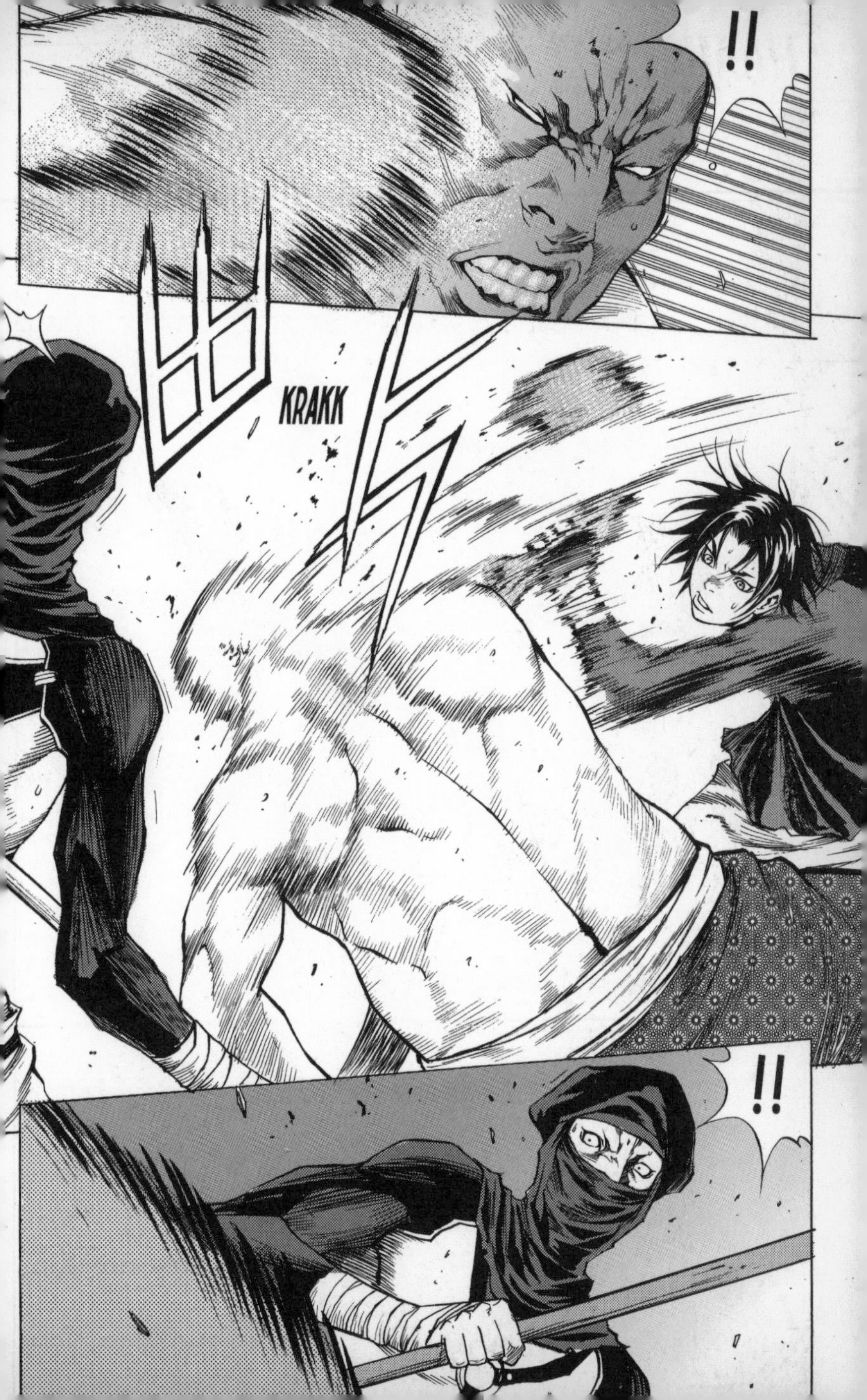
!!
KRAKK
!!

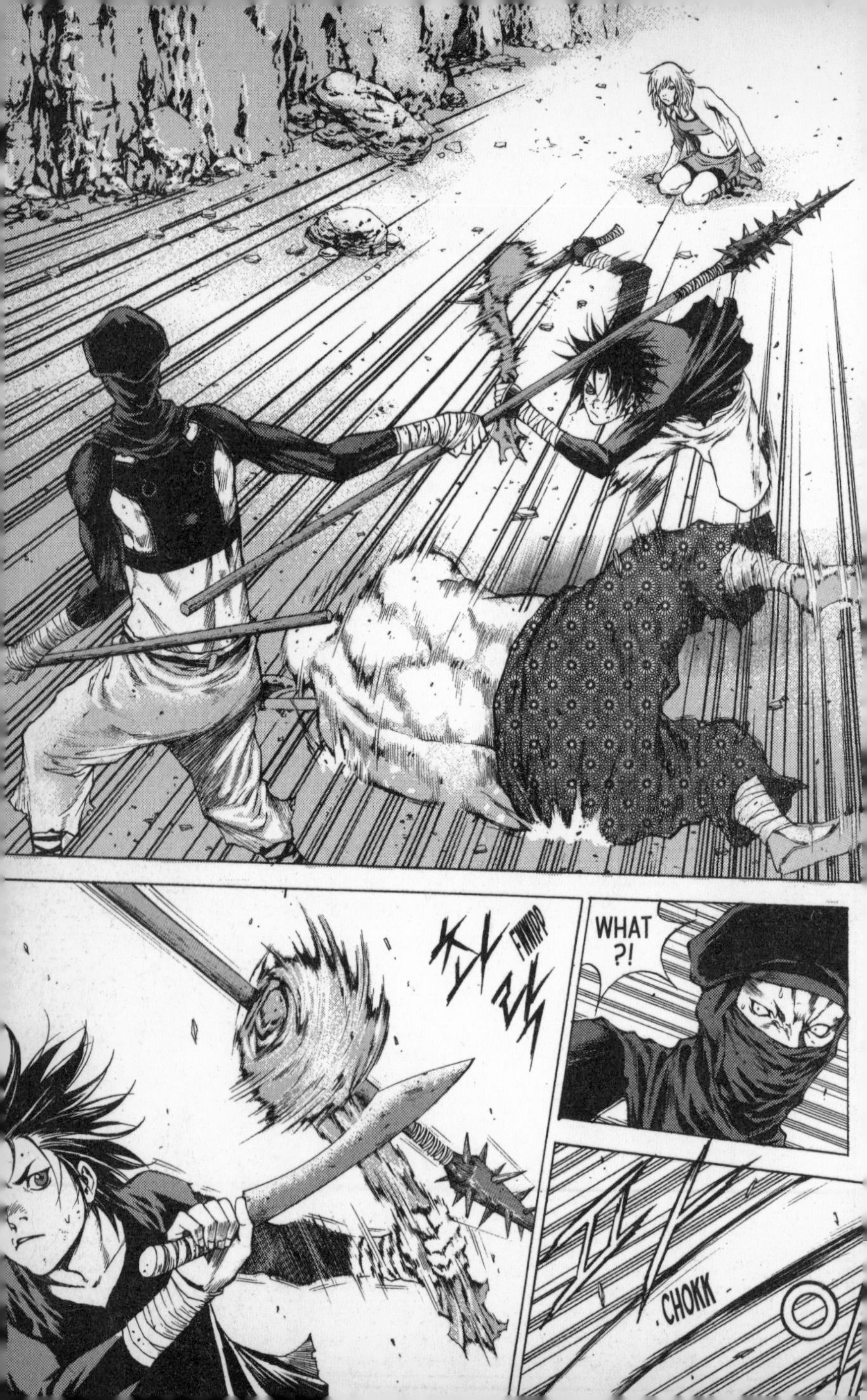
FWIPP
WHAT ?!
CHOKK

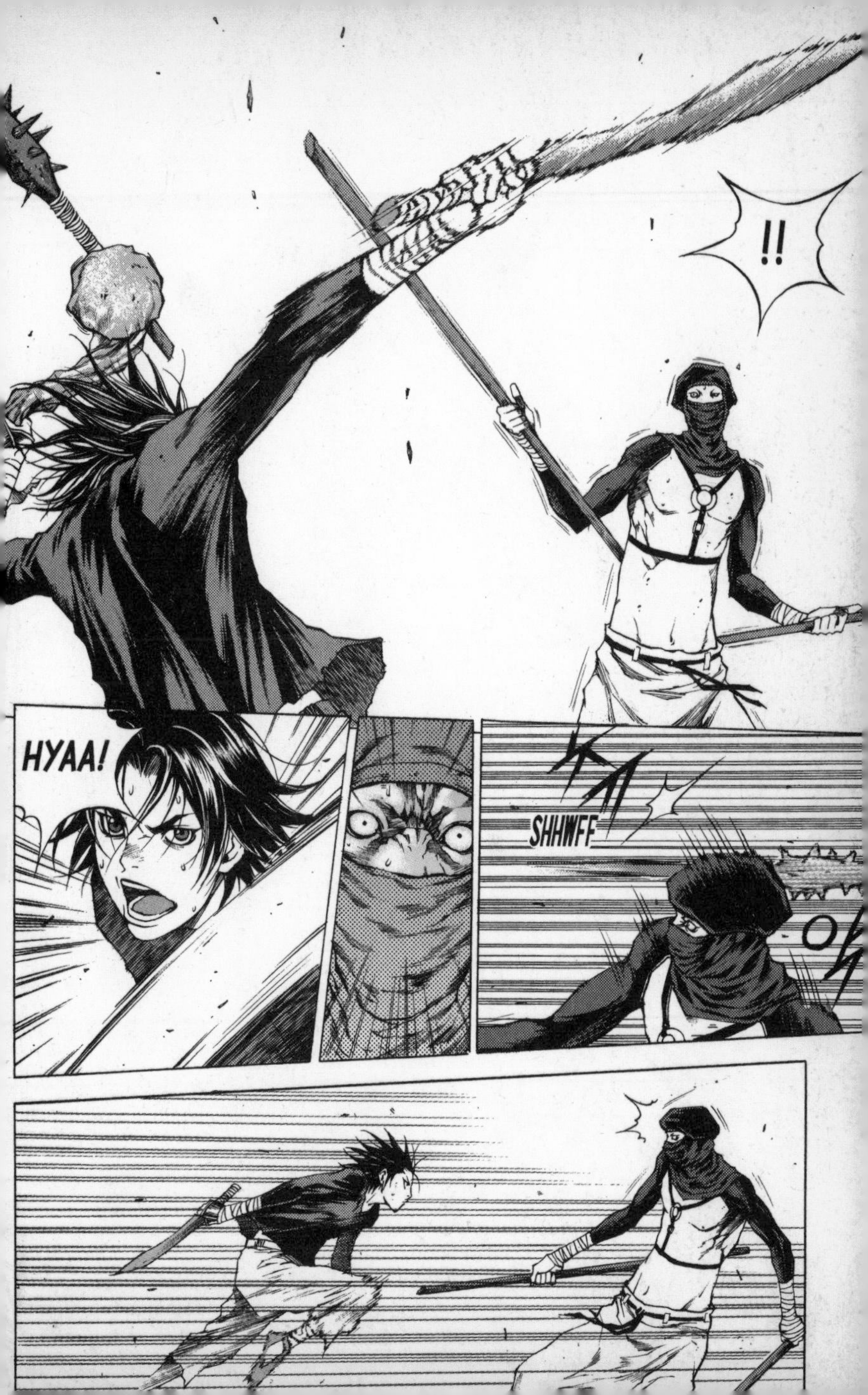
!!
HYAA!
SHHWFF

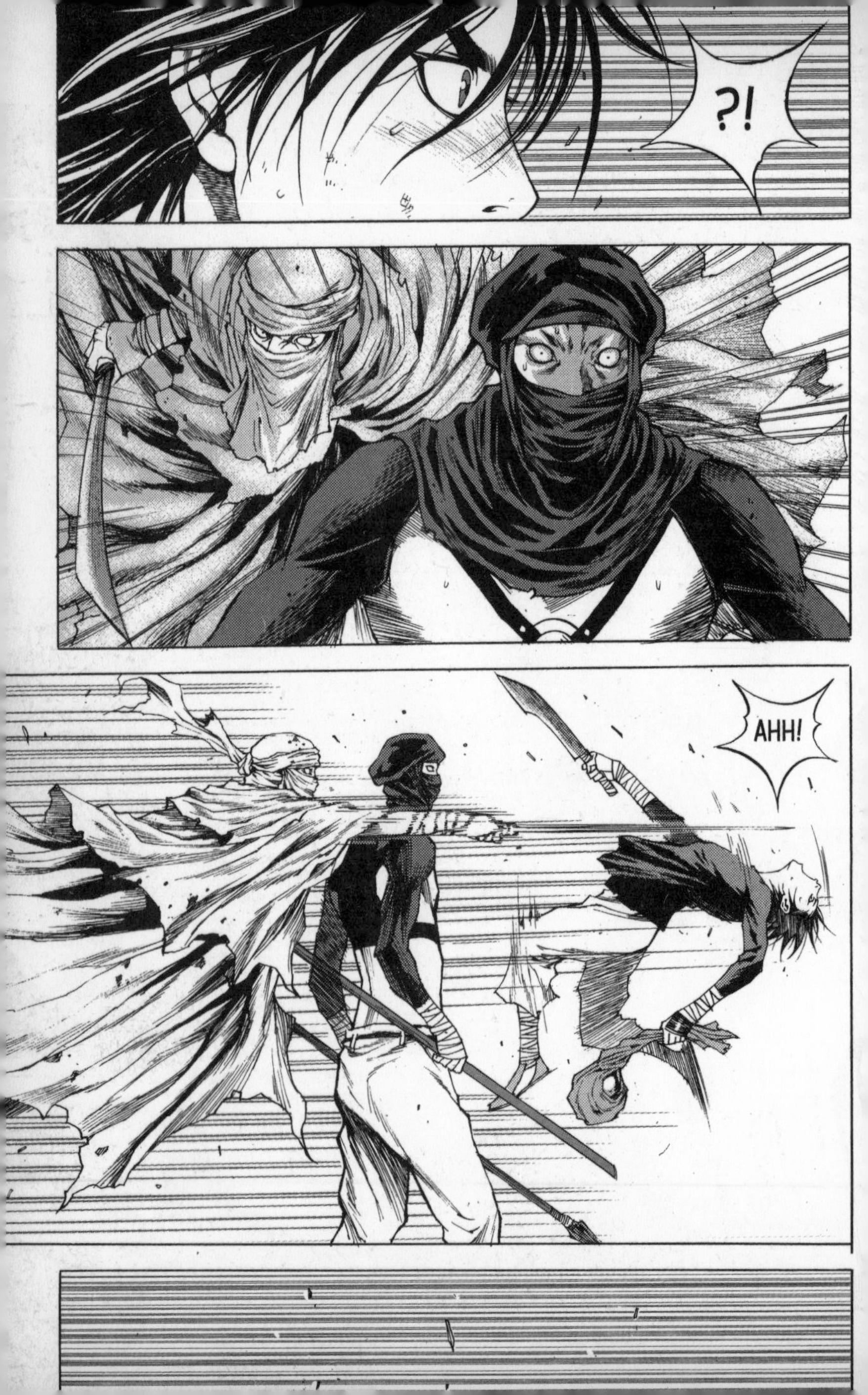
?!
AHH!

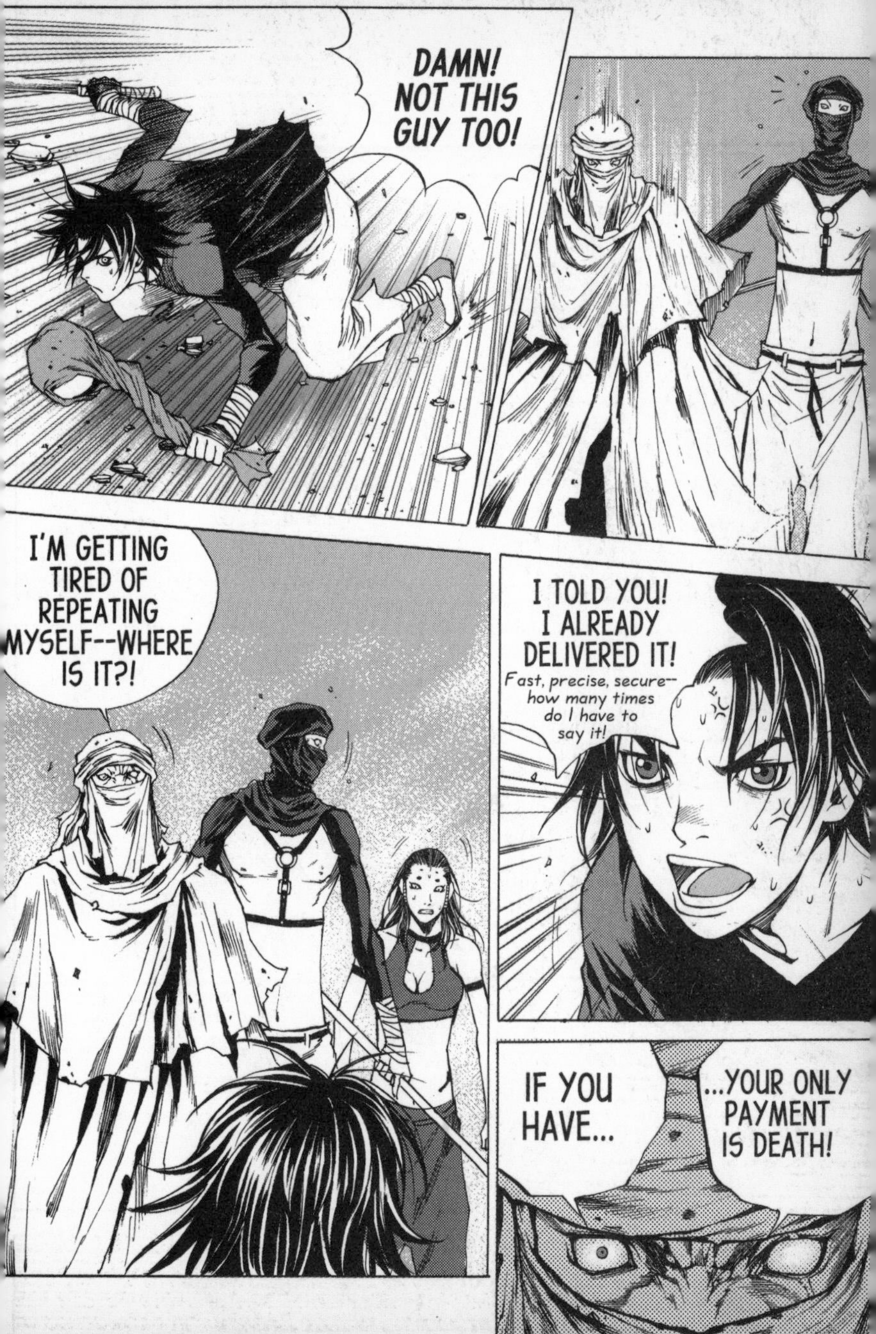
DAMN! NOT THIS GUY TOO!
I'M GETTING TIRED OF REPEATING MYSELF--WHERE IS IT?!
I TOLD YOU! I ALREADY DELIVERED IT!
Fast, precise, secure--how many times do I have to say it!
IF YOU HAVE...
...YOUR ONLY PAYMENT IS DEATH!

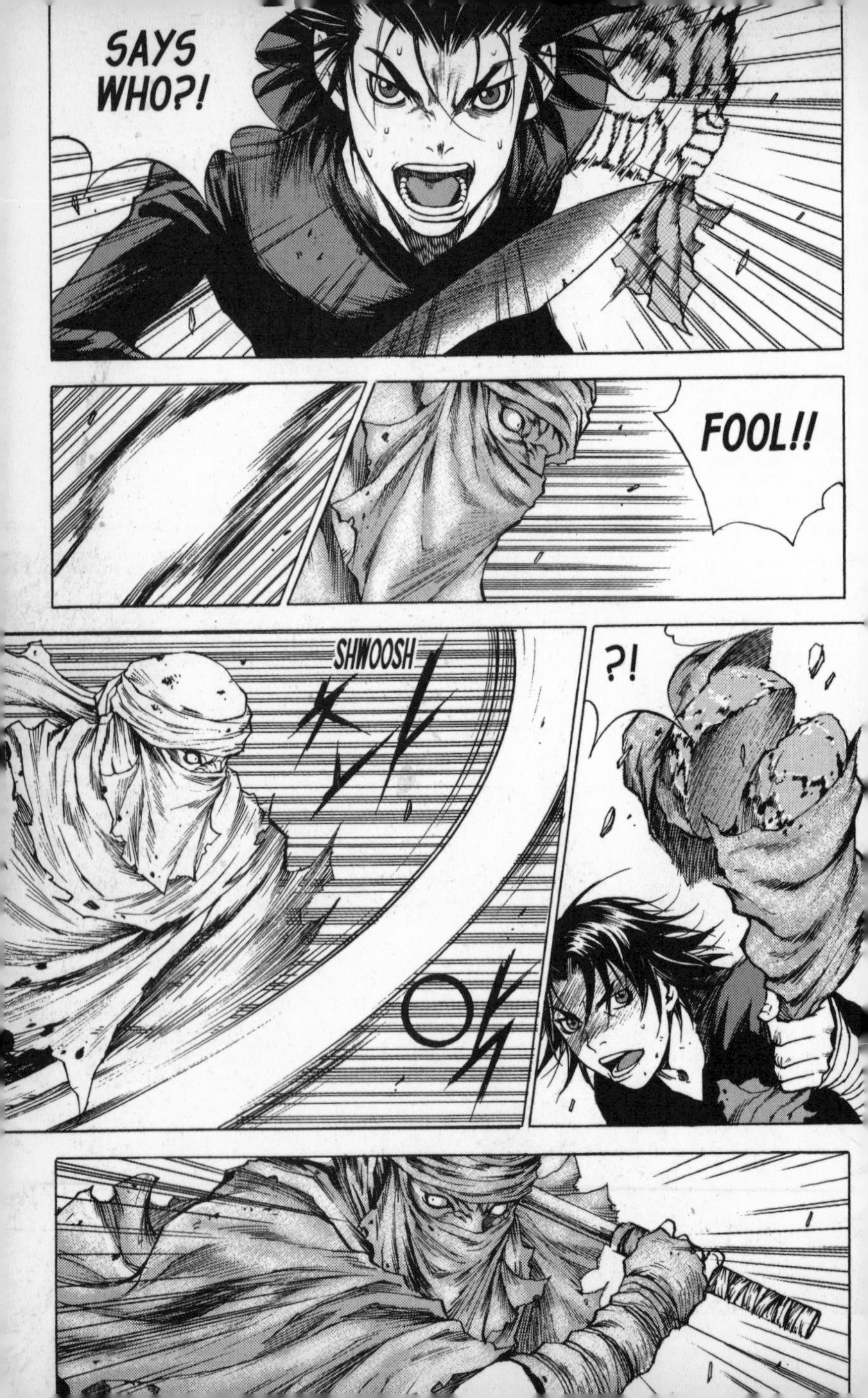
SAYS WHO?!
FOOL!!
?!
SHWOOSH

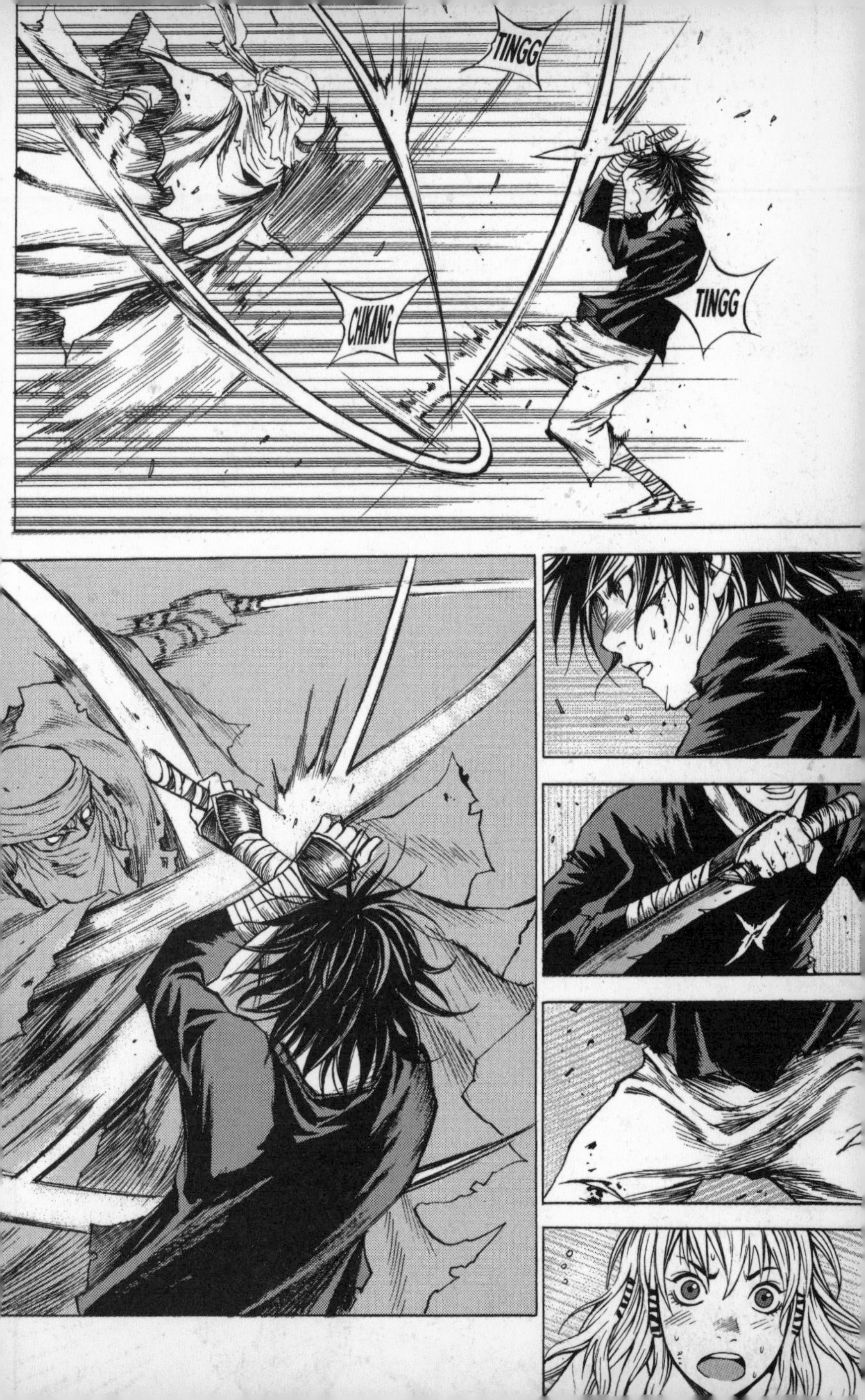
TINGG
TINGG
CHKANG

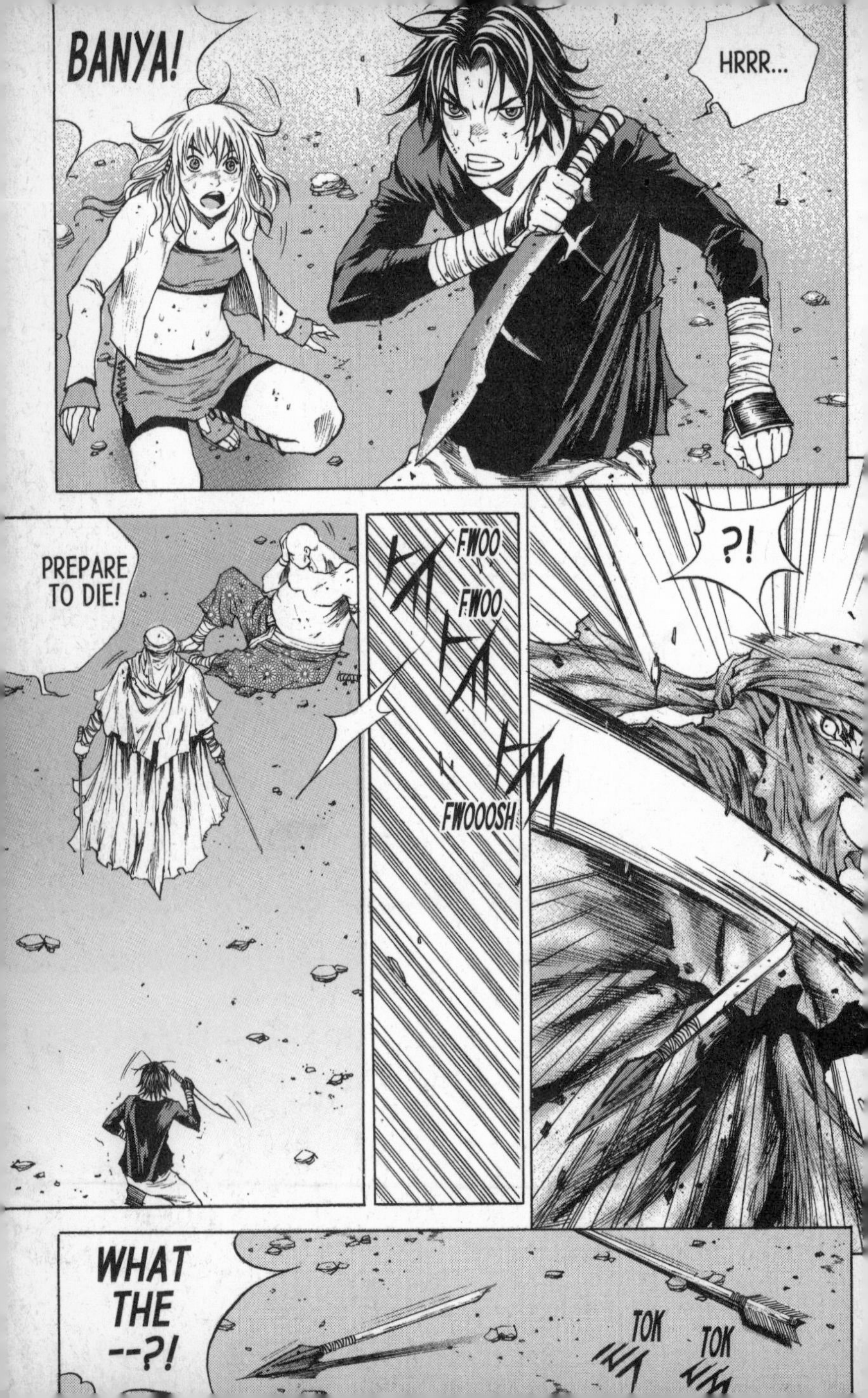
BANYA!
HRRR...
PREPARE TO DIE!
FWOO
FWOO
FWOOOSH
?!
WHAT THE --?!
TOK
TOK

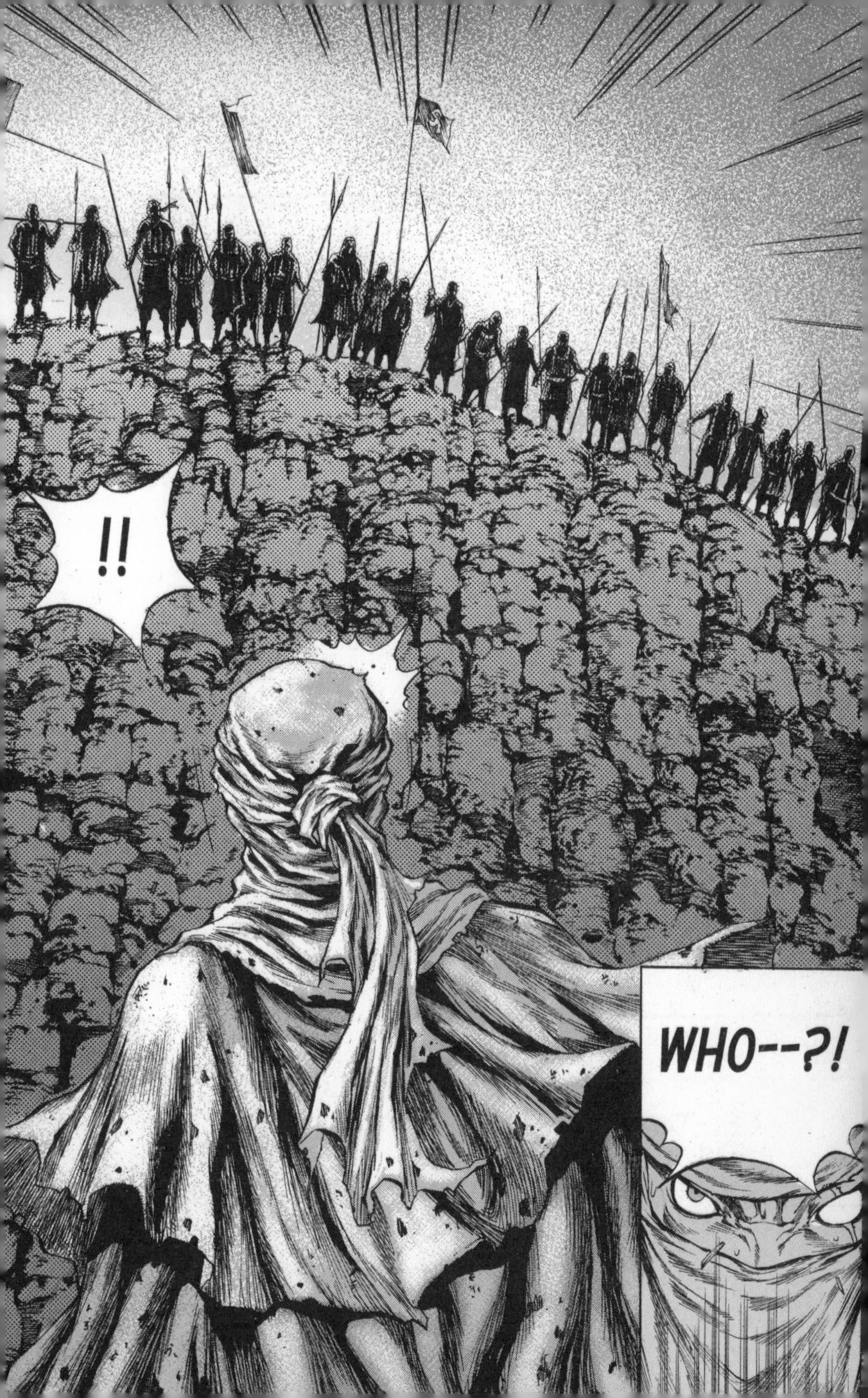
!!
WHO--?!

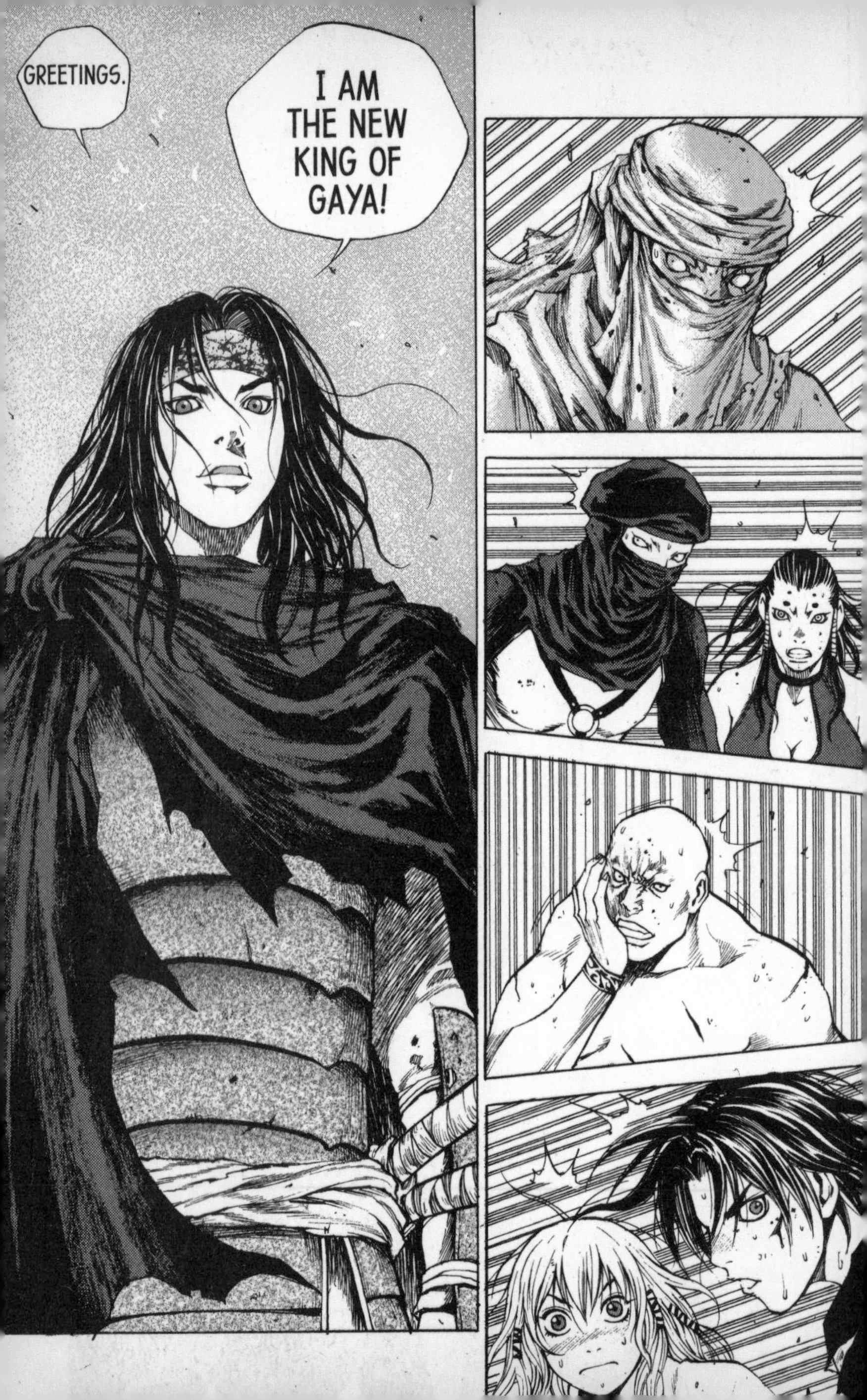
GREETINGS.
I AM THE NEW KING OF GAYA!

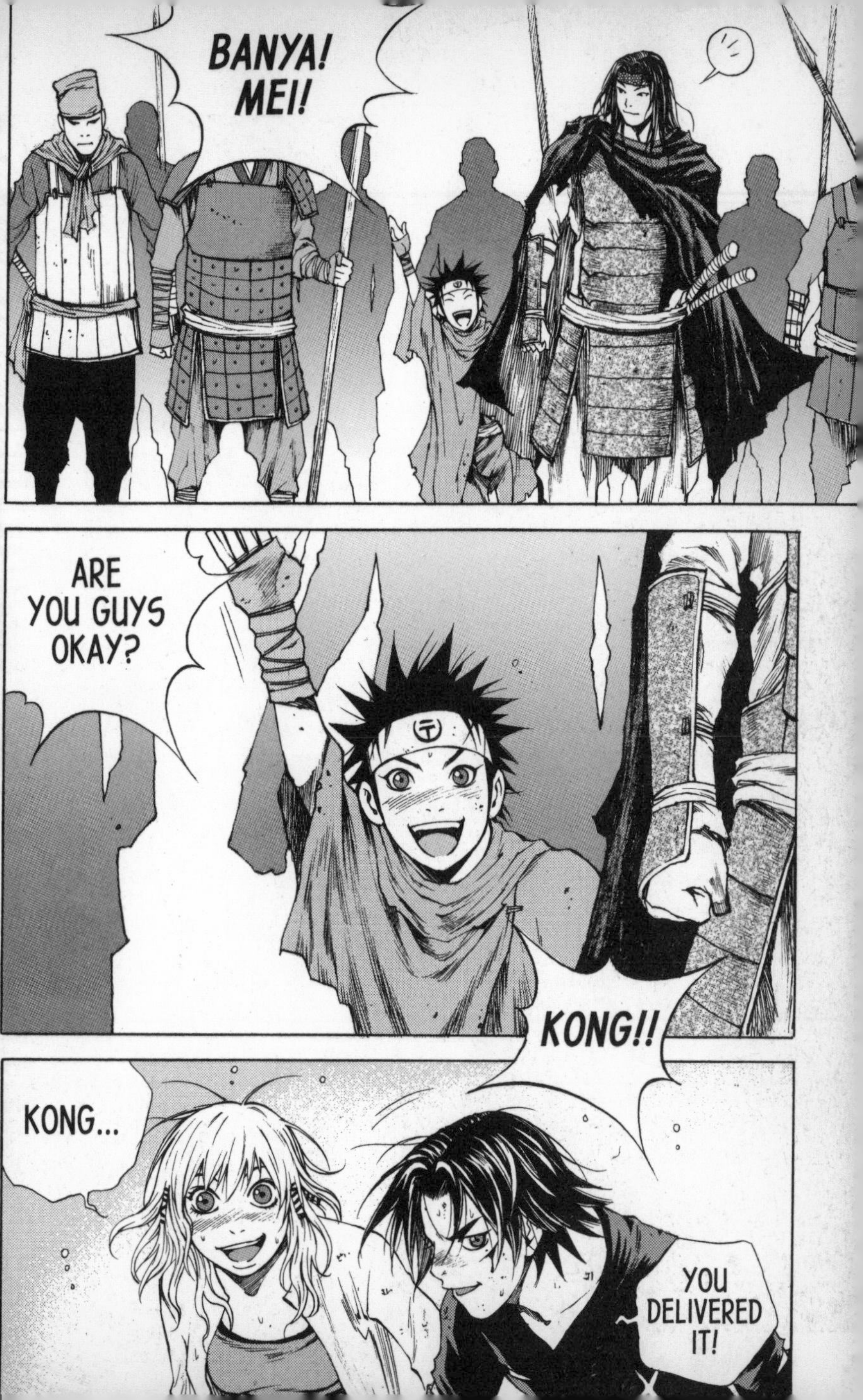
BANYA! MEI!
...
ARE YOU GUYS OKAY?
KONG!!
KONG...
YOU DELIVERED IT!

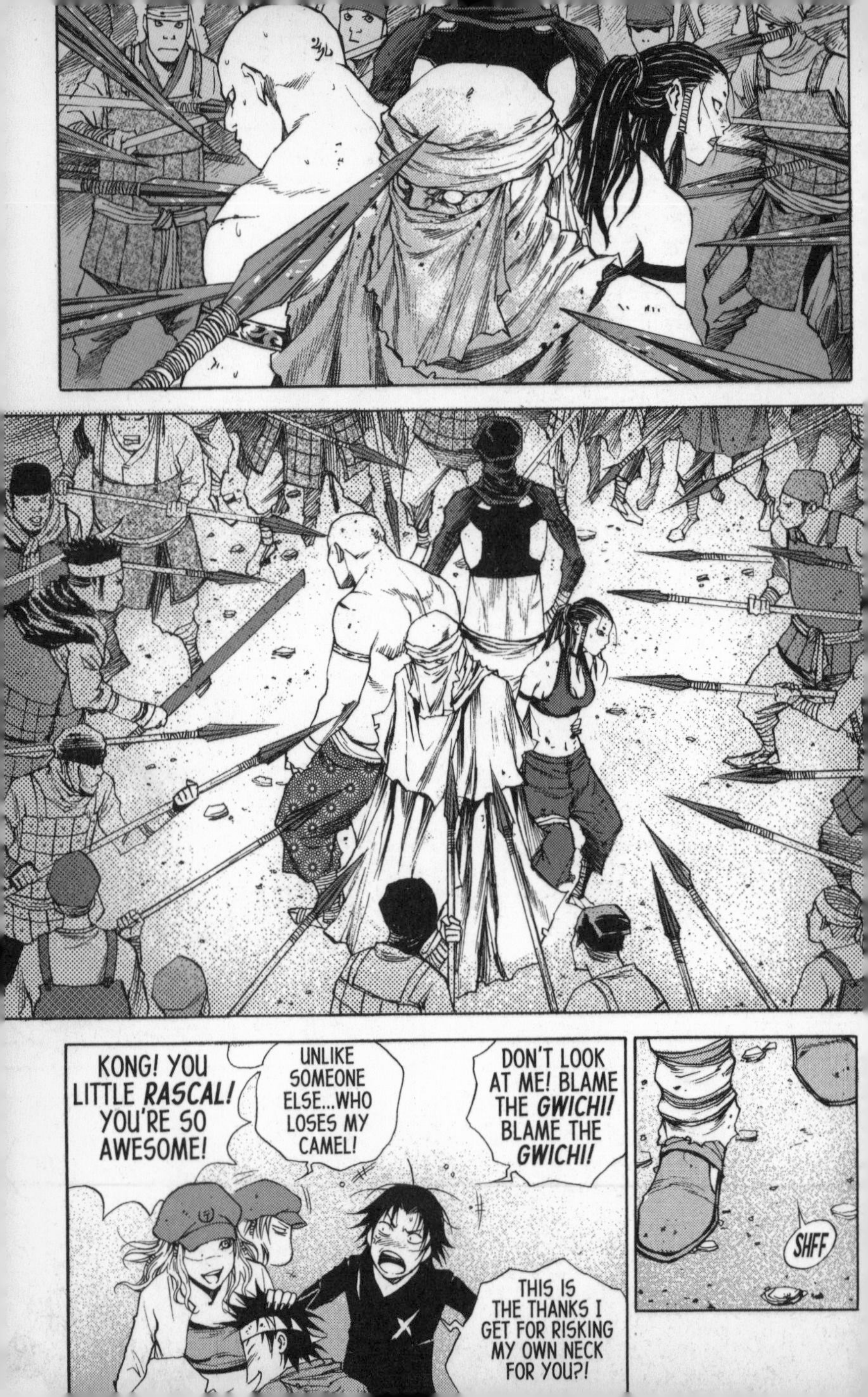
KONG! YOU LITTLE RASCAL! YOU'RE SO AWESOME!
UNLIKE SOMEONE ELSE...WHO LOSES MY CAMEL!
DON'T LOOK AT ME! BLAME THE GWICHI! BLAME THE GWICHI!
THIS IS THE THANKS I GET FOR RISKING MY OWN NECK FOR YOU?!
SHFF

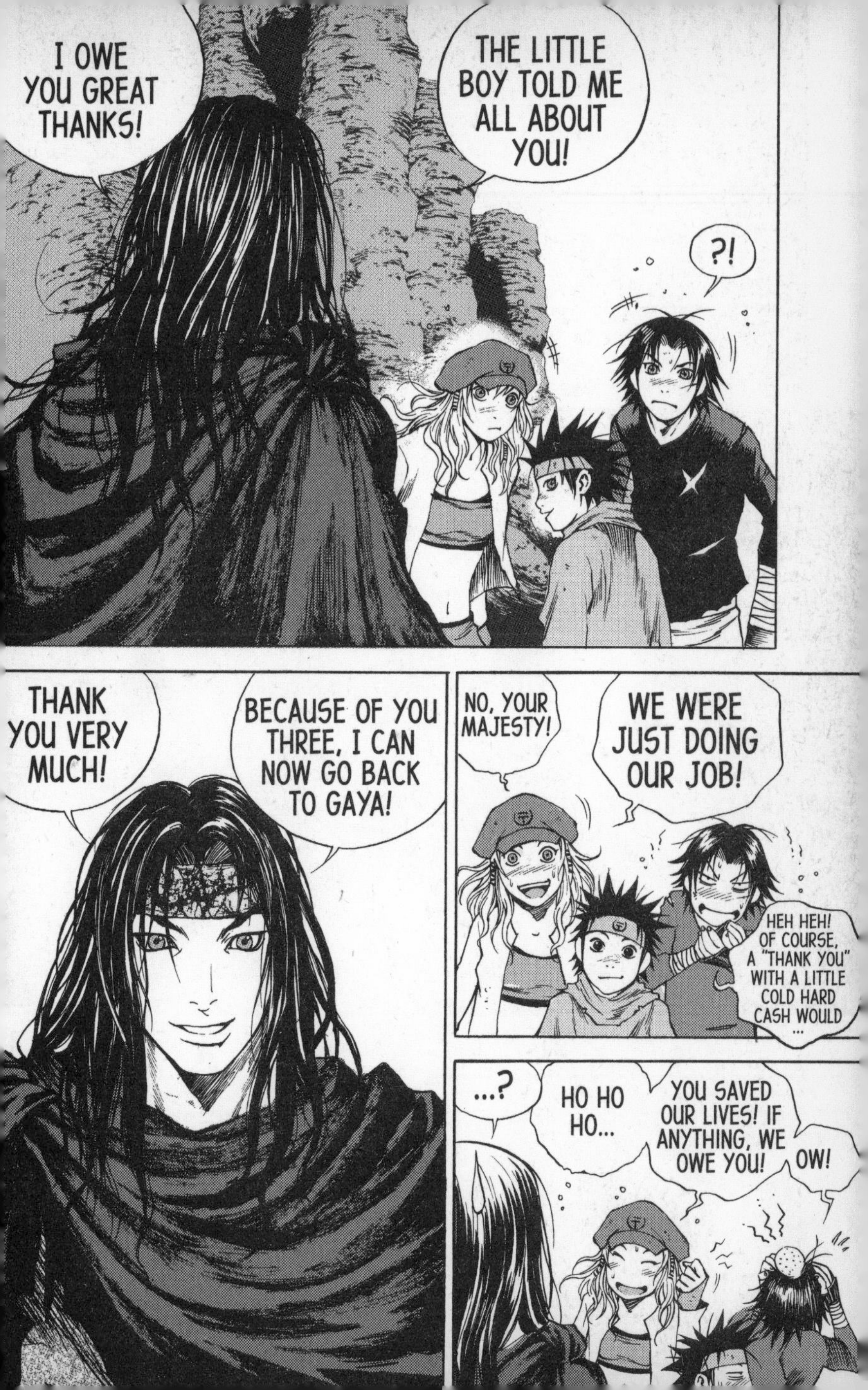
I OWE YOU GREAT THANKS!
THE LITTLE BOY TOLD ME ALL ABOUT YOU!
?!
THANK YOU VERY MUCH!
BECAUSE OF YOU THREE, I CAN NOW GO BACK TO GAYA!
NO, YOUR MAJESTY!
WE WERE JUST DOING OUR JOB!
HEH HEH! OF COURSE, A "THANK YOU" WITH A LITTLE COLD HARD CASH WOULD ...
...?
HO HO HO...
YOU SAVED OUR LIVES! IF ANYTHING, WE OWE YOU!
OW!

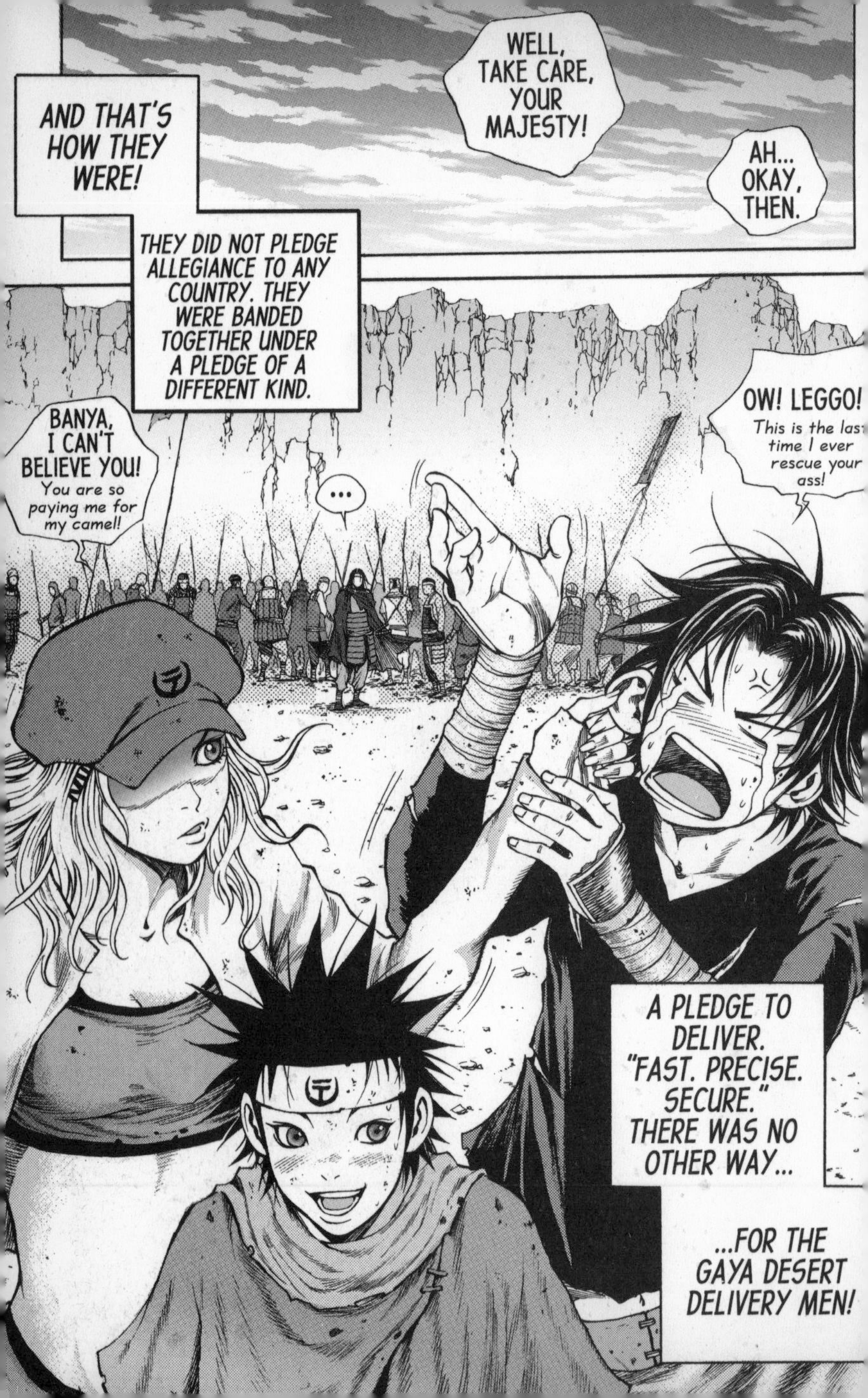

WELL, TAKE CARE, YOUR MAJESTY!
AH... OKAY, THEN.
AND THAT'S HOW THEY WERE!
THEY DID NOT PLEDGE ALLEGIANCE TO ANY COUNTRY. THEY WERE BANDED TOGETHER UNDER A PLEDGE OF A DIFFERENT KIND.
OW! LEGGO! This is the last time I ever rescue your ass!
...
BANYA, I CAN'T BELIEVE YOU! You are so paying me for my camel!
A PLEDGE TO DELIVER. "FAST. PRECISE. SECURE." THERE WAS NO OTHER WAY...
...FOR THE GAYA DESERT DELIVERY MEN!

Banya

the explosive delivery man

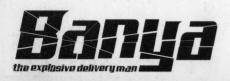

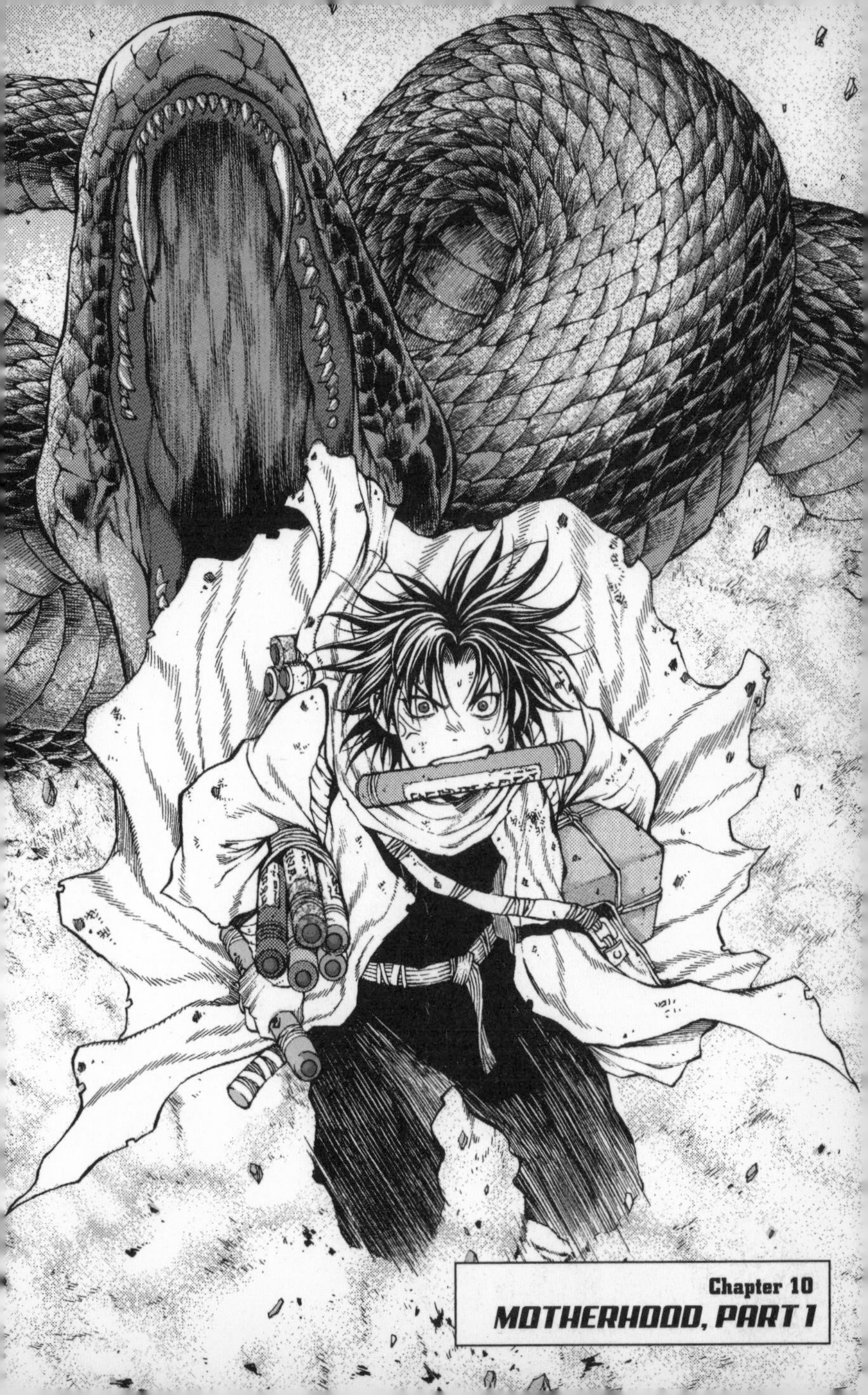
Chapter 10
MOTHERHOOD, PART 1

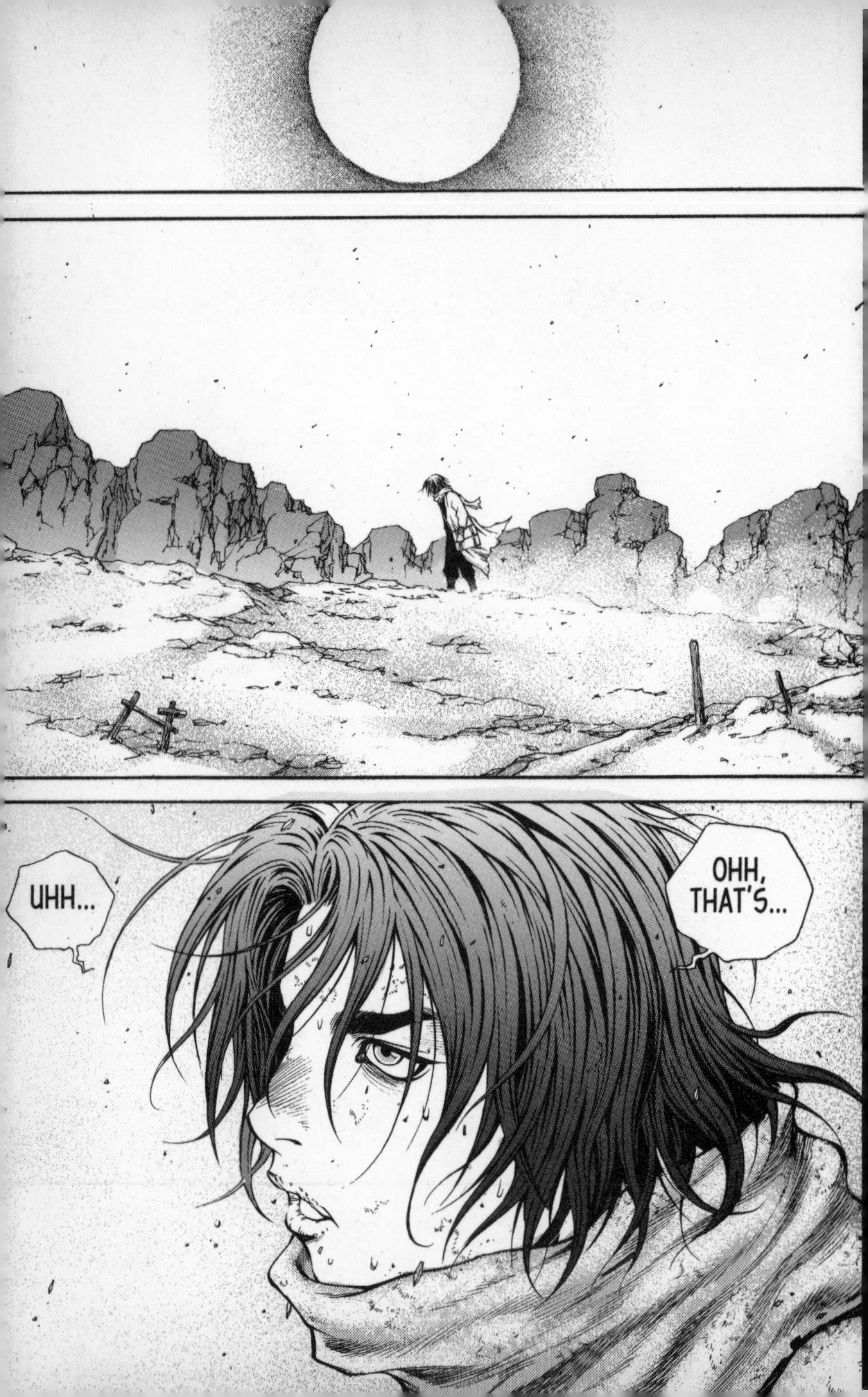
OHH, THAT'S...
UHH...

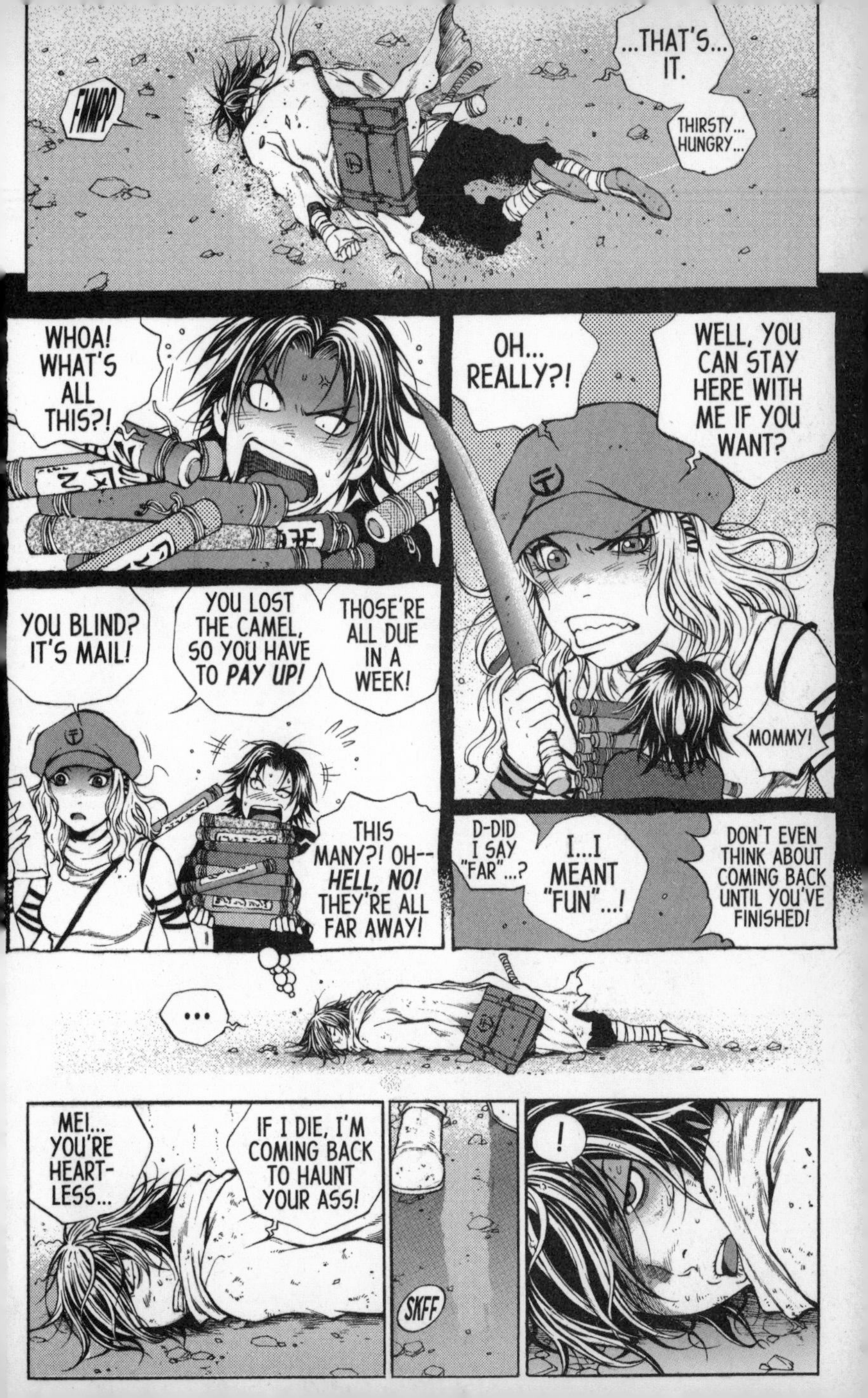
FMMPP
...THAT'S... IT.
THIRSTY... HUNGRY...
WHOA! WHAT'S ALL THIS?!
YOU BLIND? IT'S MAIL!
YOU LOST THE CAMEL, SO YOU HAVE TO PAY UP!
THOSE'RE ALL DUE IN A WEEK!
THIS MANY?! OH-- HELL, NO! THEY'RE ALL FAR AWAY!
OH... REALLY?!
WELL, YOU CAN STAY HERE WITH ME IF YOU WANT?
MOMMY!
D-DID I SAY "FAR"...?
I...I MEANT "FUN"...!
DON'T EVEN THINK ABOUT COMING BACK UNTIL YOU'VE FINISHED!
...
MEI... YOU'RE HEART-LESS...
IF I DIE, I'M COMING BACK TO HAUNT YOUR ASS!
SKFF
!

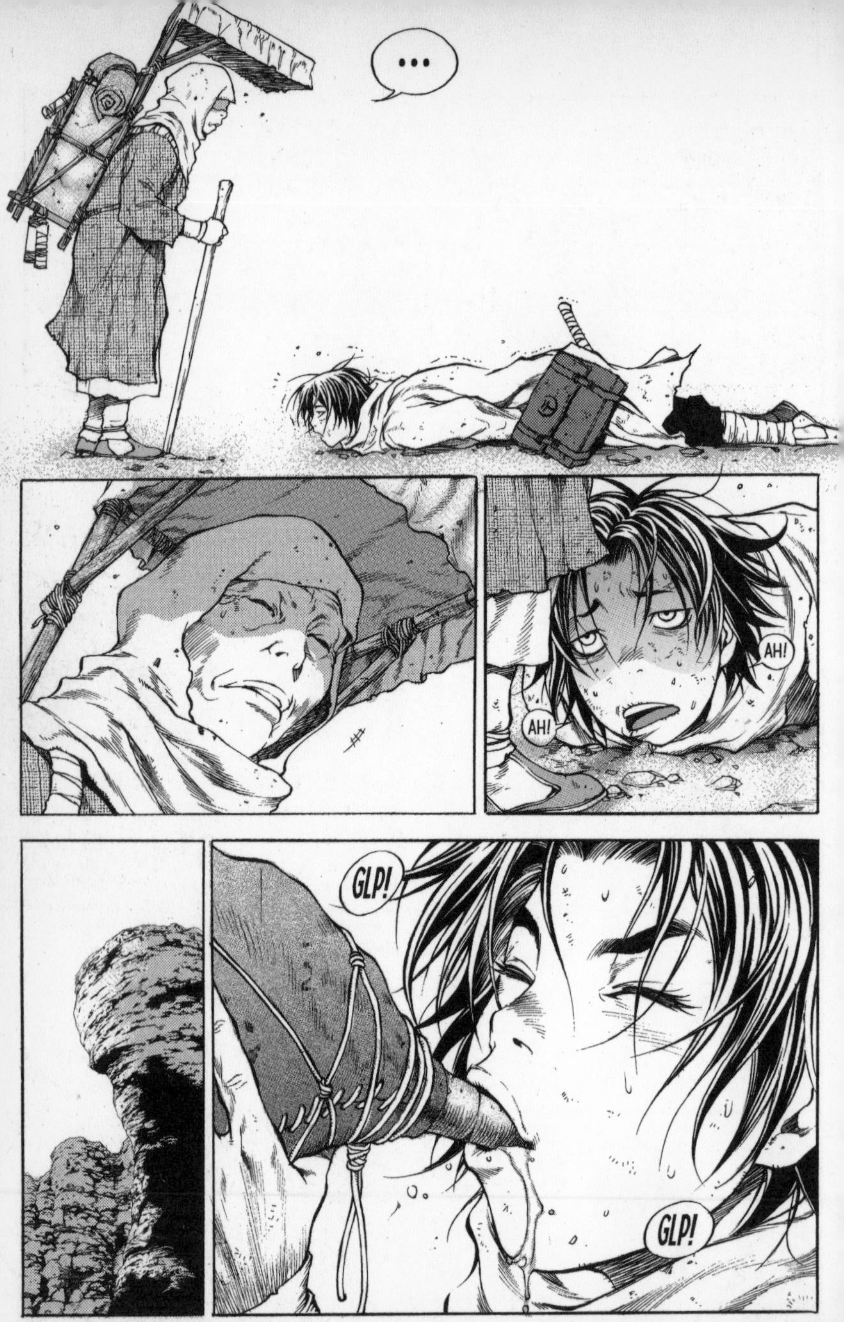
...
AH!
AH!
GLP!
GLP!

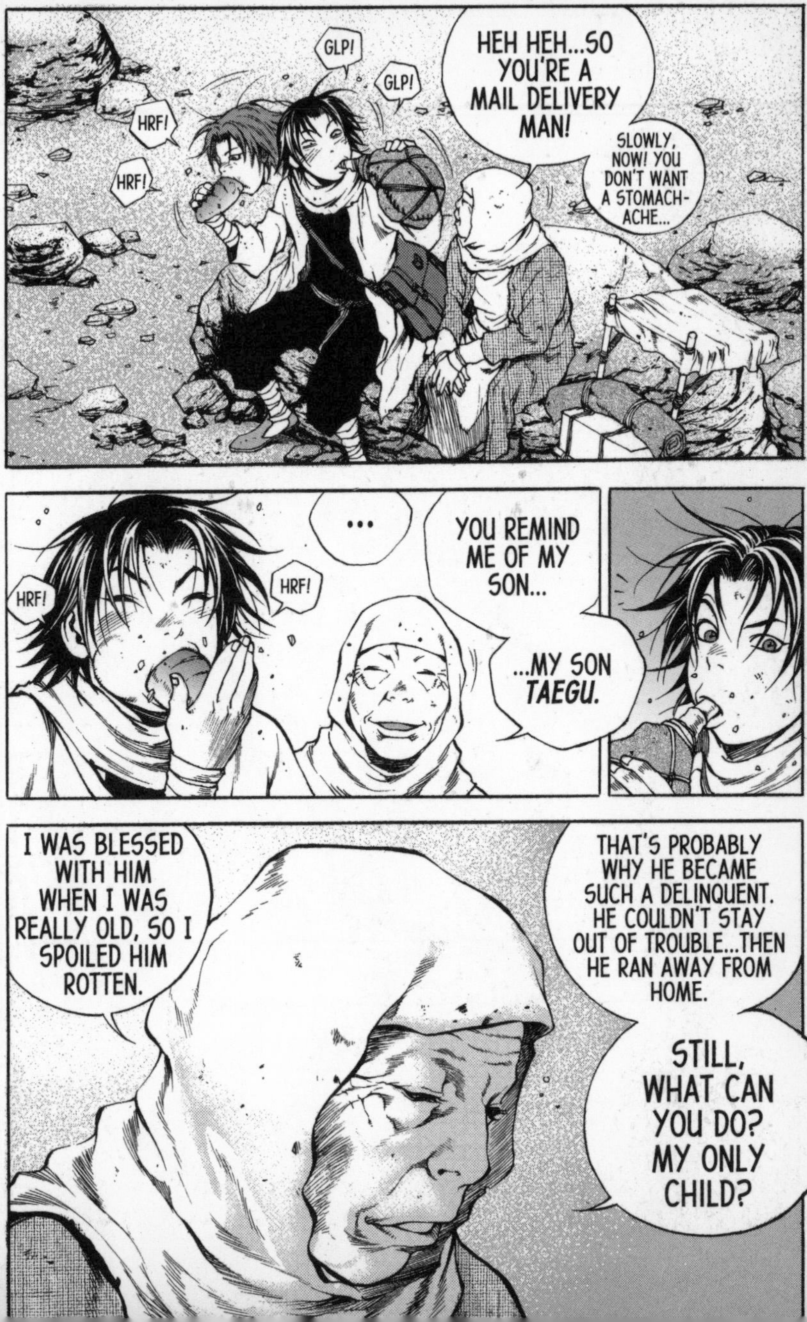
HRF!
HRF!
GLP!
GLP!
HEH HEH...SO YOU'RE A MAIL DELIVERY MAN!
SLOWLY, NOW! YOU DON'T WANT A STOMACH-ACHE...
HRF!
HRF!
...
YOU REMIND ME OF MY SON...
...MY SON *TAEGU.*
I WAS BLESSED WITH HIM WHEN I WAS REALLY OLD, SO I SPOILED HIM ROTTEN.
THAT'S PROBABLY WHY HE BECAME SUCH A DELINQUENT. HE COULDN'T STAY OUT OF TROUBLE...THEN HE RAN AWAY FROM HOME.
STILL, WHAT CAN YOU DO? MY ONLY CHILD?

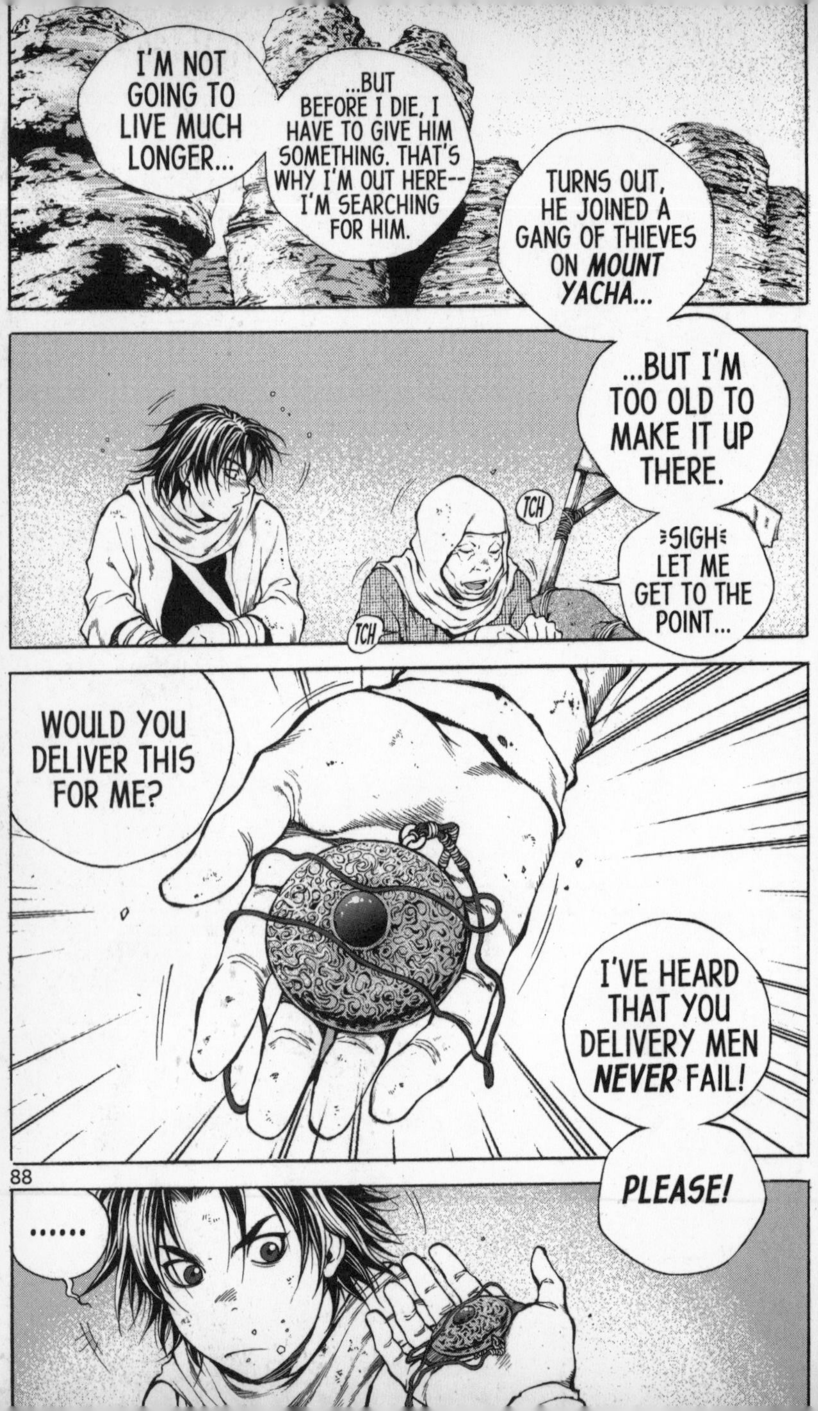

I'M NOT GOING TO LIVE MUCH LONGER...
...BUT BEFORE I DIE, I HAVE TO GIVE HIM SOMETHING. THAT'S WHY I'M OUT HERE-- I'M SEARCHING FOR HIM.
TURNS OUT, HE JOINED A GANG OF THIEVES ON *MOUNT YACHA*...
...BUT I'M TOO OLD TO MAKE IT UP THERE.
TCH
TCH
SIGH LET ME GET TO THE POINT...
WOULD YOU DELIVER THIS FOR ME?
I'VE HEARD THAT YOU DELIVERY MEN *NEVER* FAIL!
PLEASE!
......

88

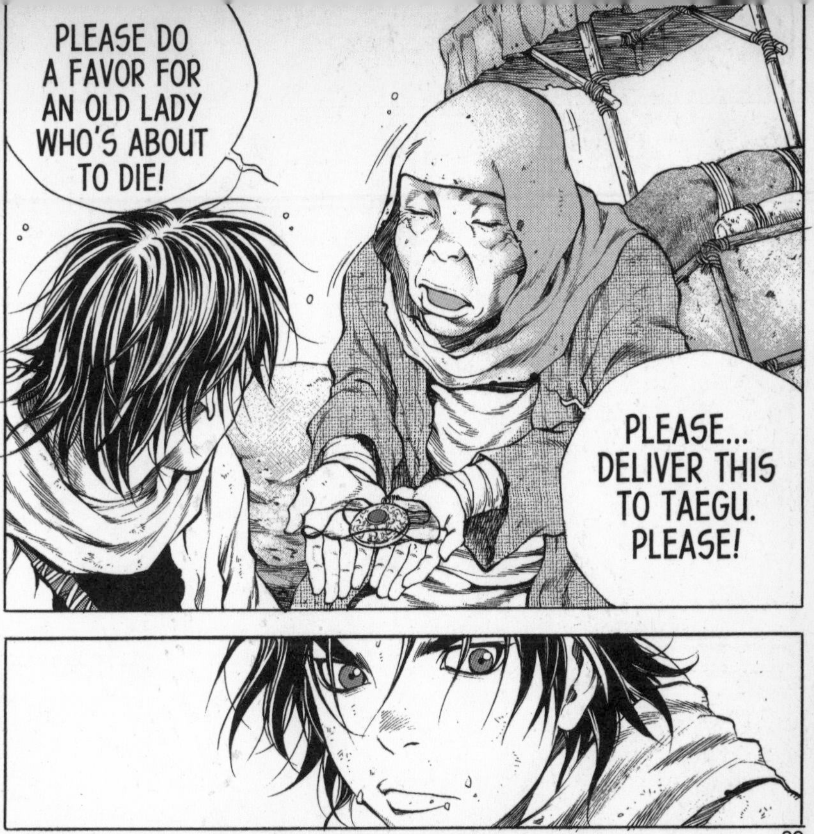
PLEASE DO A FAVOR FOR AN OLD LADY WHO'S ABOUT TO DIE!
PLEASE... DELIVER THIS TO TAEGU. PLEASE!

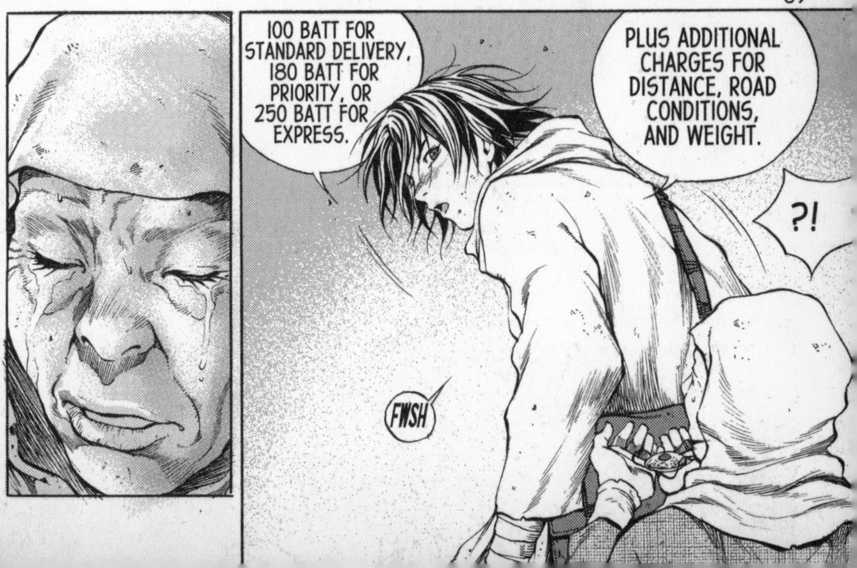
100 BATT FOR STANDARD DELIVERY, 180 BATT FOR PRIORITY, OR 250 BATT FOR EXPRESS.
PLUS ADDITIONAL CHARGES FOR DISTANCE, ROAD CONDITIONS, AND WEIGHT.
?!
FWSH

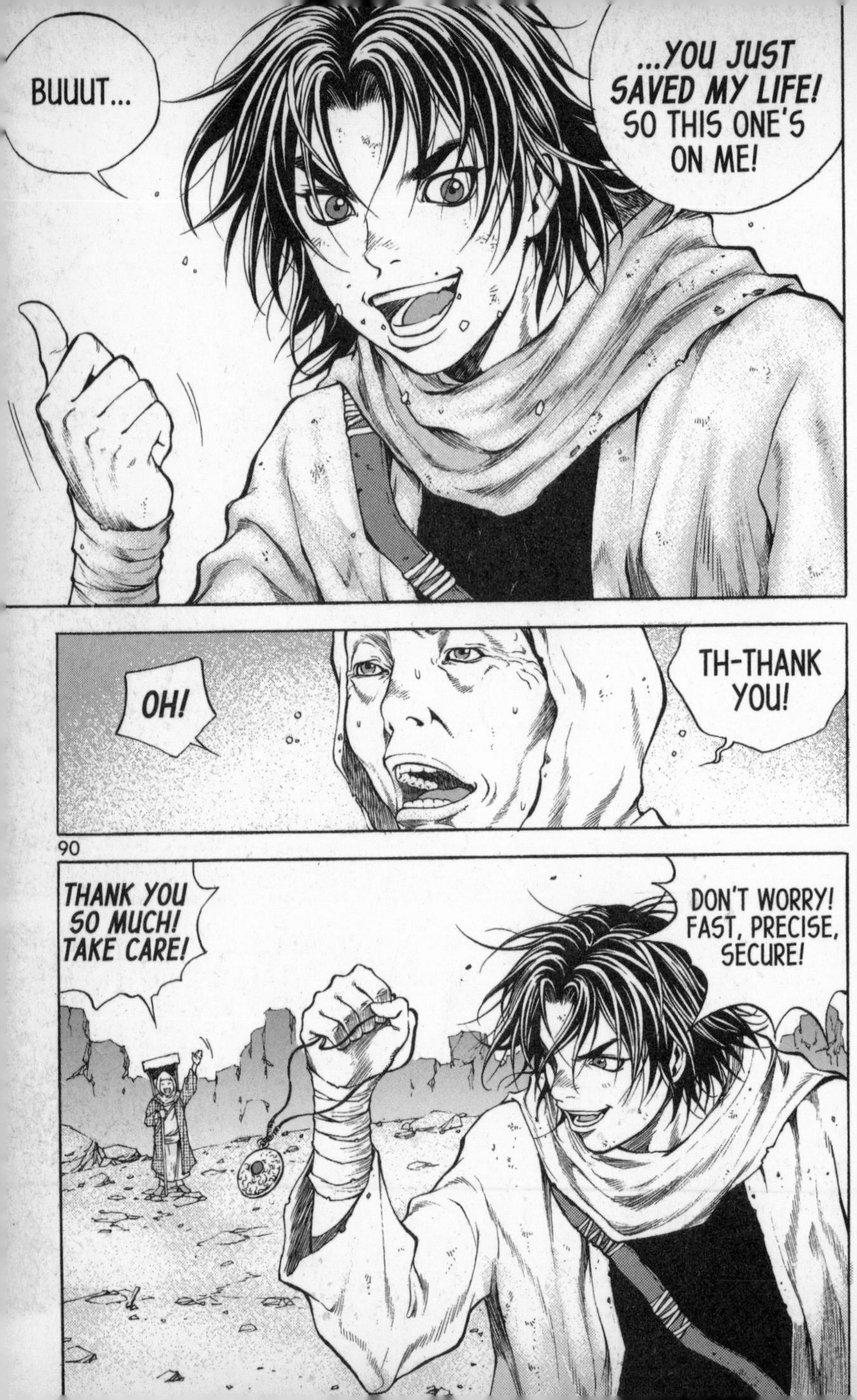
BUUUT...
...YOU JUST SAVED MY LIFE! SO THIS ONE'S ON ME!
OH!
TH-THANK YOU!
THANK YOU SO MUCH! TAKE CARE!
DON'T WORRY! FAST, PRECISE, SECURE!

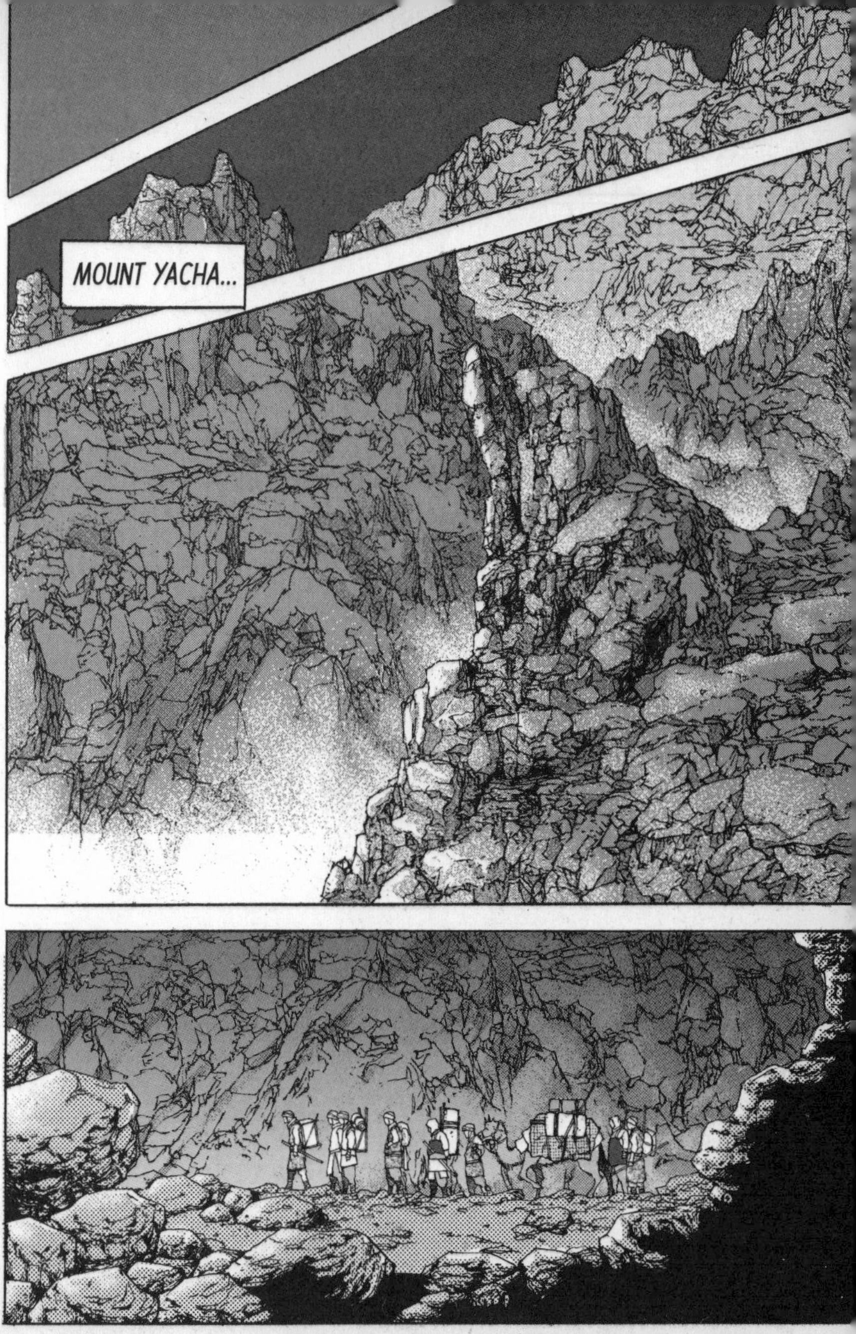
MOUNT YACHA...

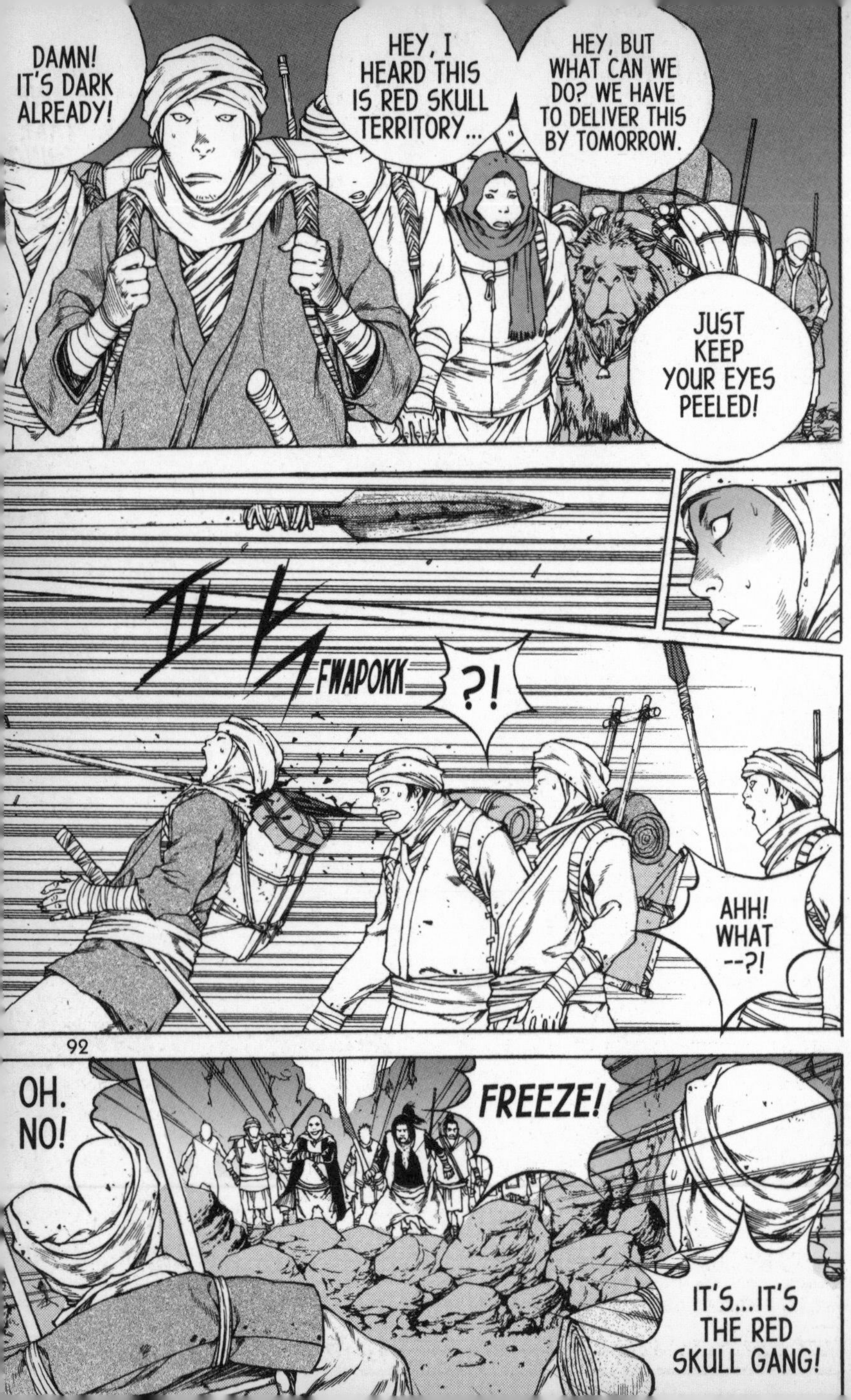
DAMN! IT'S DARK ALREADY!
HEY, I HEARD THIS IS RED SKULL TERRITORY...
HEY, BUT WHAT CAN WE DO? WE HAVE TO DELIVER THIS BY TOMORROW.
JUST KEEP YOUR EYES PEELED!
FWAPOKK
?!
AHH! WHAT --?!
OH. NO!
FREEZE!
IT'S...IT'S THE RED SKULL GANG!

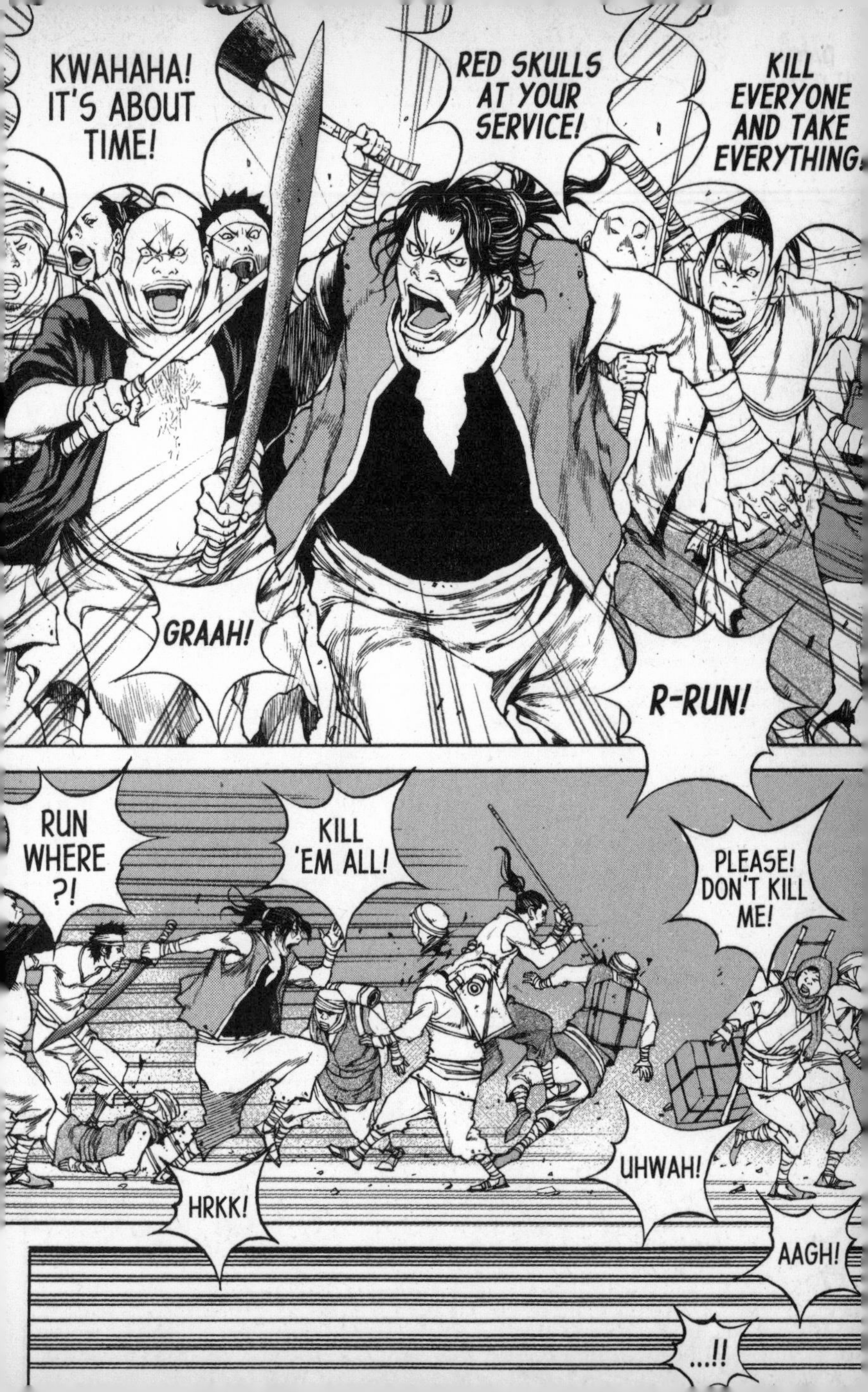
KILL EVERYONE AND TAKE EVERYTHING!
RED SKULLS AT YOUR SERVICE!
KWAHAHA! IT'S ABOUT TIME!
GRAAH!
R-RUN!
PLEASE! DON'T KILL ME!
KILL 'EM ALL!
RUN WHERE ?!
UHWAH!
HRKK!
AAGH!
...!!

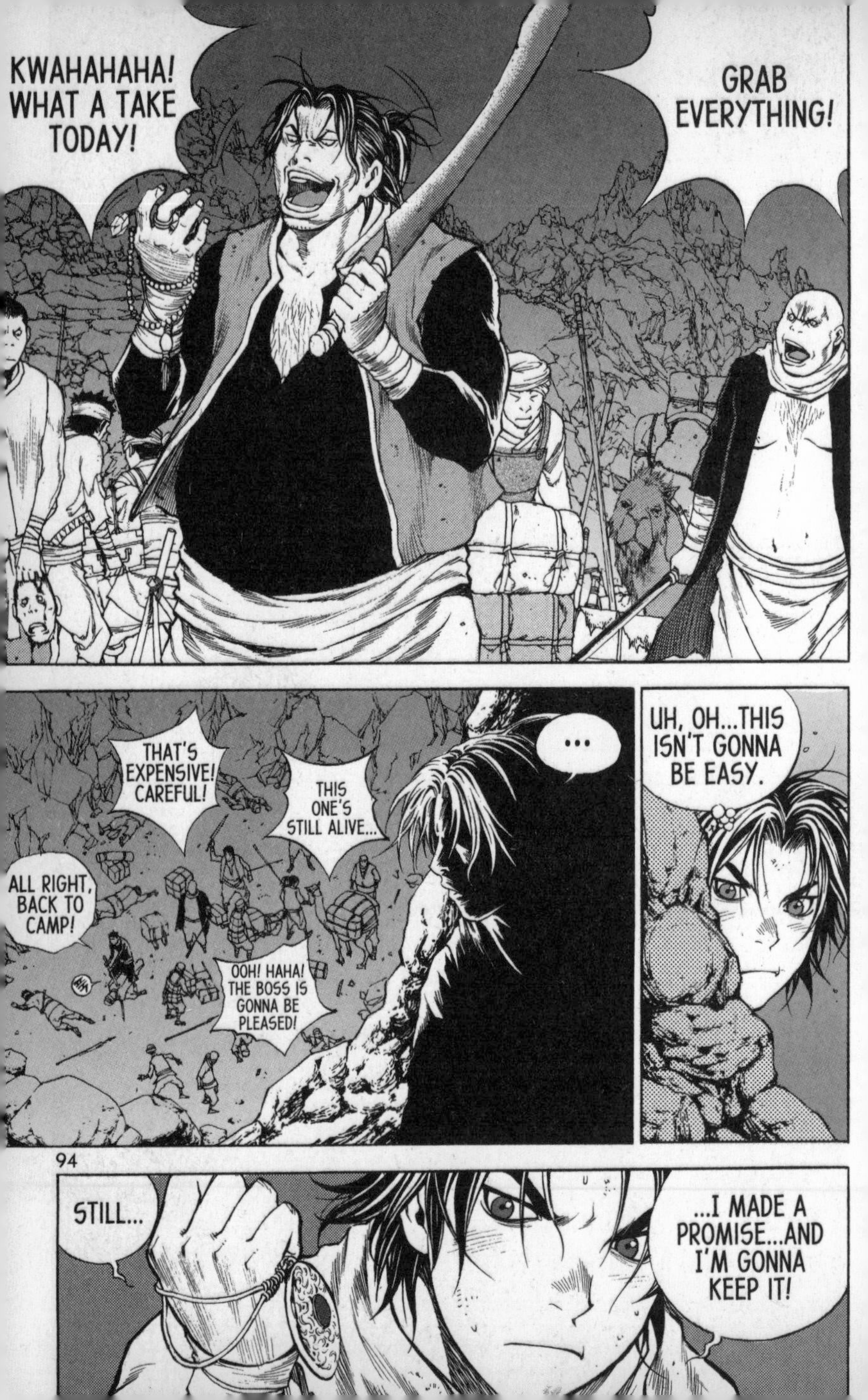
KWAHAHAHA! WHAT A TAKE TODAY!
GRAB EVERYTHING!
THAT'S EXPENSIVE! CAREFUL!
THIS ONE'S STILL ALIVE...
ALL RIGHT, BACK TO CAMP!
OOH! HAHA! THE BOSS IS GONNA BE PLEASED!
...
UH, OH...THIS ISN'T GONNA BE EASY.
STILL...
...I MADE A PROMISE...AND I'M GONNA KEEP IT!

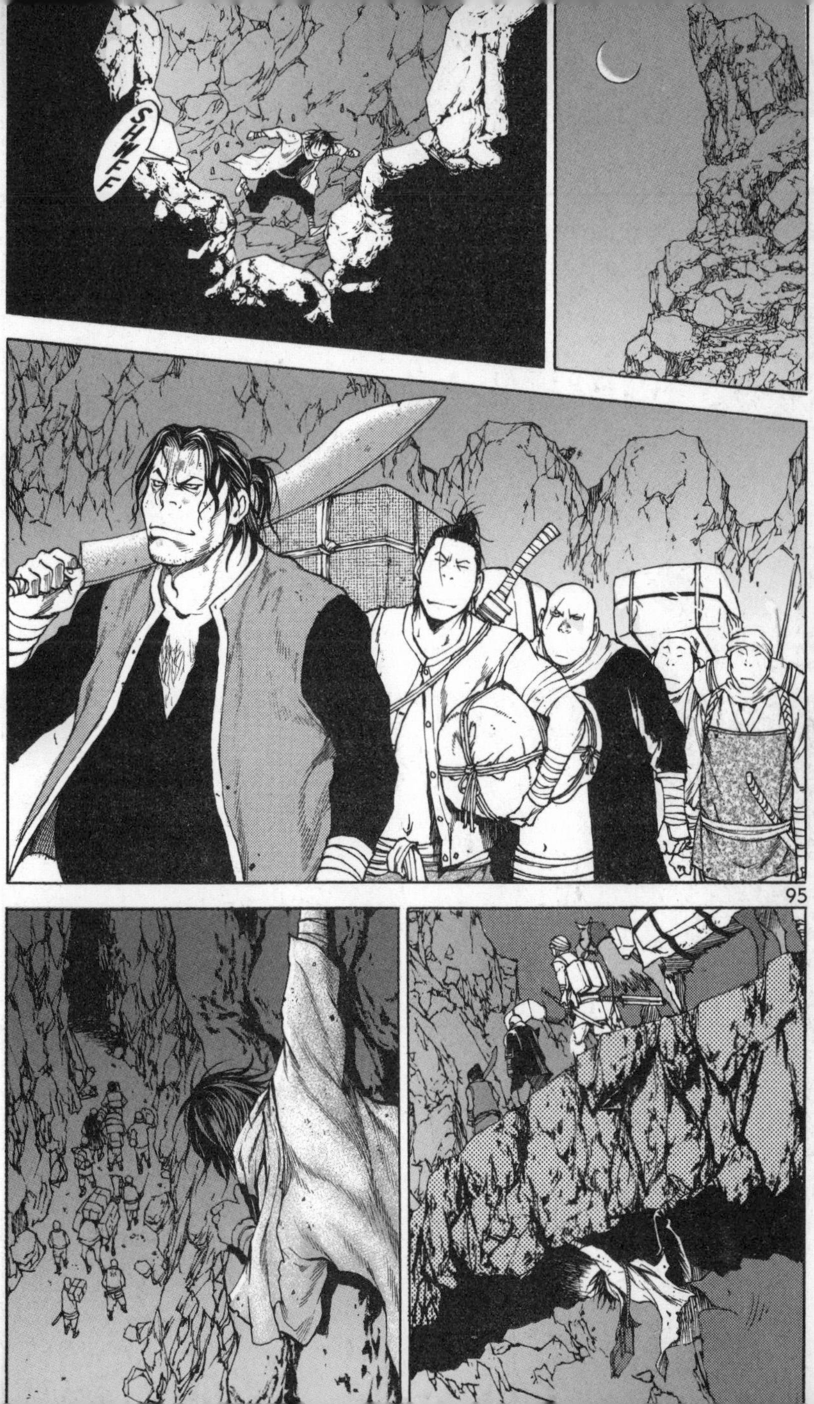
SHWEFF

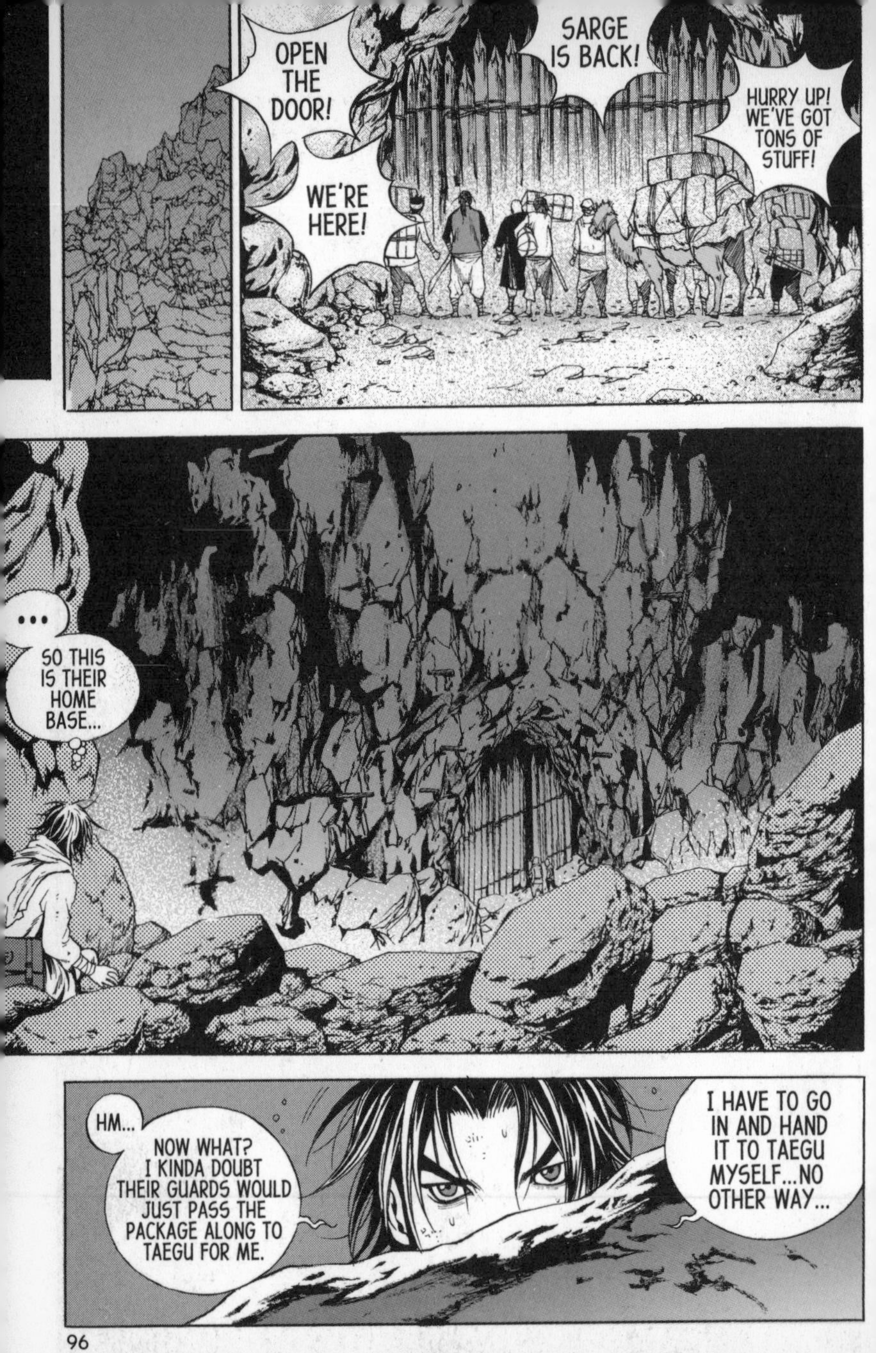
OPEN THE DOOR!
WE'RE HERE!
SARGE IS BACK!
HURRY UP! WE'VE GOT TONS OF STUFF!
...
SO THIS IS THEIR HOME BASE...
HM...
NOW WHAT? I KINDA DOUBT THEIR GUARDS WOULD JUST PASS THE PACKAGE ALONG TO TAEGU FOR ME.
I HAVE TO GO IN AND HAND IT TO TAEGU MYSELF...NO OTHER WAY...

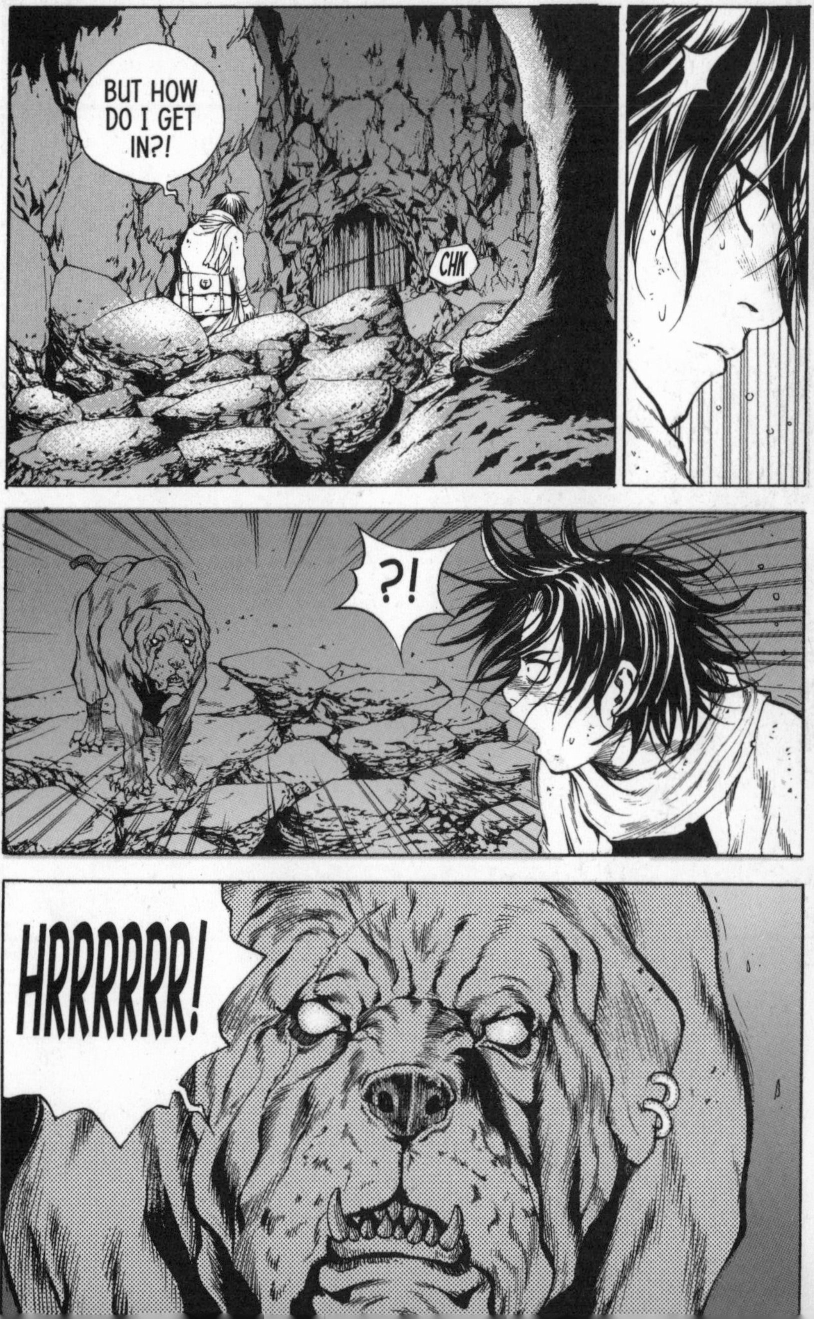

BUT HOW DO I GET IN?!
CHK
?!
HRRRRRR!

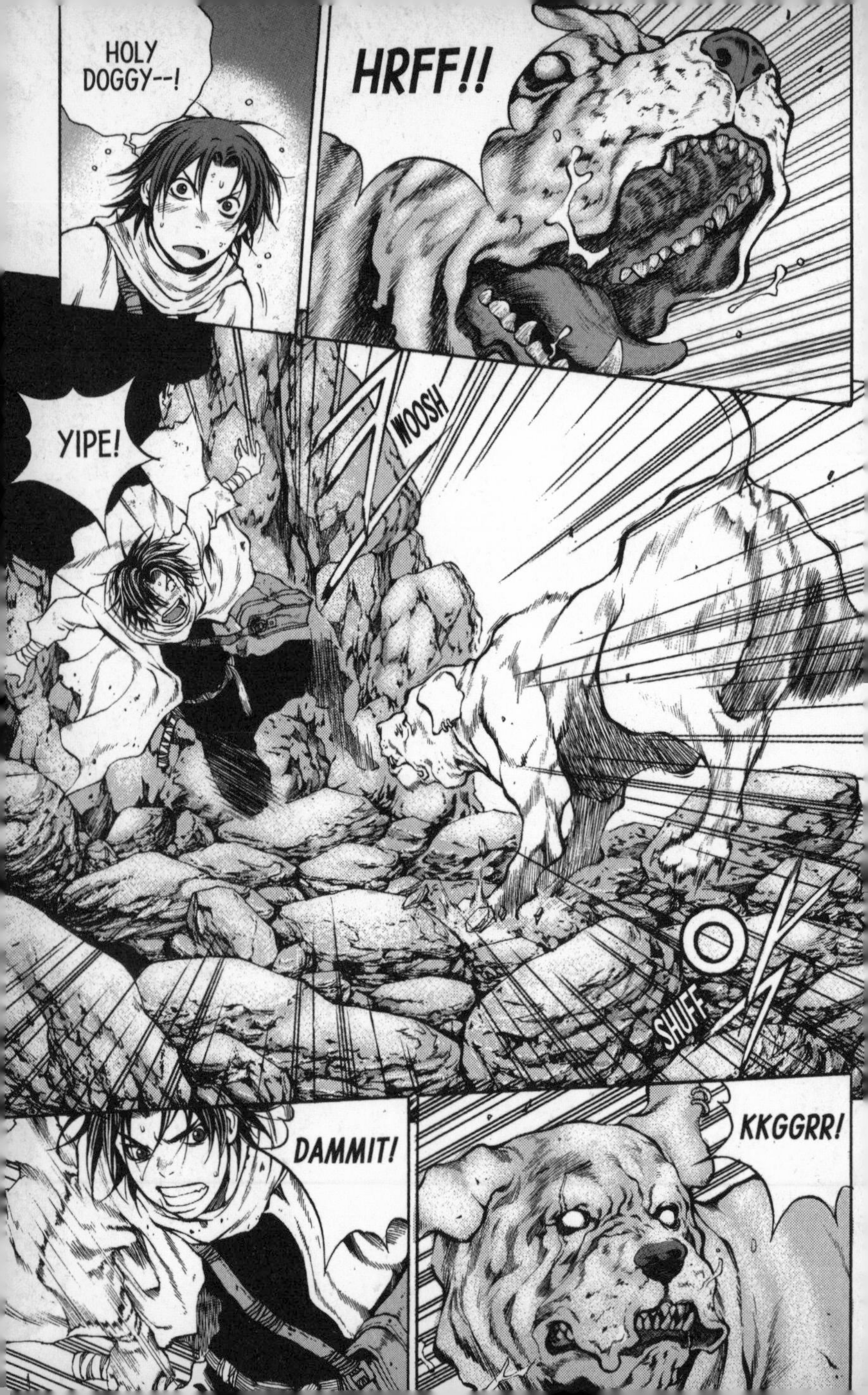
HOLY DOGGY--!
HRFF!!
YIPE!
WOOSH
SHUFF
DAMMIT!
KKGGRR!

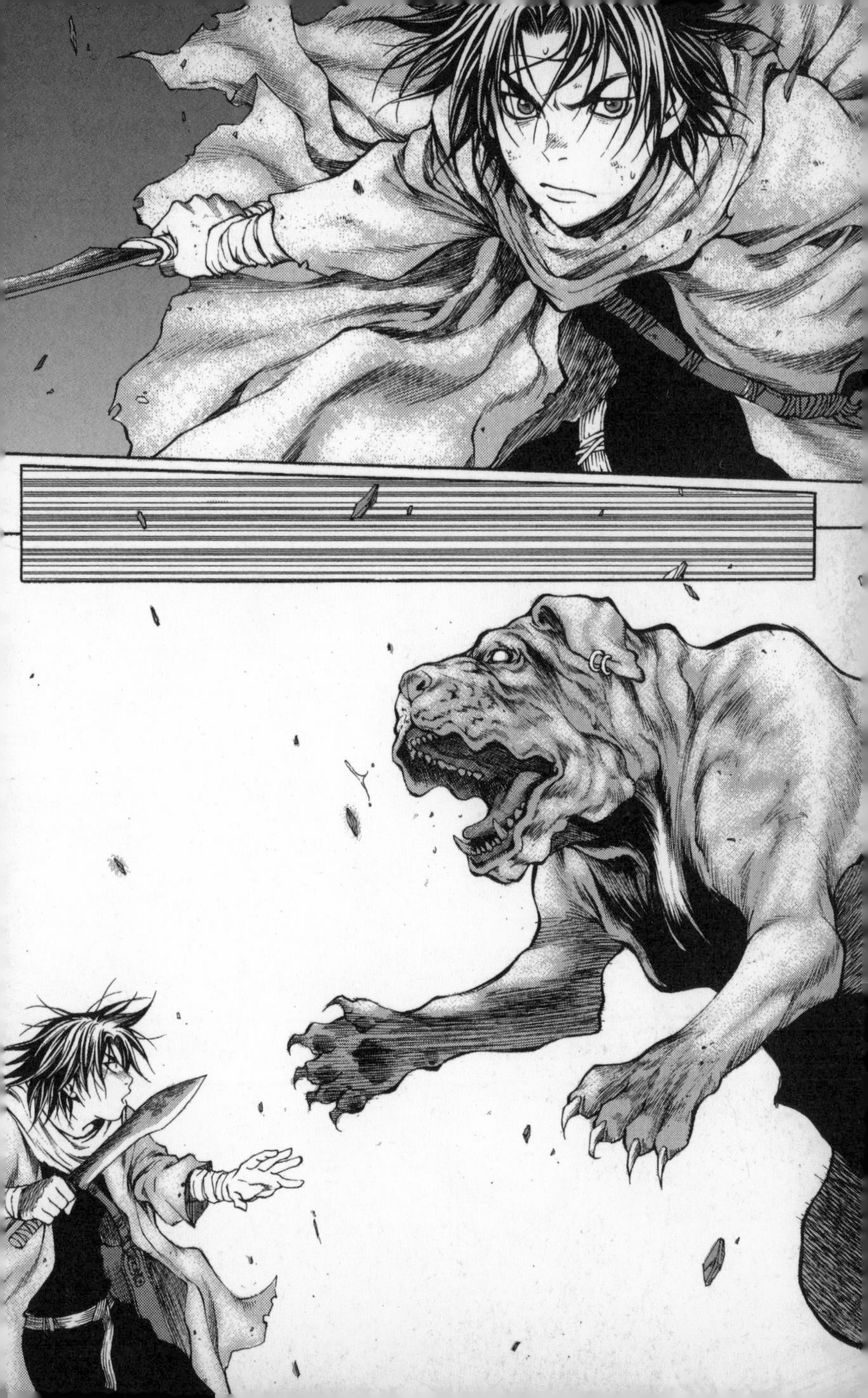

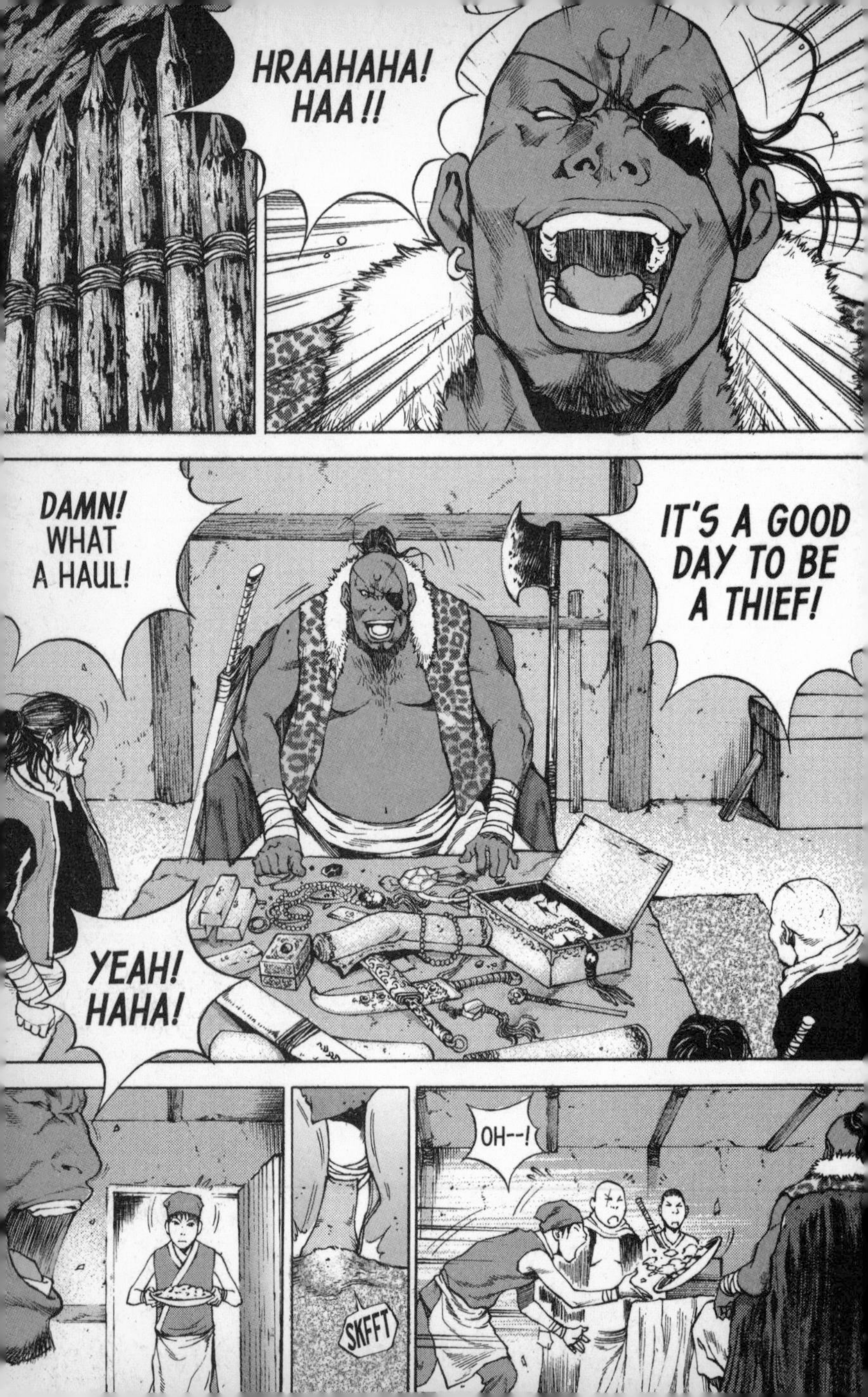
HRAAHAHA! HAA!!
IT'S A GOOD DAY TO BE A THIEF!
DAMN! WHAT A HAUL!
YEAH! HAHA!
OH--!
SKFFT

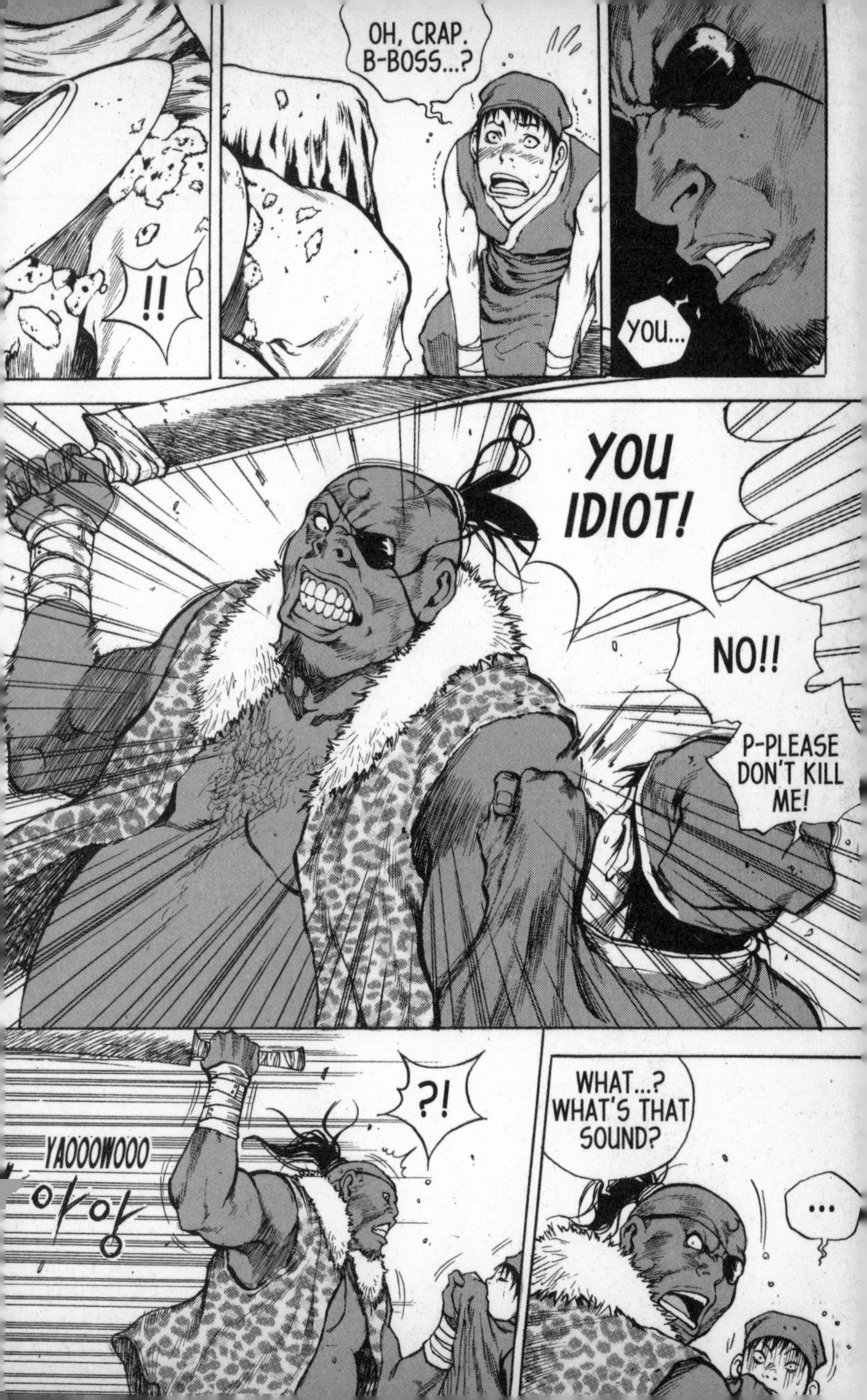
!!
OH, CRAP. B-BOSS...?
YOU...
YOU IDIOT!
NO!!
P-PLEASE DON'T KILL ME!
YAOOOWOOO
?!
WHAT...? WHAT'S THAT SOUND?
...

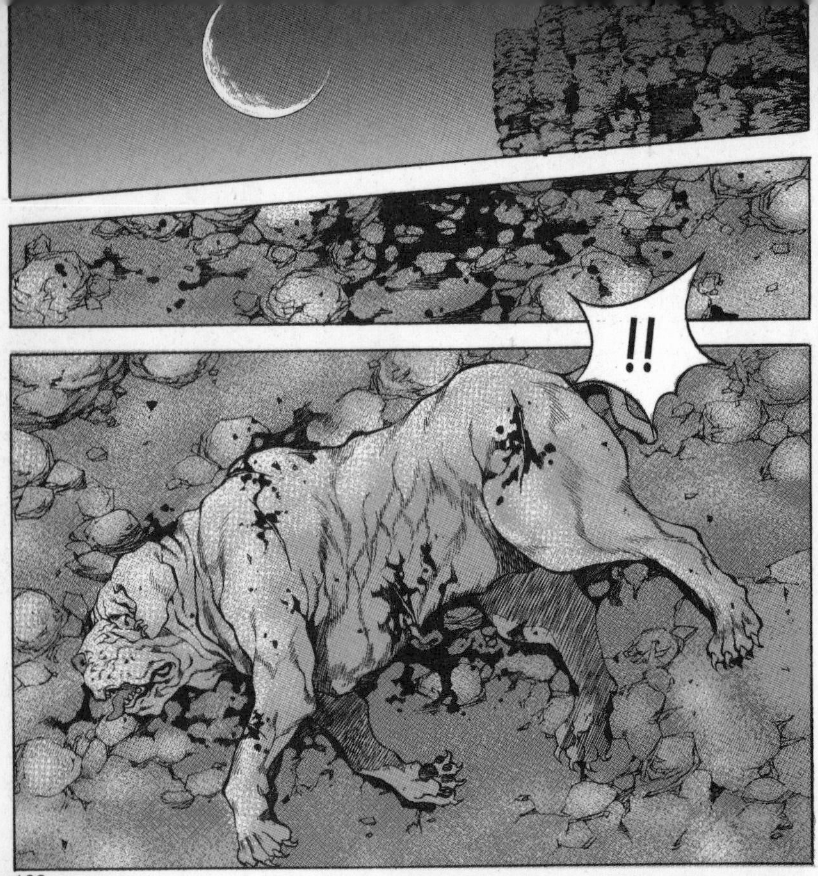
!!

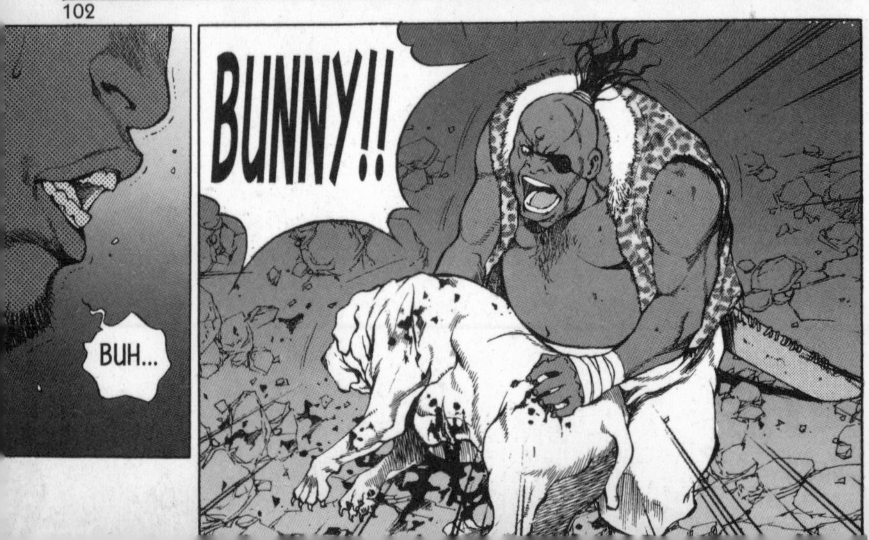
BUH...
BUNNY!!

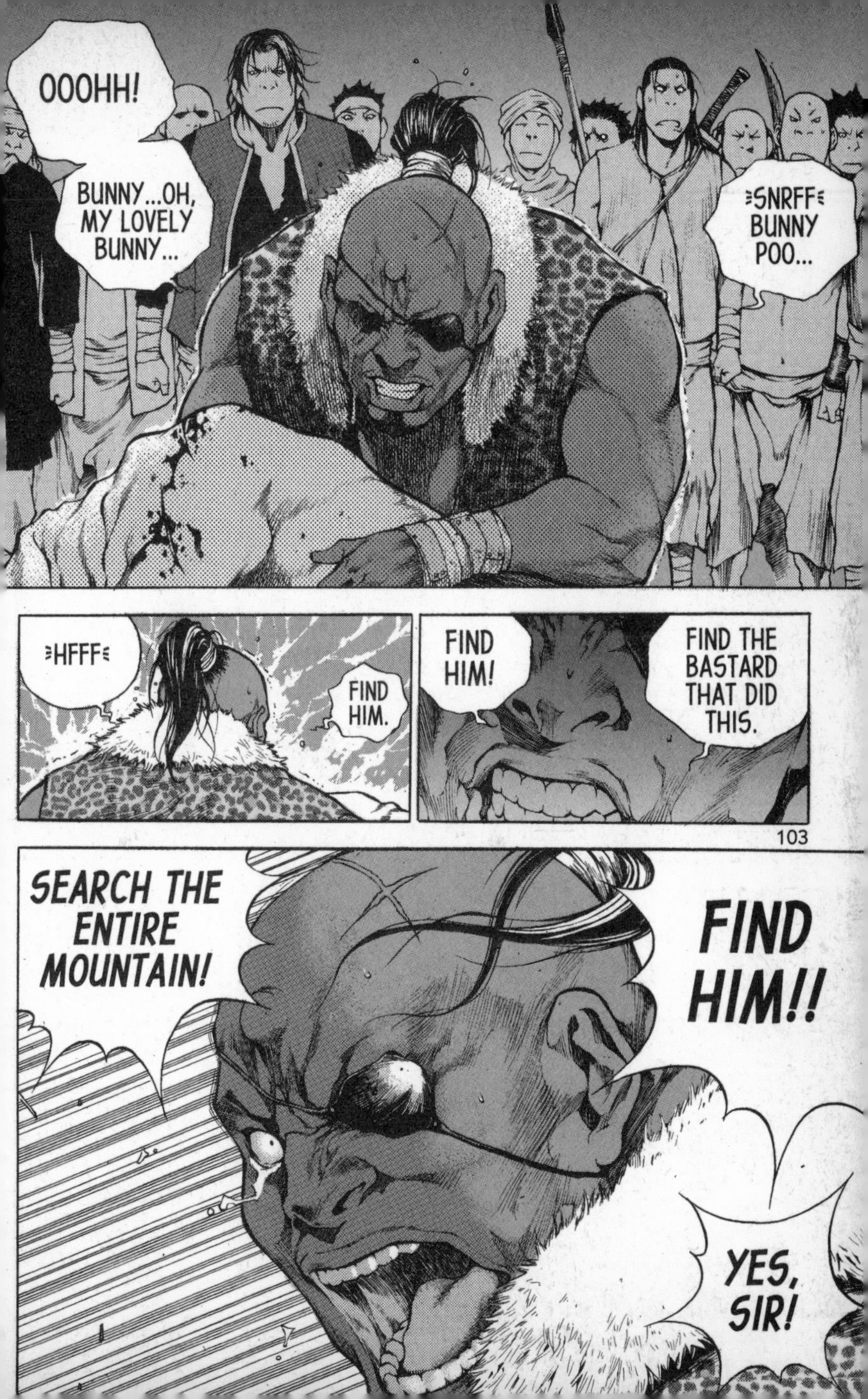
OOOHH!
BUNNY...OH, MY LOVELY BUNNY...
≡SNRFF≡ BUNNY POO...
≡HFFF≡
FIND HIM.
FIND HIM!
FIND THE BASTARD THAT DID THIS.
SEARCH THE ENTIRE MOUNTAIN!
FIND HIM!!
YES, SIR!

Banya
the explosive delivery man

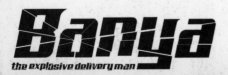

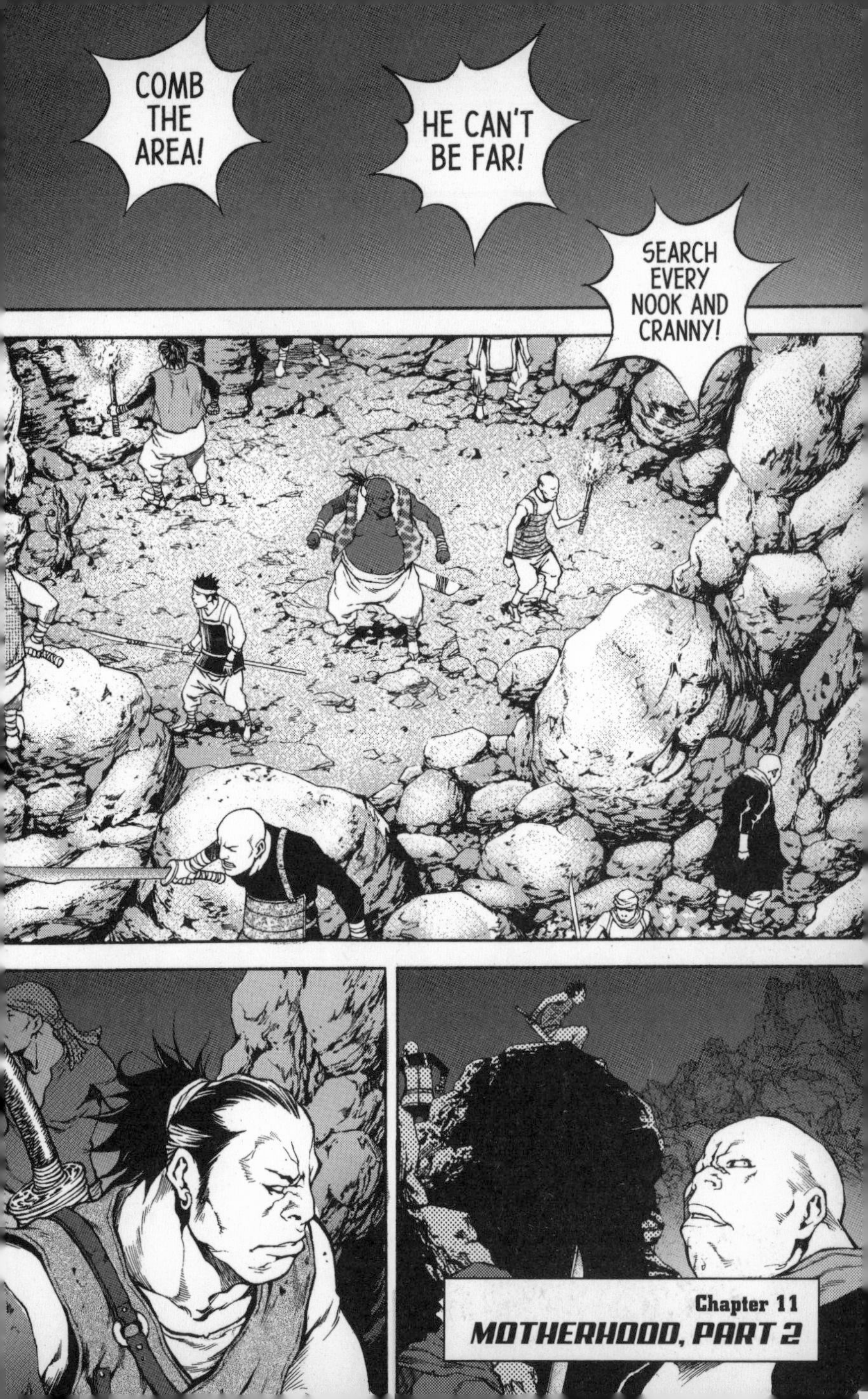
COMB THE AREA!
HE CAN'T BE FAR!
SEARCH EVERY NOOK AND CRANNY!
Chapter 11
MOTHERHOOD, PART 2

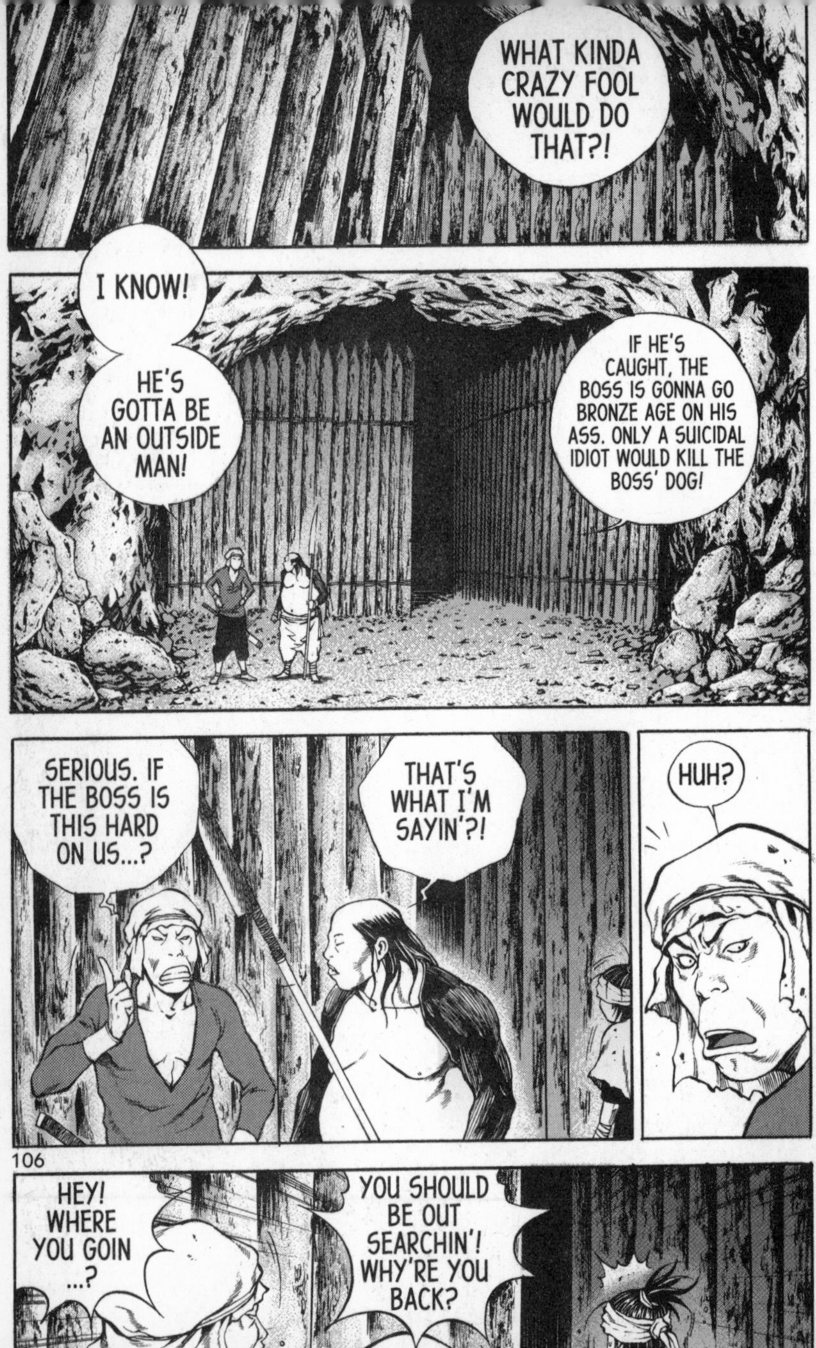
WHAT KINDA CRAZY FOOL WOULD DO THAT?!
I KNOW!
HE'S GOTTA BE AN OUTSIDE MAN!
IF HE'S CAUGHT, THE BOSS IS GONNA GO BRONZE AGE ON HIS ASS. ONLY A SUICIDAL IDIOT WOULD KILL THE BOSS' DOG!
SERIOUS. IF THE BOSS IS THIS HARD ON US...?
THAT'S WHAT I'M SAYIN'?!
HUH?
HEY! WHERE YOU GOIN ...?
YOU SHOULD BE OUT SEARCHIN'! WHY'RE YOU BACK?

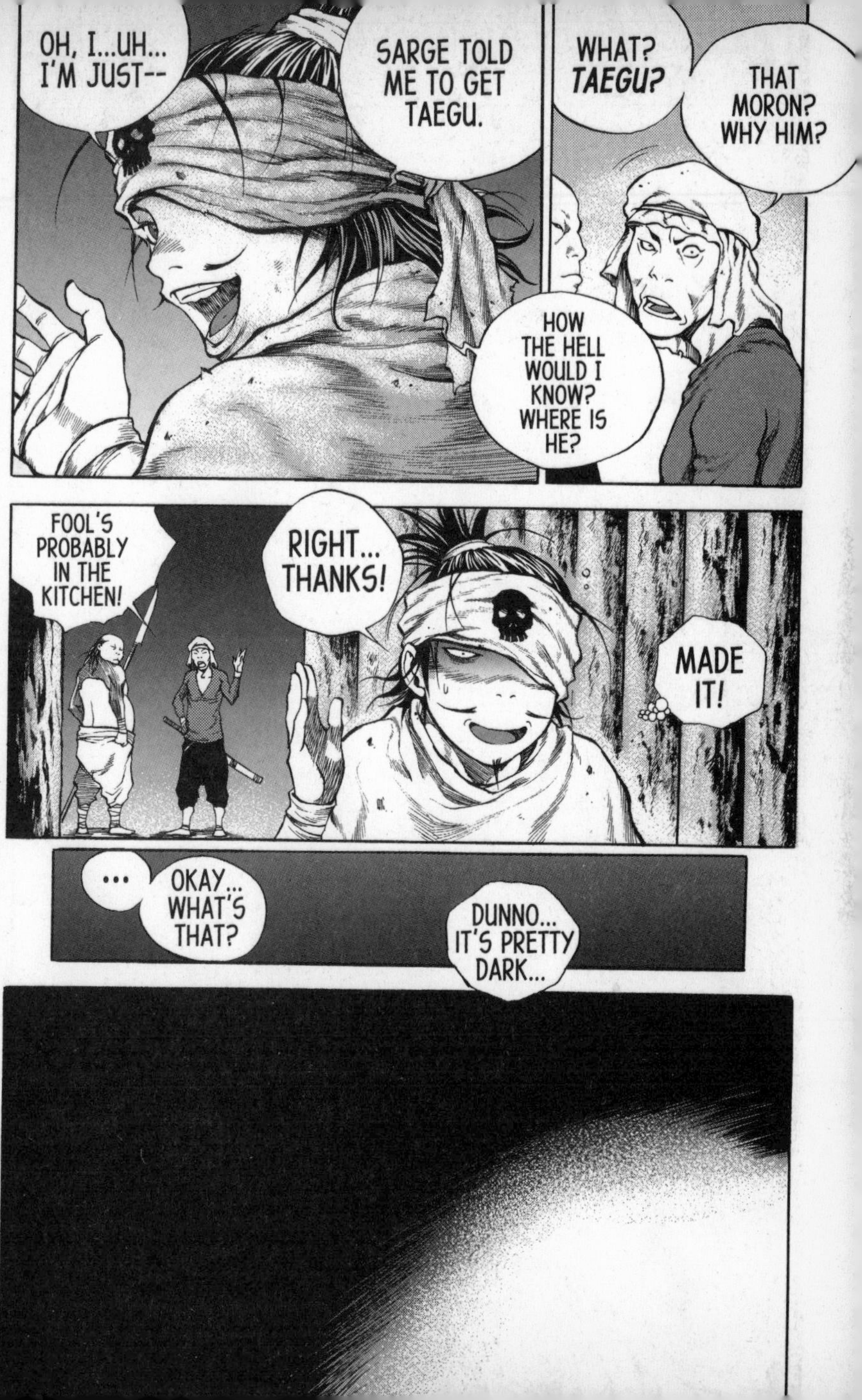
OH, I...UH... I'M JUST--
SARGE TOLD ME TO GET TAEGU.
WHAT? *TAEGU?*
THAT MORON? WHY HIM?
HOW THE HELL WOULD I KNOW? WHERE IS HE?
FOOL'S PROBABLY IN THE KITCHEN!
RIGHT... THANKS!
MADE IT!
...
OKAY... WHAT'S THAT?
DUNNO... IT'S PRETTY DARK...

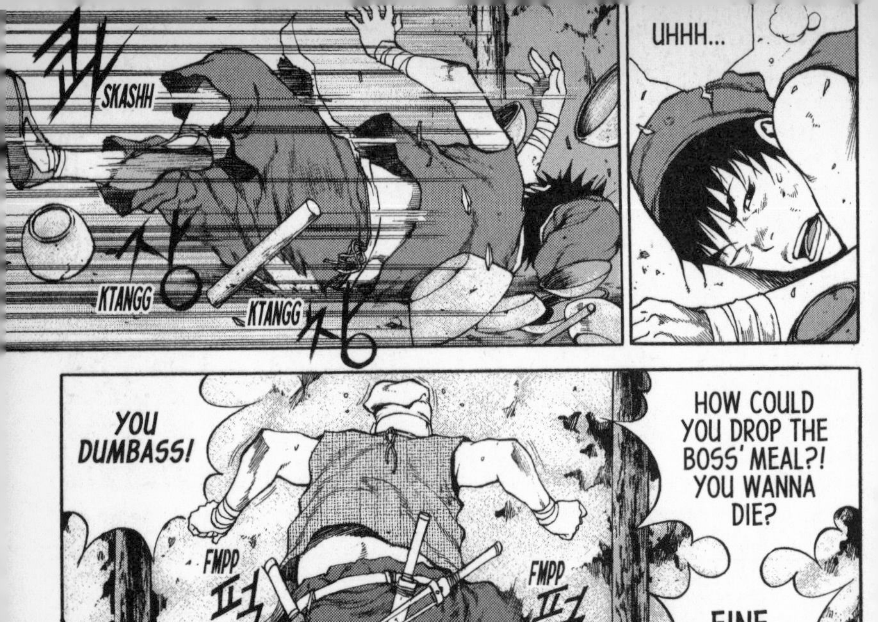

SKASHH
KTANGG
KTANGG
UHHH...
YOU DUMBASS!
HOW COULD YOU DROP THE BOSS' MEAL?! YOU WANNA DIE?
FMPP
FMPP
FINE, DIE!
OW!
OW!
FMPP
HRFF!

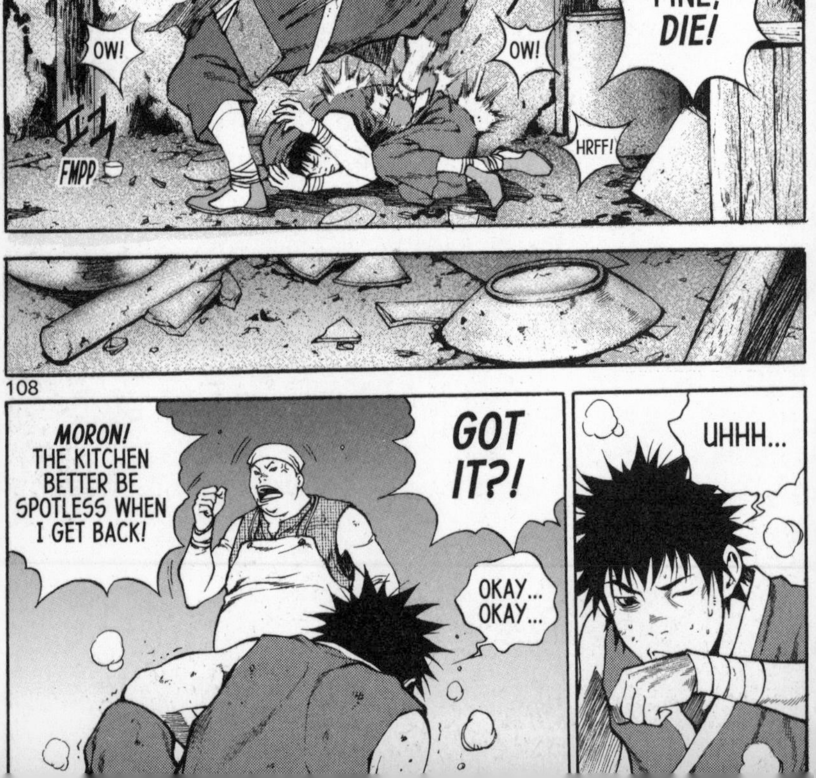

MORON! THE KITCHEN BETTER BE SPOTLESS WHEN I GET BACK!
GOT IT?!
OKAY... OKAY...
UHHH...

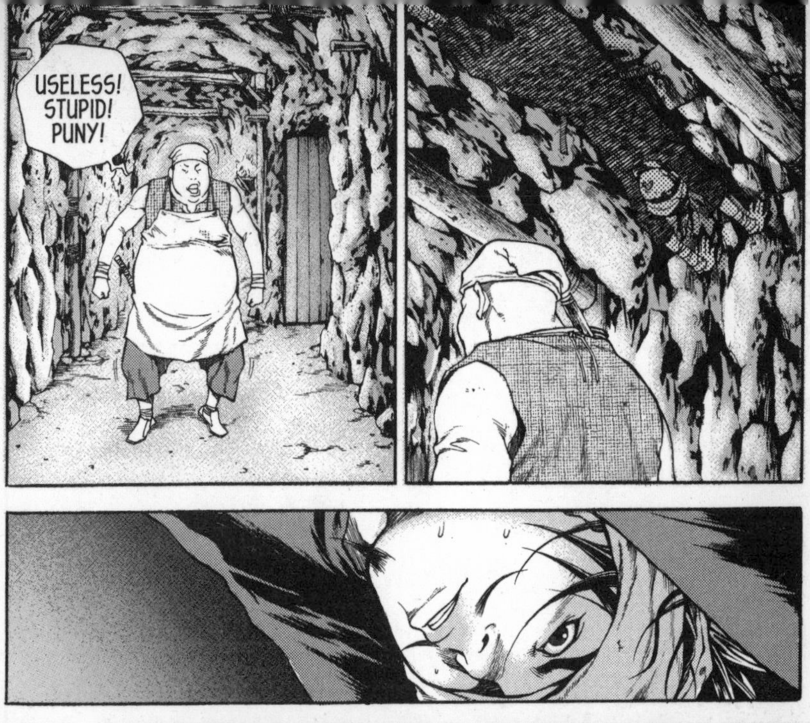
USELESS! STUPID! PUNY!
...!!
TPP

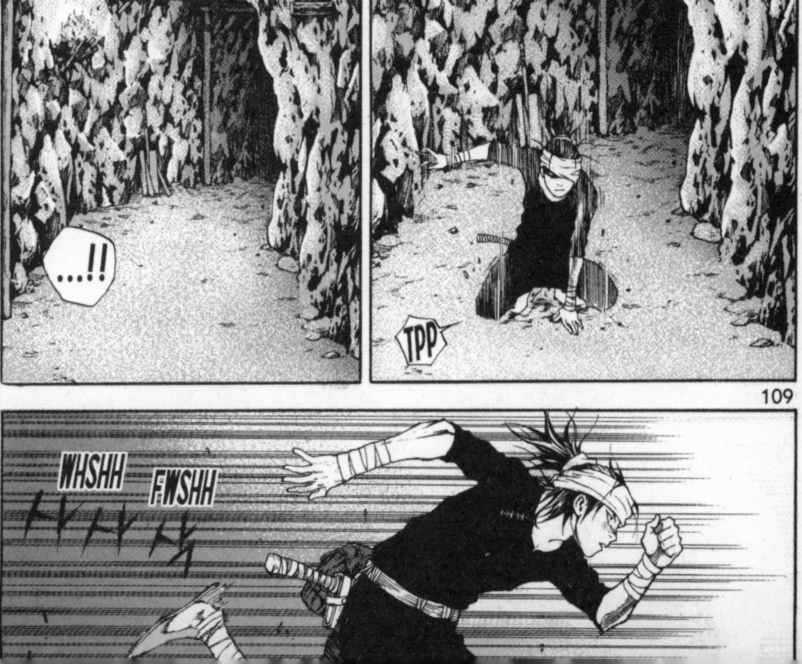
WHSHH
FWSHH

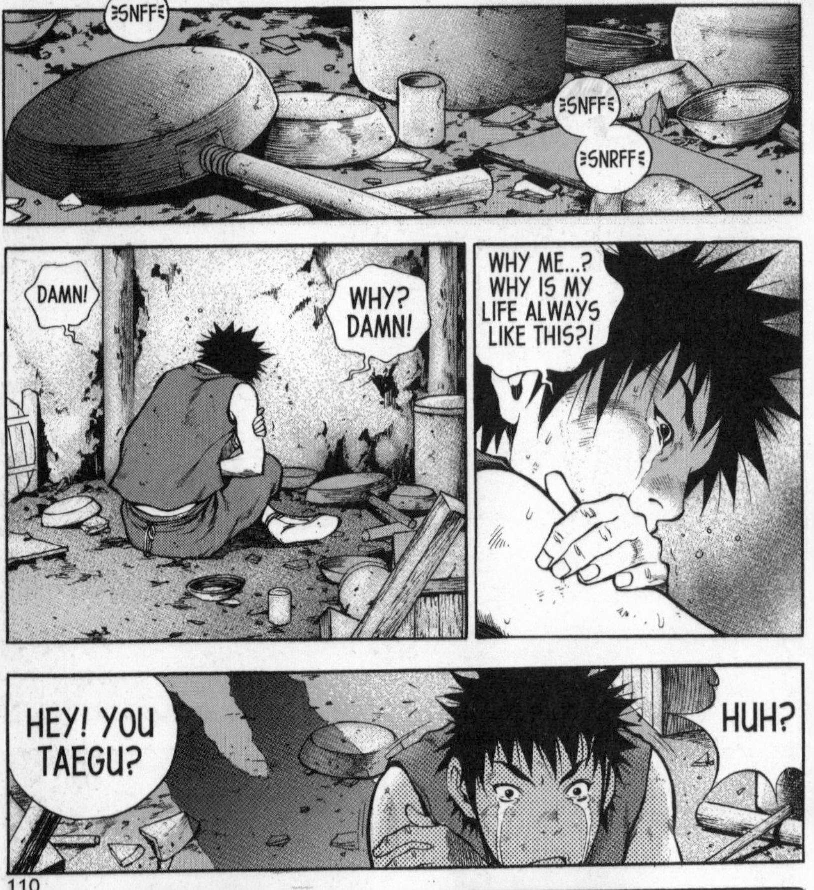
SNFF
SNFF
SNRFF
DAMN!
WHY? DAMN!
WHY ME...? WHY IS MY LIFE ALWAYS LIKE THIS?!
HEY! YOU TAEGU?
HUH?

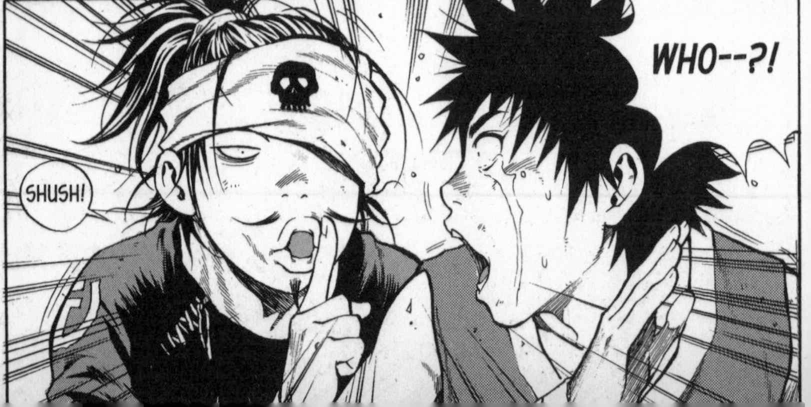
WHO--?!
SHUSH!

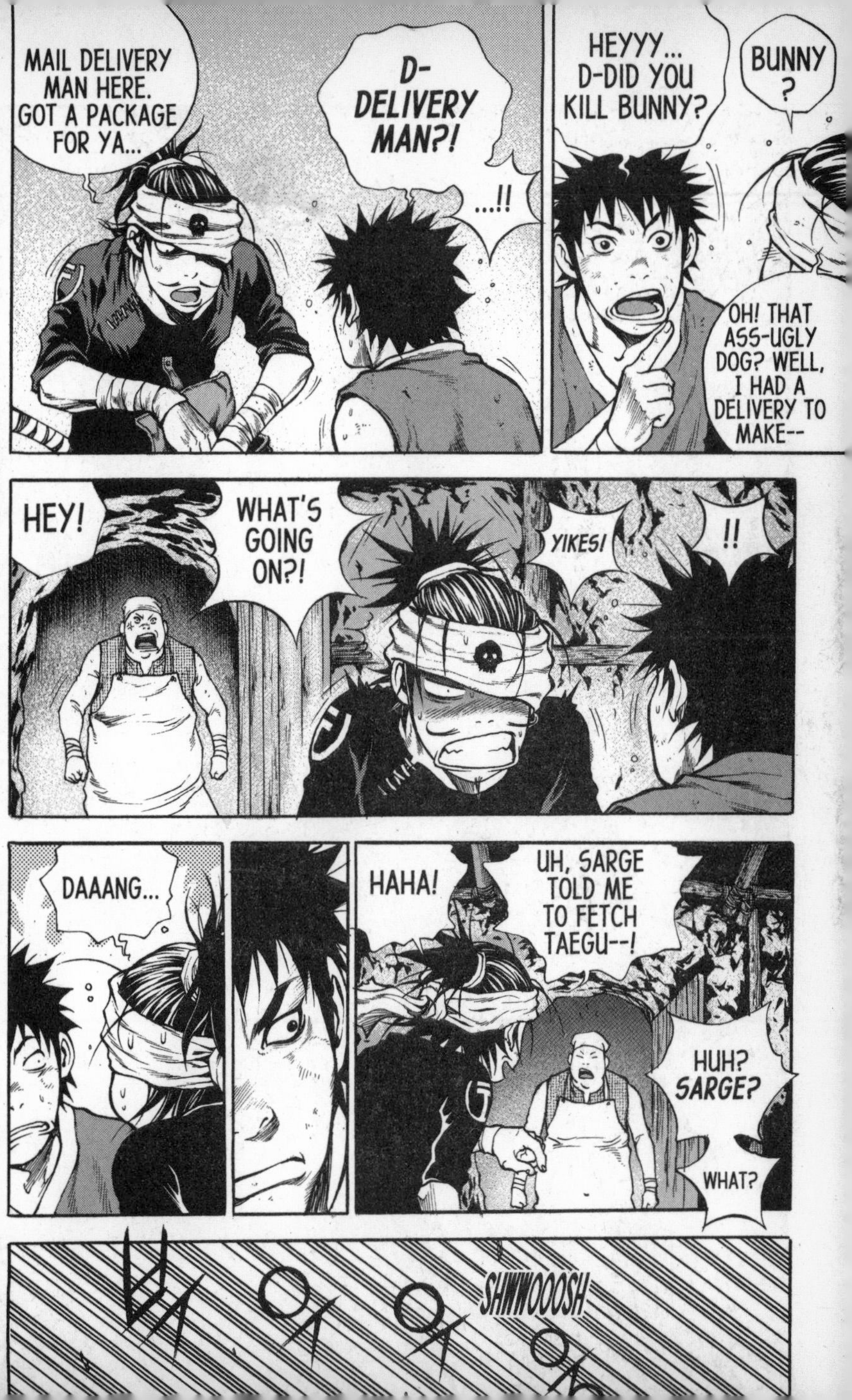
MAIL DELIVERY MAN HERE. GOT A PACKAGE FOR YA...
D-DELIVERY MAN?!
...!!
HEYYY... D-DID YOU KILL BUNNY?
BUNNY?
OH! THAT ASS-UGLY DOG? WELL, I HAD A DELIVERY TO MAKE--
HEY!
WHAT'S GOING ON?!
YIKES!
!!
DAAANG...
HAHA!
UH, SARGE TOLD ME TO FETCH TAEGU--!
HUH? SARGE?
WHAT?
SHWWOOOSH

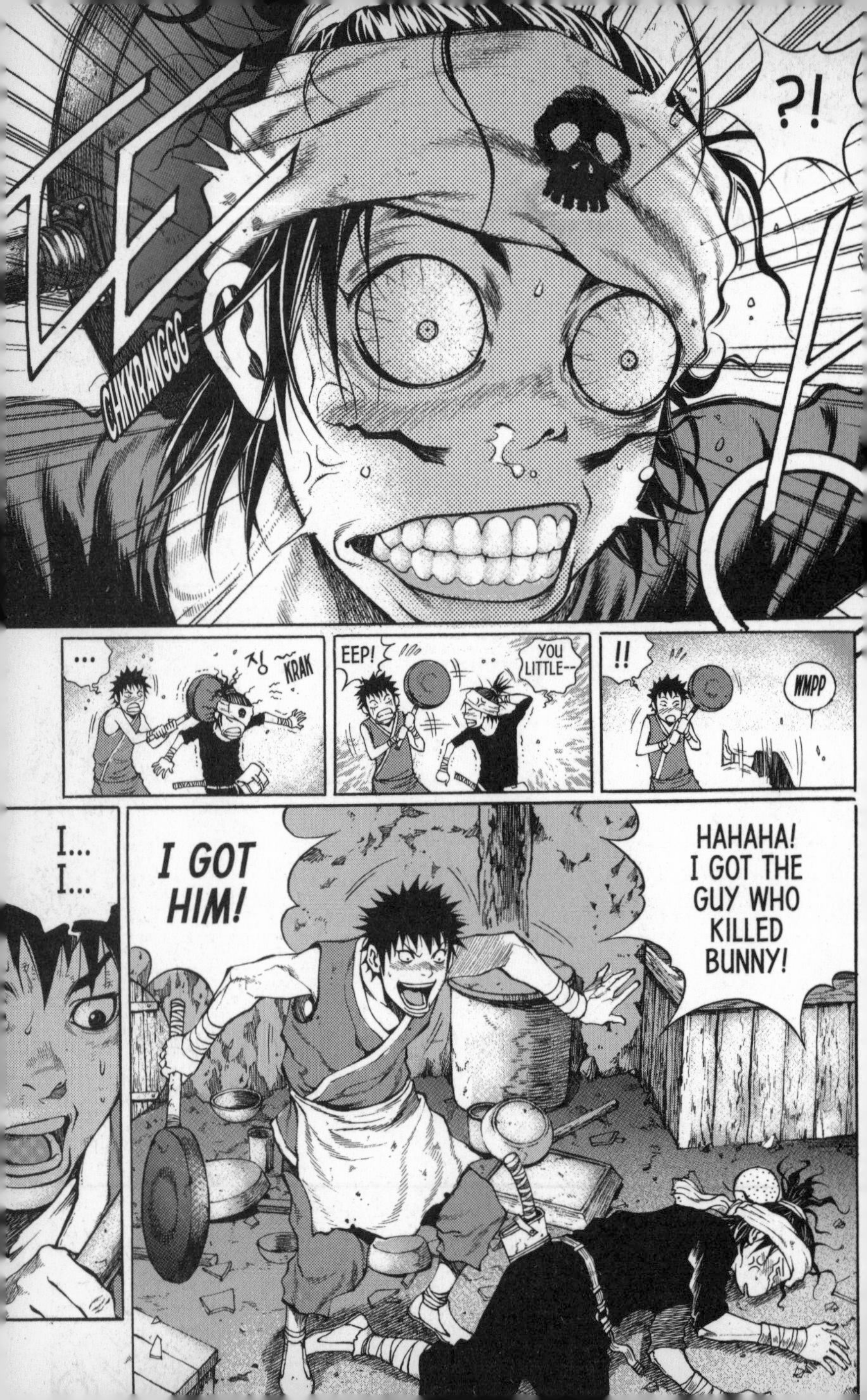
CHKKRANGGG
?!
...
징
KRAK
EEP!
YOU LITTLE--
!!
WMPP
I... I...
I GOT HIM!
HAHAHA! I GOT THE GUY WHO KILLED BUNNY!

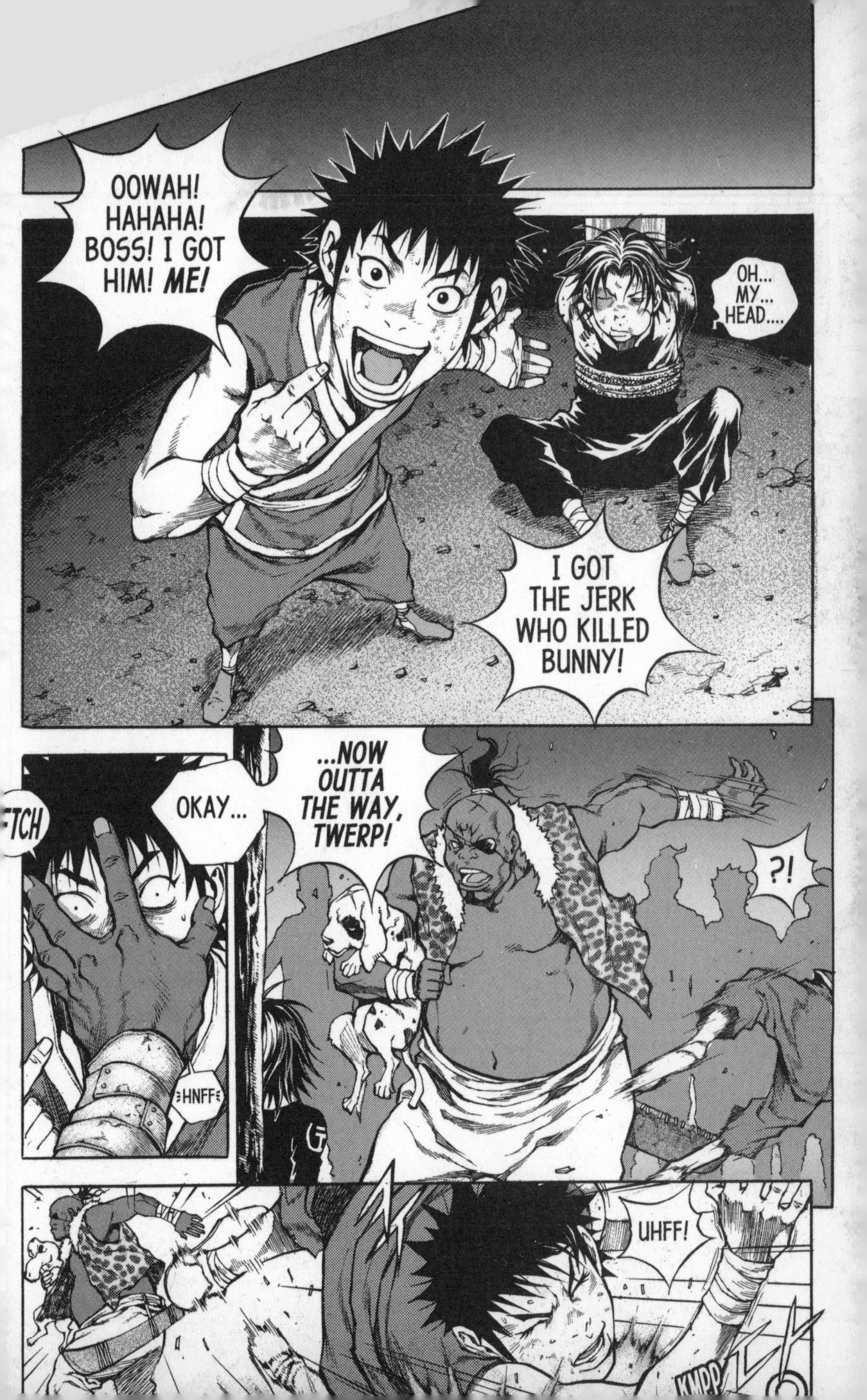
OOWAH! HAHAHA! BOSS! I GOT HIM! ME!
OH... MY... HEAD....
I GOT THE JERK WHO KILLED BUNNY!
OKAY...
...NOW OUTTA THE WAY, TWERP!
?!
HNFF
UHFF!
KMPP

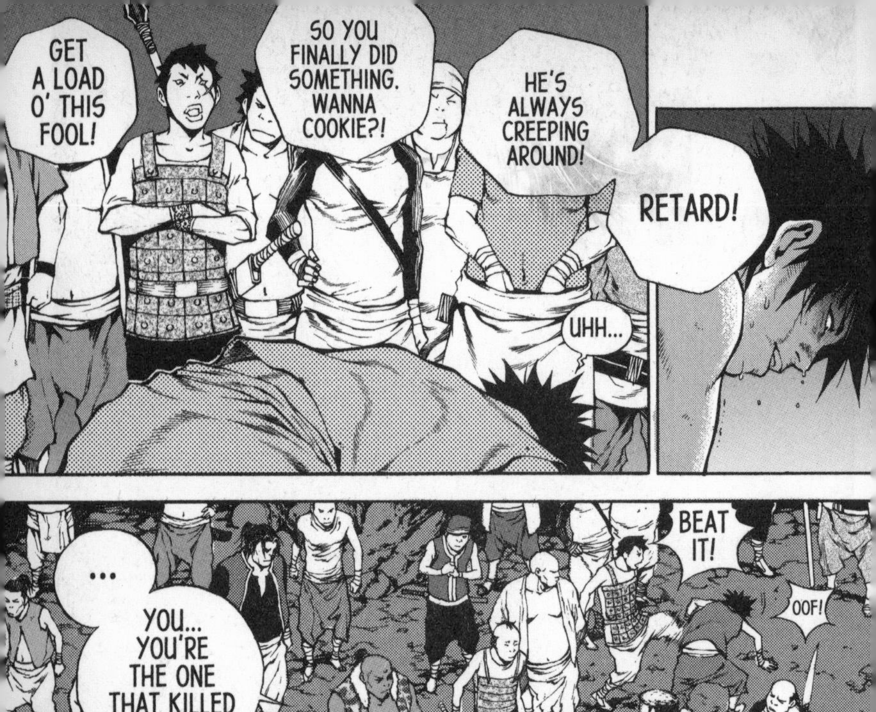
GET A LOAD O' THIS FOOL!
SO YOU FINALLY DID SOMETHING. WANNA COOKIE?!
HE'S ALWAYS CREEPING AROUND!
RETARD!
UHH...
...
YOU... YOU'RE THE ONE THAT KILLED BUNNY?
BEAT IT!
OOF!
GRRR...
...

114

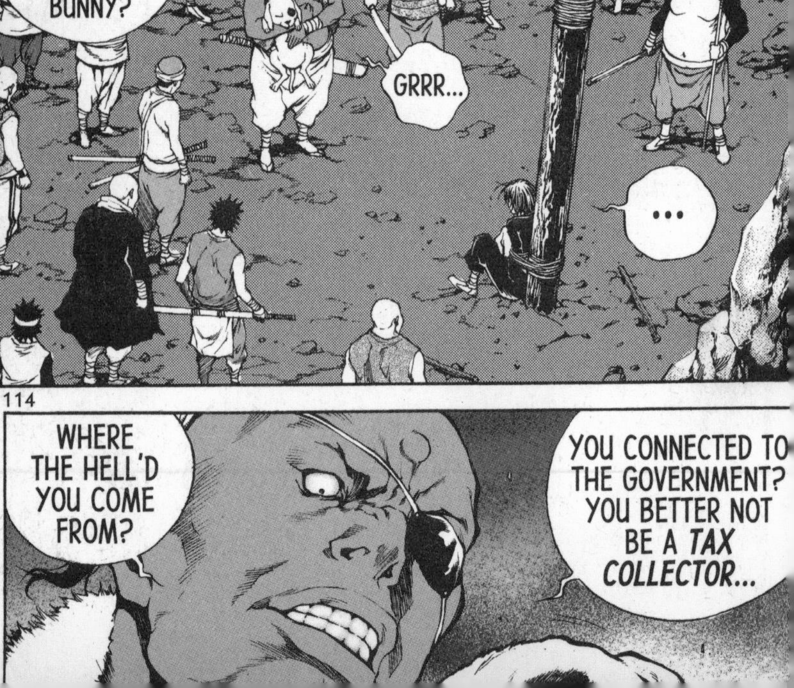
WHERE THE HELL'D YOU COME FROM?
YOU CONNECTED TO THE GOVERNMENT? YOU BETTER NOT BE A *TAX COLLECTOR*...

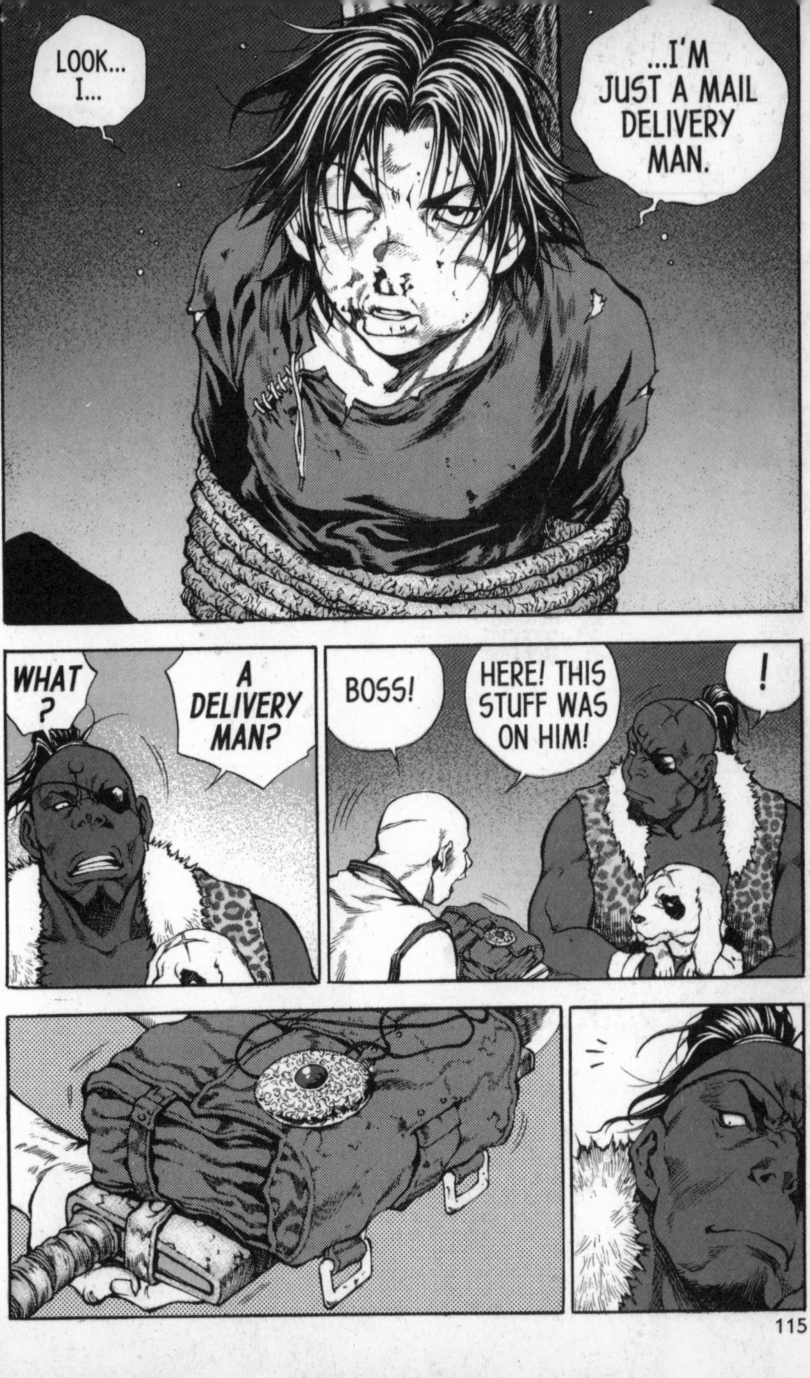
LOOK... I...
...I'M JUST A MAIL DELIVERY MAN.
WHAT?
A DELIVERY MAN?
BOSS!
HERE! THIS STUFF WAS ON HIM!
!

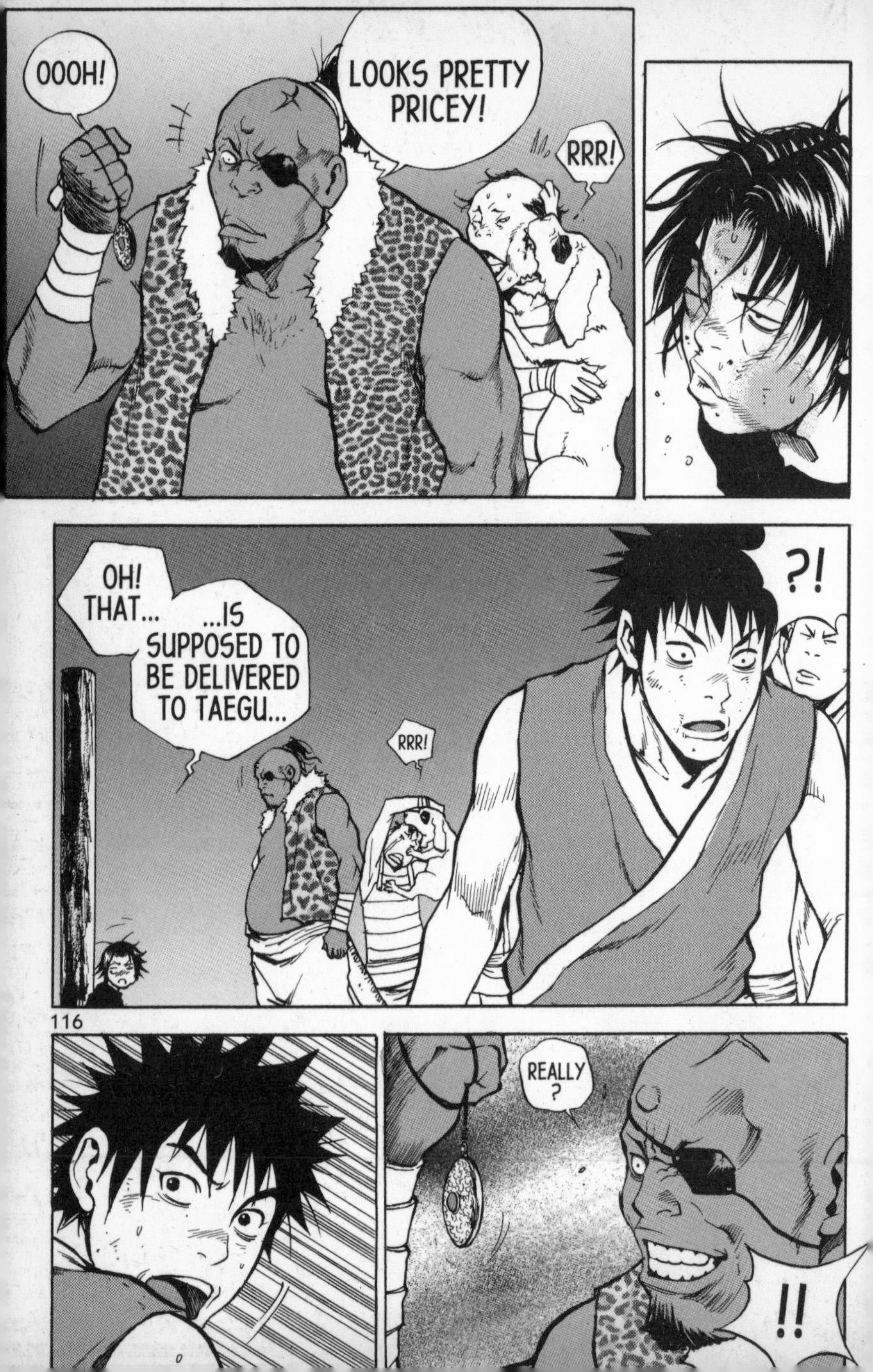
OOOH!
LOOKS PRETTY PRICEY!
RRR!
OH! THAT...
...IS SUPPOSED TO BE DELIVERED TO TAEGU...
RRR!
?!
REALLY?
!!

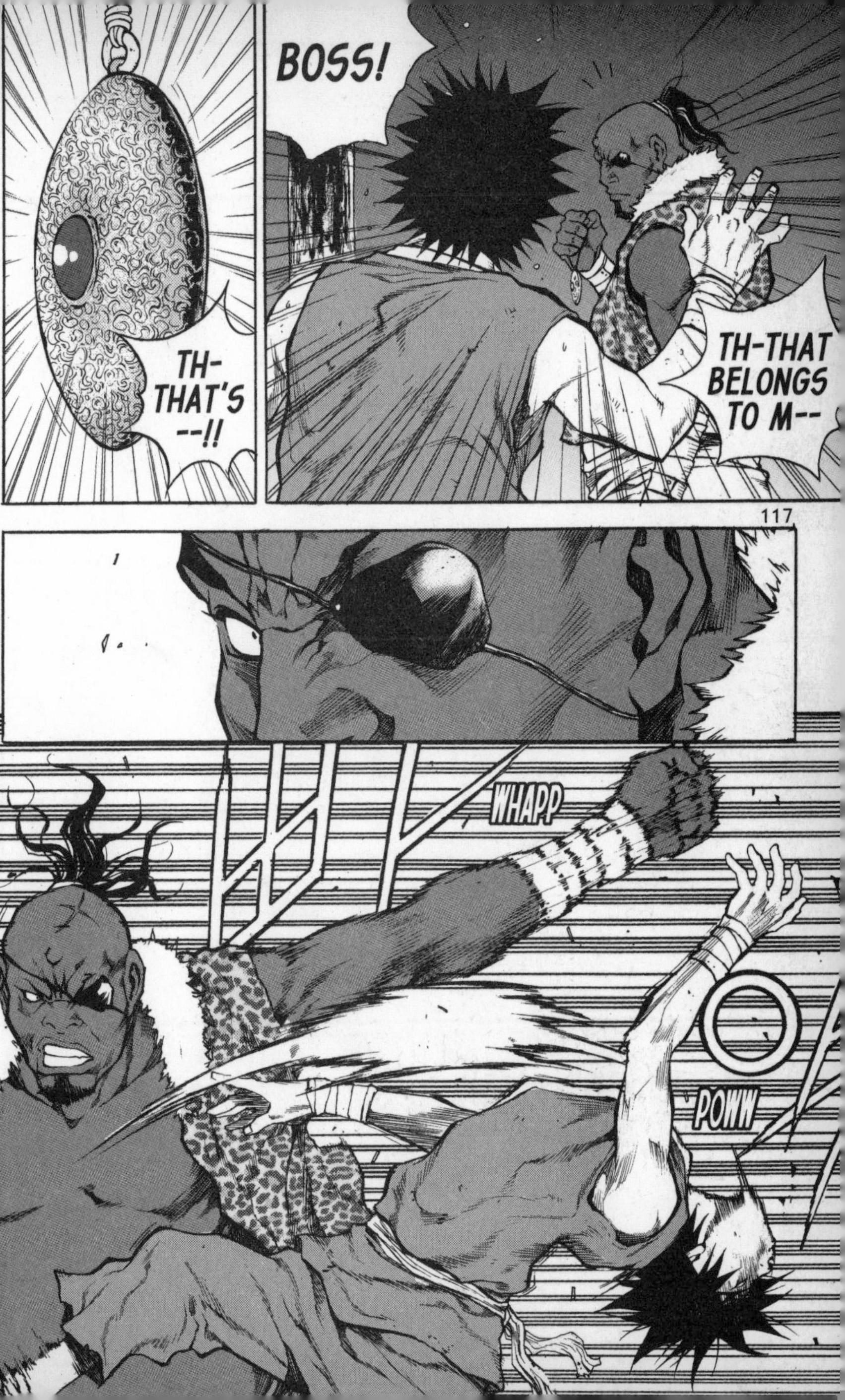
BOSS!
TH-THAT'S --!!
TH-THAT BELONGS TO M--
WHAPP
POWW

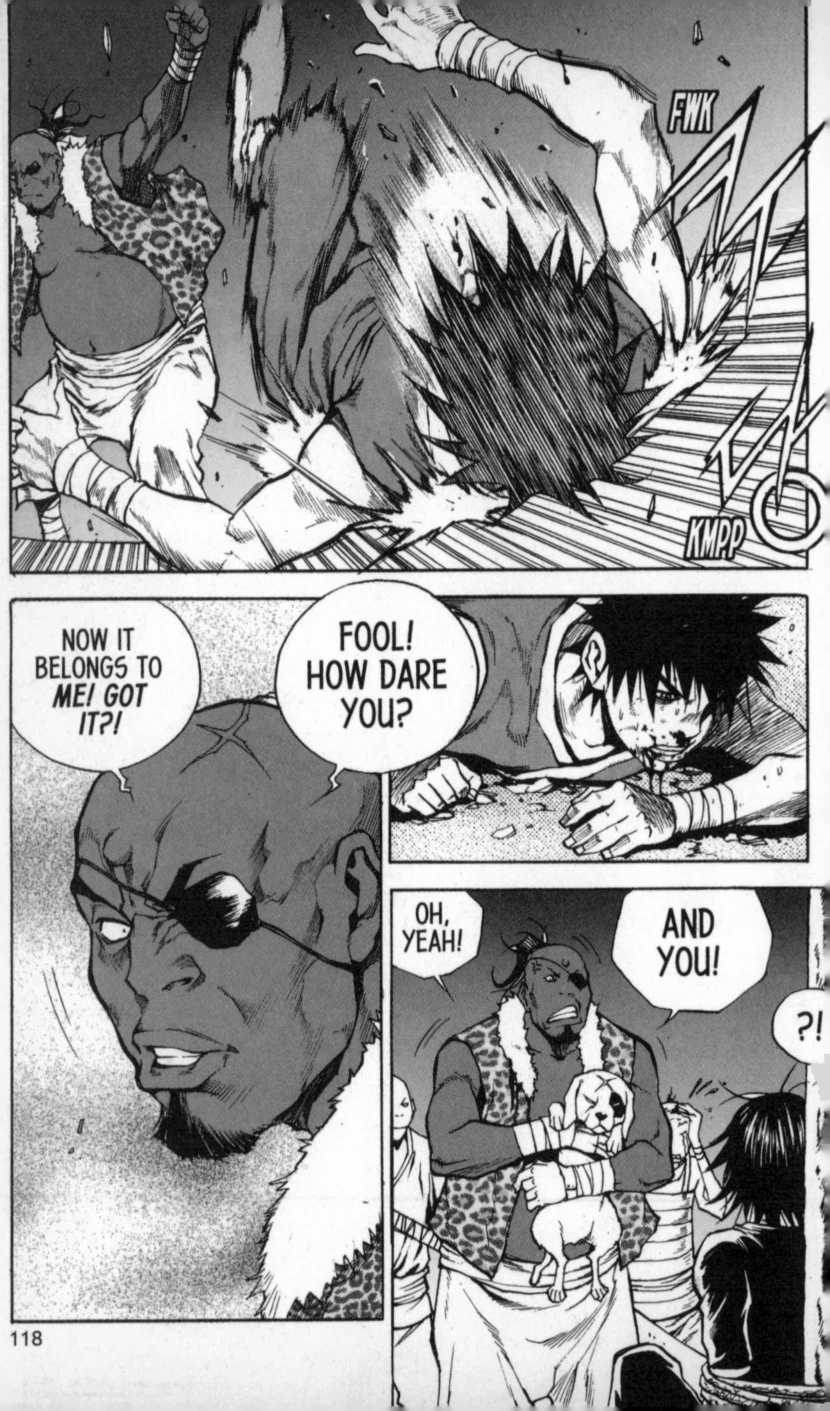

FWK
KMPP
NOW IT BELONGS TO ME! GOT IT?!
FOOL! HOW DARE YOU?
OH, YEAH!
AND YOU!
?!

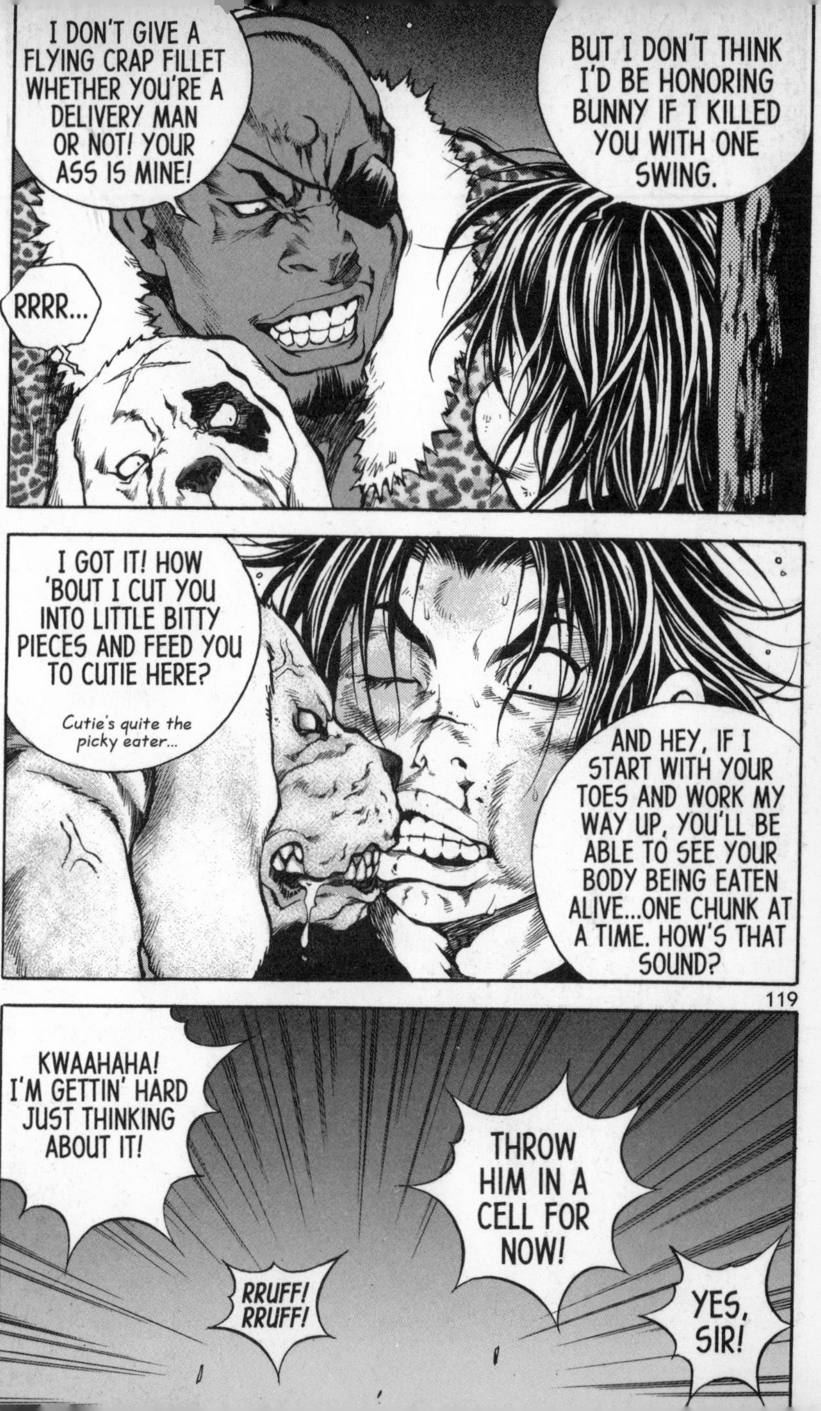

I DON'T GIVE A FLYING CRAP FILLET WHETHER YOU'RE A DELIVERY MAN OR NOT! YOUR ASS IS MINE!
BUT I DON'T THINK I'D BE HONORING BUNNY IF I KILLED YOU WITH ONE SWING.
RRRR...
I GOT IT! HOW 'BOUT I CUT YOU INTO LITTLE BITTY PIECES AND FEED YOU TO CUTIE HERE?
Cutie's quite the picky eater...
AND HEY, IF I START WITH YOUR TOES AND WORK MY WAY UP, YOU'LL BE ABLE TO SEE YOUR BODY BEING EATEN ALIVE...ONE CHUNK AT A TIME. HOW'S THAT SOUND?
KWAAHAHA! I'M GETTIN' HARD JUST THINKING ABOUT IT!
THROW HIM IN A CELL FOR NOW!
RRUFF! RRUFF!
YES, SIR!

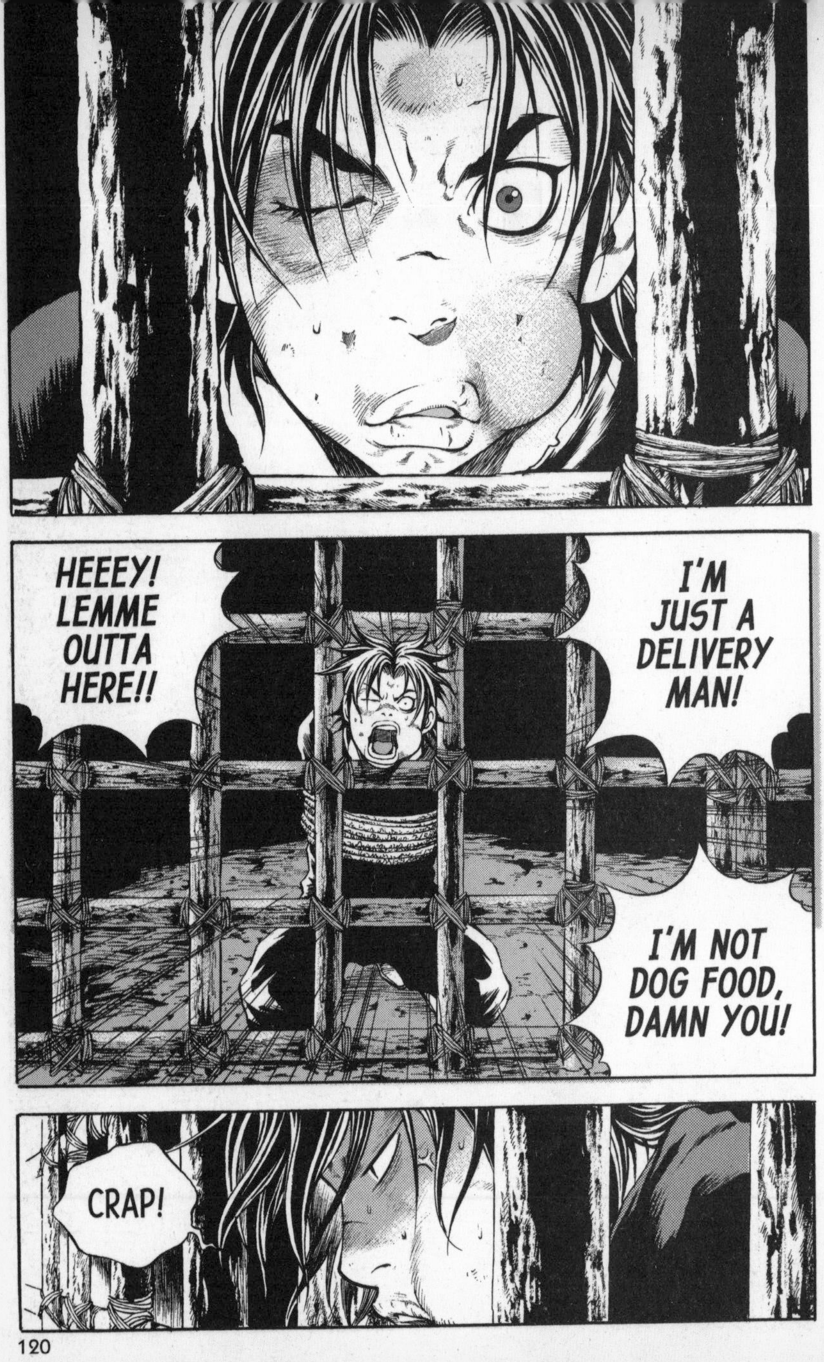
I'M JUST A DELIVERY MAN!
HEEEY! LEMME OUTTA HERE!!
I'M NOT DOG FOOD, DAMN YOU!
CRAP!

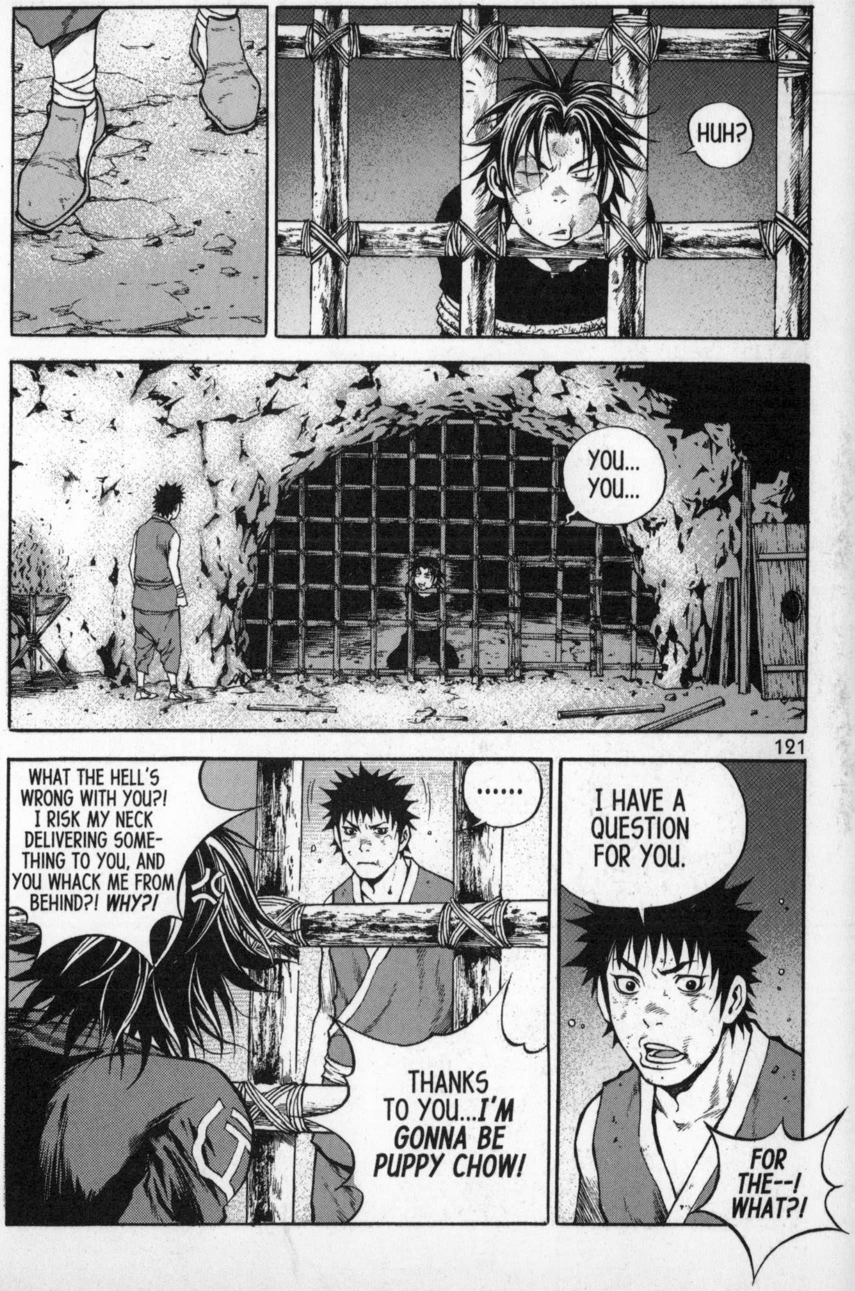

HUH?
YOU... YOU...
WHAT THE HELL'S WRONG WITH YOU?! I RISK MY NECK DELIVERING SOME-THING TO YOU, AND YOU WHACK ME FROM BEHIND?! *WHY?!*
......
THANKS TO YOU...*I'M GONNA BE PUPPY CHOW!*
I HAVE A QUESTION FOR YOU.
FOR THE--! WHAT?!

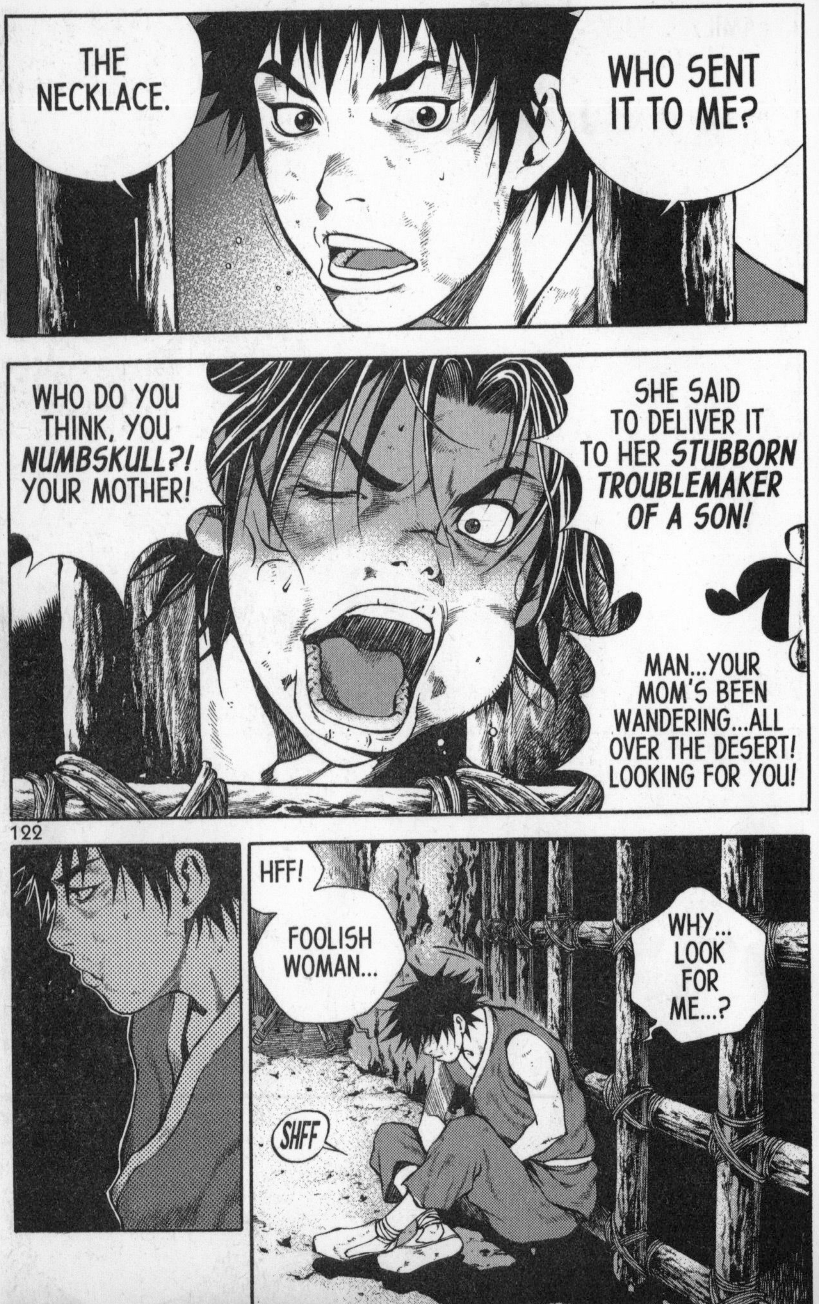
THE NECKLACE.
WHO SENT IT TO ME?
WHO DO YOU THINK, YOU *NUMBSKULL?!* YOUR MOTHER!
SHE SAID TO DELIVER IT TO HER *STUBBORN TROUBLEMAKER OF A SON!*
MAN...YOUR MOM'S BEEN WANDERING...ALL OVER THE DESERT! LOOKING FOR YOU!
HFF!
FOOLISH WOMAN...
SHFF
WHY... LOOK FOR ME...?

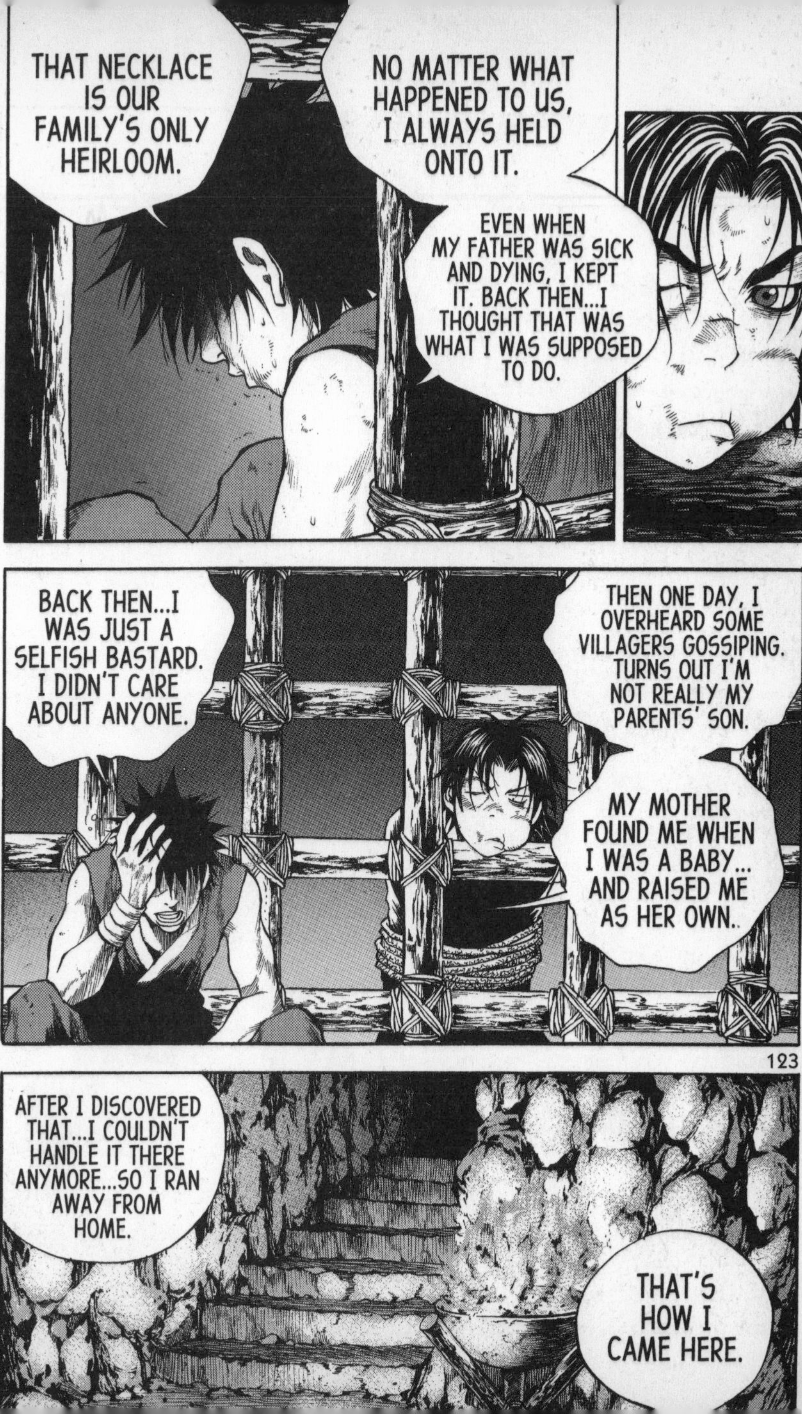
THAT NECKLACE IS OUR FAMILY'S ONLY HEIRLOOM.
NO MATTER WHAT HAPPENED TO US, I ALWAYS HELD ONTO IT.
EVEN WHEN MY FATHER WAS SICK AND DYING, I KEPT IT. BACK THEN...I THOUGHT THAT WAS WHAT I WAS SUPPOSED TO DO.
BACK THEN...I WAS JUST A SELFISH BASTARD. I DIDN'T CARE ABOUT ANYONE.
THEN ONE DAY, I OVERHEARD SOME VILLAGERS GOSSIPING. TURNS OUT I'M NOT REALLY MY PARENTS' SON.
MY MOTHER FOUND ME WHEN I WAS A BABY... AND RAISED ME AS HER OWN..
AFTER I DISCOVERED THAT...I COULDN'T HANDLE IT THERE ANYMORE...SO I RAN AWAY FROM HOME.
THAT'S HOW I CAME HERE.

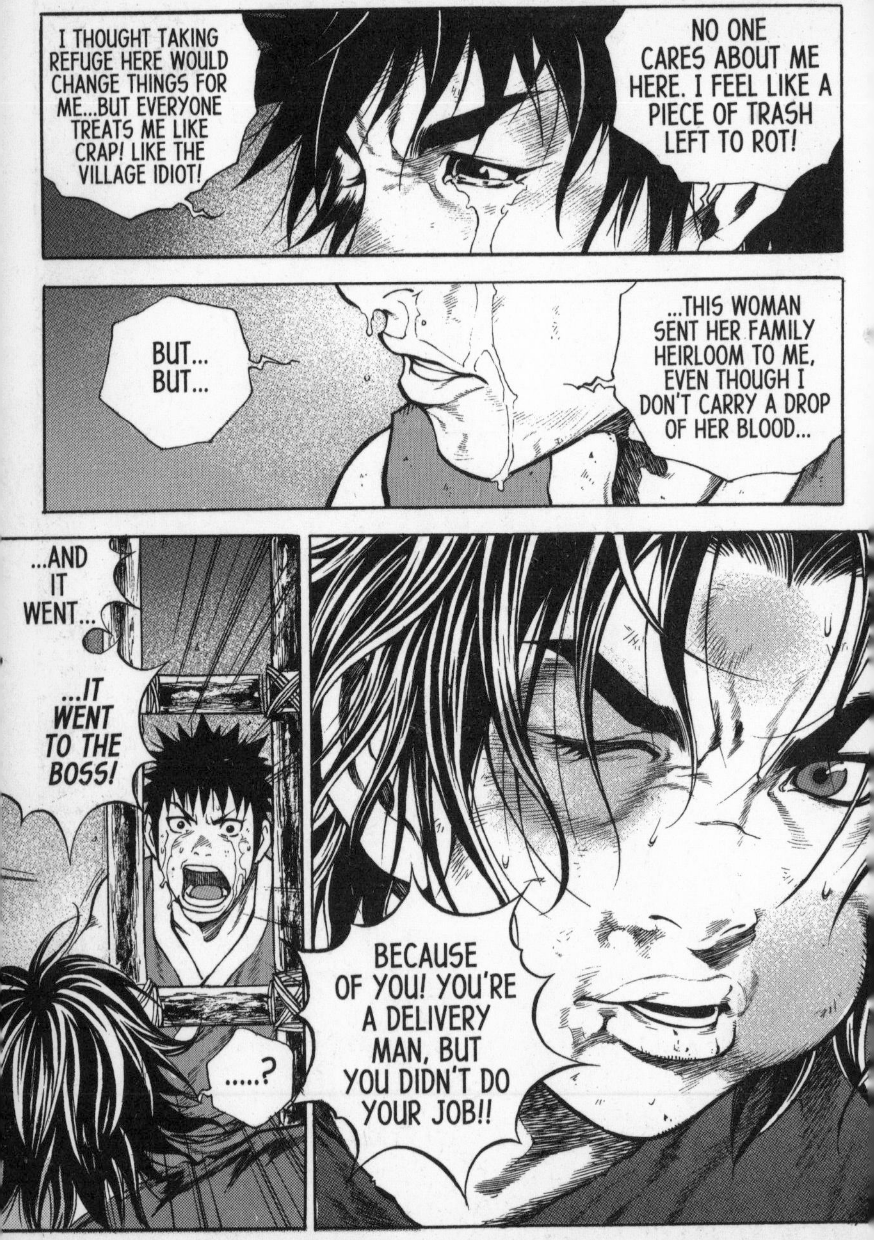
I THOUGHT TAKING REFUGE HERE WOULD CHANGE THINGS FOR ME...BUT EVERYONE TREATS ME LIKE CRAP! LIKE THE VILLAGE IDIOT!
NO ONE CARES ABOUT ME HERE. I FEEL LIKE A PIECE OF TRASH LEFT TO ROT!
BUT... BUT...
...THIS WOMAN SENT HER FAMILY HEIRLOOM TO ME, EVEN THOUGH I DON'T CARRY A DROP OF HER BLOOD...
...AND IT WENT...
...IT WENT TO THE BOSS!
.....?
BECAUSE OF YOU! YOU'RE A DELIVERY MAN, BUT YOU DIDN'T DO YOUR JOB!!

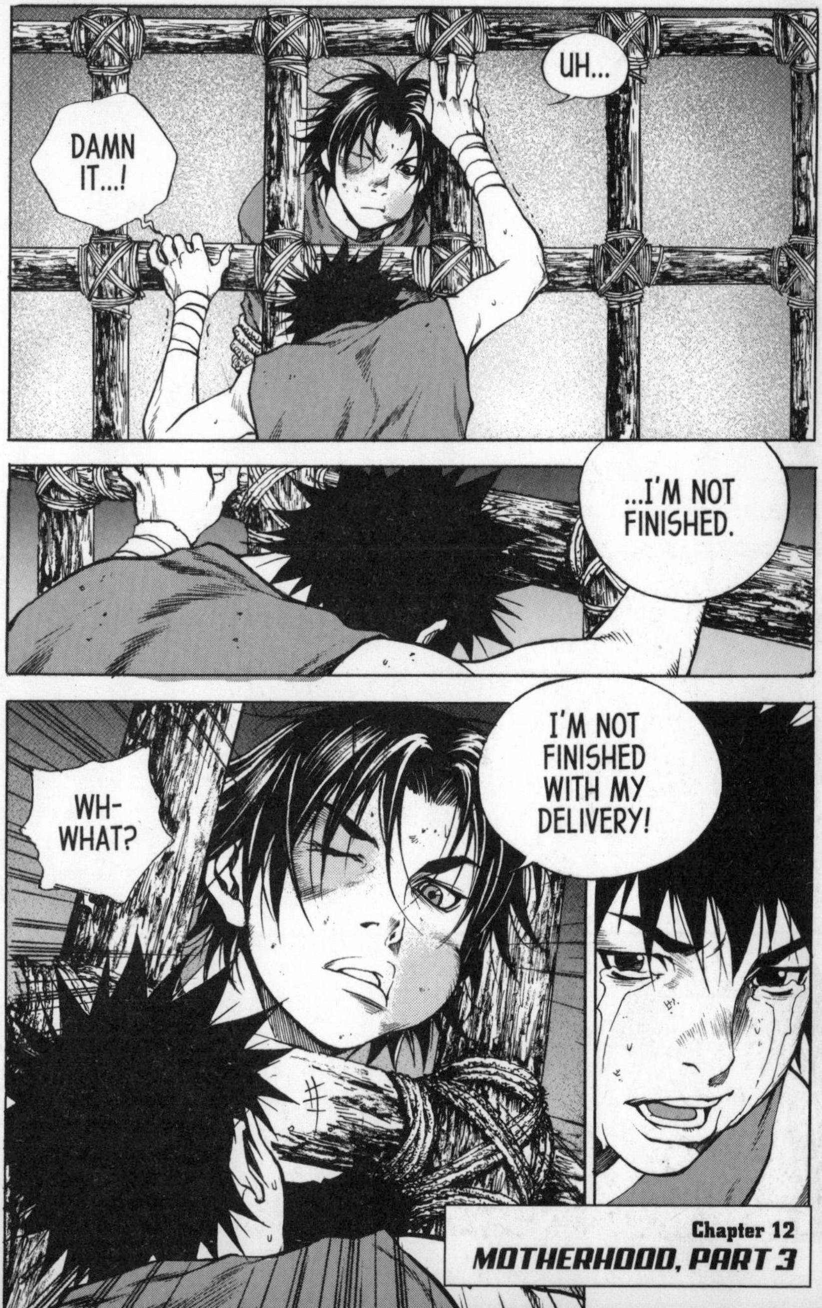
UH...
DAMN IT...!
...I'M NOT FINISHED.
I'M NOT FINISHED WITH MY DELIVERY!
WH- WHAT?
Chapter 12
MOTHERHOOD, PART 3

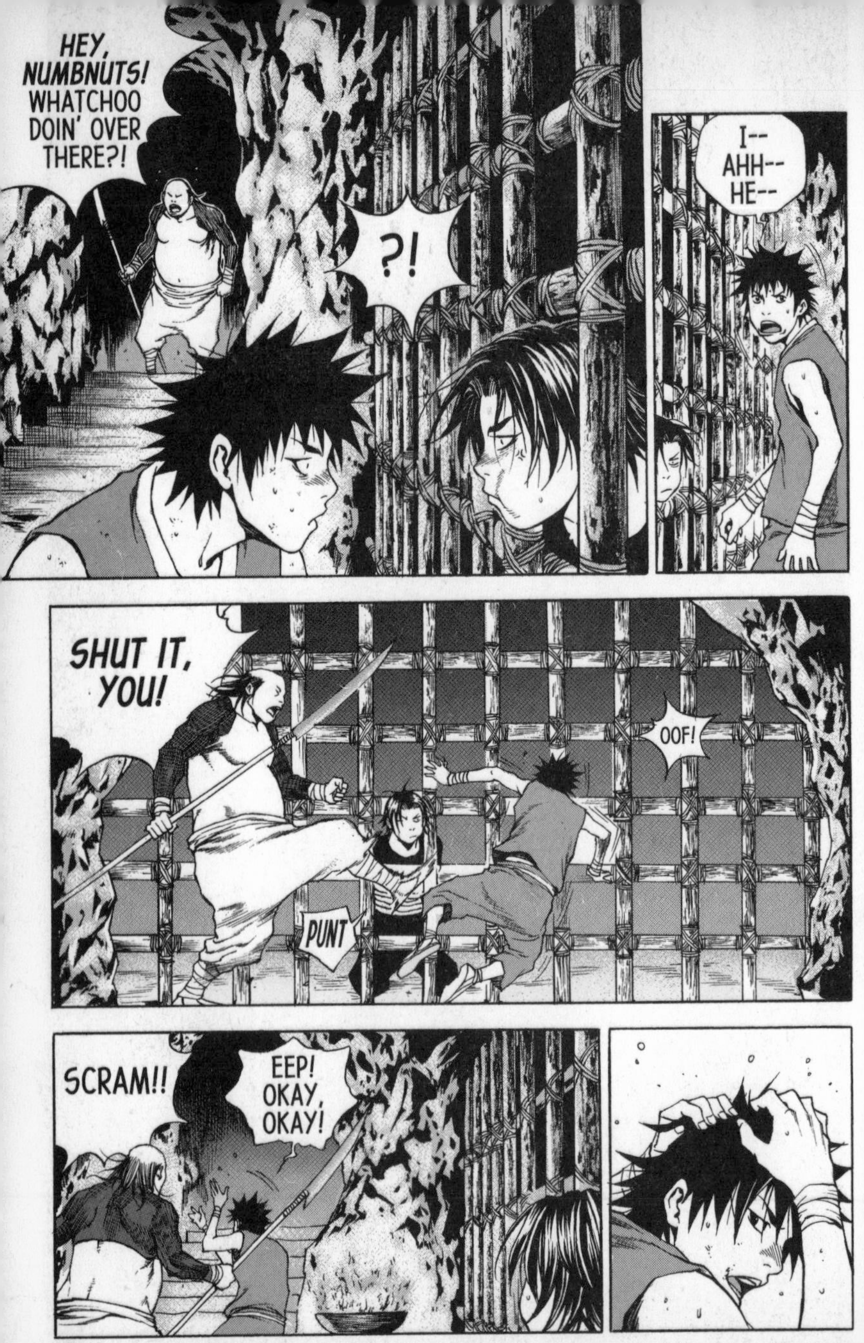
HEY, NUMBNUTS! WHATCHOO DOIN' OVER THERE?!
?!
I-- AHH-- HE--
SHUT IT, YOU!
OOF!
PUNT
SCRAM!!
EEP! OKAY, OKAY!

......

FOOO!

HKK!

ERRK!

KRRK

NNGH!

KRRK

SNNCH

SNNCH

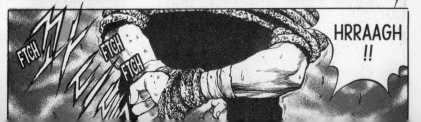

FTCH

FTCH

FTCH

HRRAAGH !!

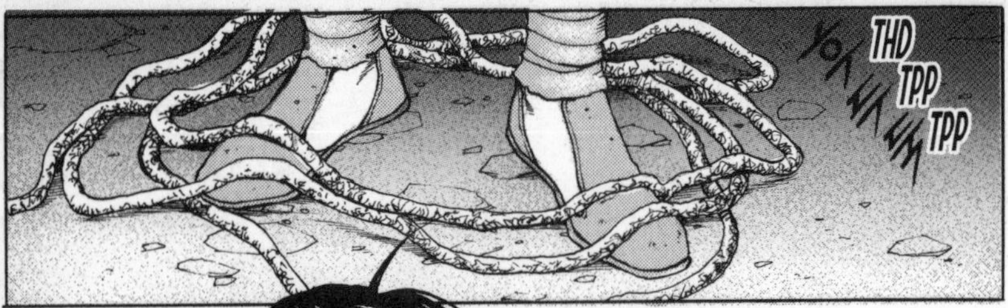
THD
TPP
TPP

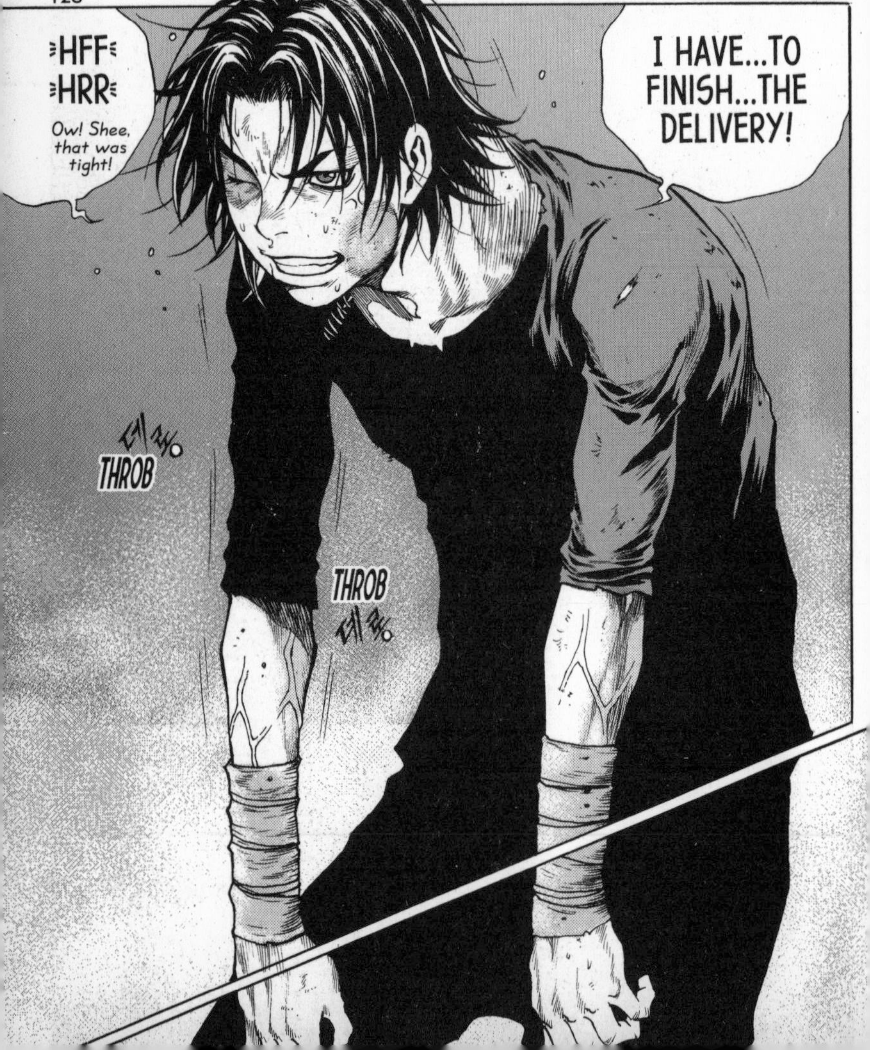
I HAVE...TO FINISH...THE DELIVERY!
HFF
HRR
Ow! Shee, that was tight!
THROB
THROB

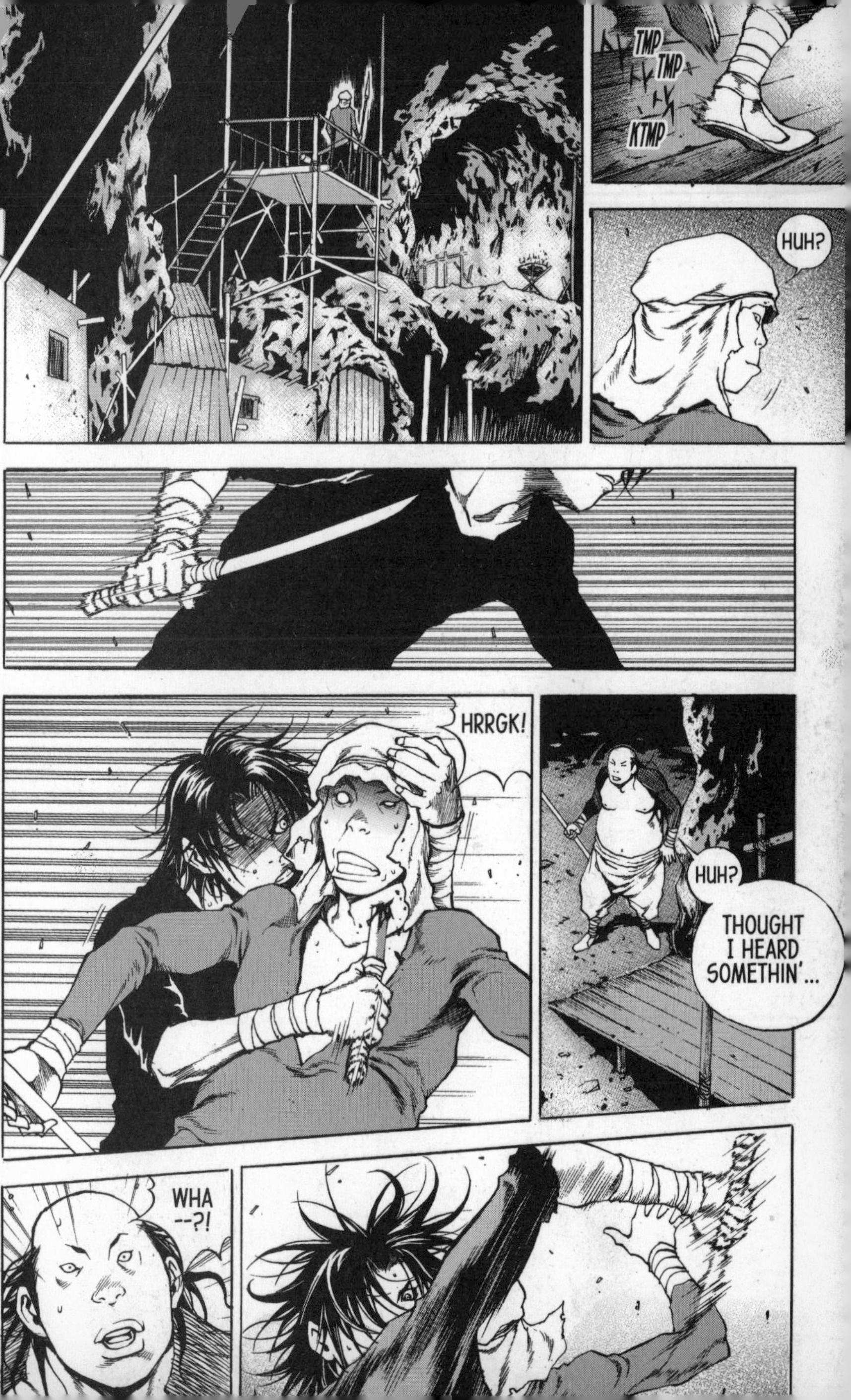
TMP
TMP
KTMP
HUH?
HRRGK!
HUH?
THOUGHT I HEARD SOMETHIN'...
WHA --?!

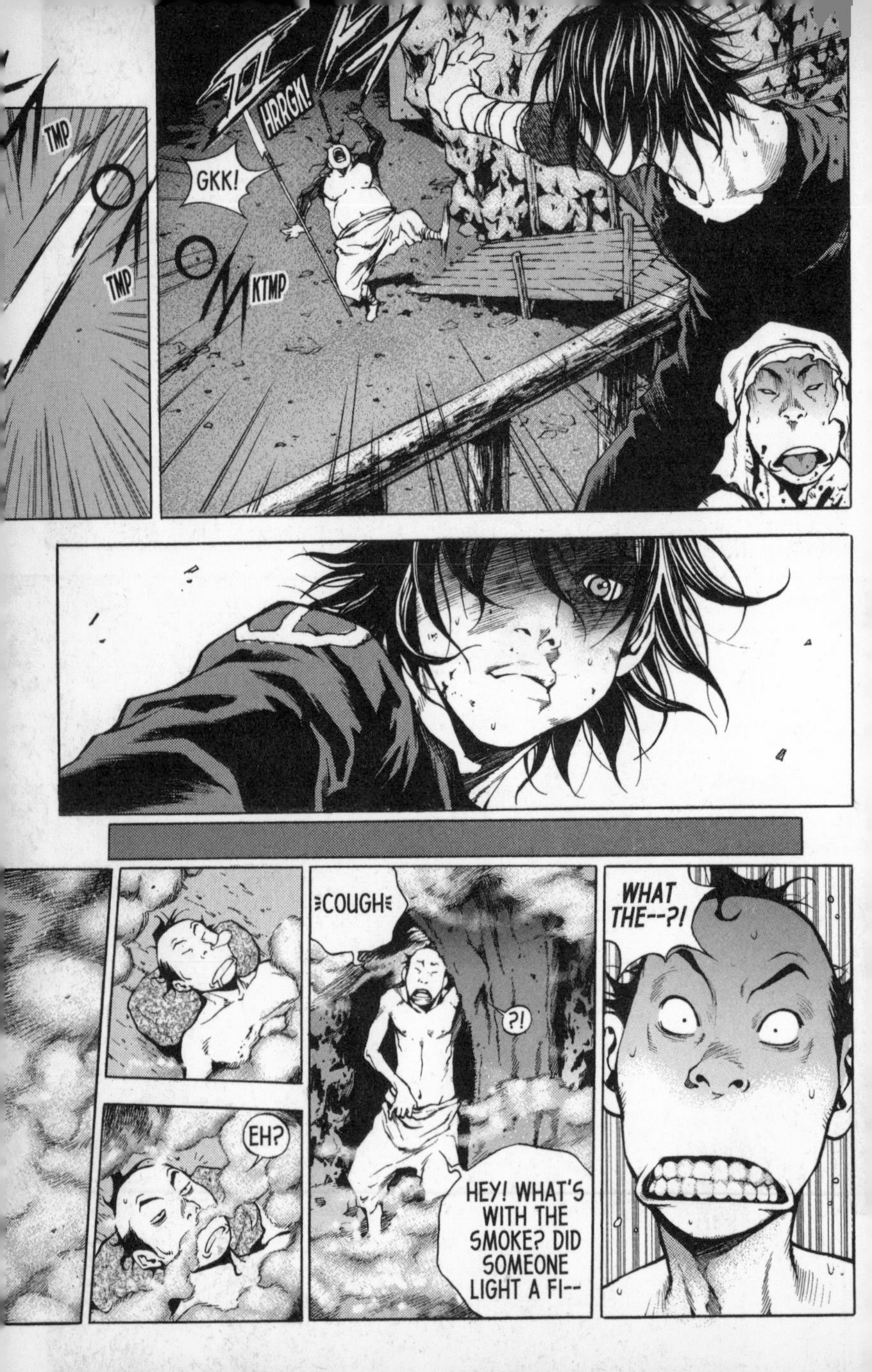
TMP
TMP
HRRGK!
GKK!
KTMP
≡COUGH≡
?!
EH?
HEY! WHAT'S WITH THE SMOKE? DID SOMEONE LIGHT A FI--
WHAT THE--?!

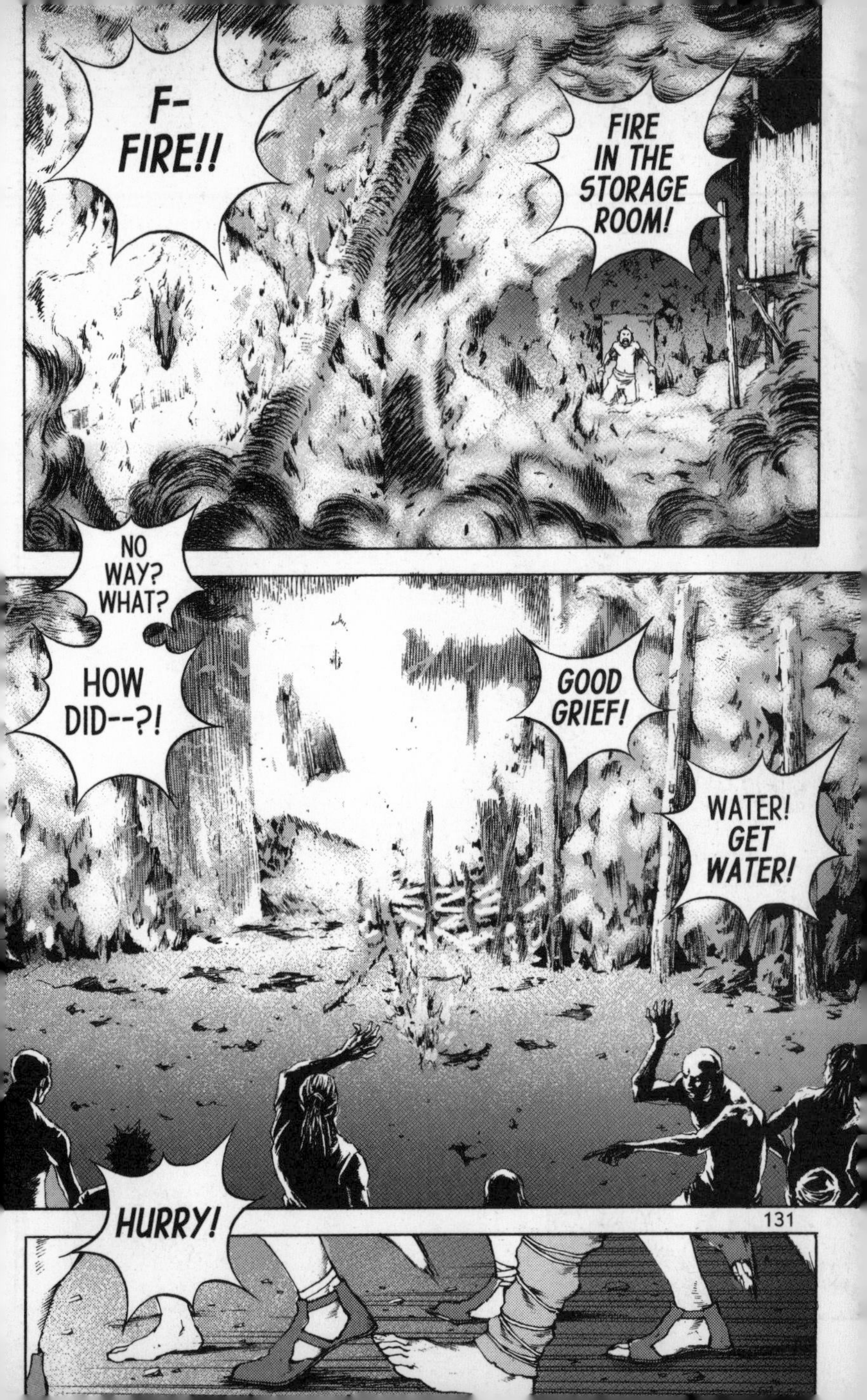
F-
FIRE!!
FIRE IN THE STORAGE ROOM!
NO WAY? WHAT?
HOW DID--?!
GOOD GRIEF!
WATER! GET WATER!
HURRY!

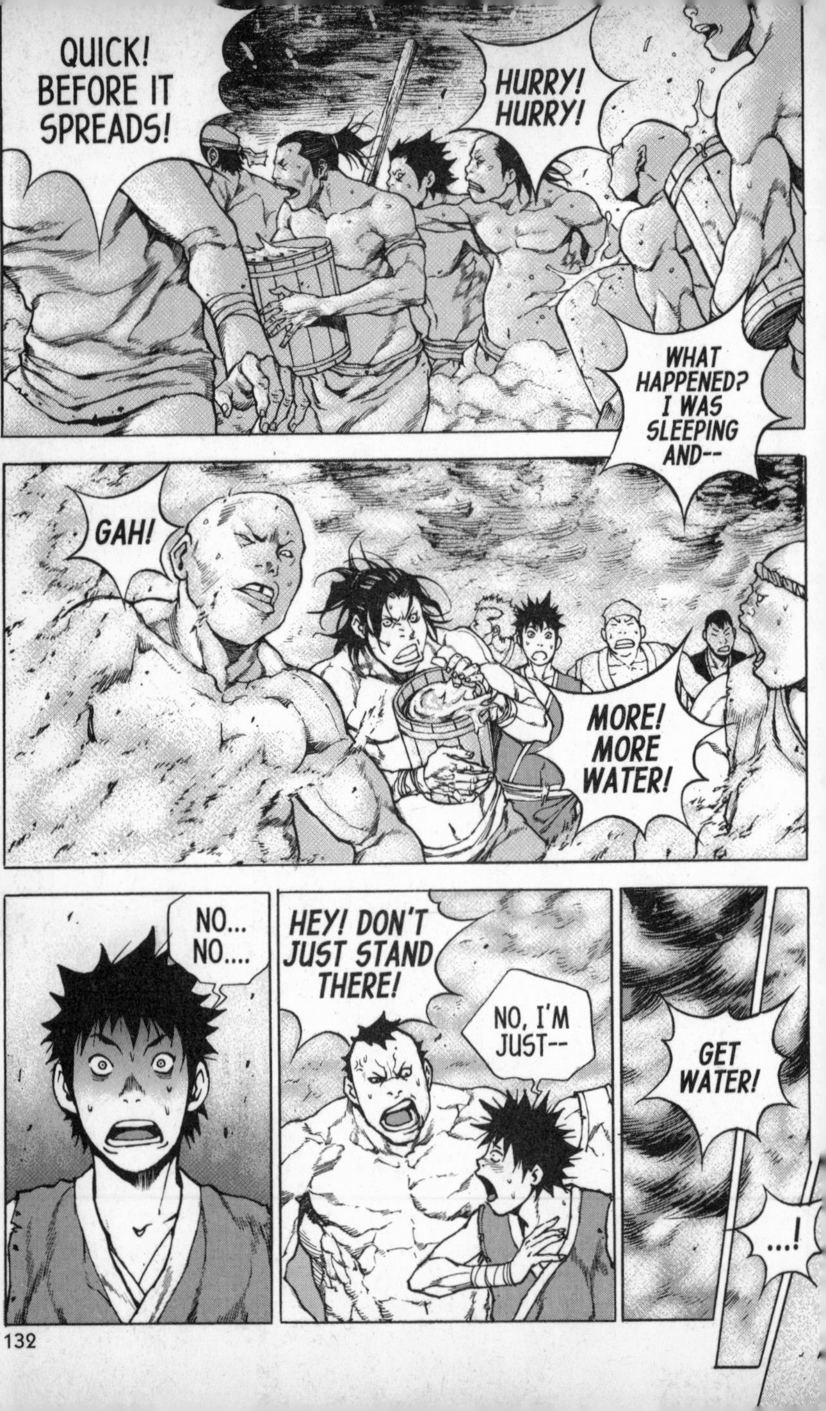
QUICK! BEFORE IT SPREADS!
HURRY! HURRY!
WHAT HAPPENED? I WAS SLEEPING AND--
GAH!
MORE! MORE WATER!
NO... NO....
HEY! DON'T JUST STAND THERE!
NO, I'M JUST--
GET WATER!
...!

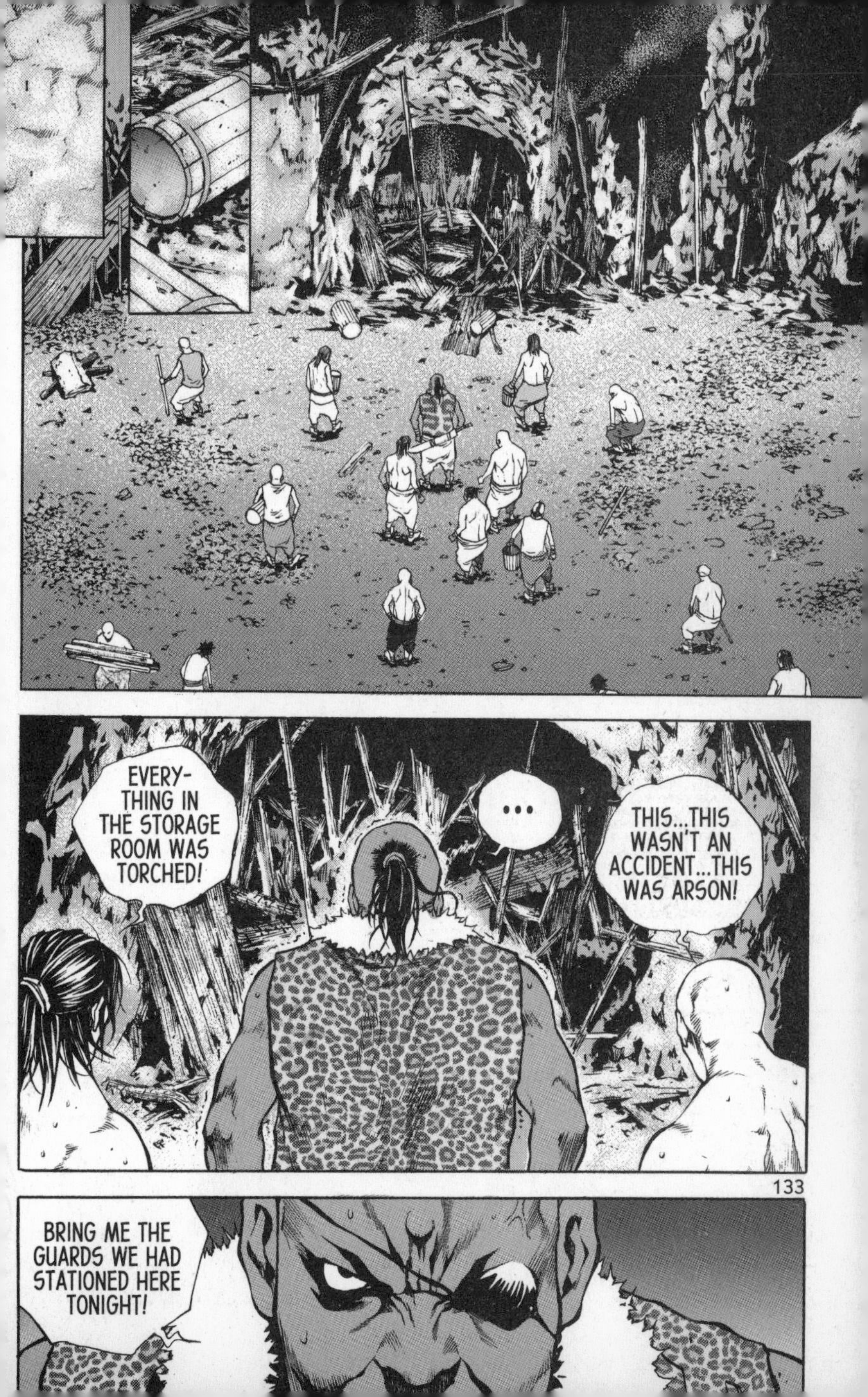
EVERY-THING IN THE STORAGE ROOM WAS TORCHED!
...
THIS...THIS WASN'T AN ACCIDENT...THIS WAS ARSON!
BRING ME THE GUARDS WE HAD STATIONED HERE TONIGHT!

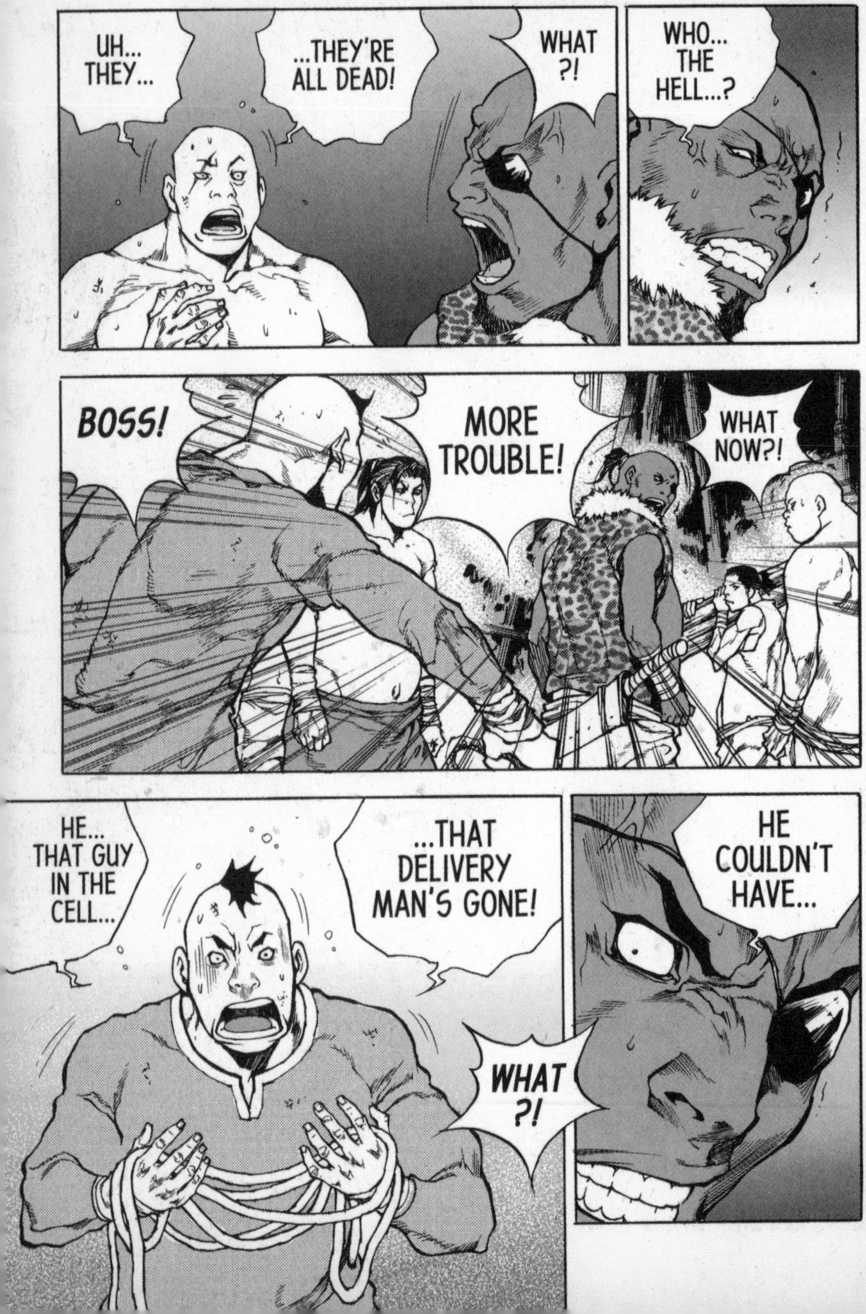
UH... THEY...
...THEY'RE ALL DEAD!
WHAT ?!
WHO... THE HELL...?
BOSS!
MORE TROUBLE!
WHAT NOW?!
HE... THAT GUY IN THE CELL...
...THAT DELIVERY MAN'S GONE!
WHAT ?!
HE COULDN'T HAVE...

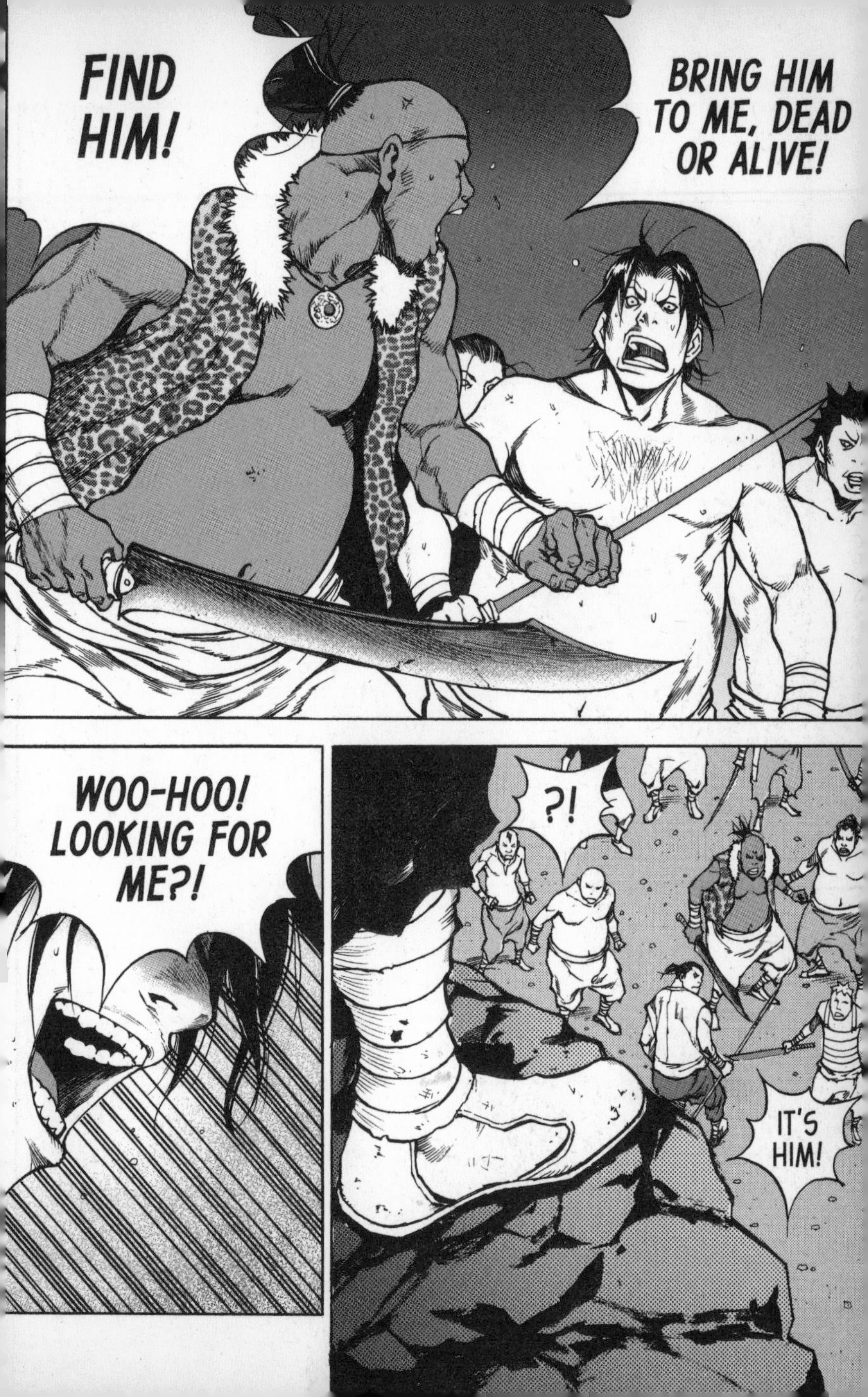
BRING HIM TO ME, DEAD OR ALIVE!
FIND HIM!
IT'S HIM!
?!
WOO-HOO! LOOKING FOR ME?!

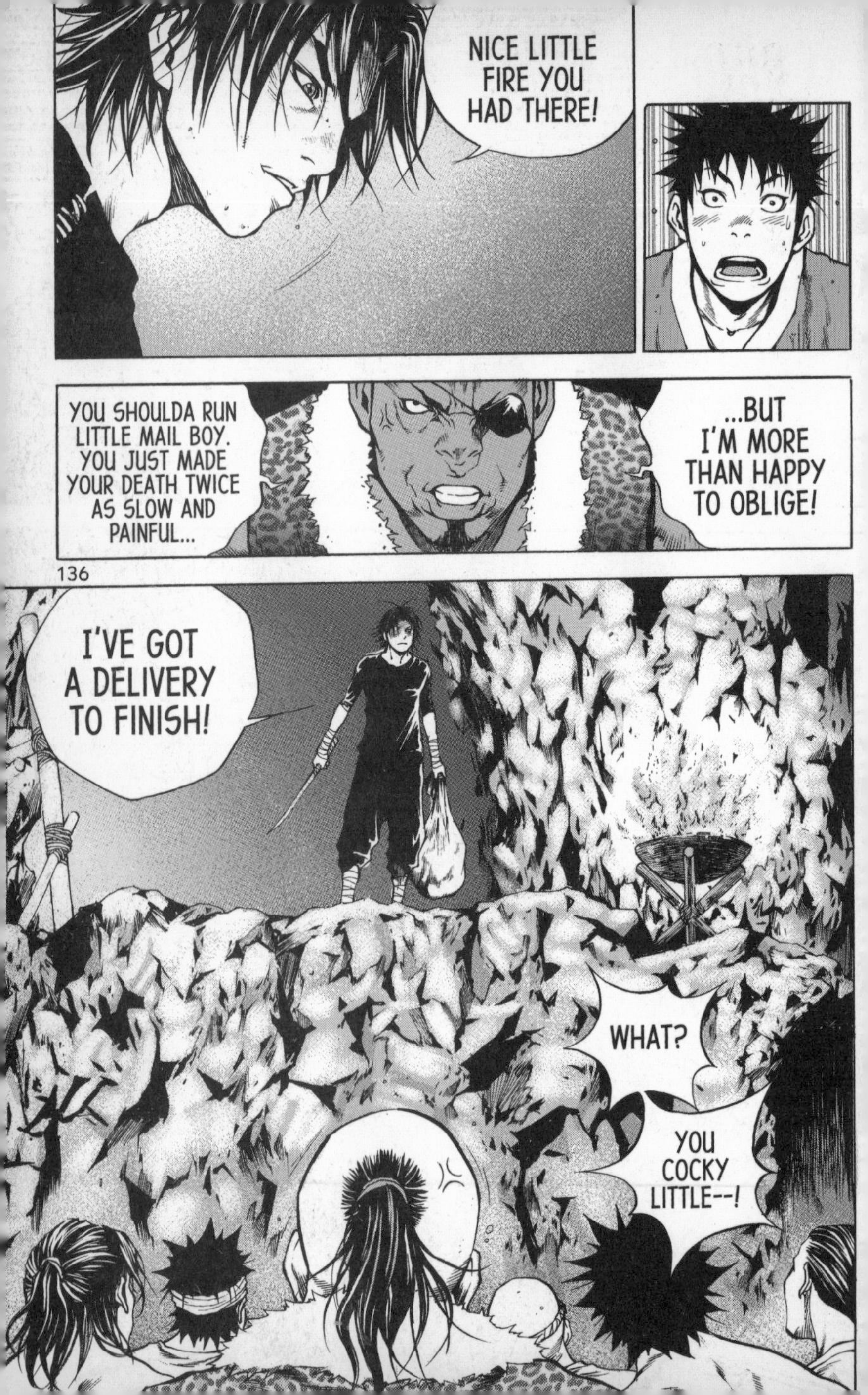
NICE LITTLE FIRE YOU HAD THERE!
YOU SHOULDA RUN LITTLE MAIL BOY. YOU JUST MADE YOUR DEATH TWICE AS SLOW AND PAINFUL...
...BUT I'M MORE THAN HAPPY TO OBLIGE!
I'VE GOT A DELIVERY TO FINISH!
WHAT?
YOU COCKY LITTLE--!

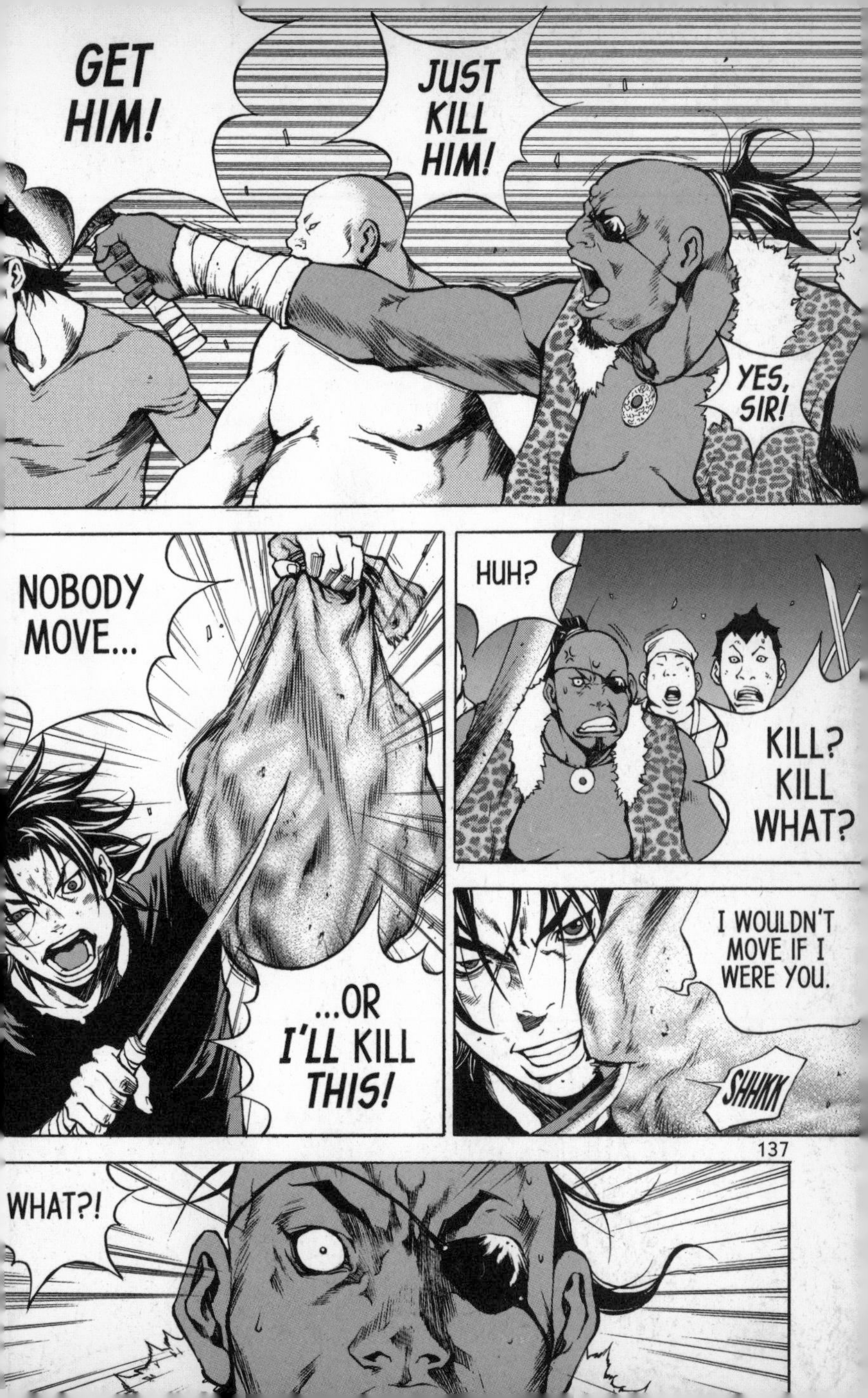

GET HIM!
JUST KILL HIM!
YES, SIR!
NOBODY MOVE...
...OR I'LL KILL THIS!
HUH?
KILL? KILL WHAT?
I WOULDN'T MOVE IF I WERE YOU.
SHHKK
WHAT?!

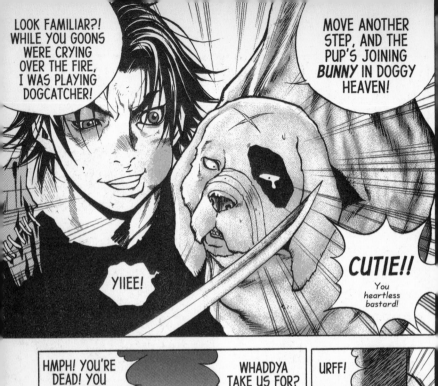

LOOK FAMILIAR?! WHILE YOU GOONS WERE CRYING OVER THE FIRE, I WAS PLAYING DOGCATCHER!

MOVE ANOTHER STEP, AND THE PUP'S JOINING *BUNNY* IN DOGGY HEAVEN!

YIIEE!

CUTIE!! You heartless bastard!

HMPH! YOU'RE DEAD! YOU CAN'T USE A STUPID DOG AS LEVERAGE!

WHADDYA TAKE US FOR? A BUNCH OF SUCKE--

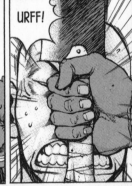

URFF!

GUH!

?!

WHAT DO YOU WANT?

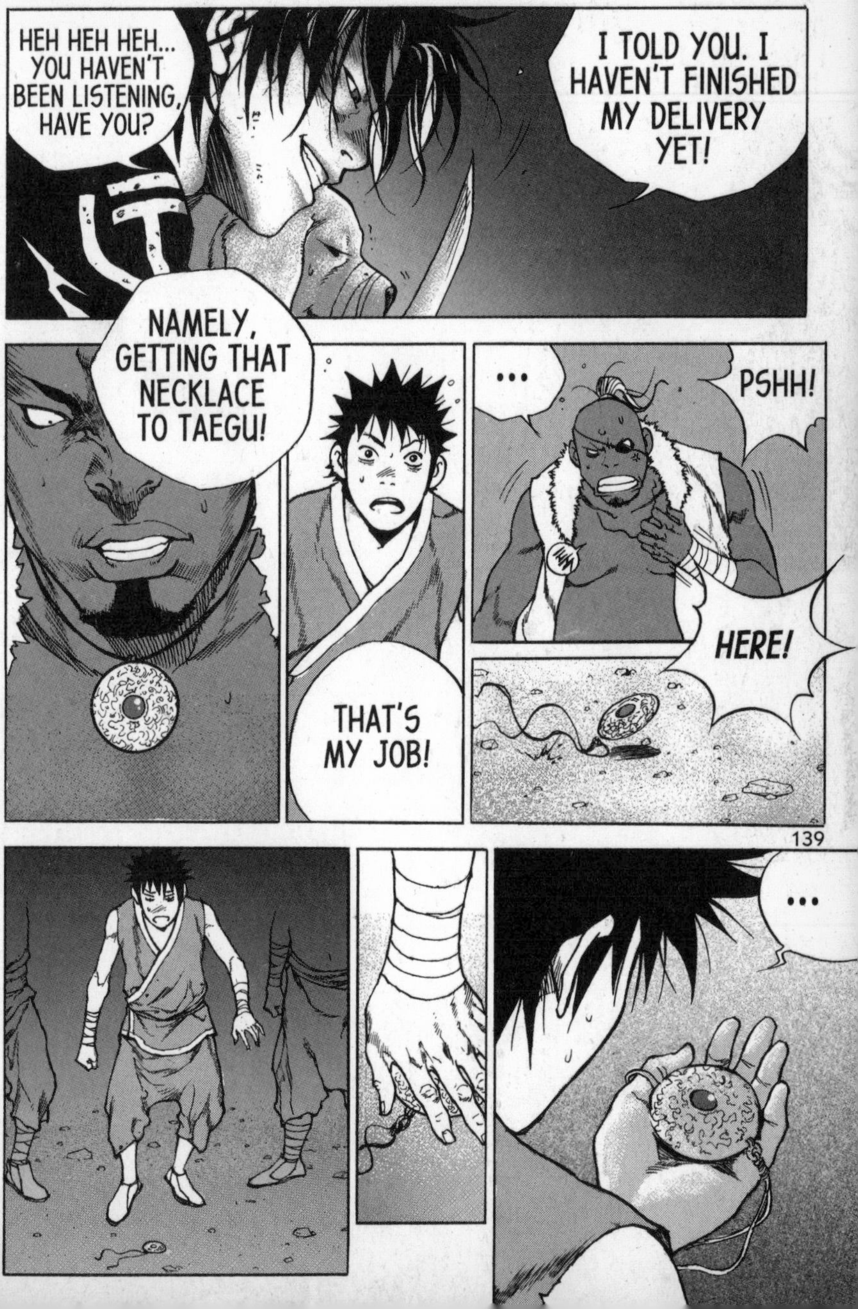
HEH HEH HEH... YOU HAVEN'T BEEN LISTENING, HAVE YOU?
I TOLD YOU. I HAVEN'T FINISHED MY DELIVERY YET!
NAMELY, GETTING THAT NECKLACE TO TAEGU!
THAT'S MY JOB!
...
PSHH!
HERE!
...

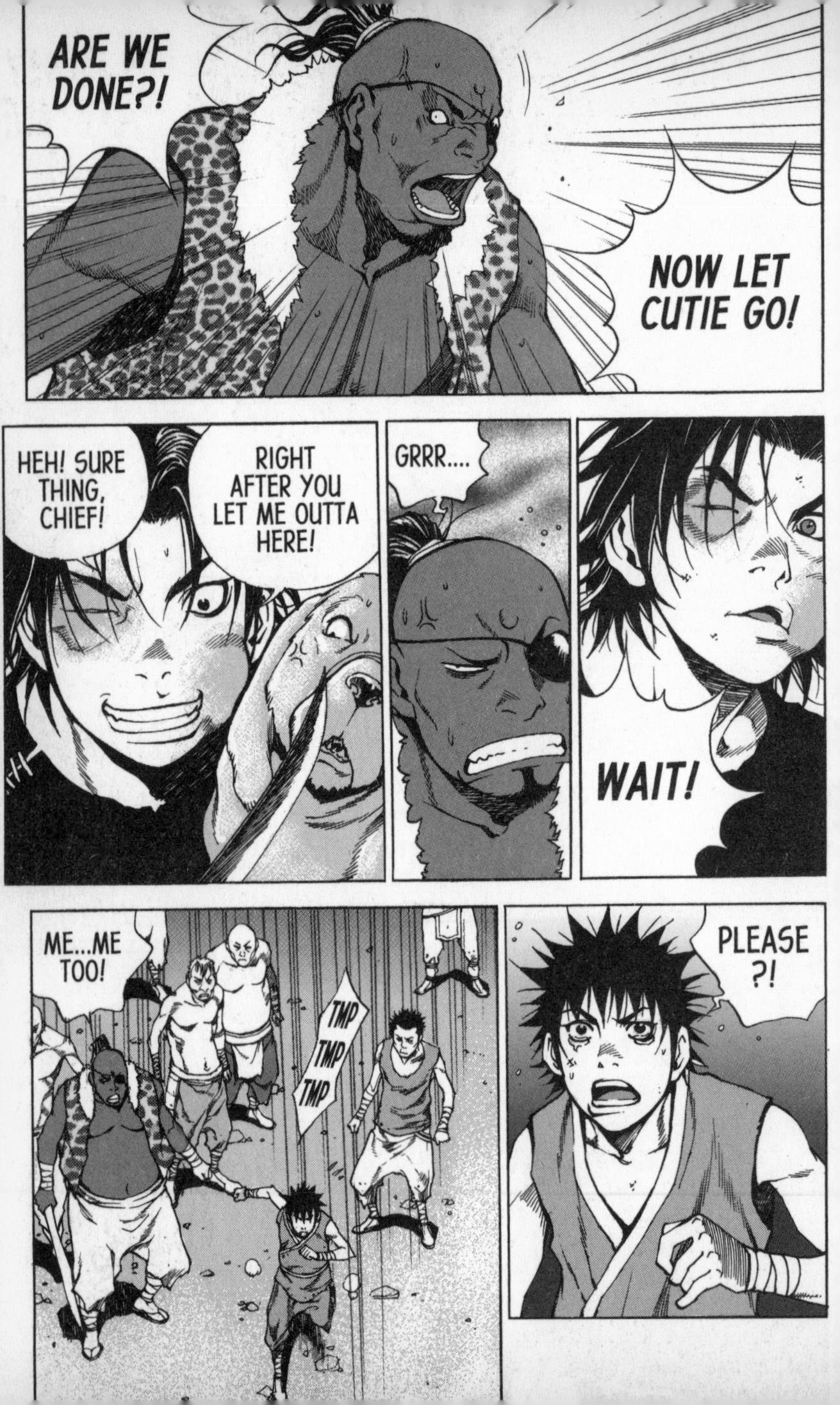

ARE WE DONE?!
NOW LET CUTIE GO!
HEH! SURE THING, CHIEF!
RIGHT AFTER YOU LET ME OUTTA HERE!
GRRR....
WAIT!
ME...ME TOO!
TMP TMP TMP
PLEASE ?!

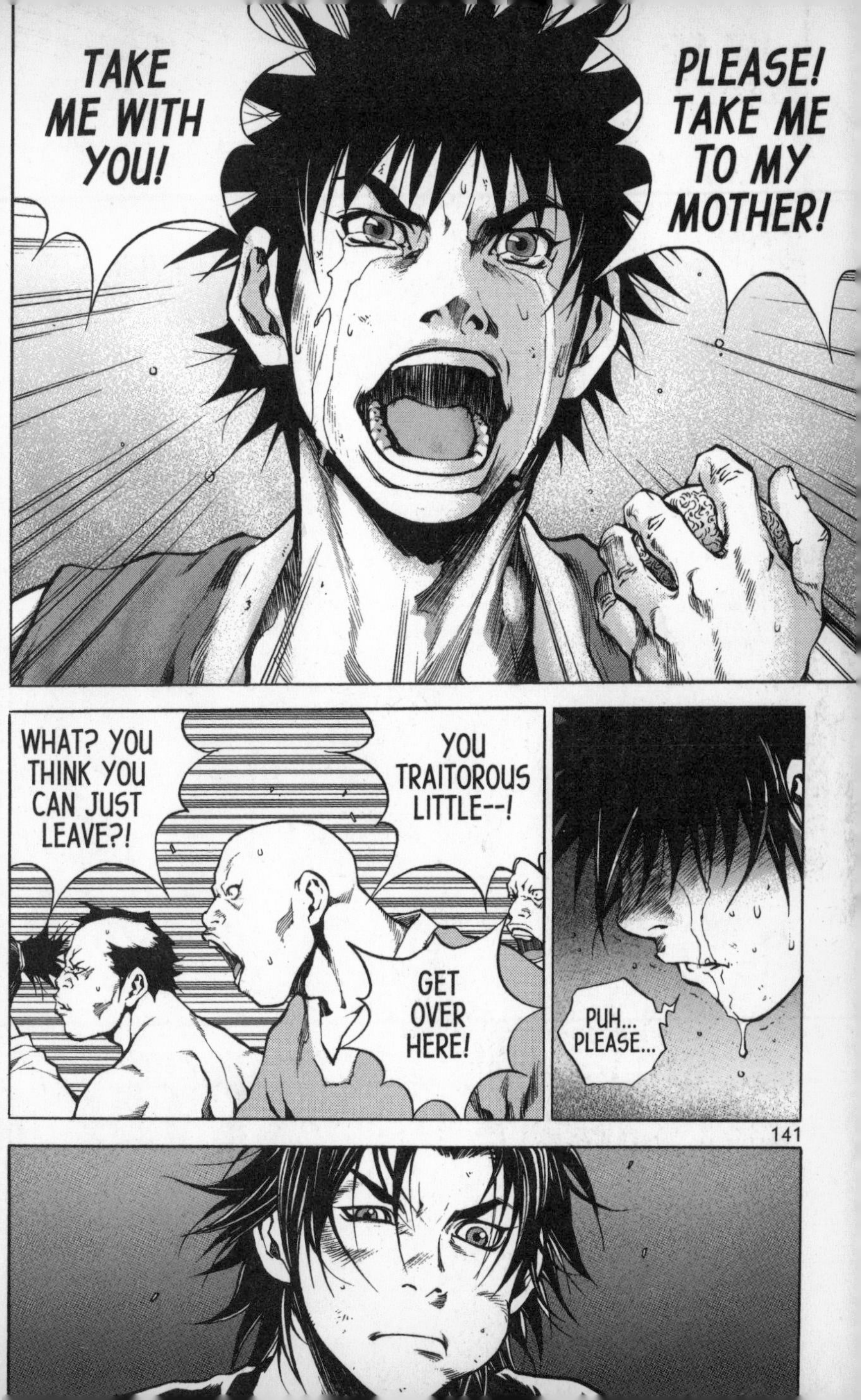
TAKE ME WITH YOU!
PLEASE! TAKE ME TO MY MOTHER!
WHAT? YOU THINK YOU CAN JUST LEAVE?!
YOU TRAITOROUS LITTLE--!
GET OVER HERE!
PUH... PLEASE...

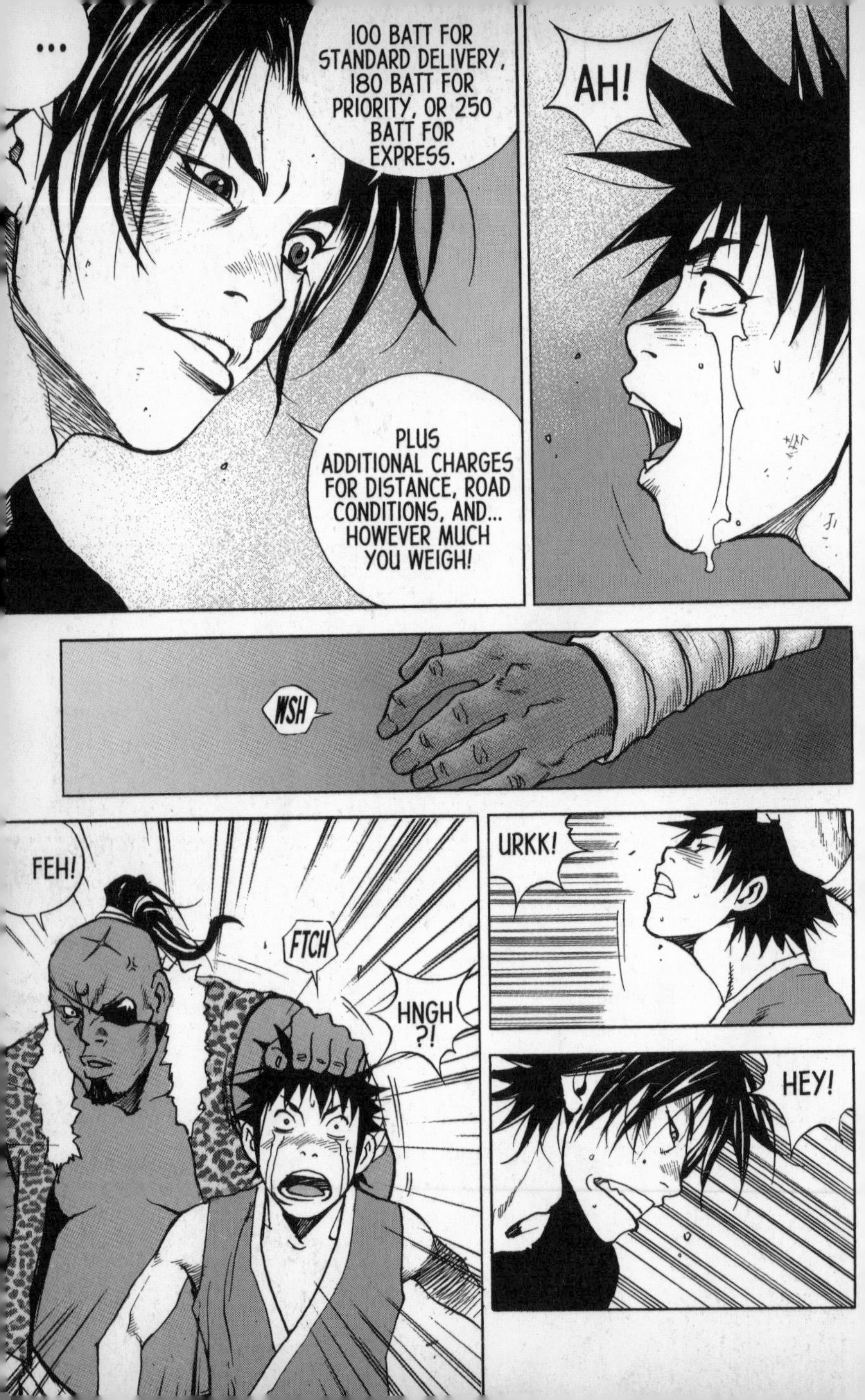

...
100 BATT FOR STANDARD DELIVERY, 180 BATT FOR PRIORITY, OR 250 BATT FOR EXPRESS.
PLUS ADDITIONAL CHARGES FOR DISTANCE, ROAD CONDITIONS, AND... HOWEVER MUCH YOU WEIGH!
AH!
WSH
FEH!
FTCH
HNGH ?!
URKK!
HEY!

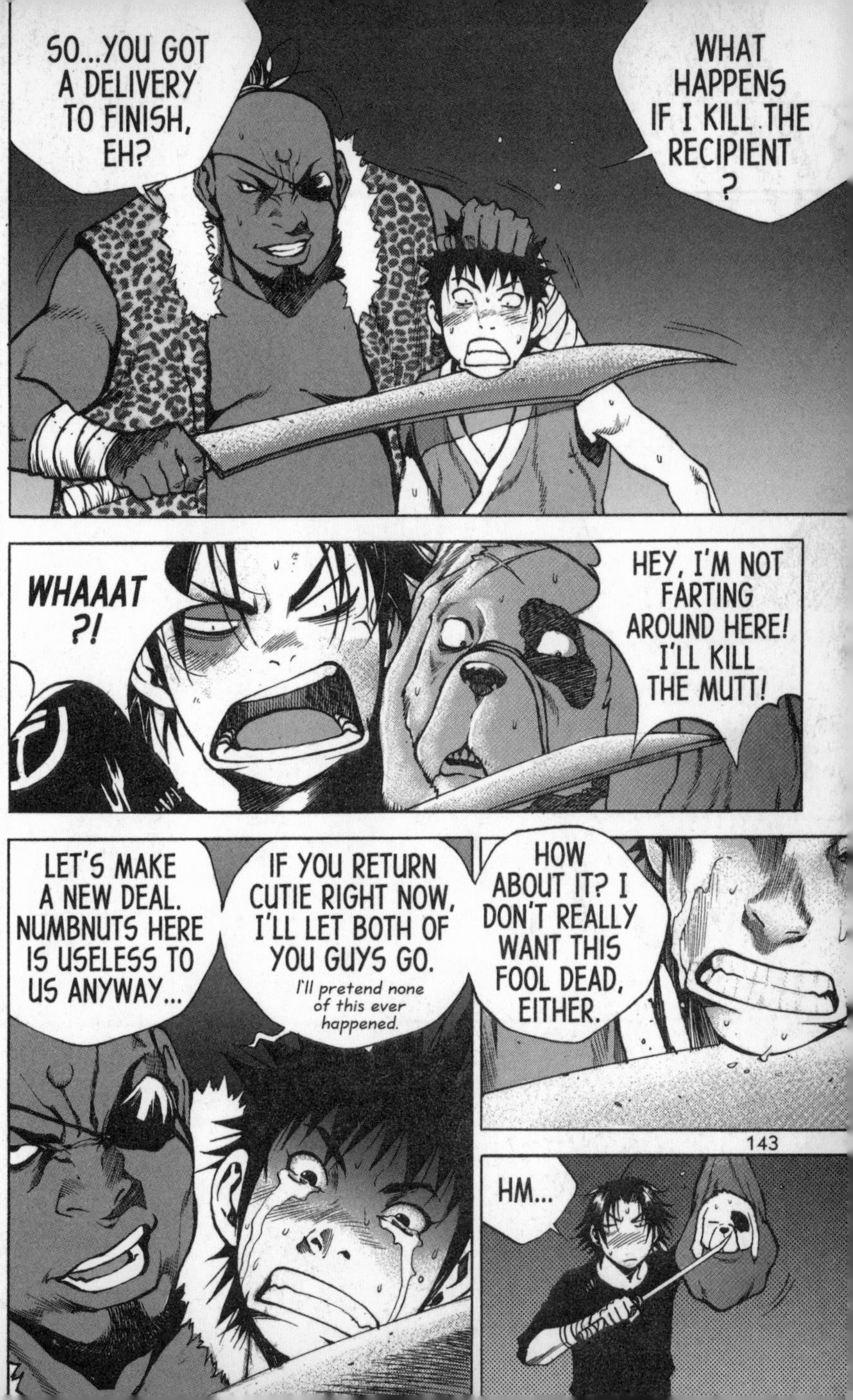
SO...YOU GOT A DELIVERY TO FINISH, EH?
WHAT HAPPENS IF I KILL THE RECIPIENT ?
HEY, I'M NOT FARTING AROUND HERE! I'LL KILL THE MUTT!
WHAAAT ?!
HOW ABOUT IT? I DON'T REALLY WANT THIS FOOL DEAD, EITHER.
IF YOU RETURN CUTIE RIGHT NOW, I'LL LET BOTH OF YOU GUYS GO.
I'll pretend none of this ever happened.
LET'S MAKE A NEW DEAL. NUMBNUTS HERE IS USELESS TO US ANYWAY...
HM...

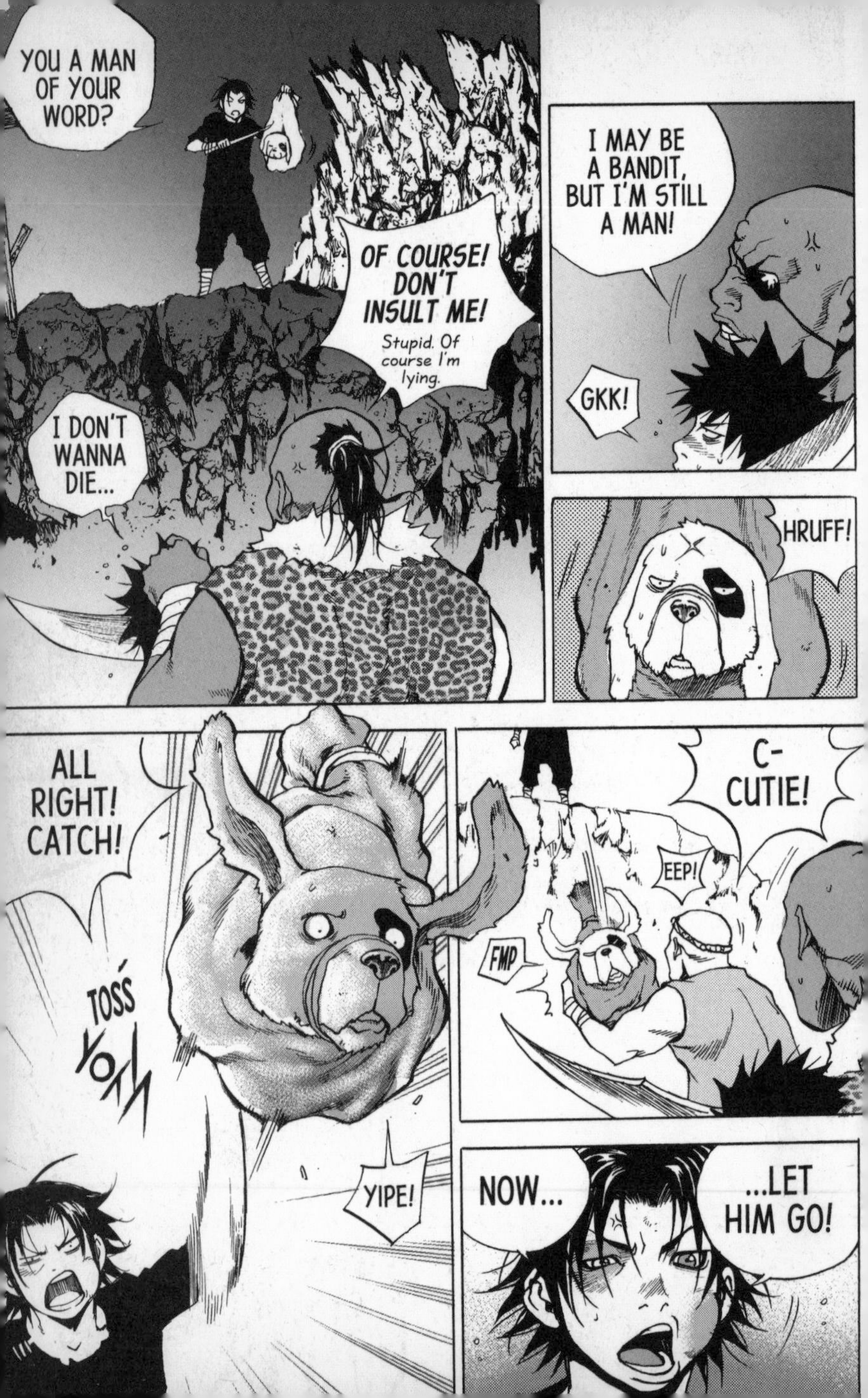
YOU A MAN OF YOUR WORD?
OF COURSE! DON'T INSULT ME!
Stupid. Of course I'm lying.
I DON'T WANNA DIE...
I MAY BE A BANDIT, BUT I'M STILL A MAN!
GKK!
HRUFF!
ALL RIGHT! CATCH!
TOSS
YOINK
YIPE!
C-CUTIE!
EEP!
FMP
NOW...
...LET HIM GO!

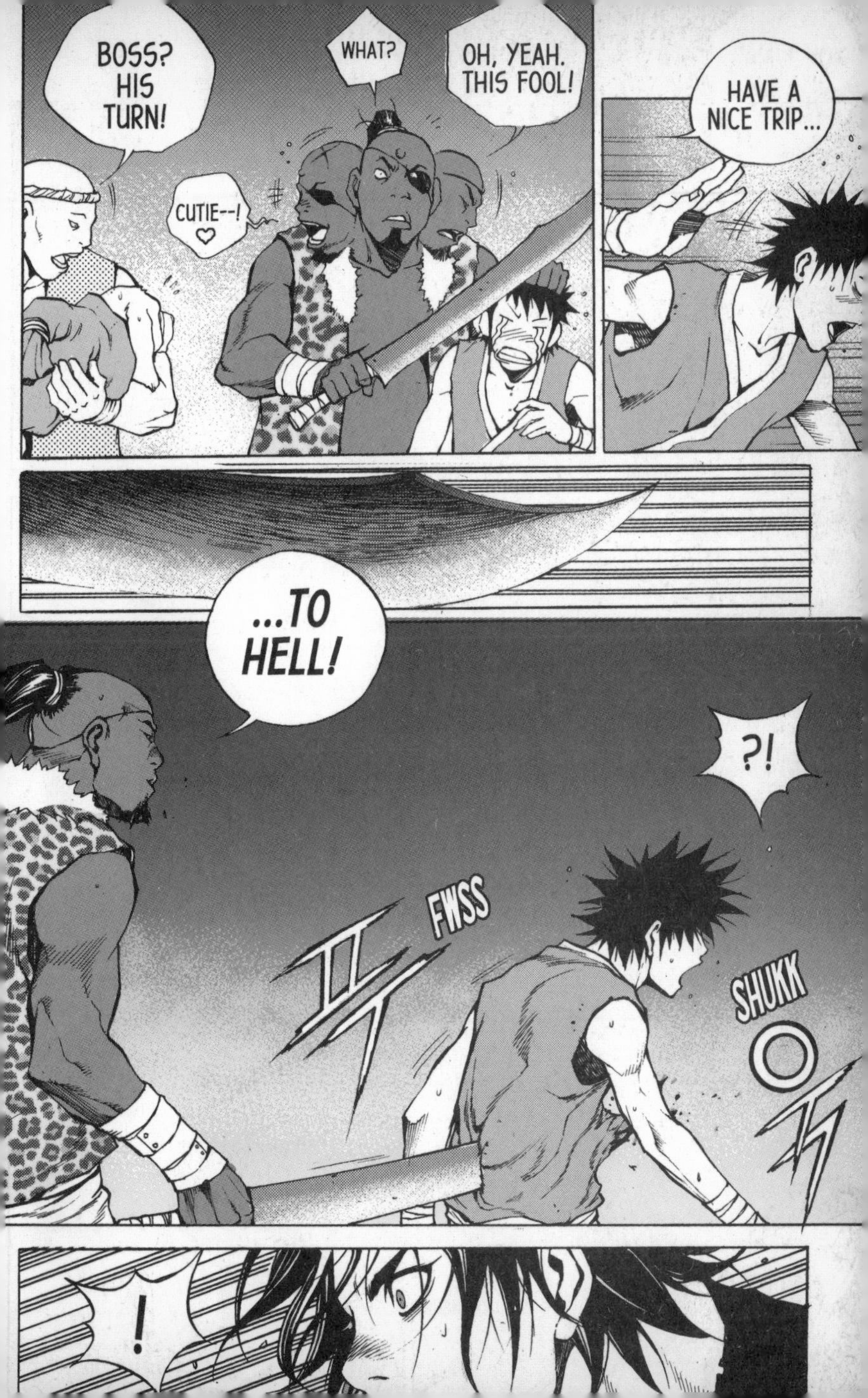

BOSS? HIS TURN!
WHAT?
OH, YEAH. THIS FOOL!
CUTIE--! ♡
HAVE A NICE TRIP...
...TO HELL!
?!
FWSS
SHUKK
!

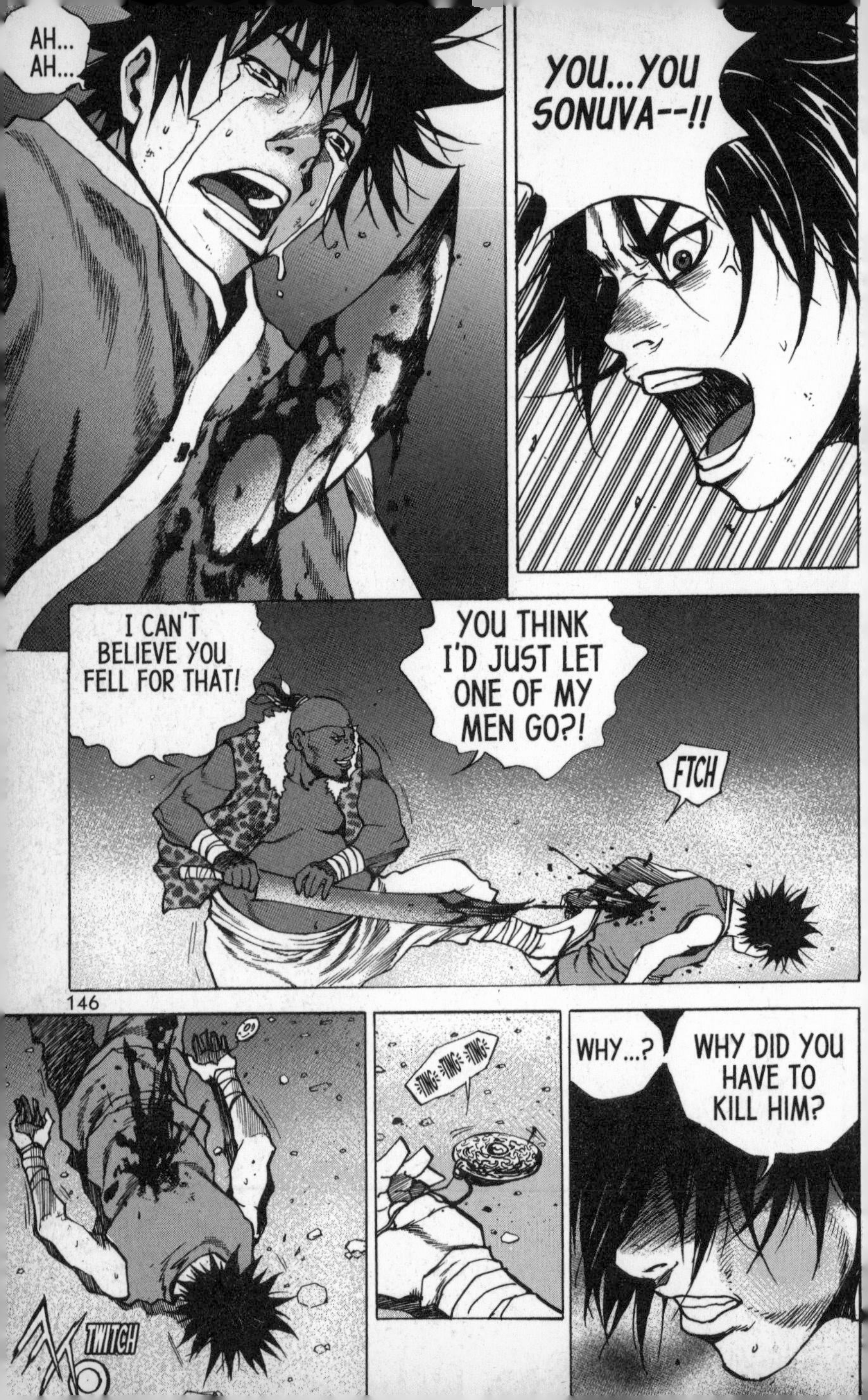
AH...
AH...
YOU...YOU
SONUVA--!!
I CAN'T BELIEVE YOU FELL FOR THAT!
YOU THINK I'D JUST LET ONE OF MY MEN GO?!
FTCH
TWITCH
TING TING TING
WHY...?
WHY DID YOU HAVE TO KILL HIM?

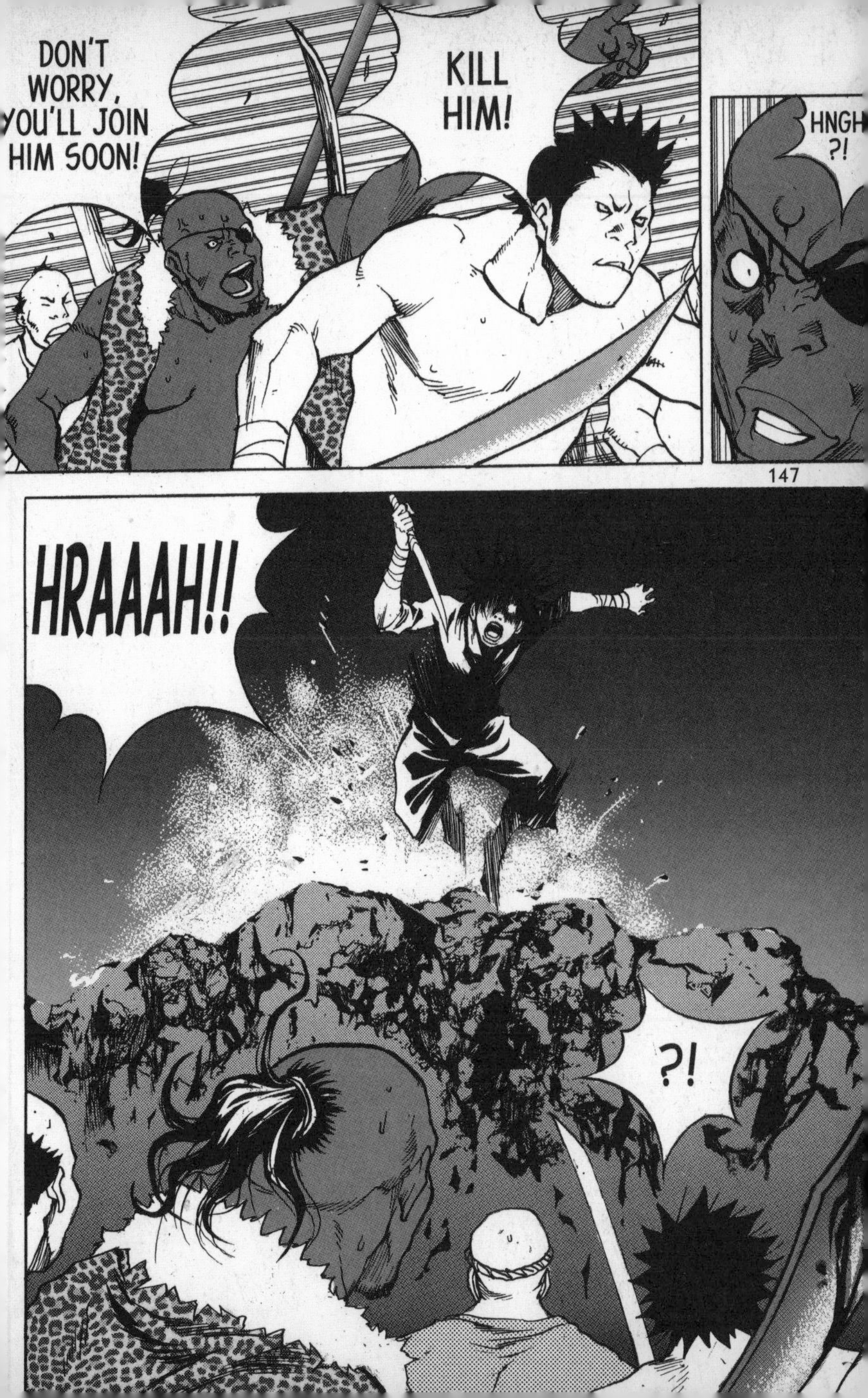
HNGH ?!
KILL HIM!
DON'T WORRY, YOU'LL JOIN HIM SOON!
HRAAAH!!
?!

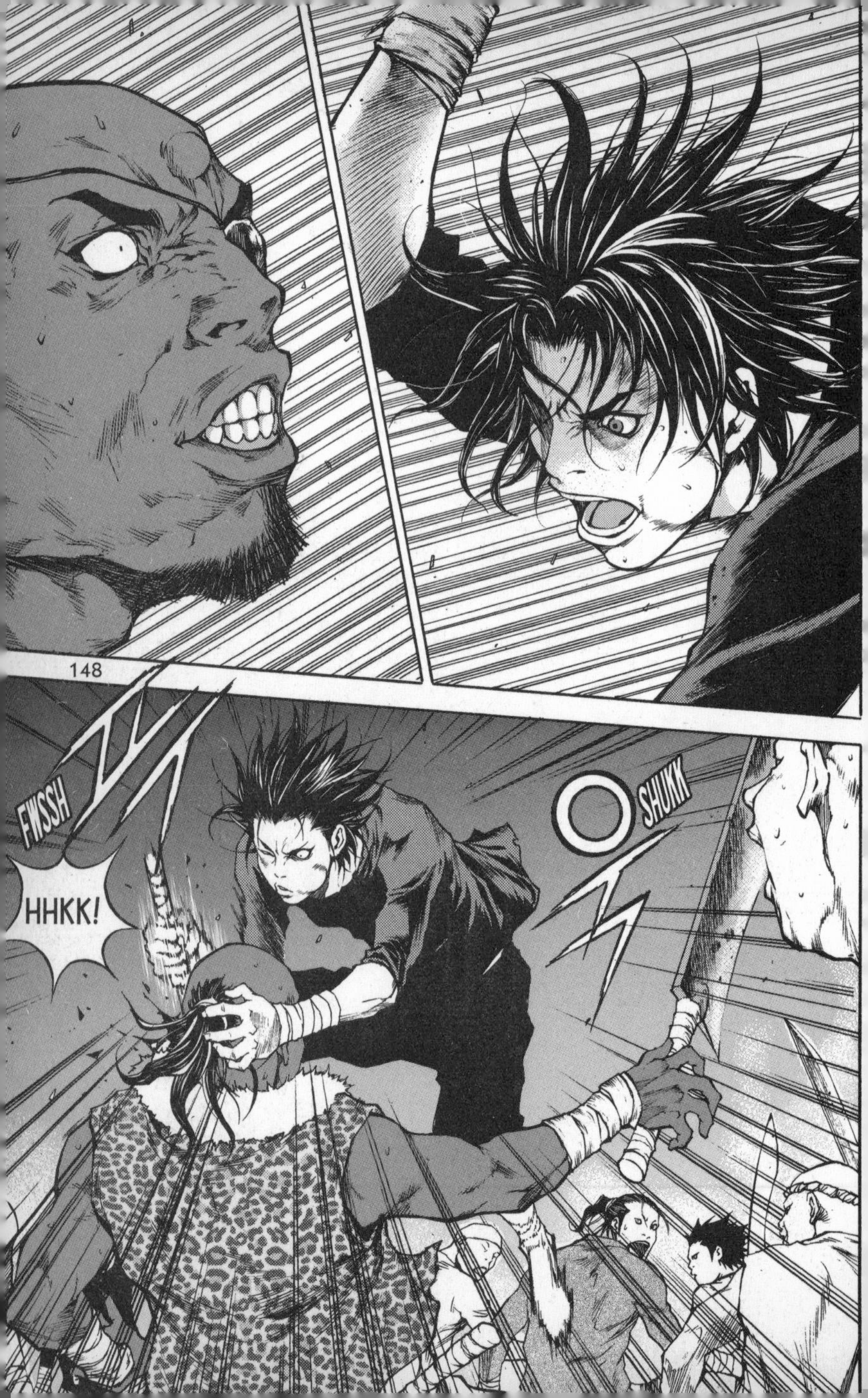
FWSSH
HHKK!
SHUKK

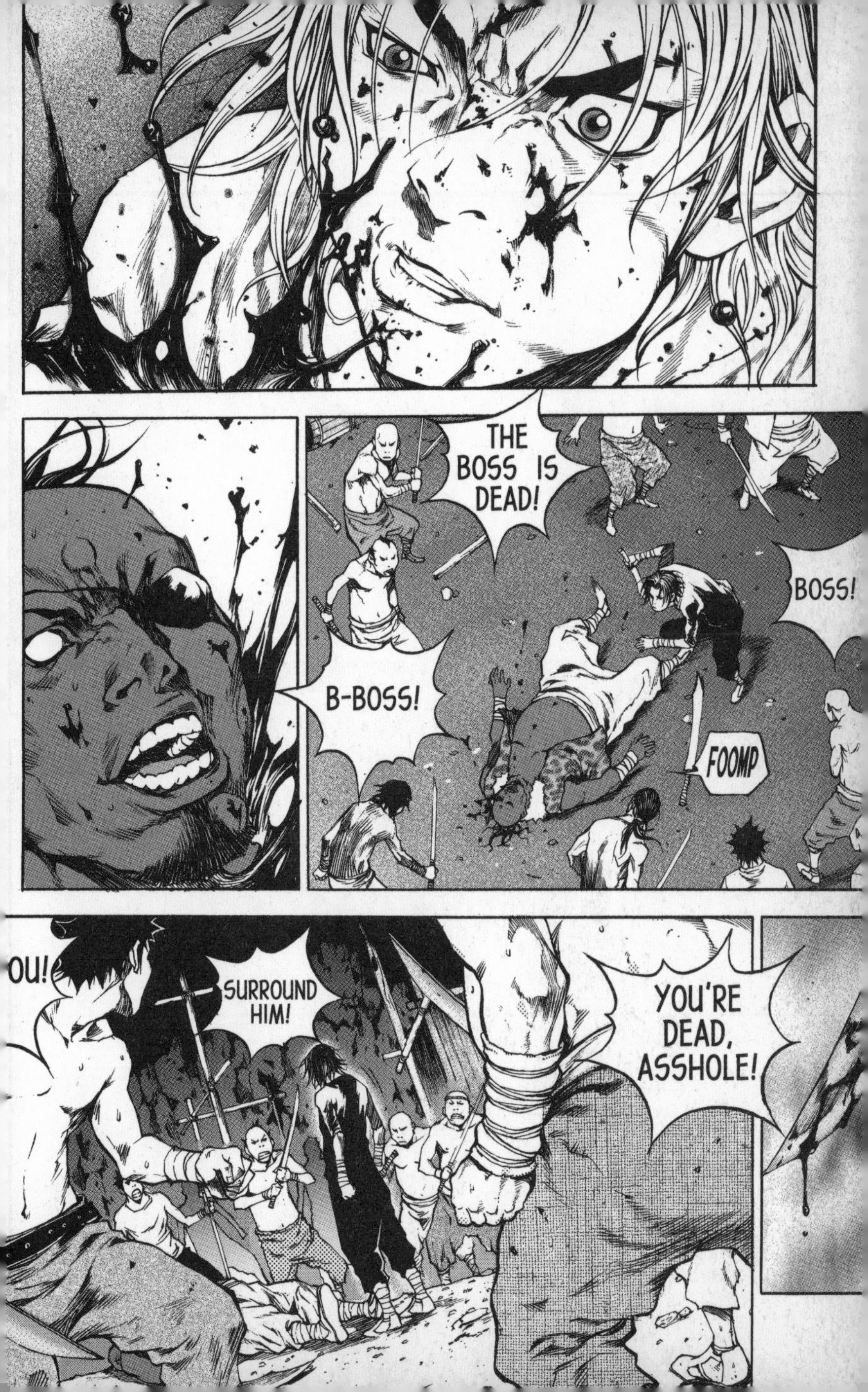
B-BOSS!
THE BOSS IS DEAD!
BOSS!
FOOMP
OU!
SURROUND HIM!
YOU'RE DEAD, ASSHOLE!

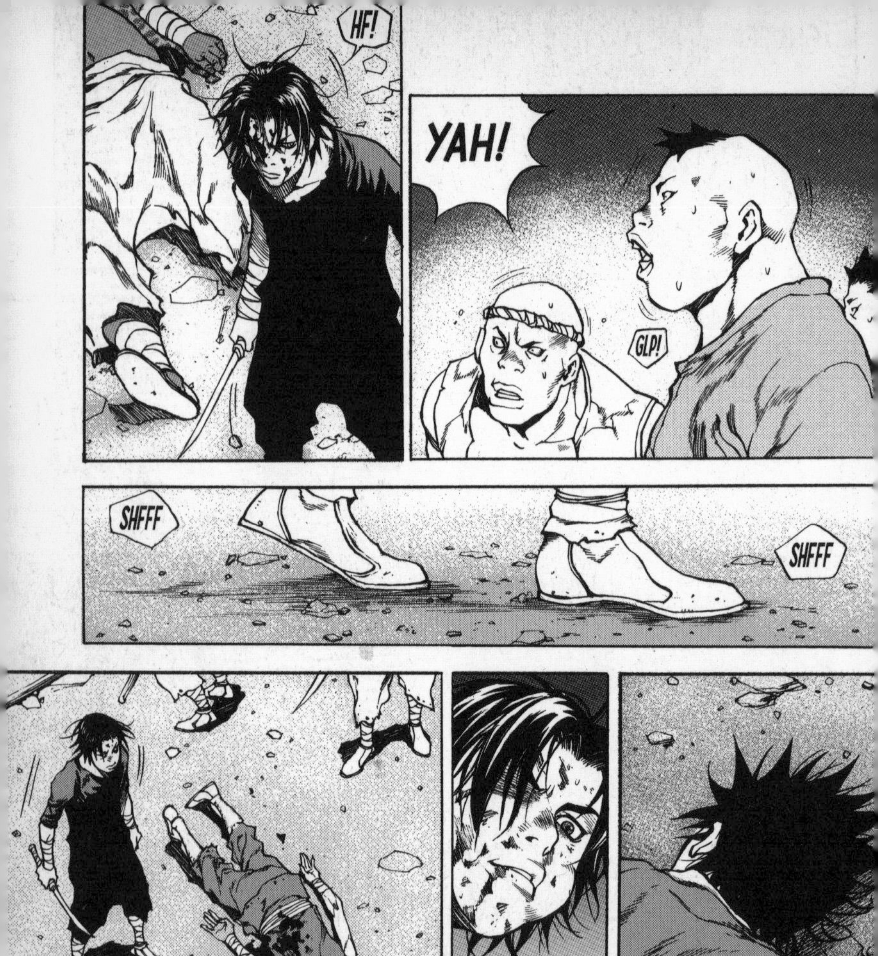
HF!
YAH!
GLP!
SHFFF
SHFFF

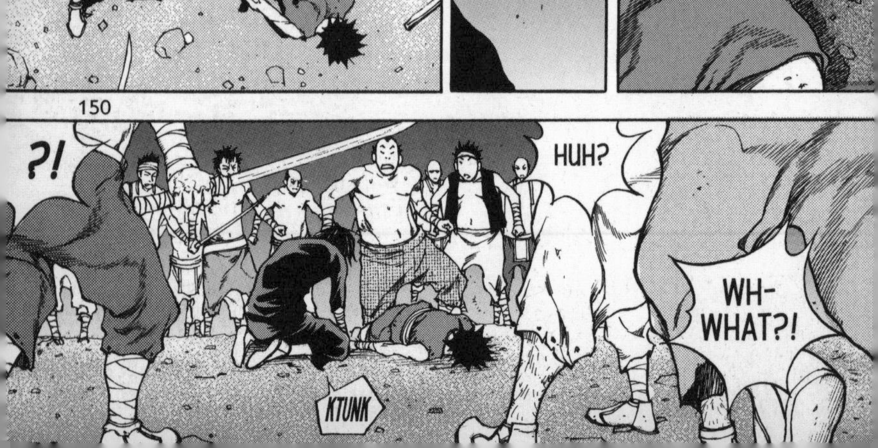
?!
HUH?
WH-
WHAT?!
KTUNK

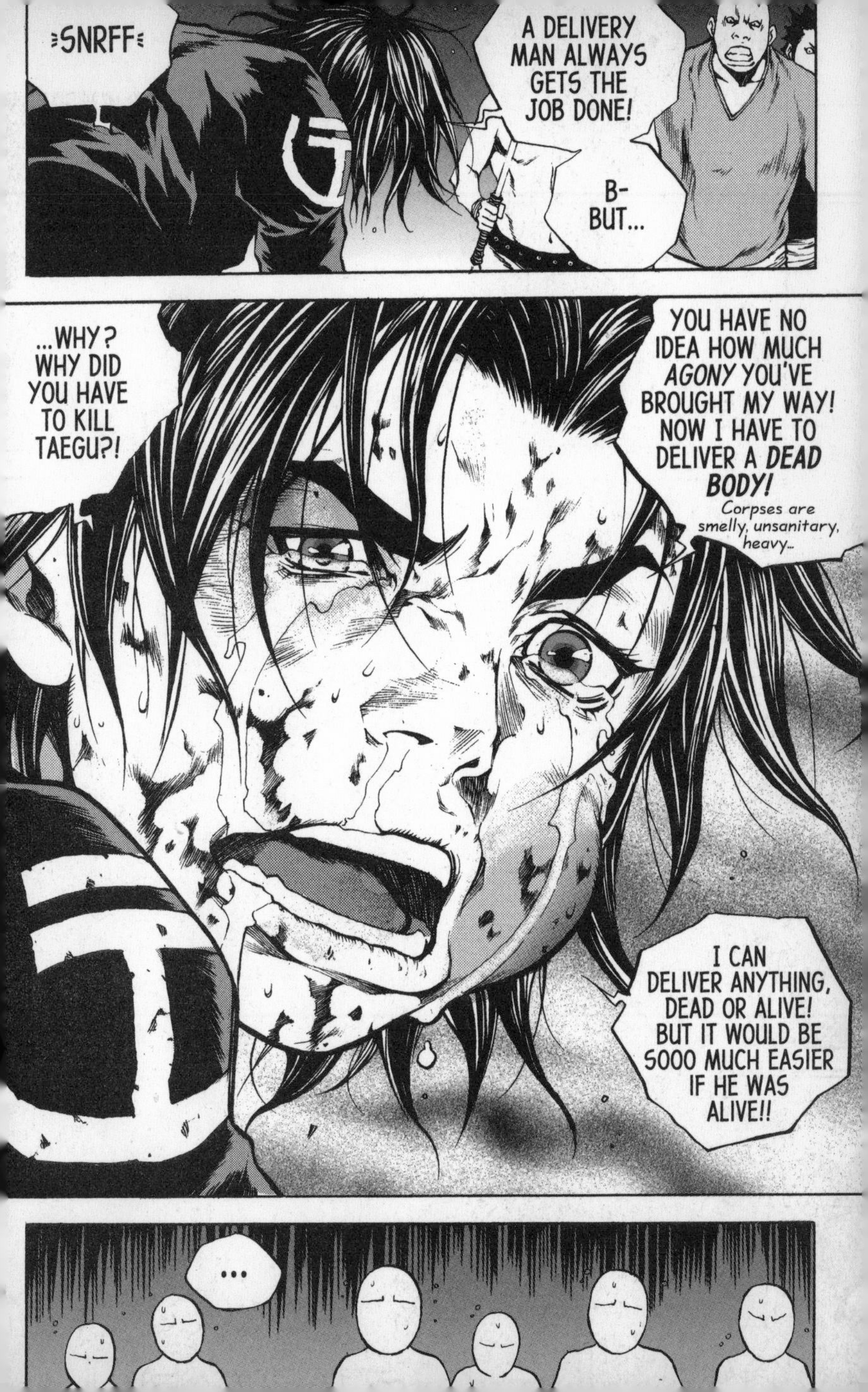
A DELIVERY MAN ALWAYS GETS THE JOB DONE!
SNRFF
B- BUT...
YOU HAVE NO IDEA HOW MUCH AGONY YOU'VE BROUGHT MY WAY! NOW I HAVE TO DELIVER A DEAD BODY!
Corpses are smelly, unsanitary, heavy...
...WHY? WHY DID YOU HAVE TO KILL TAEGU?!
I CAN DELIVER ANYTHING, DEAD OR ALIVE! BUT IT WOULD BE SOOO MUCH EASIER IF HE WAS ALIVE!!
...

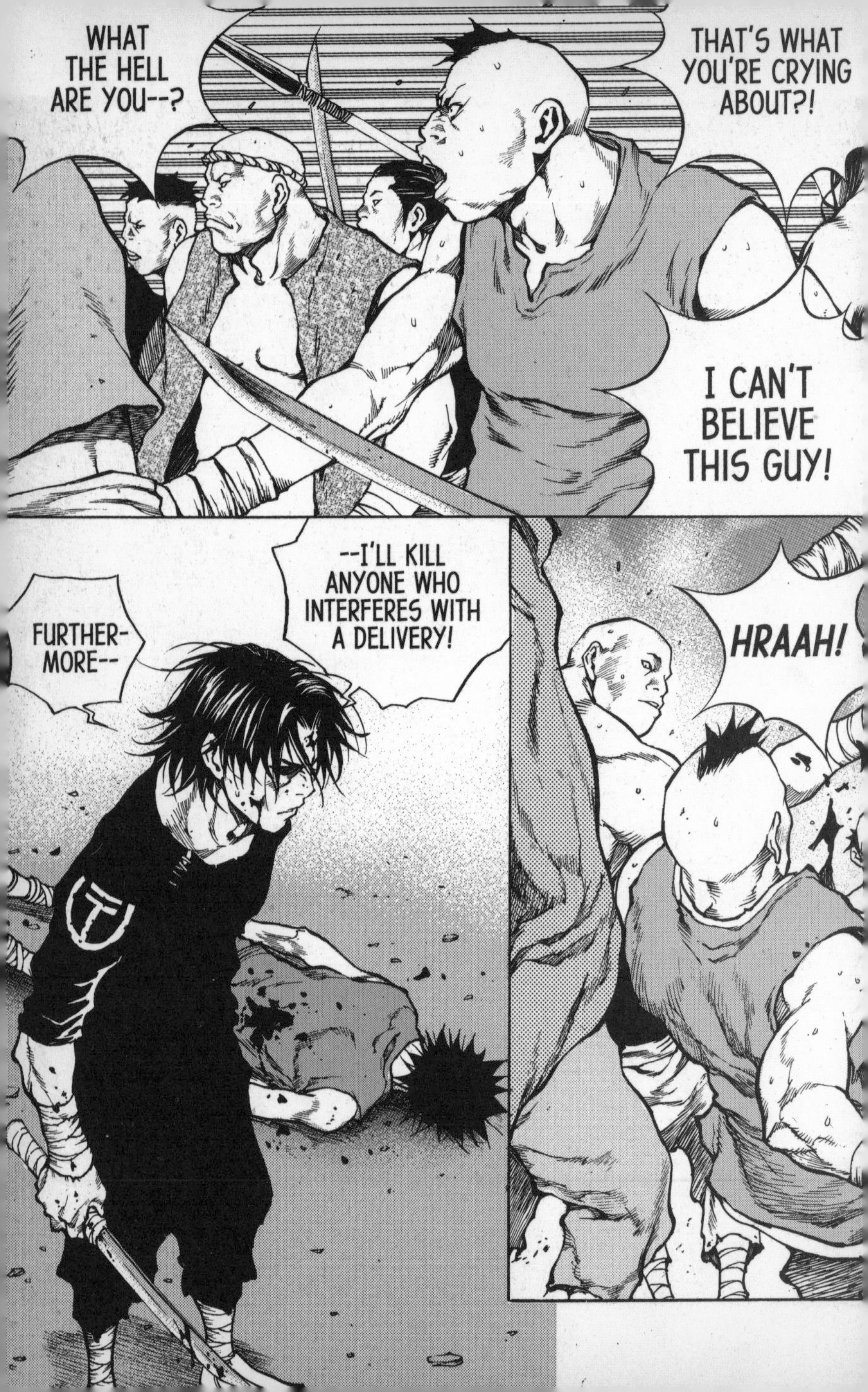
THAT'S WHAT YOU'RE CRYING ABOUT?!
WHAT THE HELL ARE YOU--?
I CAN'T BELIEVE THIS GUY!
HRAAH!
--I'LL KILL ANYONE WHO INTERFERES WITH A DELIVERY!
FURTHER-MORE--

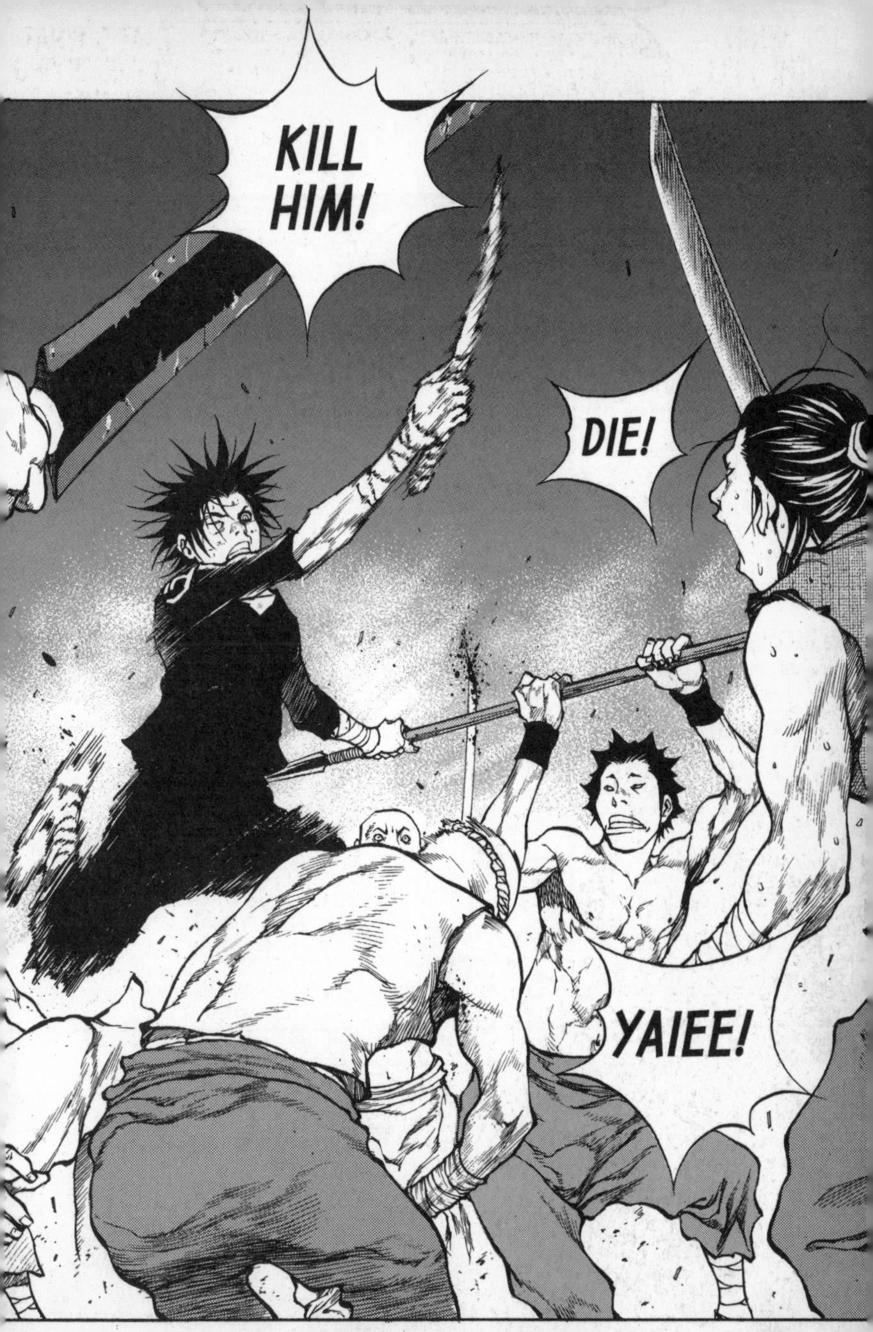
KILL HIM!
DIE!
YAIEE!

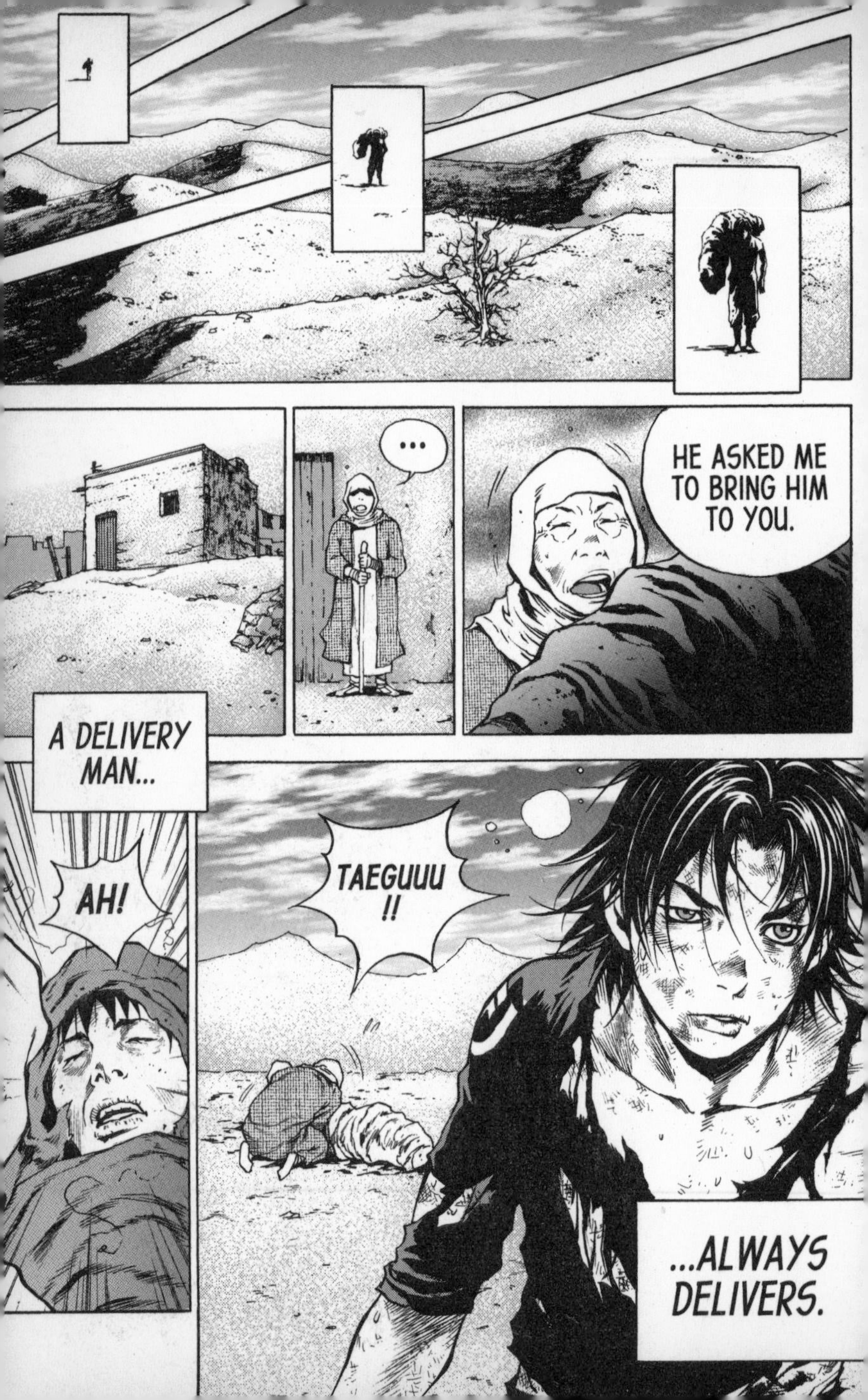
...
HE ASKED ME TO BRING HIM TO YOU.
A DELIVERY MAN...
AH!
TAEGUUU !!
...ALWAYS DELIVERS.

Banya

the explosive delivery man

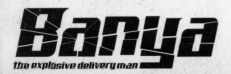

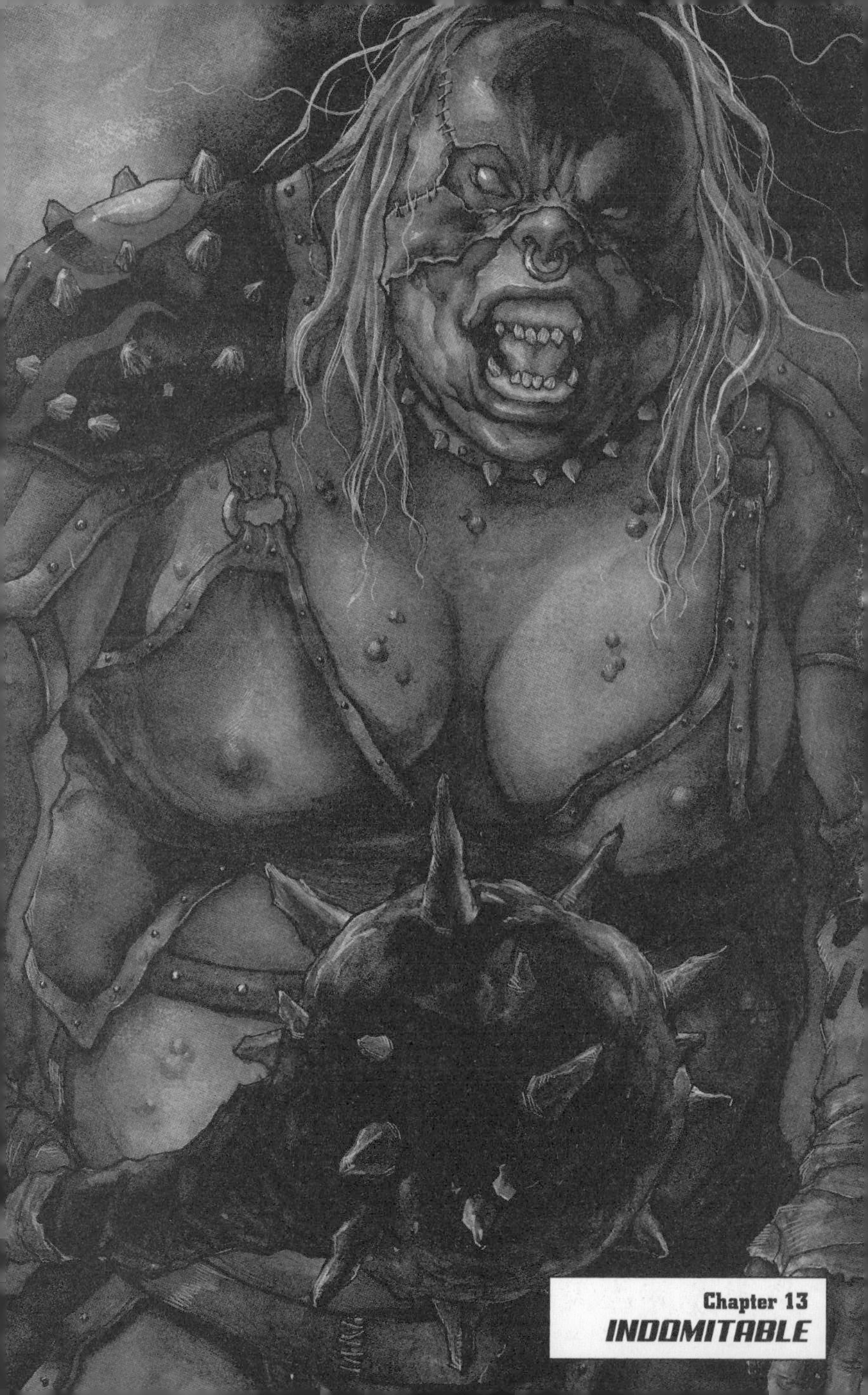

Chapter 13
INDOMITABLE

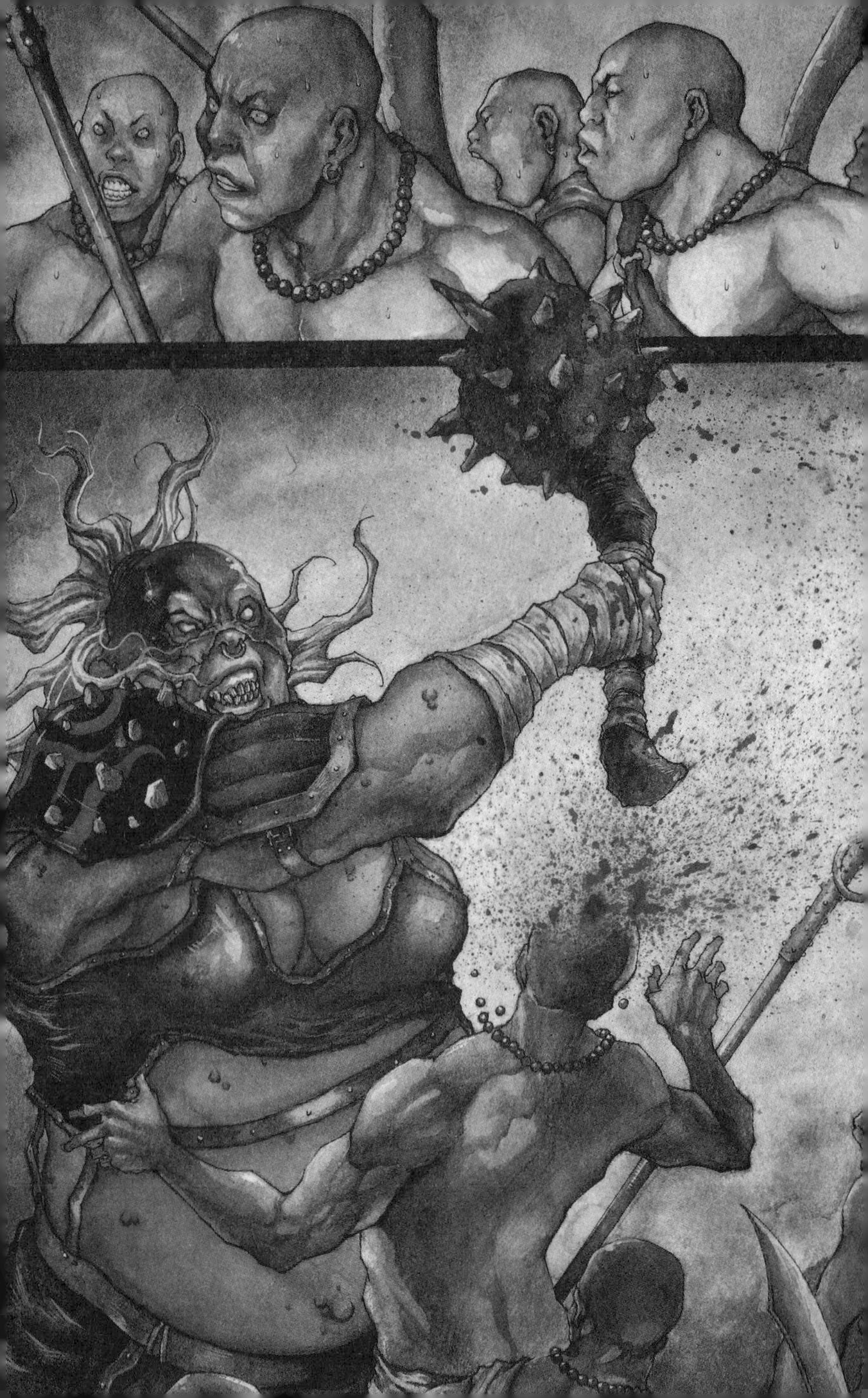

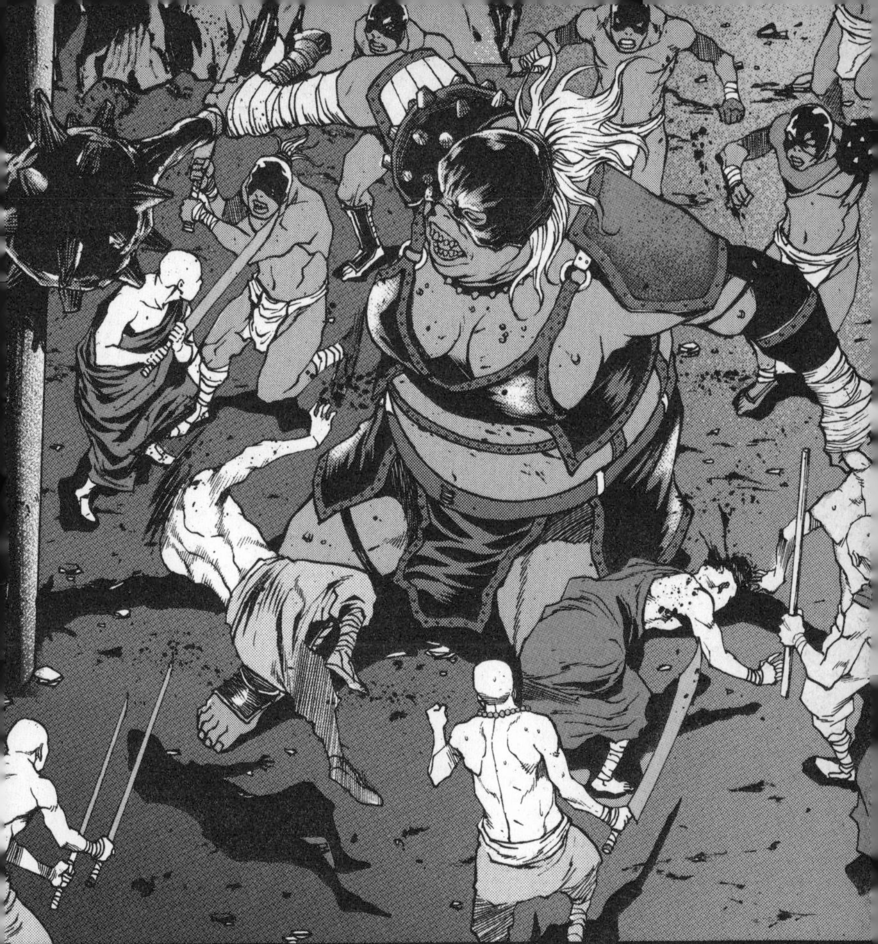
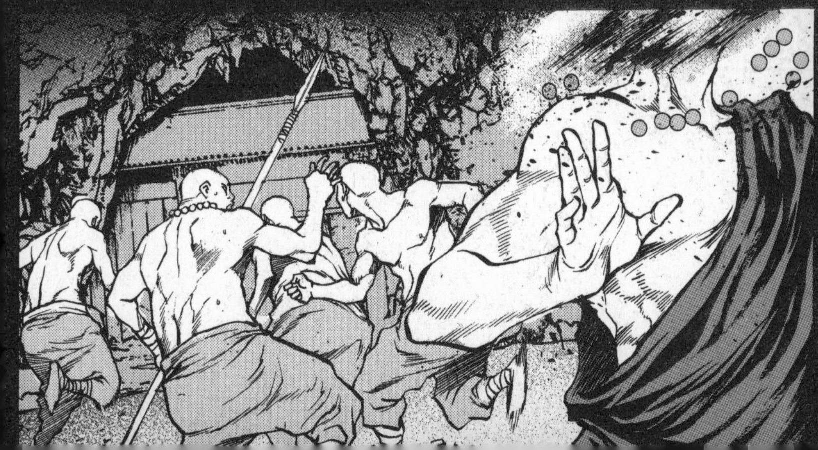

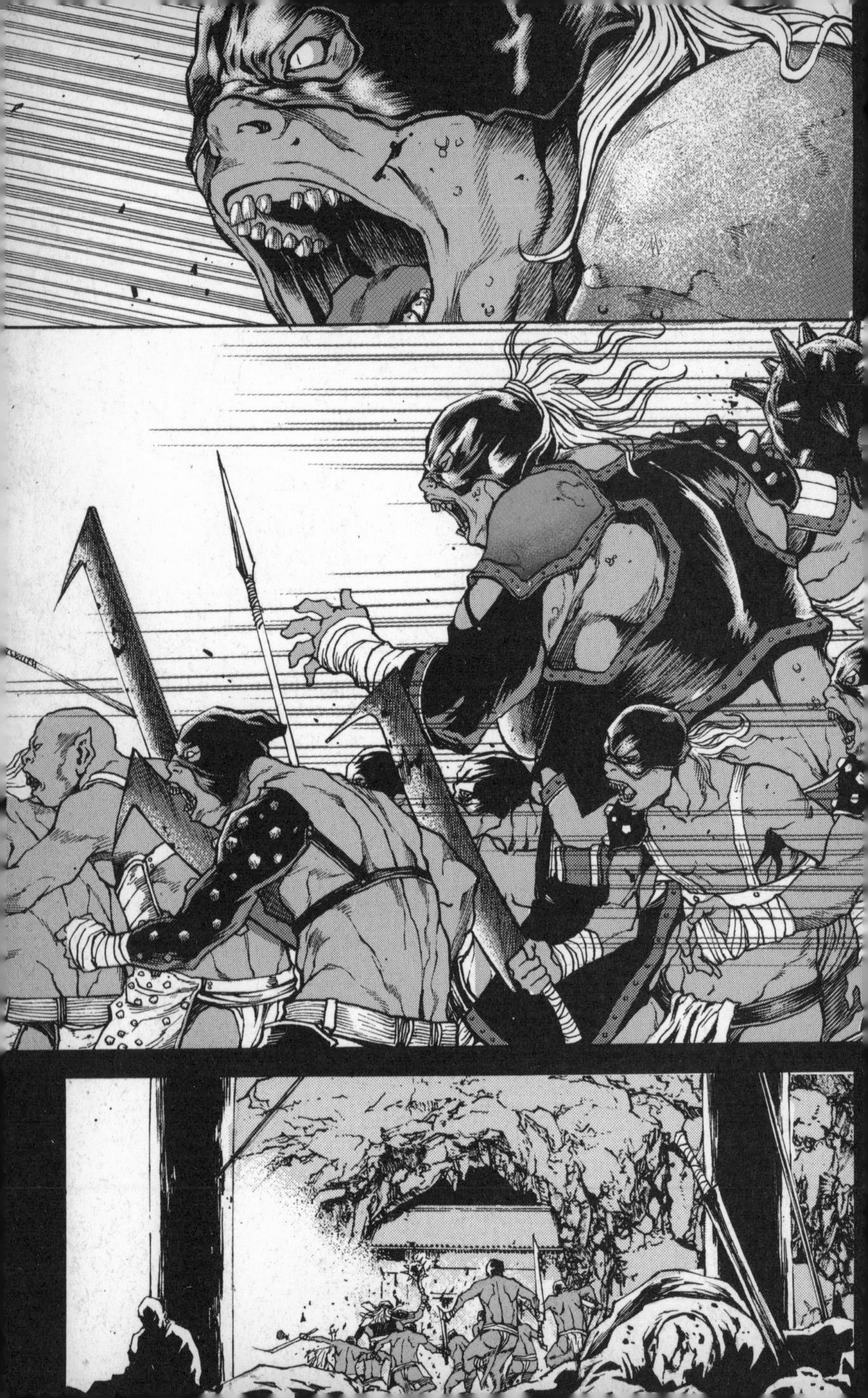

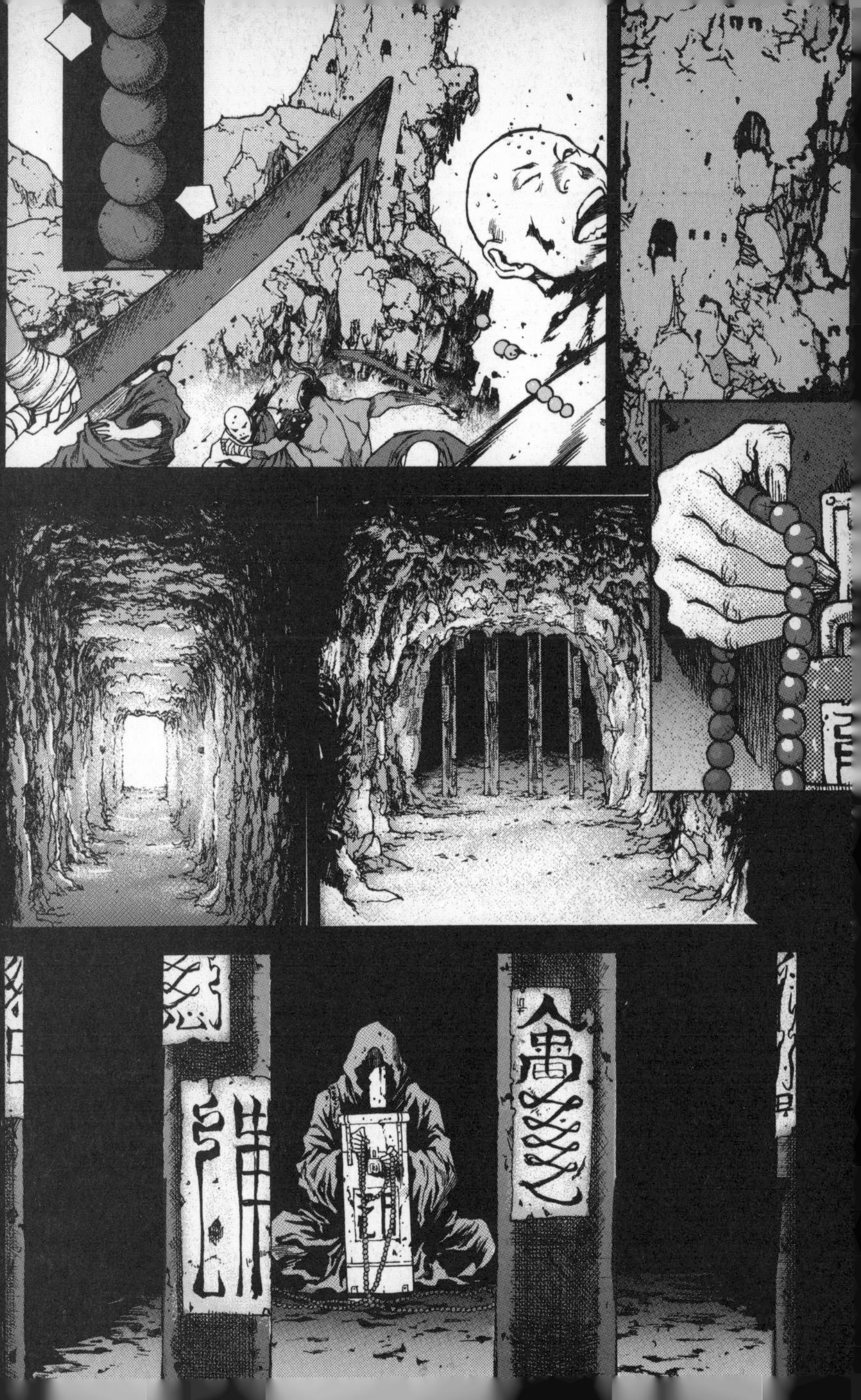

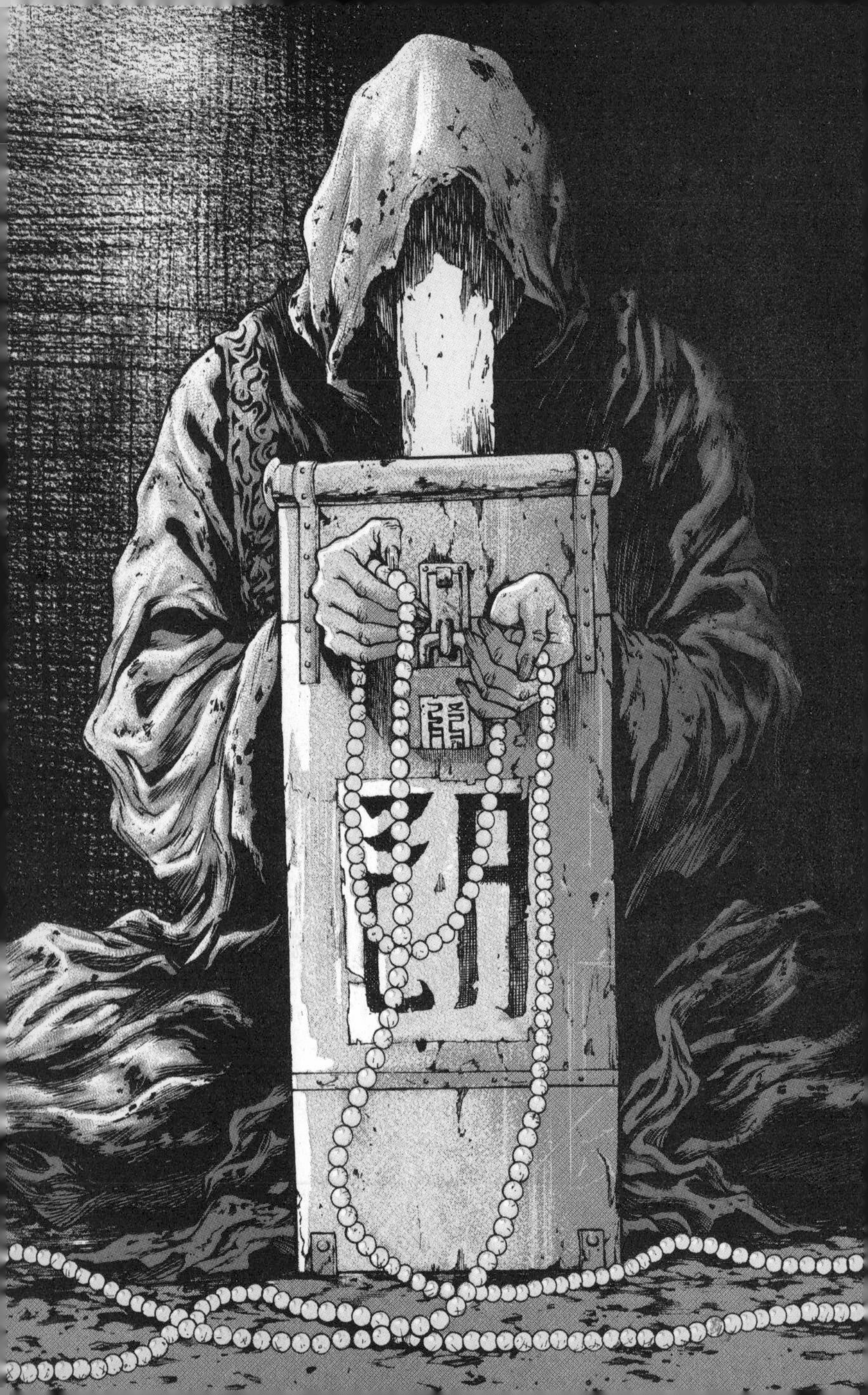

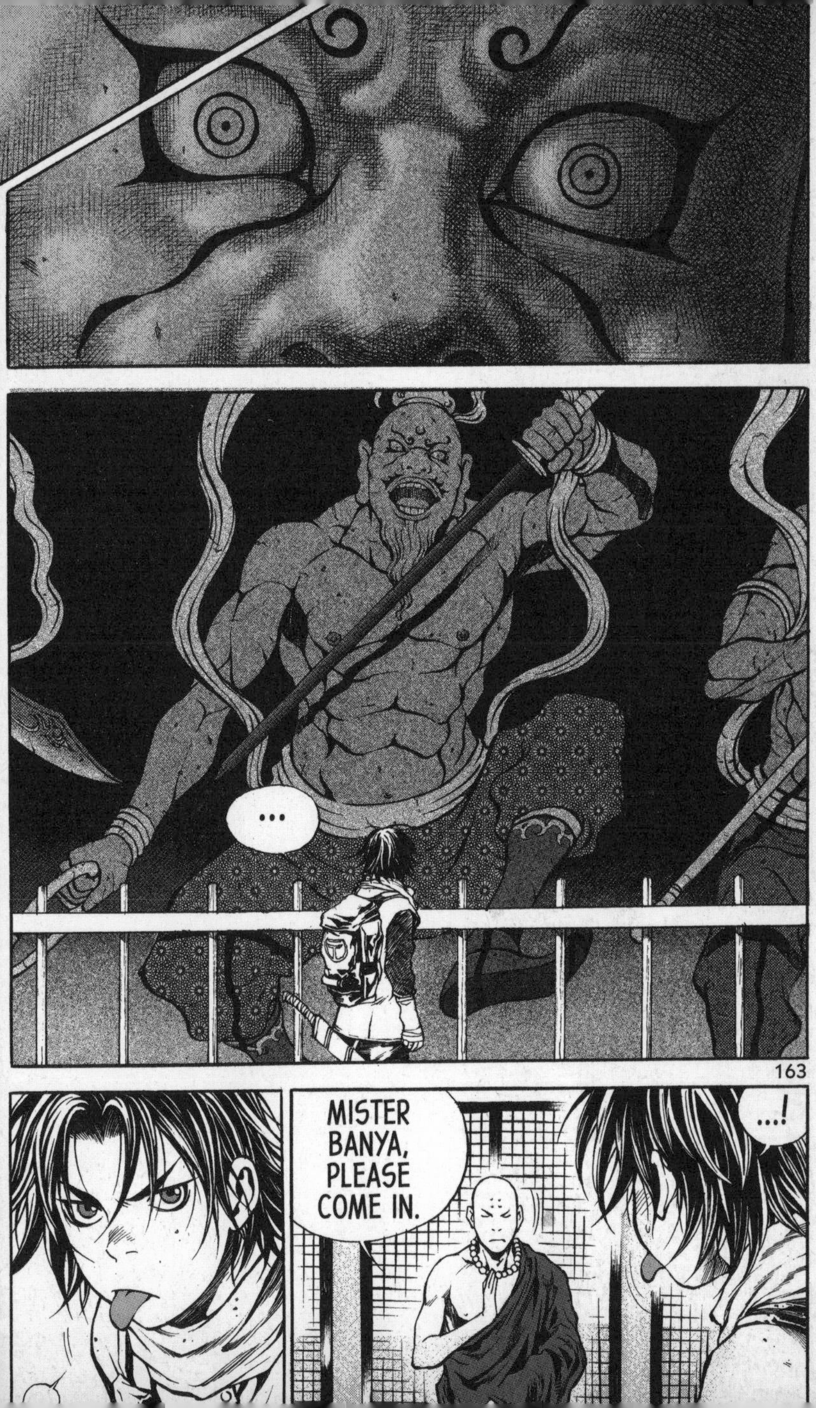
...
MISTER BANYA, PLEASE COME IN.
...!

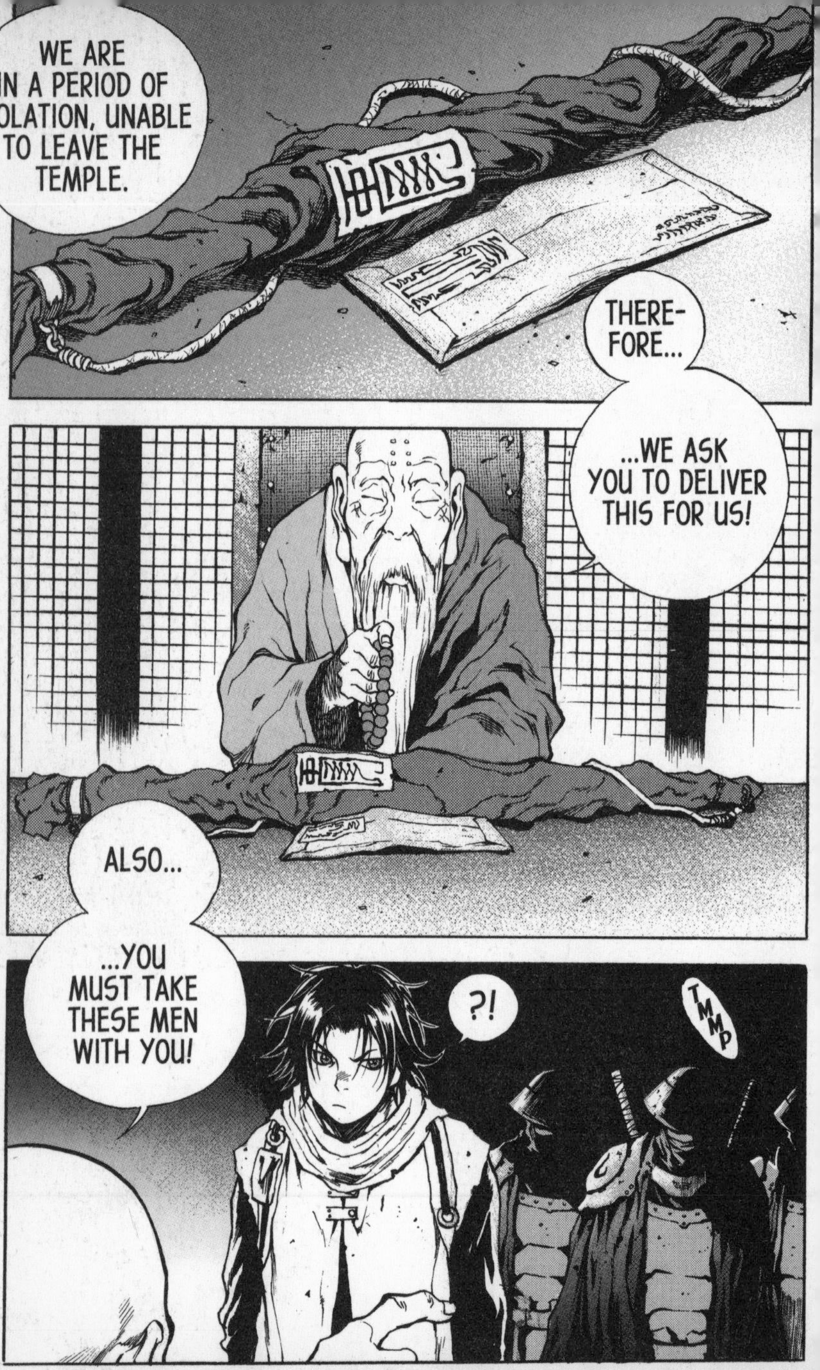
WE ARE IN A PERIOD OF ISOLATION, UNABLE TO LEAVE THE TEMPLE.
THERE-FORE...
...WE ASK YOU TO DELIVER THIS FOR US!
ALSO...
...YOU MUST TAKE THESE MEN WITH YOU!
?!
TMMP

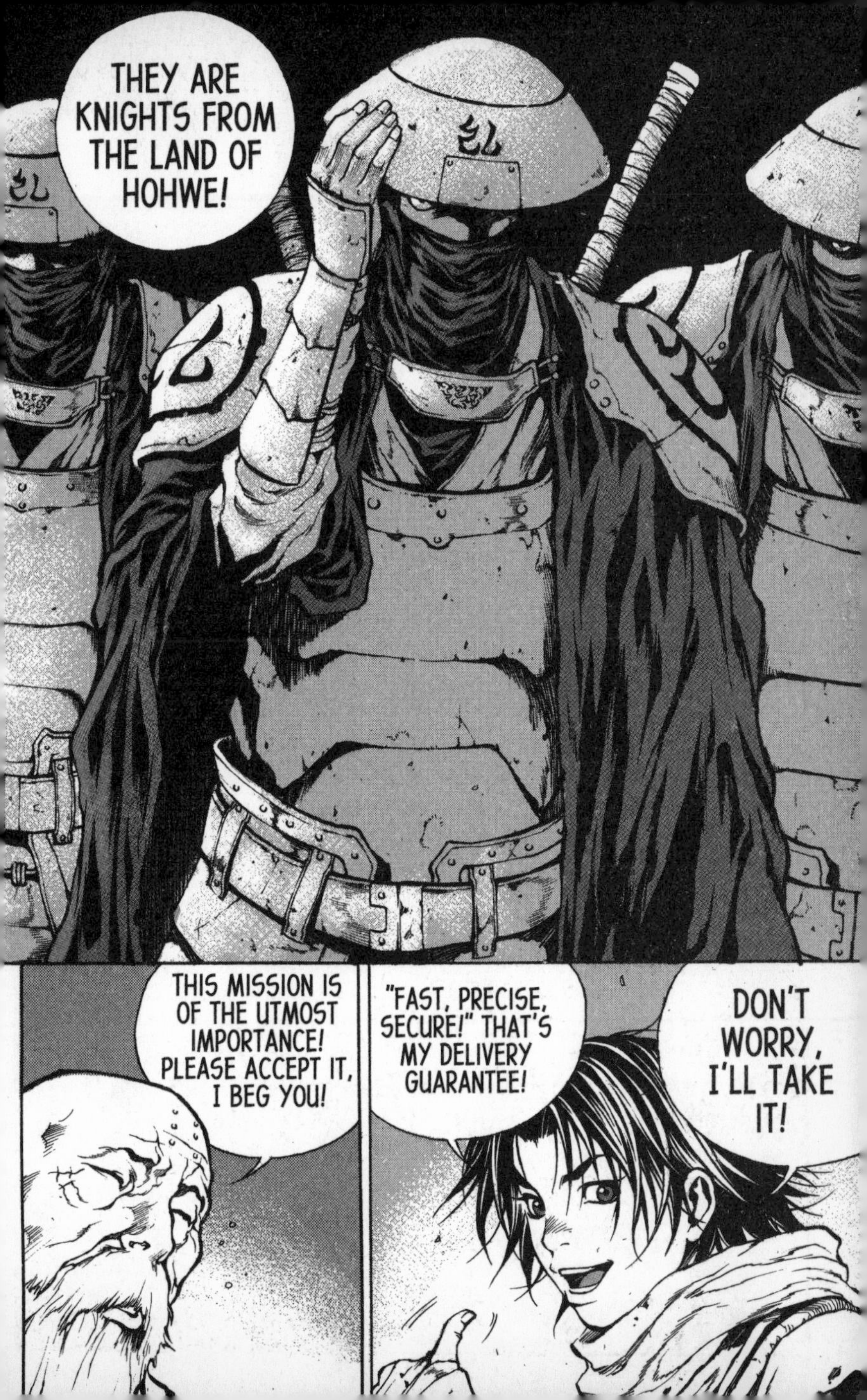
THEY ARE KNIGHTS FROM THE LAND OF HOHWE!
THIS MISSION IS OF THE UTMOST IMPORTANCE! PLEASE ACCEPT IT, I BEG YOU!
"FAST, PRECISE, SECURE!" THAT'S MY DELIVERY GUARANTEE!
DON'T WORRY, I'LL TAKE IT!

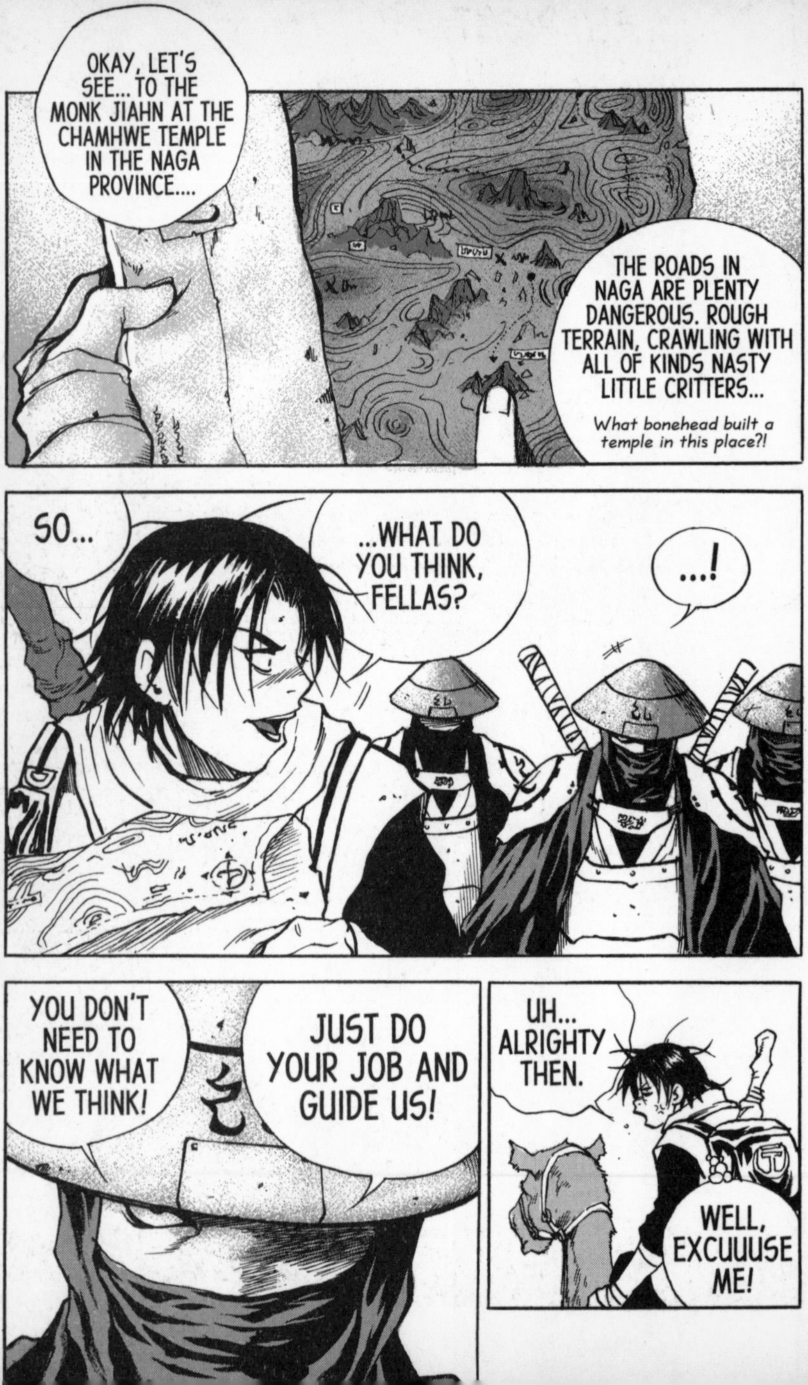
OKAY, LET'S SEE... TO THE MONK JIAHN AT THE CHAMHWE TEMPLE IN THE NAGA PROVINCE....
THE ROADS IN NAGA ARE PLENTY DANGEROUS. ROUGH TERRAIN, CRAWLING WITH ALL OF KINDS NASTY LITTLE CRITTERS...
What bonehead built a temple in this place?!
SO...
...WHAT DO YOU THINK, FELLAS?
...!
YOU DON'T NEED TO KNOW WHAT WE THINK!
JUST DO YOUR JOB AND GUIDE US!
UH... ALRIGHTY THEN.
WELL, EXCUUUSE ME!

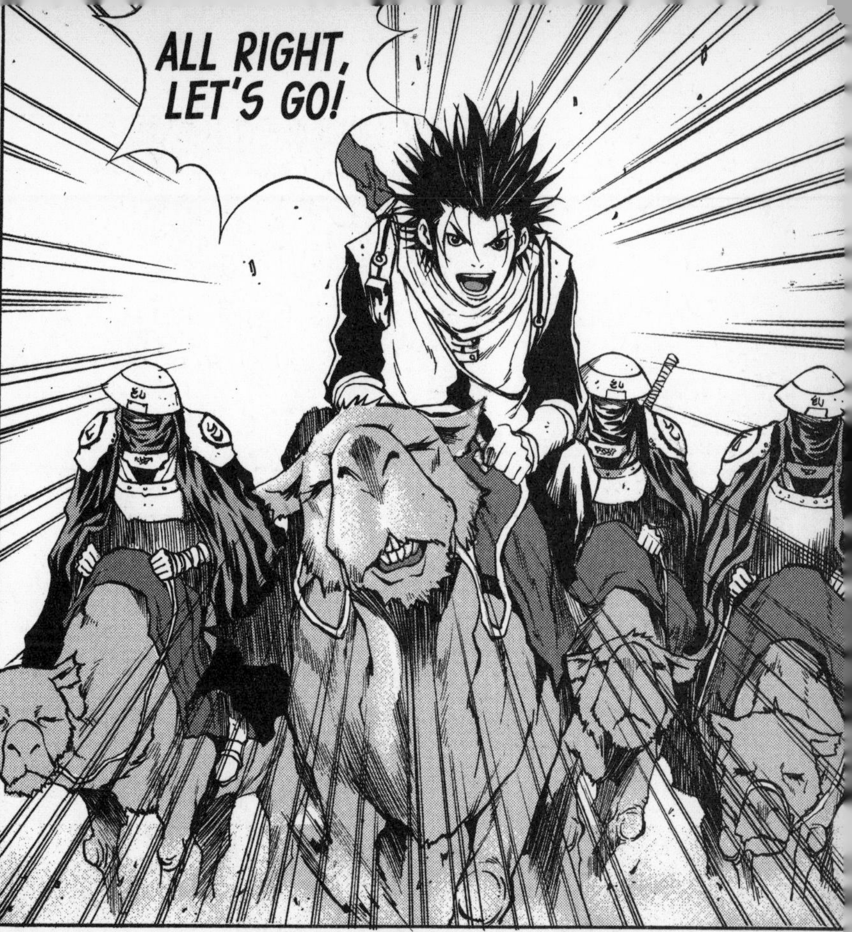
ALL RIGHT, LET'S GO!

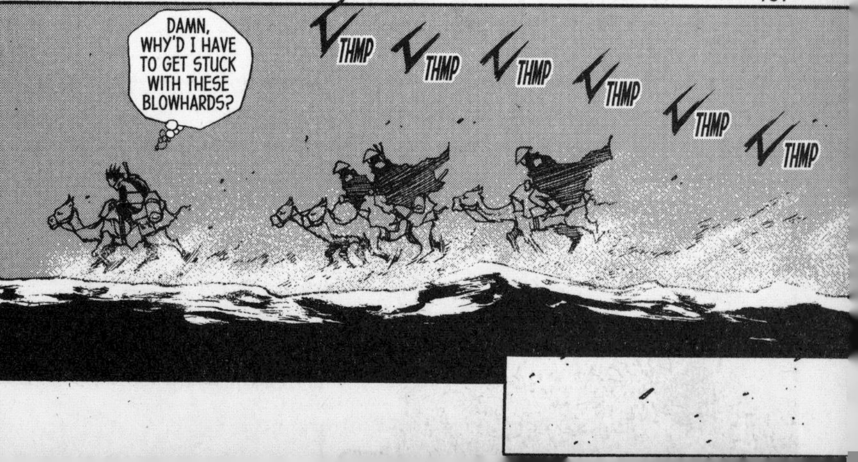
DAMN, WHY'D I HAVE TO GET STUCK WITH THESE BLOWHARDS?
THMP
THMP
THMP
THMP
THMP
THMP

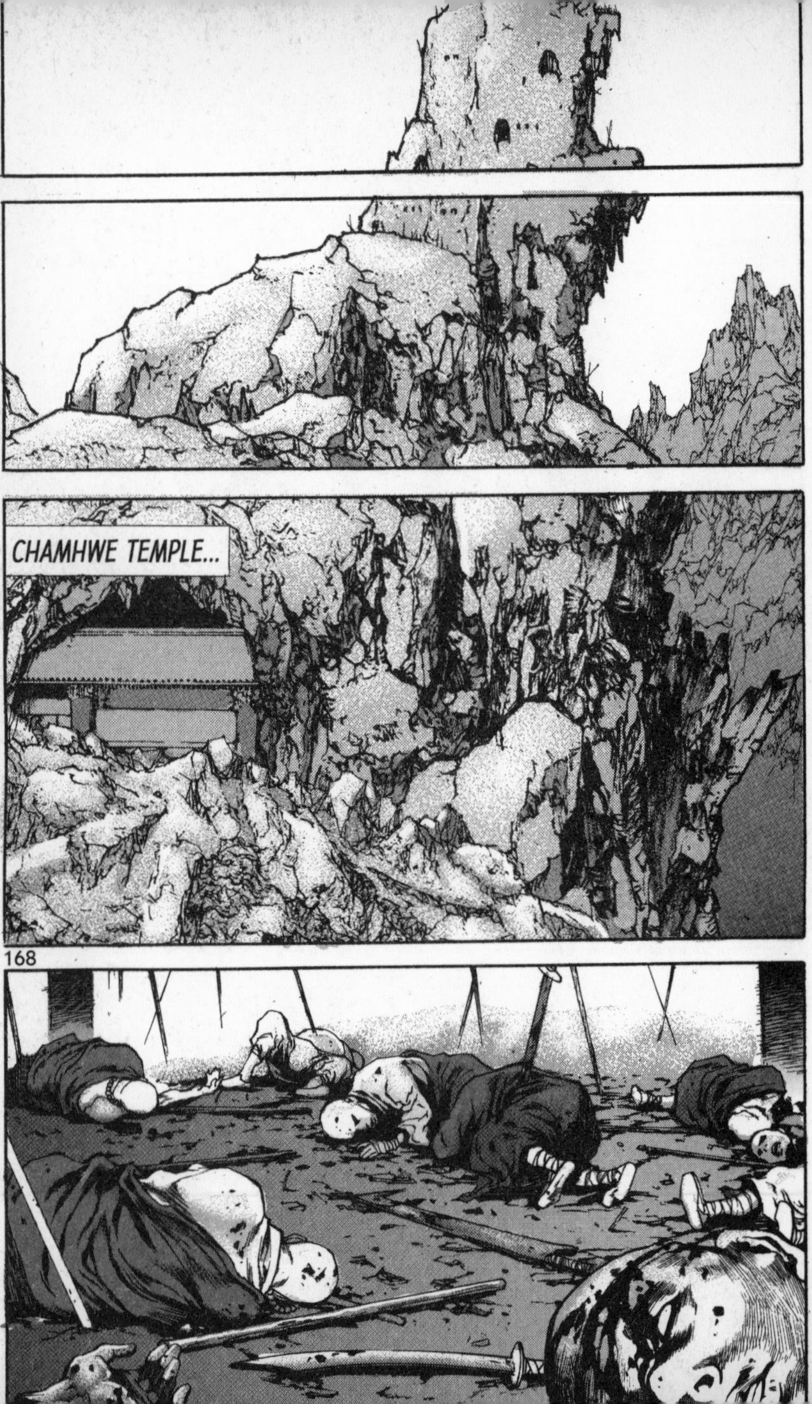
CHAMHWE TEMPLE...

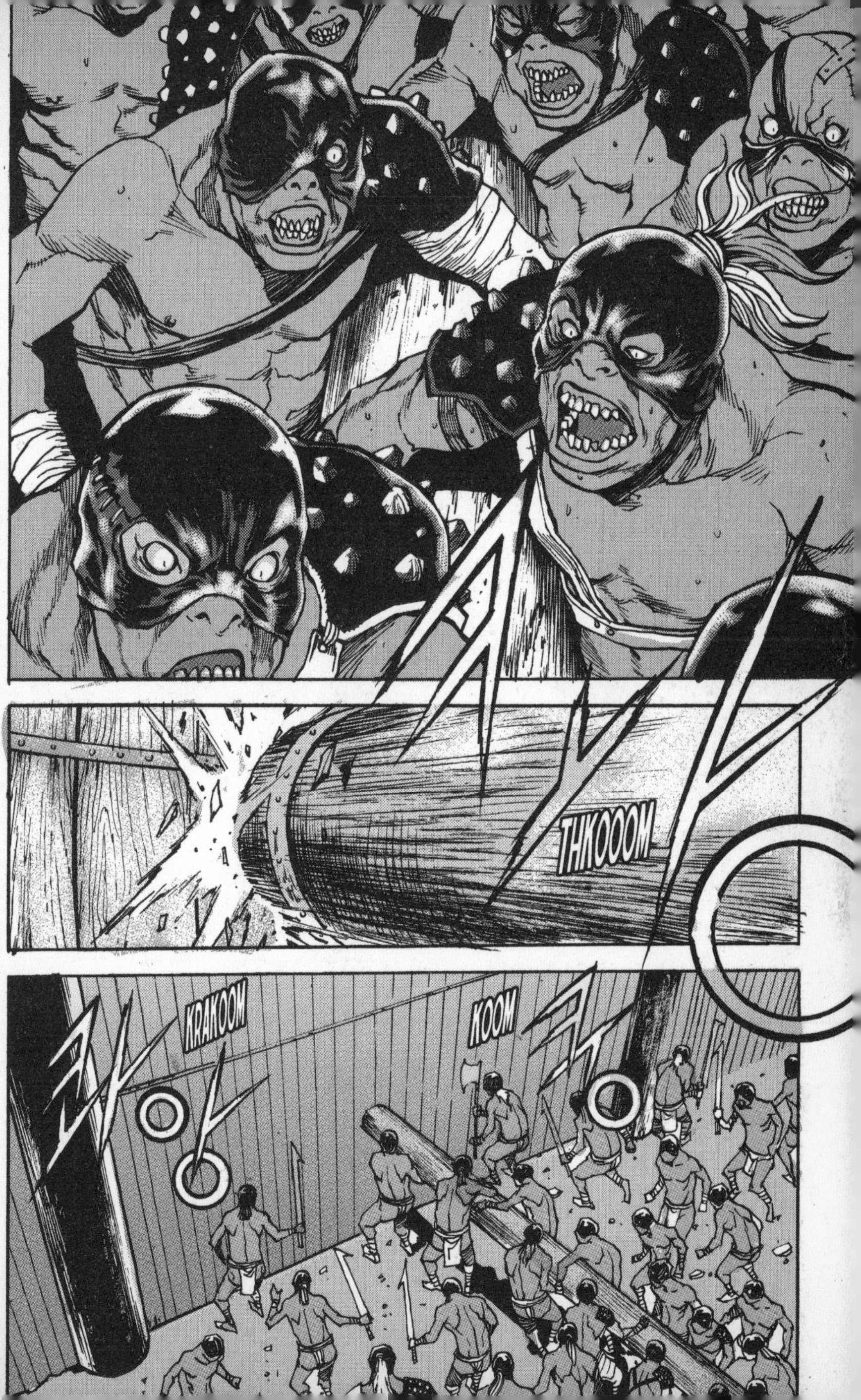
THKOOOM
KRAKOOM
KOOM

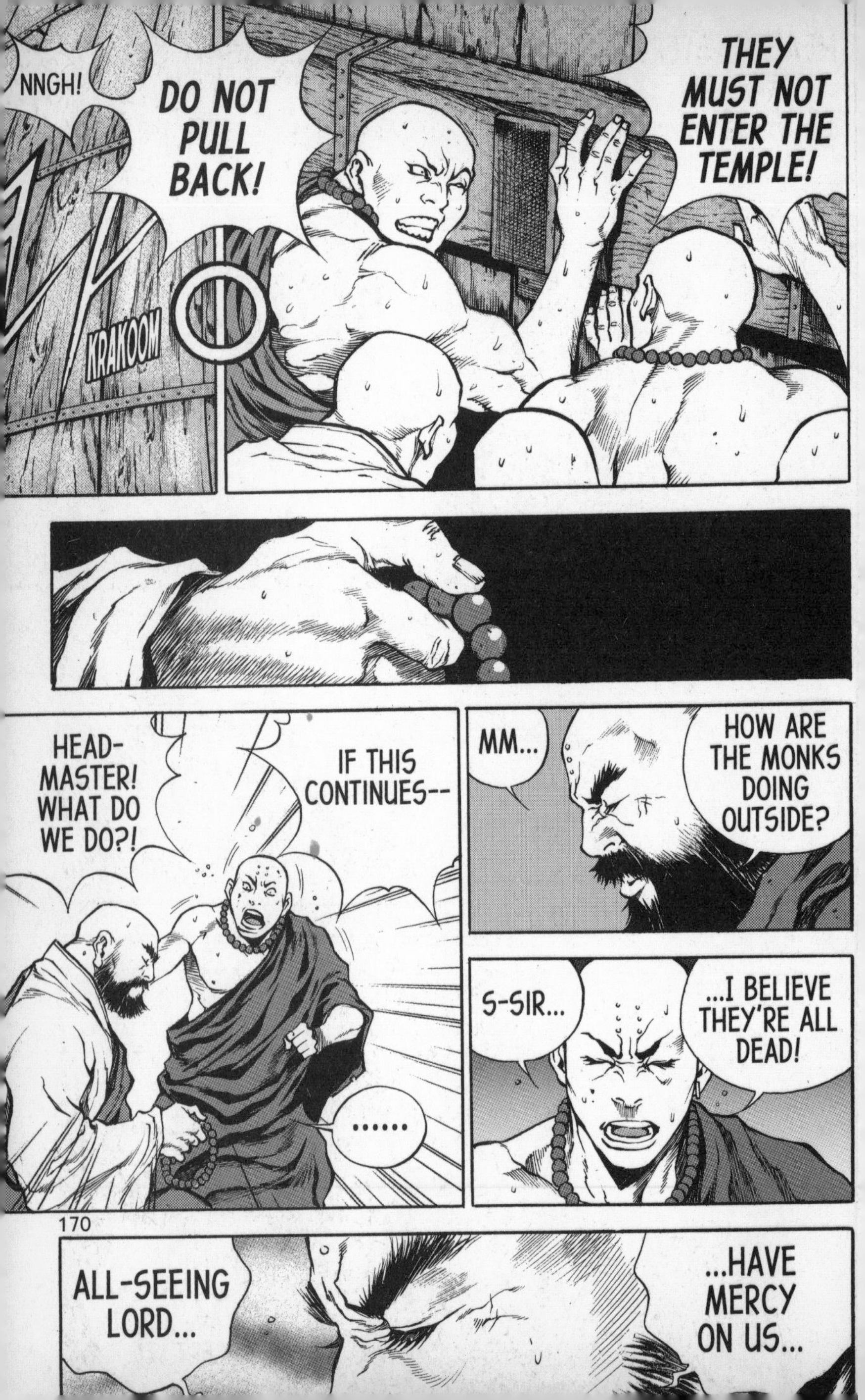

NNGH!
DO NOT PULL BACK!
THEY MUST NOT ENTER THE TEMPLE!
KRAKOOM
HEAD-MASTER! WHAT DO WE DO?!
IF THIS CONTINUES--
......
MM...
HOW ARE THE MONKS DOING OUTSIDE?
S-SIR...
...I BELIEVE THEY'RE ALL DEAD!
ALL-SEEING LORD...
...HAVE MERCY ON US...

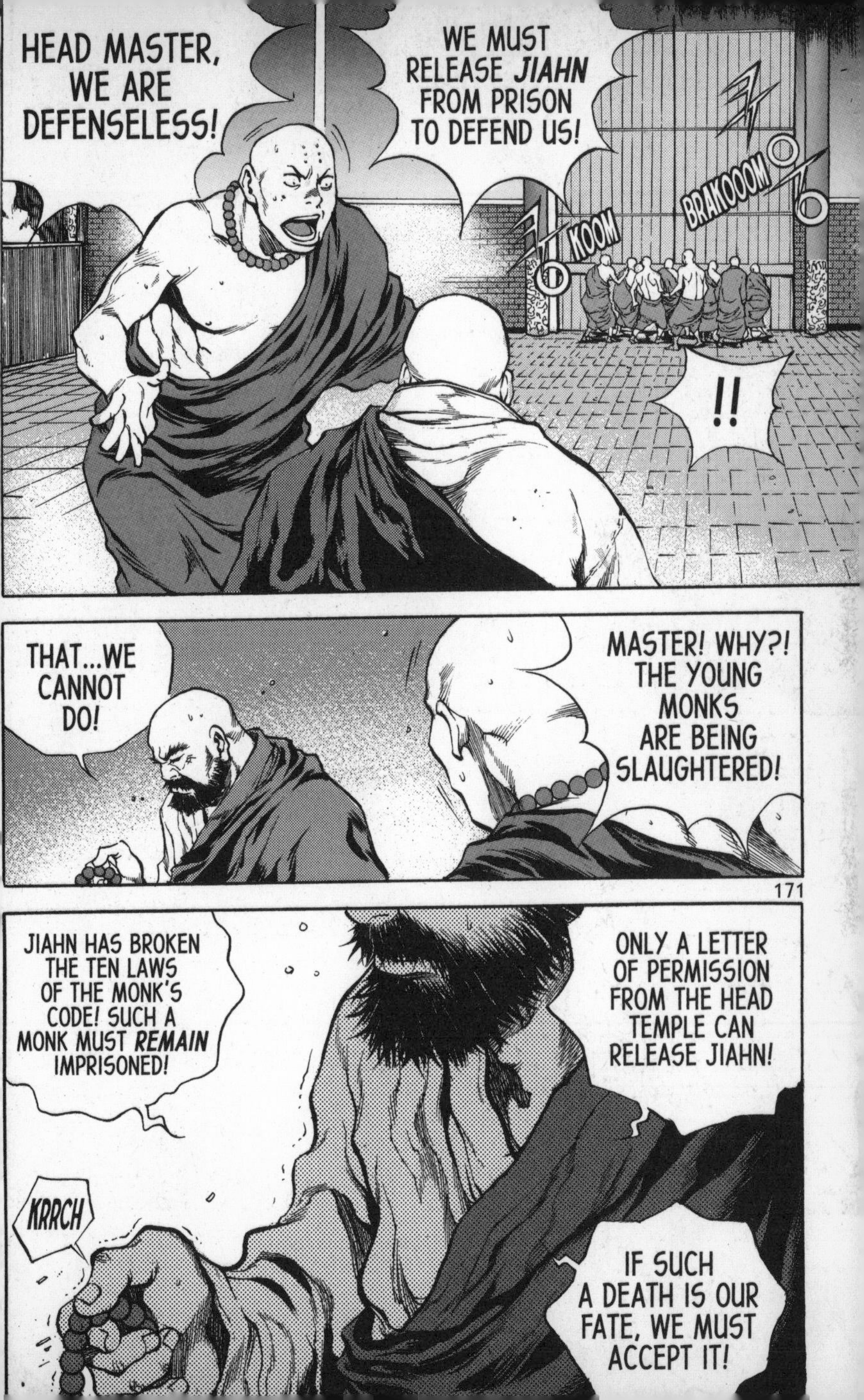

HEAD MASTER, WE ARE DEFENSELESS!
WE MUST RELEASE *JIAHN* FROM PRISON TO DEFEND US!
KOOM
BRAKOOOM
!!
THAT...WE CANNOT DO!
MASTER! WHY?! THE YOUNG MONKS ARE BEING SLAUGHTERED!
JIAHN HAS BROKEN THE TEN LAWS OF THE MONK'S CODE! SUCH A MONK MUST *REMAIN* IMPRISONED!
ONLY A LETTER OF PERMISSION FROM THE HEAD TEMPLE CAN RELEASE JIAHN!
KRRCH
IF SUCH A DEATH IS OUR FATE, WE MUST ACCEPT IT!

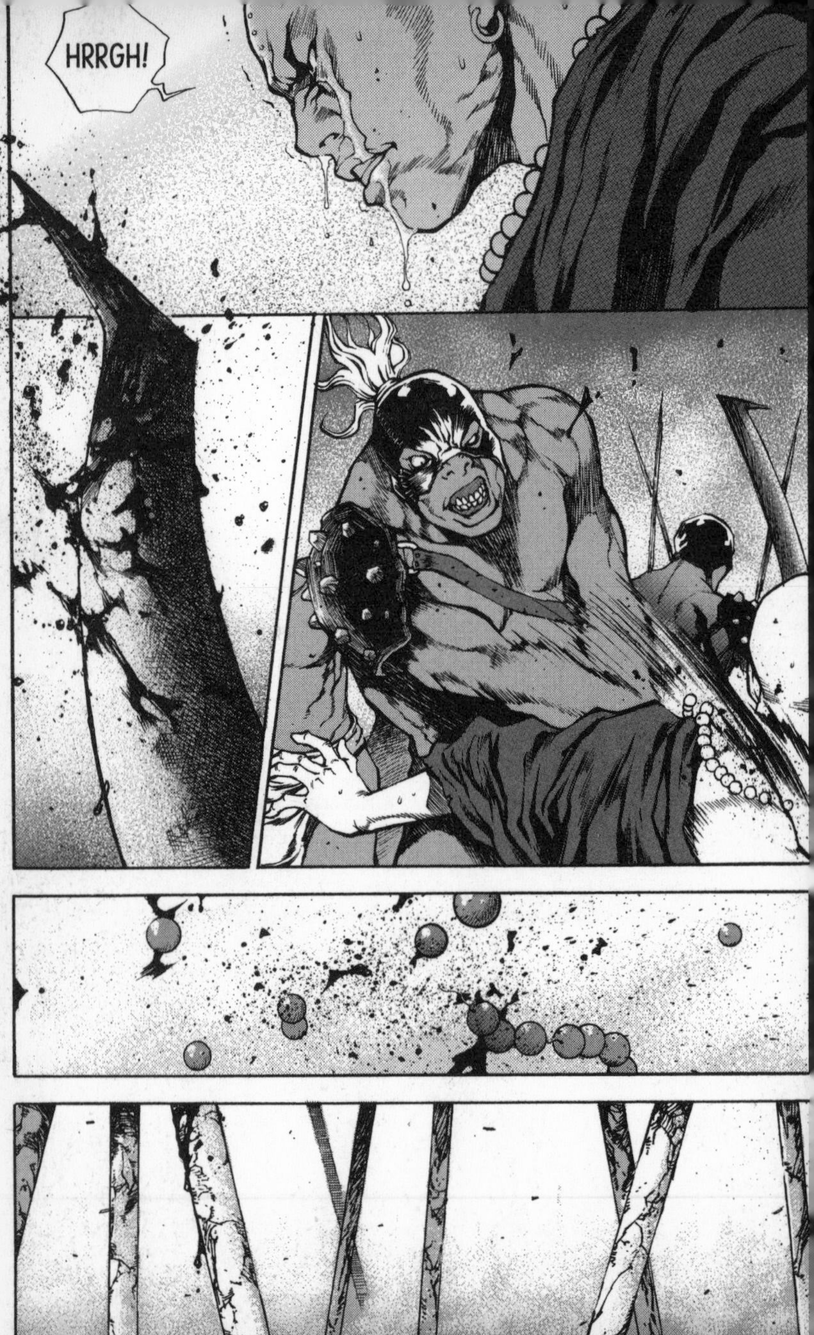
HRRGH!

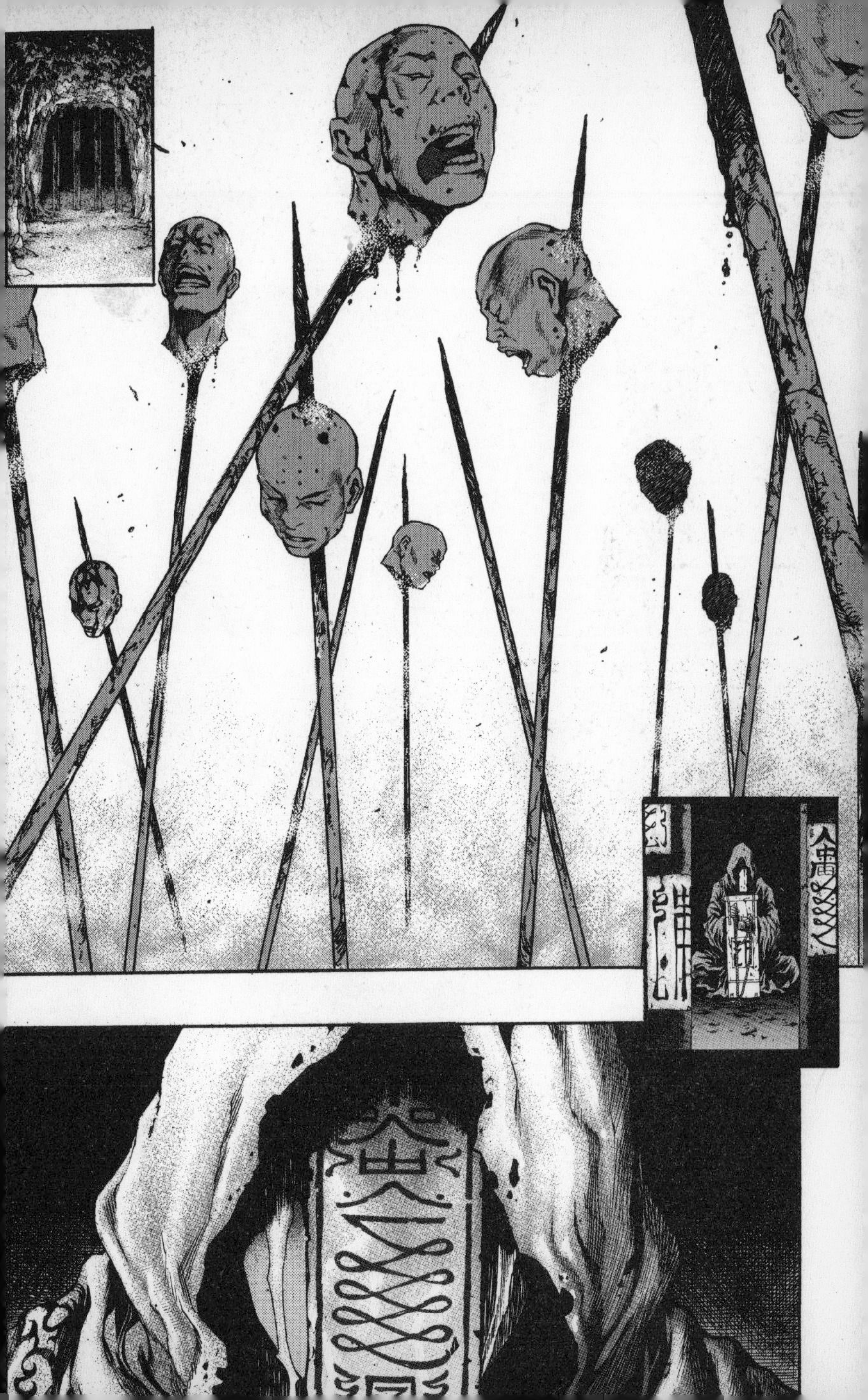

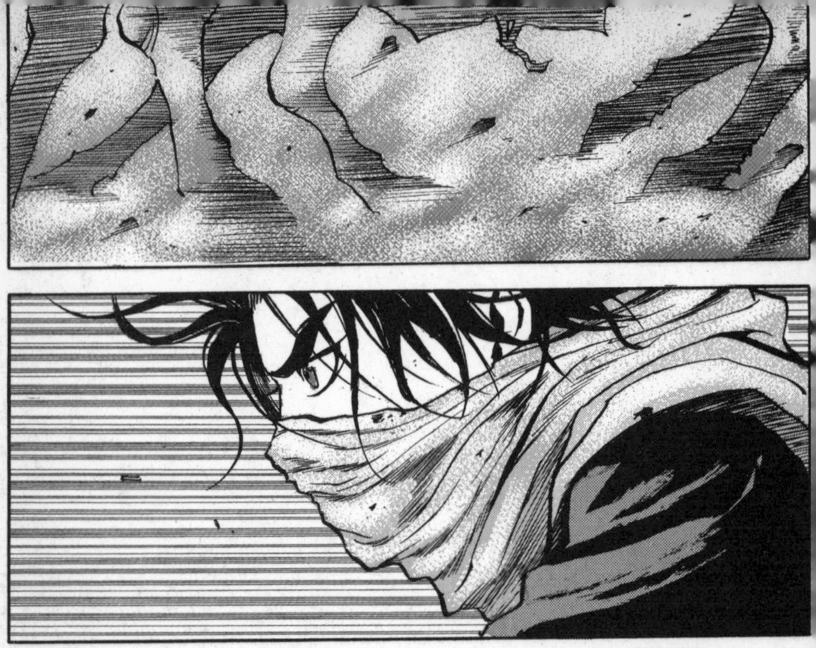

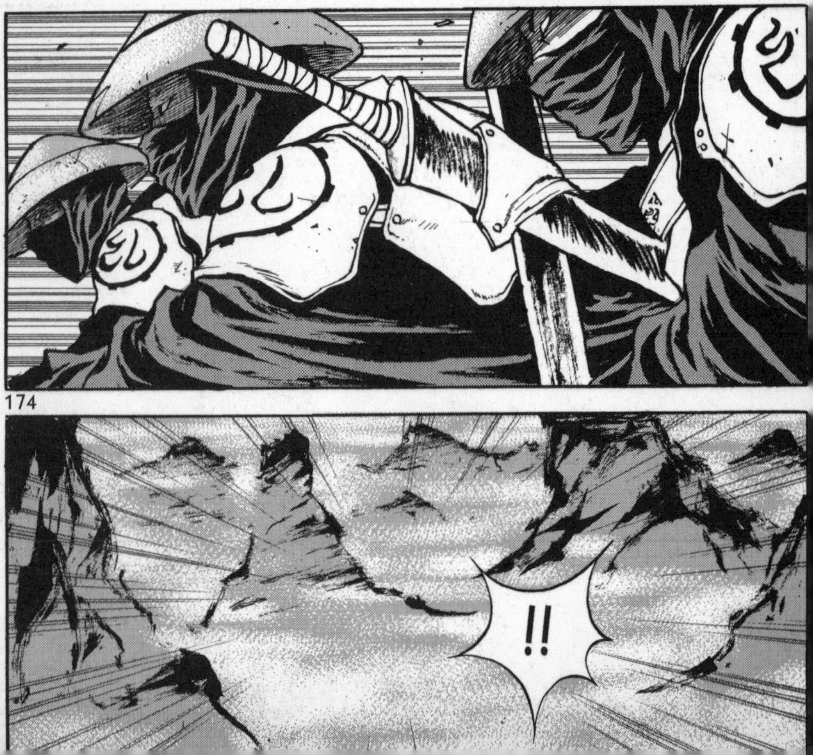
!!

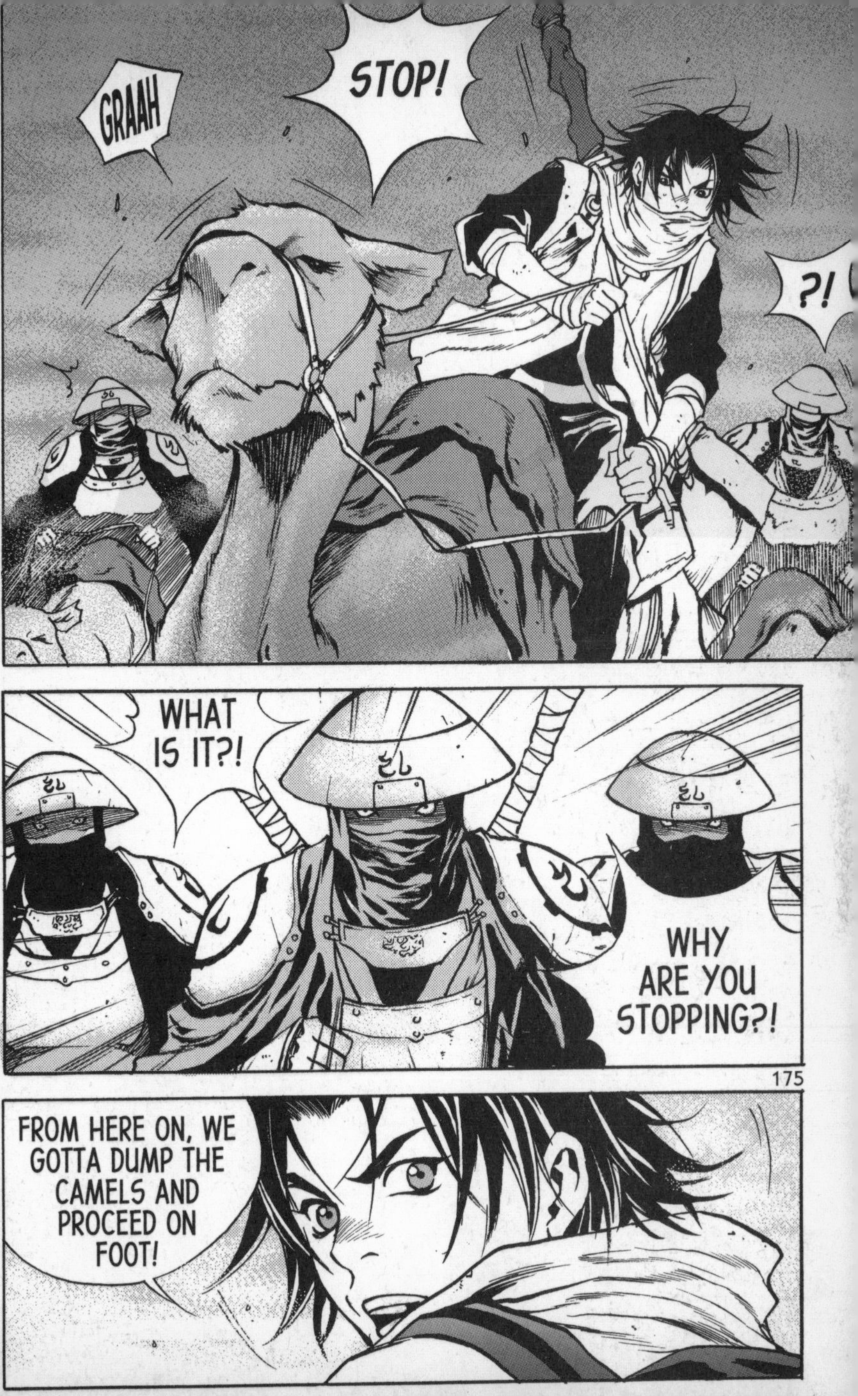
GRAAH
STOP!
?!
WHAT IS IT?!
WHY ARE YOU STOPPING?!
FROM HERE ON, WE GOTTA DUMP THE CAMELS AND PROCEED ON FOOT!

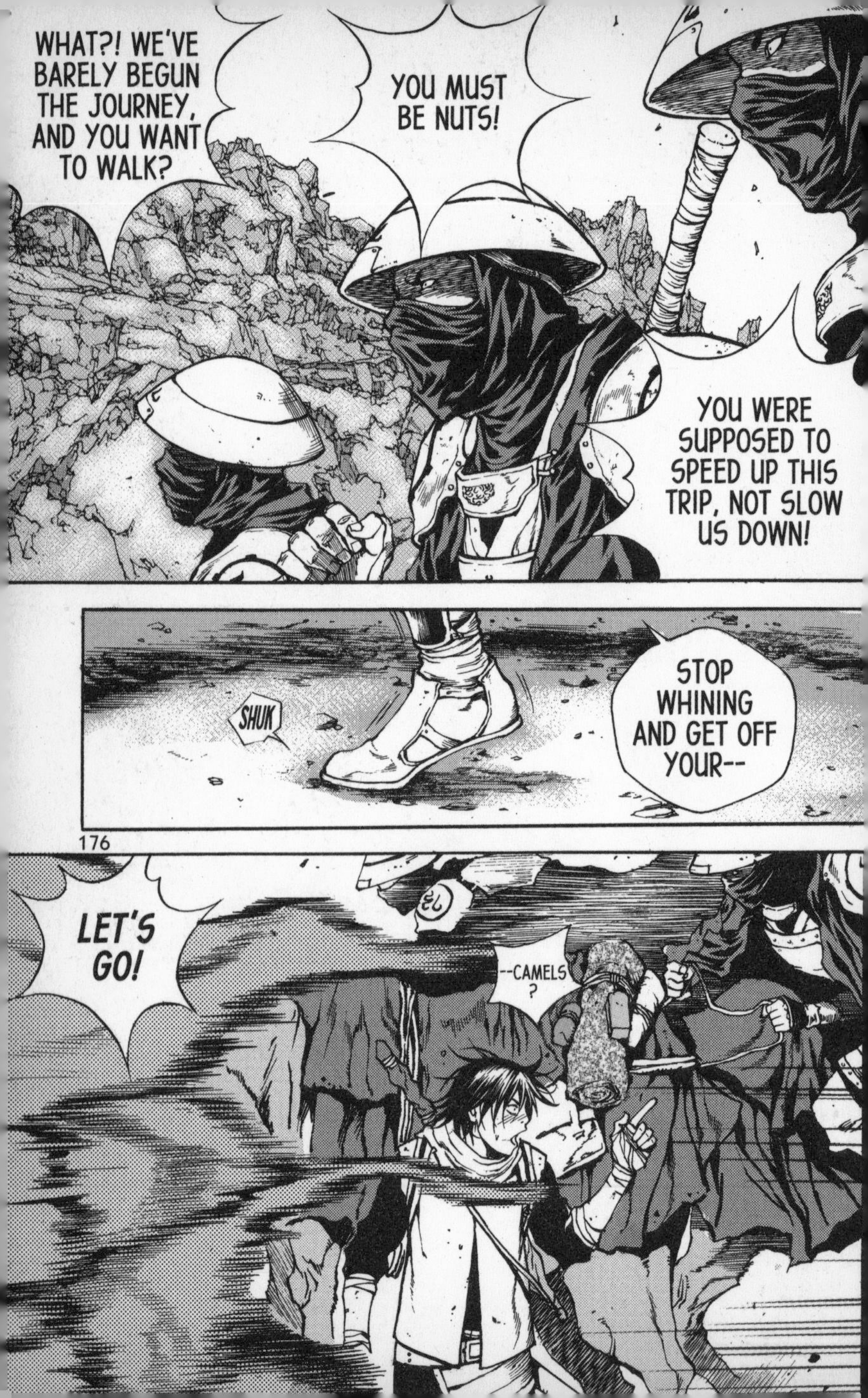
WHAT?! WE'VE BARELY BEGUN THE JOURNEY, AND YOU WANT TO WALK?
YOU MUST BE NUTS!
YOU WERE SUPPOSED TO SPEED UP THIS TRIP, NOT SLOW US DOWN!
SHUK
STOP WHINING AND GET OFF YOUR--
LET'S GO!
--CAMELS?

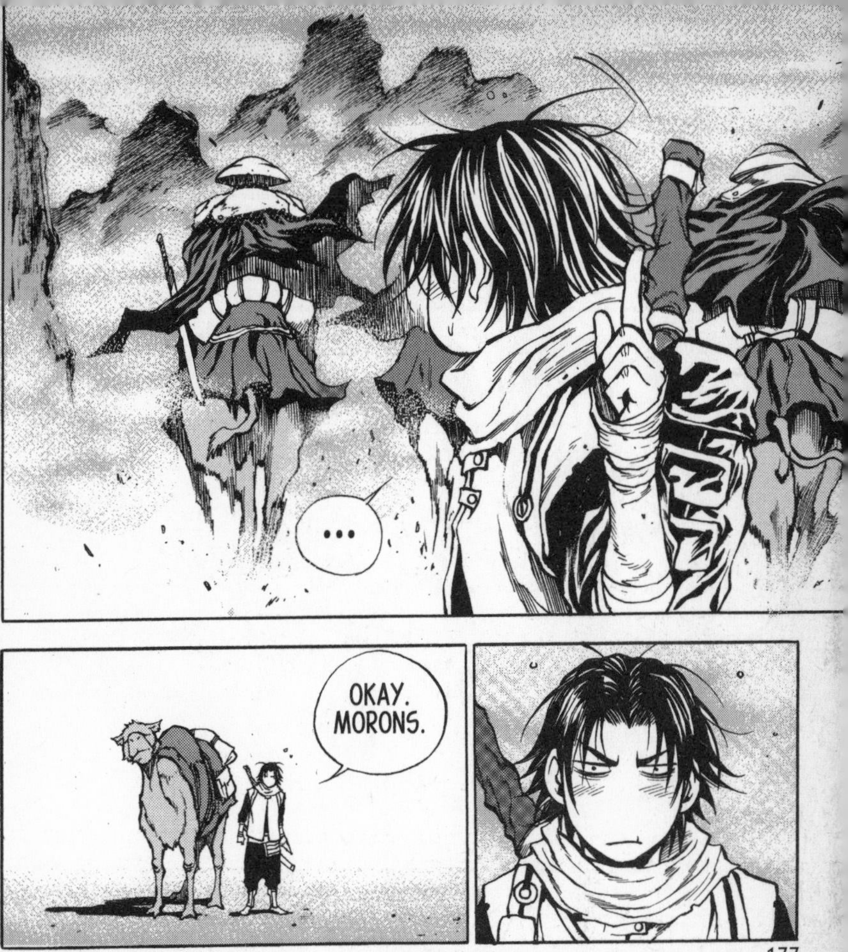
...
OKAY. MORONS.

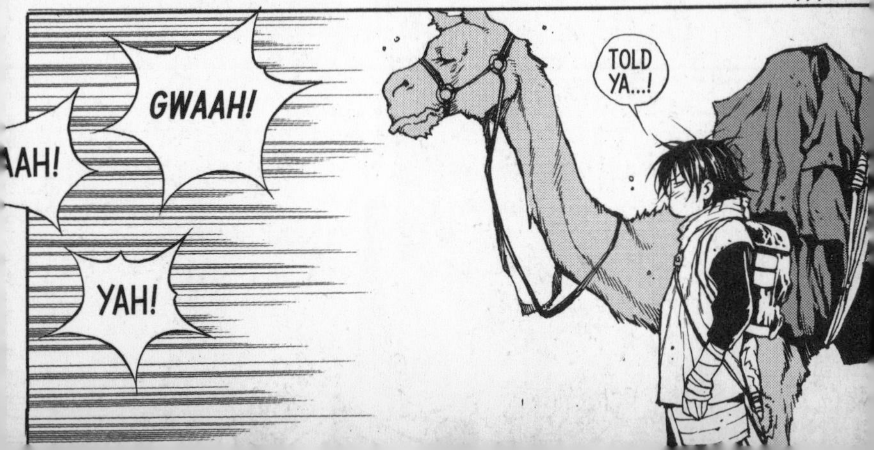
TOLD YA...!
GWAAH!
AH!
YAH!

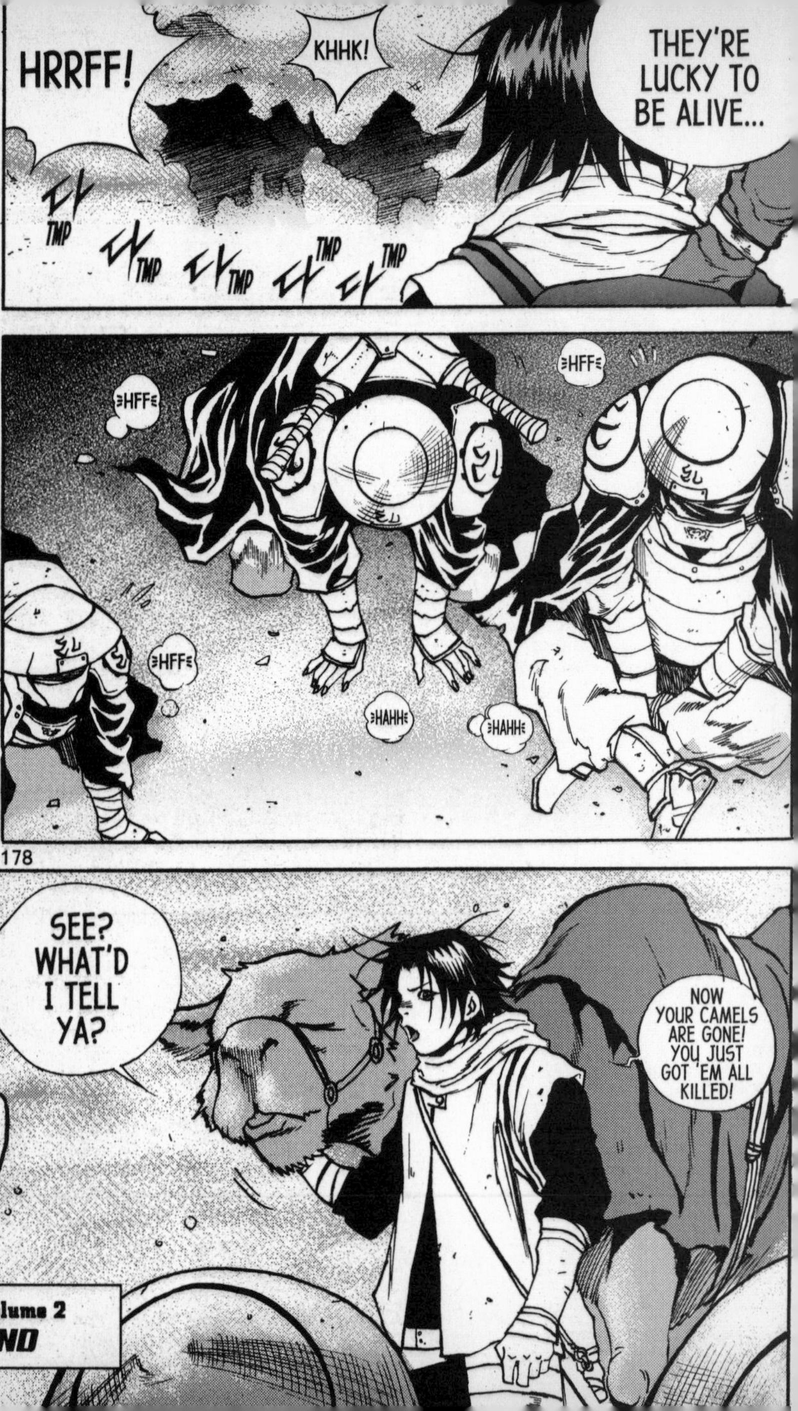
HRRFF!
KHHK!
THEY'RE LUCKY TO BE ALIVE...
TMP
TMP
TMP
TMP
TMP
HFF
HFF
HFF
HAHH
HAHH
SEE? WHAT'D I TELL YA?
NOW YOUR CAMELS ARE GONE! YOU JUST GOT 'EM ALL KILLED!
Volume 2
END

publisher
MIKE RICHARDSON

editor
PHILIP SIMON

editorial assistants
JEMIAH JEFFERSON and RYAN JORGENSEN

collection designer
M. JOSHUA ELLIOTT

art director
LIA RIBACCHI

Special thanks to Michael Gombos, Ryan Hill, Dr. Won Kyu Kim, J. Myung Kee Kim, and Julia Kwon.

English-language version produced by DARK HORSE COMICS.

BANYA: THE EXPLOSIVE DELIVERY MAN Volume 2

DARK HORSE MANHWA
A division of Dark Horse Comics, Inc.
10956 S.E. Main Street
Milwaukie OR 97222

darkhorse.com

To find a comics shop in your area, call the
Comic Shop Locator Service toll-free at 1-888-266-4226

First edition: December 2006
ISBN-10: 1-59307-688-6
ISBN-13: 978-1-59307-688-7

10 9 8 7 6 5 4 3 2 1
Printed in Canada

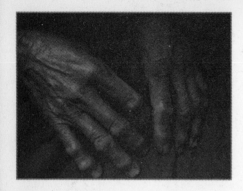

AUTHOR'S NOTE

The most beautiful hands in the world . . .
though they are as rough as an old tree,
with deep wrinkles at every joint . . .

These hands are made for loving a rascally child.
In this world, these warm hands
are the most beautiful.

She puts her own needs behind,
to take care of the child . . .
to embrace the child.

Through cold winters and hot summers,
going from dry farms to wet paddies,
just making enough money to survive
and working with an aching back . . .
this is how these beautiful hands lived,
and how they showed their love!!

To Mother . . . I love you!!

By Kim Young-Oh
Photograph by Noh Min-Yong

(Author's Note translated by Dr. Won Kyu Kim and J. Myung Kee Kim)

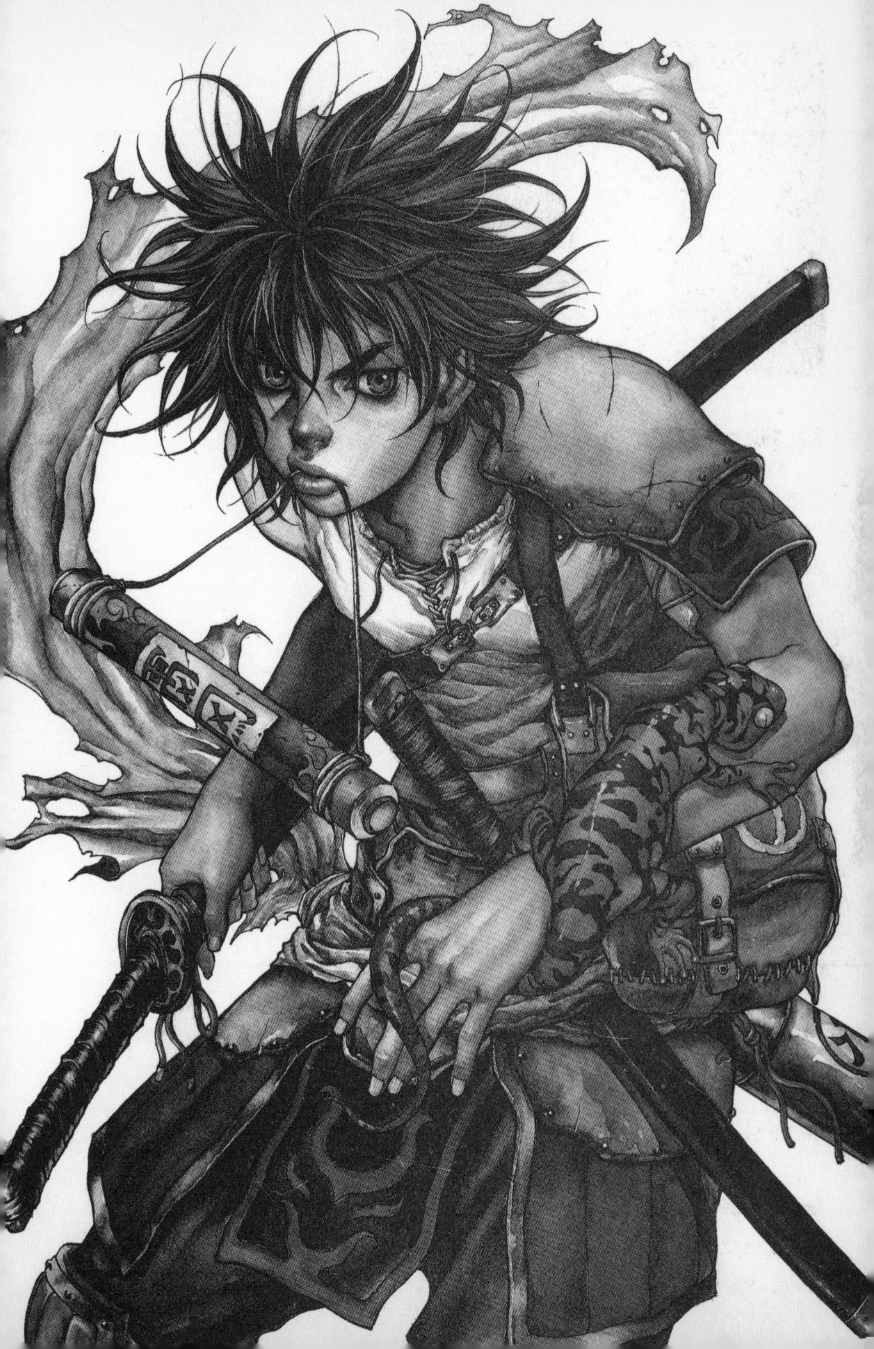

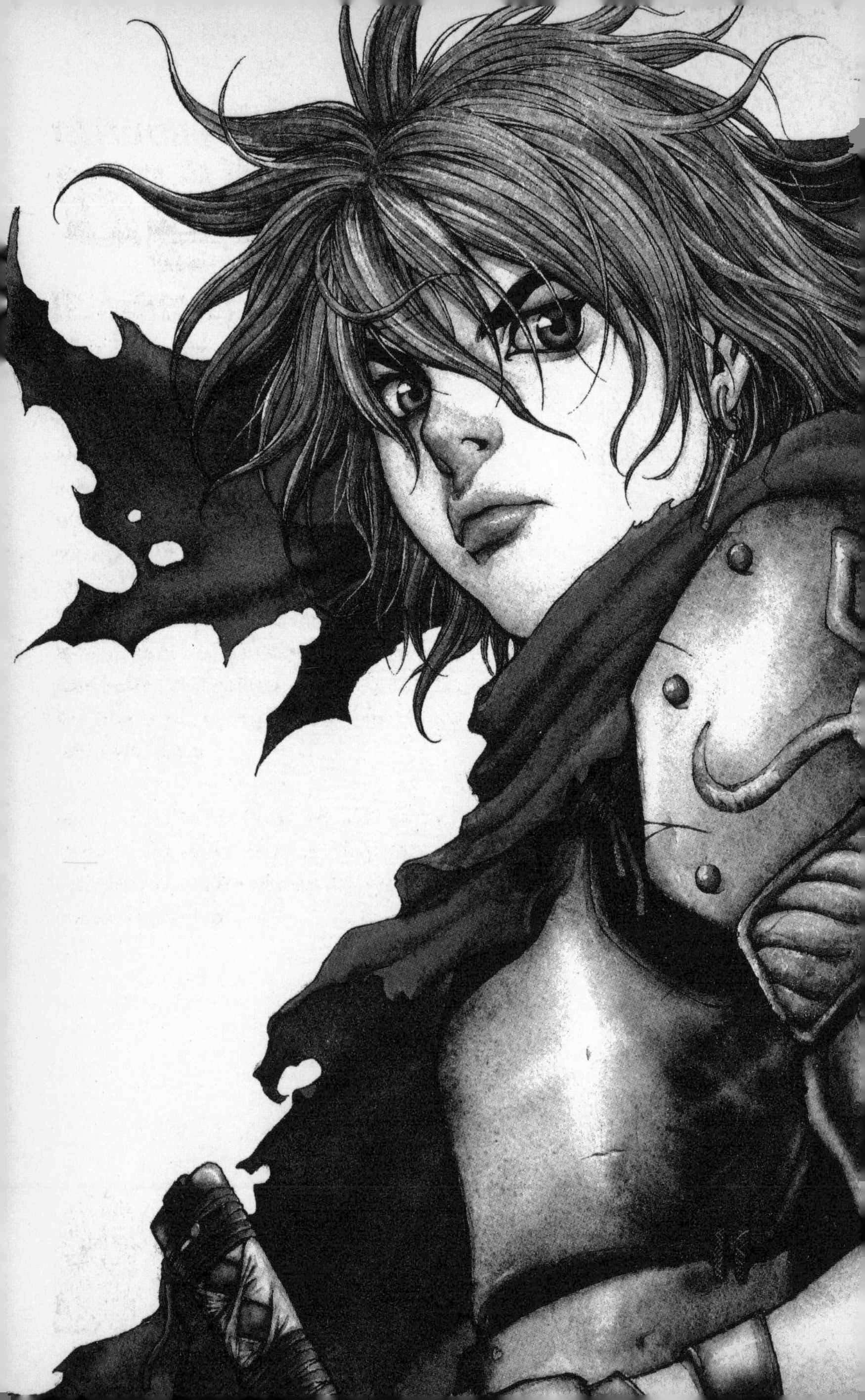

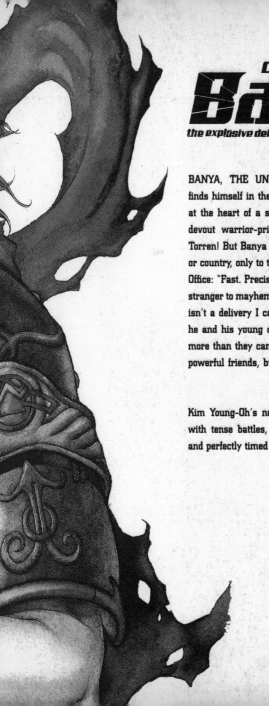

coming soon in
Banya
the explosive delivery man
volume 3!

BANYA, THE UNSTOPPABLE DELIVERY MAN, finds himself in the middle of a mysterious dispute at the heart of a sacred temple—trapped between devout warrior-priests and the vicious, ruthless Torren! But Banya pledges allegiance to no religion or country, only to the motto of the Gaya Desert Post Office: "Fast. Precise. Secure." Banya's certainly no stranger to mayhem, and he proudly asserts, "There isn't a delivery I can't make!" This time, however, he and his young cohort Kong may have bitten off more than they can chew! Also, Kong makes some powerful friends, but will they be able to save him from a grisly fate?

Kim Young-Oh's next action-packed romp is filled with tense battles, horrific villains and monsters, and perfectly timed comedic moments. Coming soon from Dark Horse Manhwa!

DARK
HORSE
MANHWA

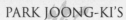

PARK JOONG-KI'S

S·H·A·M·A·N
WARRIOR

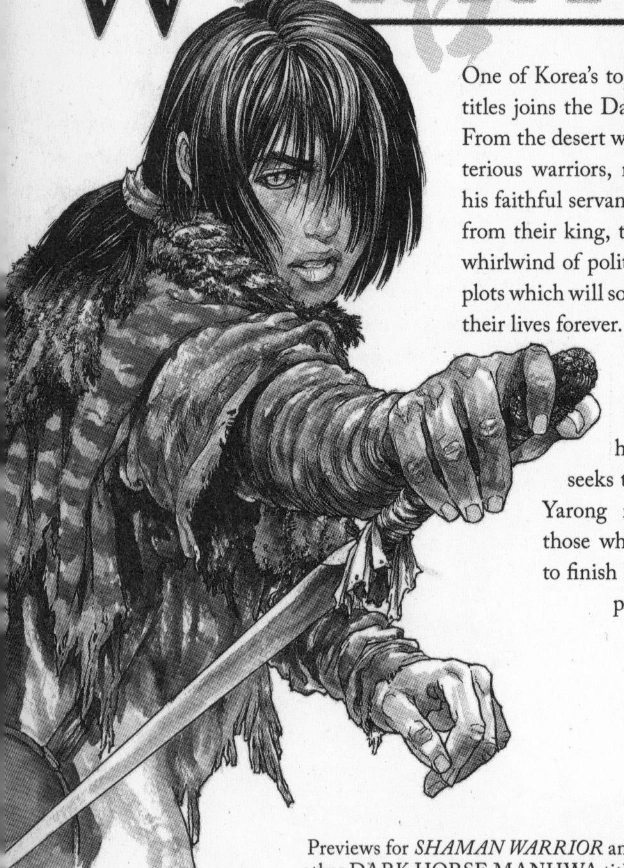

One of Korea's top five best-selling manhwa titles joins the Dark Horse Manhwa lineup! From the desert wastelands emerge two mysterious warriors, master wizard Yarong and his faithful servant Batu. On a grave mission from their king, they have yet to realize the whirlwind of political movements and secret plots which will soon engulf them and change their lives forever. When Yarong is injured in battle, Batu must fulfill a secret promise to leave Yarong's side and protect his master's child. As Batu seeks to find and hide the infant, Yarong reveals another secret to those who have tracked him down to finish him off—the deadly, hidden power of a Shaman Warrior!

Volume 1
ISBN-10: 1-59307-638-X
ISBN-13: 978-1-59307-638-2

Volume 2
ISBN-10: 1-59307-749-1
ISBN-13: 978-1-59307-749-5
Coming soon!

Previews for *SHAMAN WARRIOR* and other DARK HORSE MANHWA titles can be found at darkhorse.com!

$12.95 EACH!

DARK HORSE MANHWA